RUINING DAHLIA

C.R. JANE

MAFIA WARS

~ A DARK MAFIA ROMANCE ~

Proof: Jasmine Jordan
Interior: Nutty Formatting

Grandma, if you've opened this book…turn away right now. I repeat, do not go any further…

TRIGGER WARNING

Please Read…

This is a dark mafia reverse harem standalone which means the main character will end up with multiple love interests. It may have triggers for some as it has intense angst, mention of previous non-consent, dark love-hate themes, scenes of self harm, sexual scenes, and some violence, and is not for the faint of heart.

Prepare to enter the world of the Cosa Nostra...you've been warned.

BLURB

I was sold to my enemies

And not just my enemies. *I was sold to monsters.*

I should know all about how to survive monsters though, I come from a family of them. We aren't Butchers in name only, after all.

I'm shipped away to New York City to the powerful head of the Cosa Nostra, the Rossi Family.

My first meeting with them is bloody and wild, just like they are. Lucian, Raphael, and Gabriel Rossi...they own me now. And they won't let me forget it.

A dahlia has always bloomed best in the light, but they're determined to keep me in the dark.

The thing they don't realize is that I'm more than what I seem.

It's a race to the ending, me against them.

They want to ruin me. And I'm afraid I just might like it.

Ruining Dahlia
Soundtrack

Ruining Dahlia Soundtrack

It'll Be Okay - *Shawn Mendes*
Killer Queen - *Queen*
like that - *Bette Midler*
So What - *P!nk*
Hurts Like Hell - *Feurie, Tommee Profitt*
Him & I (with Halsey) - *G-Eazy*

I Fell In Love With The Devil - *Avril Lavigne*
Infinity - *Jaymes Young*
Young and Beautiful - *Lana Del Rey*
Take Me To Church - *Hosier*
All Too Well (10 Min Version) - *Taylor Swift*

PREFACE

Since the dawn of time, waging war on those who have wronged us has been embedded in the very fiber of mankind's true nature. The thirst for vengeance and retribution has always prevailed over turning the other cheek to one's enemies. Creating chaos and bloodshed is preferable to being subjected to vapid dialogues of peaceful negotiation.

None hold this way of life more sacred than *made men*.

Honor.

Loyalty.

Courage.

These are the codes of conduct of every mafia family.

However, the same cannot be said when dealing with their enemies.

Through recent decades, in the midst of civil evolution, an ancient war was being fought. From both sides of the globe, blood was spilled in the name of honor, while the brutal carnage each family bestowed upon the other was anything but noble.

Soldiers, kin, and innocent lives were lost on all sides, and the inevitable extinction of the Mafioso way of life was fast approaching.

In the most unlikely scenarios, six families came together in an undisclosed location to negotiate a peace treaty. As the leaders of the most influential crime families in the world, they recognized that a cease-fire was the only way to guarantee their endurance. Should this attempt fail, then their annihilation was all but inevitable.

The treaty was effectively simple.

Each family would offer up one of their daughters as a sacrifice to their enemies. Marriage was the only way to ensure that the families wouldn't retaliate against one another. It would also guarantee that the following successor's bloodline would be forever changed, creating an alliance that would continue through generations to come.

Not all in attendance were happy with the arrangement.

The deep scars gained from years of plight and hatred can't be so easily healed or erased. However, even the cynical and leery knew that this pact was their best chance of survival. Although the uncertainty of the treaty's success was felt by every mob boss there, one by one swore an oath that would bind them to it forever.

And as the words spilled from their lips and the scent of blood hung in the air, they made sure innocent lives would yet again be deemed collateral damage to their mafia wars—one last time.

Their daughters would have to pay the price for peace.

Whether they wanted to or not.

PROLOGUE

Ten years ago

LUCIAN

I was bored.

And perhaps, we were all going to drown.

There was a fucking hurricane outside, and the whole place was shaking. Bermuda and hurricane season.

My father had a wicked sense of humor when he set this up, but I could see the strategy behind it. A little harder to kill everyone when you were in a hotel conference room.

The wind banged against the shutters, and any minute now we were going to be showered with glass when the windows finally gave out.

Maybe the storm will take everyone out, and we won't have to bother with this fucking treaty.

The bosses were seated around the table, chests puffed up like the arrogant pricks they were.

Deciding my fate.

And their daughters' fates.

But I guess this was how the world worked. The ones in power decide the lives of the ones who were not.

I studied the faces of each man seated around the round table, scenting for weakness, or blood…or treachery that would spell a knife in someone's back.

Preferably my father's.

Athair looked like he'd spent his years watching the Giants in an old armchair, a six-pack of beer never far away. Guinness, of course.

The perfect cover for him to slit your throat. I did admire the Irish's tactics.

The Firm's boys had arrived late, covered in blood. I had heard okay things about Benny, but Danny, he was the sort of asshole who needed to be crushed.

And then there were the Russians, the Cartel, and The Outfit, fucking bastards. All equally unlikeable.

"We all know why we have come together today," my father, Carlo Rossi, announced, gaining the room's attention. As I listened to him talk about peace and sacrifice, it was all I could do not to laugh hysterically.

Carlo Rossi was the biggest cockroach in the room.

And someday, hopefully soon, he was going to be squished.

I listened, bored, as the men bickered, the Irish heir adding flames to the fire as he mouthed off to the Russians. Maybe Volkov would shoot him. I'd love to get into Hell's Kitchen; it was the last piece of New York not under our control.

"We came here to ensure peace and to ensure we can continue our livelihood. That will not happen if sacrifice and pride cannot be set to the side," Carlo continues with less vehemence in his tone.

I really wanted to know who'd written this script for him. He sounded like a fucking preacher, begging his flock of unruly sheep for repentance.

I tuned out until Carlo started discussing the deal—the blood that sealed this treaty, if you will.

"We all have daughters, and a woman's reason for being has always been to use for alliances purposes, so it fits that they are the ones to be sacrificed here."

"Once the girls are of age, they must marry the leaders of their family, or soon to be Dons. This exchange must be done all within the same time frame. We don't want to have anyone back out because they got cold feet and are no longer interested in the union. Can we agree on those terms?"

Everyone's silent, sealing the agreement in place.

"Good. Now seeing as my daughter is only eight and the youngest of the girls, I propose marriage should only occur in ten years' time when she's of age."

My insides burned thinking about Valentina. She was still playing with fucking Barbies, for God's sake. And here we were discussing trading her like it was nothing.

I listened to the men bicker, all of their daughters different ages, and then Athair got up and walked calmly to the table where a breakfast spread was set out. He grabbed one of the large fruit bowls and walked back to the table.

After emptying it, he grabbed a yellow pad of paper and wrote his name down before dropping it into the bowl.

Simple. I liked it.

"We all pick a name. Should the name pulled out be of our own daughter, we pick again until we have a new name."

Ten years.

It was blaring in my head like a neon light in Times Square, the names in the bowl somehow making it all seem more real.

My father almost spits blood when Giovanni from The Outfit picks Valentina's name. His face goes purple, and I'm sure mine looks the same.

They would be the last place we'd want Valentina to go.

It's the shock of a lifetime when Carlo doesn't start a fight.

They go around the room pulling names, and then it's my turn. Carlo digs in the bowl and picks out:

Butcher

The twins flash their teeth at me, but it's nothing. I'm too busy envisioning my life with a woman I'll hate.

Ten years. Ten years until I'm in prison for life, stuck with a woman that's been forced upon me.

Gabriel and Raphael will be so amused.

Carlo coughs, and I realize I've just been standing here like a fool for who knows how long.

"On my blood, I swear to protect and care for the woman who will ensure the life of the Cosa Nostra. Let her sacrifice bring union to the *famigghia*," I spit out, the words sour in my mouth.

Because what do these men know of honor?

If they had any, they would know that women don't last long in our family.

The Butcher girl was going to be ruined.

ONE

DAHLIA

I t was dark.

Isn't that how all these tales go?

Maybe everything had always been dark for me though, since the moment I took my first breath as a baby. Always somber. Always sad.

An ache inside of me that the doctors and the medicine could never fix.

I laid in bed that night, listening to the sounds of the party that my parents were throwing to celebrate some deal that The Firm had managed to enter into.

There was a nightlight across the room, its light a beacon that I would stare at every night until finally I drifted off to sleep.

I had always been scared of the dark. Which was a strange thing in itself since I just confessed to living in it.

But ever since I could remember, I'd needed a light on.

At first, I'd been allowed to have the closet light on, but then my father had insisted that "no child of his was going to be afraid of the dark," and from that moment on, it wasn't allowed. He'd gone so far as to unscrew my lightbulb at night so I could "get over my fears." It was only my continual screaming at night that got him to allow me a small nightlight. When I was away at school, I always kept the light on in my room, but here I was, back home on holiday, the nightlight my only saving grace.

A small creak sounded in the room. I flinched at the noise, my eyes desperately searching the darkness to see what monster was waiting in the dark corners of my room. I watched in terror as the door to my closet inched open, the sound of its creaking scraping down my spine, and a massive form stepped out from its depths.

I opened my mouth to scream, just praying that the music wasn't too loud and that someone would be able to hear me before it was too late.

"It's just me, pet," my uncle's voice whispered in the darkness.

I trembled beneath my blankets, sliding farther away from him until I hit the wall, because I knew even at eight there was no good reason for my uncle to be hiding in my closet.

His footsteps were soft as he ambled towards me, his features becoming clear as he walked into the nightlight's purvey.

"Please get out," I hoarsely begged, not sure what to do. My Uncle Robert was my father's right hand. A skilled killer whose name was synonymous with The Firm.

My father would never believe me over him.

"Don't be afraid, Dahlia," he whispered as he reached my bed.

I whimpered and pulled the covers up closer to my chin.

I cried when he slid into the bed with me, his hands traveling over my skin.

I shattered into a million pieces when he first stroked his finger across my knickers. The darkness that lived inside me spread through my veins, until any light that had been trying to survive was extinguished, leaving me an empty husk.

But I didn't cry after that.

Or the time after that.

Or the time after that.

I didn't cry ever again.

Twelve Years Later

"Bollocks," I murmured as a busy passerby shoulder-swiped me as they walked past, the white chocolate mocha in my hand going flying all over the pristine white blouse that I'd mistakenly chosen for this flight. For some inane reason, I'd thought that getting all dressed up before my eight-hour flight made sense.

Not that the man waiting for me at the end of the flight would care if I was dressed up or not. He probably wouldn't care if I showed up in a paper bag...or if I showed up at all.

Butterflies swarmed inside me just thinking of what lay ahead. I'd stopped in the middle of the walkway to assess the damage, so it wasn't a surprise when someone knocked into me again, spilling the rest of my drink.

"Fuck," I griped as I finally did the sensible thing and scurried out of the way of the thousands of people milling around in the Heathrow airport today. I'd never been in a public airport before. I'd always been on a private plane courtesy of the wealth of my father, Trevor Butcher. But he was gone now, and my brother…along with my new fiancé had apparently thought that commercial was the way to go.

For a moment, I imagined melding into the crowd and setting off for some exotic locale to be lost in. I imagined golden beaches, and drinks with the little umbrellas in them…or maybe an idyllic lake setting where I'd spend my days on a dock, watching wisteria grow over my bare feet, writing the next great novel which would never see the light of day.

I would have thought them all foolish to send me on my own. A girl even an ounce braver than me would be running for the hills, desperate not to marry a perfect stranger. After all, they didn't know the nightmares that waited for me here in England were far worse than anything I could comprehend waiting for me in New York. They didn't know how close I'd been to trying to get away…permanently.

Or maybe they did. My stomach clenched at the thought. Maybe they saw the ruin in me. Either way, my warped, damaged self somehow held some loyalty to "The Firm"…so here I was, the obedient daughter to the very end.

I shook my head, trying to push away the memories and images that seemed to be permanently etched into my mind.

That was all behind me now. This was my fresh start. I threw my now empty cup away and looked around to see if there were any airport shops I could get a new shirt from, since my bags and belongings were all either checked already or shipped to New York ahead of me. I wandered through the airport, glancing at the stores, searching for anything that might sell clothing, until I stopped and turned around, not wanting to get too far from my gate.

See…the perpetual good girl to a fault.

I weighed my options as I spotted a shirt sporting the Union Jack in one of the gift shops. Which was worse, meeting my future husband with a brown stain that resembled shit all over my shirt…or wearing that?

Union Jack it was.

My hand reached for the shirt at the same time another hand did, and our skin brushed against each other, until I yanked my hand away like I'd been burned.

I turned my head to apologize, but my words got lost at the blond Adonis standing next to me.

Everyone was looking at him. It was impossible not to. He was beautiful. Like Chris Hemsworth and Henry Cavill had merged into one being and then been touched by Midas.

And that description wasn't an exaggeration.

It was his eyes that caught me first. They were the color of a thousand dancing waves, the exact color of pictures I'd seen showing the Caribbean. Or maybe not the Caribbean. They seemed to change the longer I stared. Maybe they were more like the hot blue flicker of a flame, burning my insides until a warm, achy feeling overtook me. Something I'd never experienced before, not even with Leo.

The color was startling against his golden features. Golden skin. Golden hair that reminded me of a field of golden wheat in the peak of the summer, right before fall hit and it was ready to harvest. His aristocratic nose would have had Prince William weeping with envy. And those lips…I knew a thousand women who would give their left ovaries…or both ovaries…to get a pair.

"I'm sorry, what did you say?" I asked, realizing that the beautiful stranger had just spoken.

He looked at me, amused and unimpressed at the same time.

I blushed furiously under his gaze, feeling like an errant school girl who'd never seen a man before.

I quickly yanked my gaze back to the offensive-looking shirt in front of me, wondering idly why this perfect creature would be wanting anything to do with this shirt.

"I was saying we seem to have the same taste in horrible clothing," he said with a practiced grin that melted my insides. His accent was American, and the timbre of his voice was like honey, like he'd been biologically made to attract a mate in any way possible.

I could only imagine his scent. I resisted the urge to lean forward and try and capture it.

That would be too much, right?

He looked amused again and I belatedly gestured to my ruined shirt, only then realizing that not only was it stained... It was also see-through. When I quickly crossed my arms in front of my chest to try to hide the fact that my nipples were standing at attention, I almost missed the flash of heat in his gaze, followed by a surprised expression that looked out of place on his face. I'm sure a guy like him had seen a million boobs.

And with that thought, I turned my attention back to the shirt, dismissing whatever errant thoughts I'd had about him.

But a piece of me wondered...could a man like him make me feel?

"I'm sorry if I offended you. I'm sure the shirt would look amazing on you," he said quickly, blinding me with another perfect grin.

"I know why I'm buying this blight of patriotism, but why are you?" I asked, examining the expensive-looking black dress shirt and slacks he was sporting, the dark color making his golden appearance even more noticeable.

He brushed his hand through his hair, almost sheepishly. "It's a thing I do. Well, a thing I collect," he explained. "I try to get a trashy t-shirt from every country I visit."

"How many do you have?" I asked, giggling at the thought of this veritable god having a closet somewhere stuffed with corny t-shirts. I tried picturing him in one, but my mind couldn't quite wrap around the thought.

He chuckled, probably at the look on my face. The sound reverberated right through me, stoking the flames inside that I was trying desperately to suppress. I didn't want to jump the man after all, and I was really close to that.

"Fifty-three?" he mused, stroking his lips with his thumb as he thought about it...I found myself strangely jealous of that thumb. "Well, I guess fifty-four as soon as this piece of art is paid for."

"Well, your reason for buying this shirt is far better than my clumsiness."

I rifled through the shirts, looking for my size. Once I found it, I turned around and almost dropped it when I found him staring at me intensely, all the earlier lightheartedness completely gone. He was studying me closely...clinically, like he was tearing off the layers of my skin to see what was inside.

I hoped he didn't venture too far down, he would only be disappointed when he got to my insides and found there was nothing but empty space.

What did it say about me that this small glimpse of the darker side of him only made me more attracted?

"Well," I began awkwardly. "Enjoy your shirt," I finished lamely, wanting to slap myself in the face for not being able to come up with something wittier.

"I hope you can find another coffee before your flight," he

said charmingly as he reached past me and began to look through the shirts.

I was far more reluctant to leave his side than I would've liked as I headed towards the cashier stand to pay for my shirt. The bored-looking clerk quickly rang up my purchase, snapping her gum loudly as she did so. I forced myself not to wince. I'd always hated the sound of chewing. Chewing gum. Chewing food. It all drove me mad. Just another one of the little idiosyncrasies that set me apart from the rest of society.

I grabbed the shirt, not bothering to have her bag it since I would just be putting it on, and strode towards the exit, furtively looking around to see if I could get one more glimpse of him. He was still by the shirts, and he didn't turn around when I strode past him.

That was really okay, though; the backside of him was almost as good as the front.

As soon as I stepped out of the store, it all came rushing back. Where I was going. The fact that technically I was an engaged woman... It would take a minute to get used to that. I waited for the rush of guilt to hit me, since I'd spent the last two weeks after finding out about this whole arranged marriage trying to wrap my mind around the idea of becoming a stranger's wife.

Nope. Nothing. Not a flicker of guilt that I was just lusting crazily over a stranger.

My mum would be so disappointed, God bless her distracted, oblivious soul.

Rosemary Butcher was a lot of things, but oblivious was probably the most apt description for her. Oblivious to my father's sins, oblivious to my brothers following in his footsteps, oblivious to her daughter's pain.

I stepped into the bathroom stall, thinking of how excited she'd been for me as we said our farewells. She'd thought that this was the most amazing thing that could have happened to me. It would've been amazing if she was actually right.

But Rosemary Butcher was never right.

About anything.

I shook my head and pulled off my blouse, trying to push away the memory of that last hug she'd given me before she'd "spotted out for tea." It was amazing how someone could love you so much, and at the same time, not see you at all.

I should've just stuffed my shirt in my bag. I'm sure someone could have gotten the stain out, but instead, I impulsively threw it into a trashcan in the stall. I tore off the tag to the Union Jack shirt and slipped it on, immediately realizing that I'd somehow managed to get a size too small. I blamed it on being distracted and cringed as I pictured showing up to New York in a skin-tight t-shirt sporting the Union Jack flag.

Deciding I didn't have a choice but to buy another size, I peered into the trashcan to see if I could grab my blouse so I could take this one off and exchange it.

Of course, I muttered to myself, when I saw that I'd managed to throw the blouse right into an open diaper filled with poop.

I guess I was about to be the proud owner of *two* Union Jack shirts. Maybe there were better ones in there that I could find.

Two

As soon as I stepped out of the bathroom, an announcement blared out from above me that "flight 41182 to JFK" was about to board.

Nausea burst into play inside of me. The butterflies from earlier turned into veritable fireworks, threatening to send the sandwich I'd eaten an hour before all over the floor.

I looked longingly towards the store, a part of me obviously noting that the scorching hot stranger I'd met there wasn't inside, and then I hustled to my gate like the good girl I was.

I probably had time, but since this was my first time traveling commercial, I didn't want to risk it. I had no idea how much time there was between announcements like that and the plane actually taking off.

I sighed in relief…or misery, when I saw that the gate doors were indeed still open, and there was a line in front of them to get on the plane. I double-checked that my tickets were still in my bag. Looking around, I saw that everyone else had their tickets on their phone, but I was terrible at technology, and it felt much safer to have tangible tickets rather than something on my phone that could disappear with my clumsy fumbling.

Plus, I wasn't quite sure that the paper tickets would work on my phone.

Part of being a member of *The Firm* meant that there were a million firewalls on my phone to prevent hacking—not that there was actually anything interesting on my phone to be hacked. Pa had always gone on and on about security though.

My thoughts scattered as the line moved forward, and then it was my turn to give the tickets to the gate agent. My hand was trembling as I handed her the tickets, but she didn't say anything. She just shot me a polite, tight smile and nodded at the guest behind me to hand her their tickets. I rolled my shoulders back, becoming aware once again of just how tightly the shirt stretched across my chest, and started down the gangway...or at least I think that's what it was called.

The walk felt a mile long. I wondered if that's how prisoners felt when they were walking the plank—that it stretched on for miles...yet wasn't long enough.

Except then I thought about what I was leaving behind, and some of my anxiety disappeared. Every step meant I was farther from *him*. And even though my brother, Benny, had cast my uncle out as soon as my father died, for reasons unrelated to me, in my head he was still right behind me.

My fingers itched for a razor-blade at the thought.

I don't do that anymore, I reminded myself as I finally got to the entrance of the plane and stepped inside. That was another part of my fresh start. I didn't make myself bleed so I could stop feeling.

I wondered how long it would take to not crave the feeling of release as dear to me as water was to a desperate man.

There was a smiling flight attendant at the entrance handing out antiseptic packets, and I nodded my thanks as I took one. I wondered what I looked like to her. If I appeared as pale and out of sorts as I felt. Or if I just looked daft.

"I like your shirt," she said with a smile and an American accent. Which of course made me immediately think of the stranger in the store. There had been a few American students at my boarding school, and I'd always been fascinated by their accents...as fascinated as they were with mine.

I smiled in response, knowing she really didn't mean it— because really, who would?—and I turned to go farther into the plane. My jaw dropped. I was sure that this airline was far nicer than most because the first-class cabin had what looked like little square pods lined up down the aisle. I could see the tops of people's heads and not much else inside of them. I'd been imagining myself squished in a middle seat like in the movies with some drunk guy leaning his head on mine and snoring loudly as he drooled.

At least I would have some privacy. My rich mafia boss fiancé had sprung for first-class...the gentleman. Excuse my sarcasm.

I examined my ticket then started to scan the seats for 10C. Someone bumped me from behind, obviously not believing in personal space, and I walked a little bit faster down the row.

From this angle, I could see into most of the seats as I passed, since most people hadn't put up their privacy screens yet. The brown leather seats matched the outside of the pod and were at least three people wide. There was a tray off to the side and tons of space in front of the seat, I assumed so you could make the seat into a bed. Flight attendants were walking along the rows of first-class with trays laden with bubbly-filled glasses.

Getting drunk sounded good about now.

I found 10C and slid in gratefully, tossing my bag to the ground with a sigh and sinking back into the surprisingly comfortable seats.

"It'll do for eight hours," a familiar voice commented from next to me, and I shot up in my seat, heat flushing through me as the screen separating me from the pod next to me slid down.

It was him. The beautiful stranger from the shop.

Maybe the heavens really did love me. Or they hated me. I guess I would find out in the next eight hours as I did my best to shield this guy from the full force of my awkwardness...and darkness.

Not that I assumed he would want to talk to me for eight hours. If anything, having him next to me would distract me from what awaited me at the end of the flight.

10C was located in the center of the plane. The seats on the sides of the plane were solo seats not connected to anyone else, but the ones in the center of the plane were side by side with another pod.

Not that I was complaining.

"You're not much of a talker, I take it," he commented, breaking me out of my head where I seemed to spend most of my time.

"I'm a talker. I love to talk," I spit out, wanting to find the nearest acid bath and jump in as soon as my word vomit came out.

He didn't seem to be put off. Instead, he leaned forward over the partition. "Well, that's good to know. I wouldn't want to have to sit the whole flight in silence." He winked at me, and I swore that my knickers melted. They just melted right off. I bet if I looked at the ground, there would just be a puddle of melted fabric.

I resisted the urge to take a look.

"So, is New York your final destination?" he asked, clearly better at conversing than I was.

"Yes. New York's going to be my new home, actually."

He smirked at that answer, like it delighted him or something.

"Do you live in New York?" I asked, not sure if I wanted him to answer yes. I didn't even know what my new husband looked like. Although I'd been assured by my brother Benny that "he didn't resemble an arsehole" and he wasn't an old man, I was still picturing a decrepit man in a wheelchair a la Anna Nicole Smith.

It might be torture to know that the Adonis next to me was walking the streets in the same city where I lived.

Don't get me wrong, I'd tried to find pictures of Lucian Rossi aka the future "Boss" of the famed Cosa Nostra, but he'd somehow had zero web presence. No Facebook. No Instagram. No TikTok. I'd found one mention of someone at a society event with his name, but of course, there was no picture attached.

"Yes. I've lived there my whole life, actually," he answered, doing that thing where he brushed his lips with his thumb. He was studying me again, and I once more had the urge to put on extra layers of clothing…just so he wouldn't find me lacking…or find out the truth.

"Champagne?" a flight attendant asked from next to me, making me jump in my seat as she pulled me from whatever spell my seat neighbor had weaved around me.

"Yes, please," I murmured as she handed me a glass. I took a big gulp, trying not to choke on the bubbles.

"Sir?" she whispered in a voice that had somehow transformed from the professional tone she'd used for me into one that would suit her well if she was a phone sex operator.

Jealousy clawed at my insides, and I frowned at myself for being so weirdly proprietary about a man I didn't even know.

I didn't get jealous. Leo had tried that in an effort to get me to care, but he'd soon learned that I just didn't. I didn't get attached. I didn't get upset. And I didn't cry.

So, this was new.

"Why not?" he answered with a wink so sexy that I swore I heard a soft moan come from the flight attendant's lips.

Hussy.

He took the flute from her, and I cocked my head as I studied his movements. The practiced, charming smile was there, but there was a certain blankness in his eyes as he thanked the woman. It wasn't the warm look he gave me, not even the cold one I'd witnessed for a brief moment in the store.

It was just blank...

Intriguing.

She didn't seem to notice, judging by the way she was panting next to me.

I took a moment to check my phone while she tried to small talk him over my head.

I miss you.

Leo's text should have done something to me, given me a pang of longing...regret. But I'd just used him as a distraction. A place to lay my lips for a moment when the memories became too much. He was a fool for believing it was anything more.

I didn't answer his message, and after checking to make sure there wasn't anything from my mum, or my brothers...which there wasn't, I threw my phone in my bag.

An announcement rang through the cabin, and the Captain began speaking, forcing the flight attendant to drag herself away from my side as she moved to ready the cabin.

I was sure that she'd be back as often as possible.

"Why the move?" he commented, dragging my attention back to his face.

I opened my mouth, but the words I should have said didn't come out. "Just needed a change," I answered, and his eyes glimmered as if my vague answer amused him.

"We all do sometimes," he responded, once again brushing his lips with his thumb. This close up, his lips looked so soft. I wondered if they would feel that soft against mine.

The plane began to move then, and I gripped the edge of my seat, working to relax myself as I prepared for takeoff. I let go of the seat long enough to drain the rest of the champagne that I'd set on the side tray. I set the flute down sharply as the plane began to pick up speed.

"Not a fan of flying?" he asked, his hand reaching over to brush mine.

"I love flying, actually," I whispered, the plane shaking as it raced forward. "It's just the takeoff I hate."

His fingertips brushed soothingly against my arm

"What's your name?" I asked in a choked voice, figuring that I should probably get his name at this point, since he was touching me...

Not that I minded his touch. The surprising roughness of his fingers was doing a nice job of distracting me. A more sane person probably would have politely pulled away, but I'd learned early on in life I was far from sane.

"Raphael," he said softly. I found myself smiling even though the plane was taking off...because of course he would be named after an angel. It was the most fitting name I'd ever heard for a person.

"You're laughing at me," he mused as his fingers kept up their maddening stroke across my skin.

"Just a little," I giggled a little crazily.

"Evidently, I came out with a full head of blonde hair. It was sticking straight up. My mother inanely thought it looked like an angel's halo, hence Raphael." He shook his head, "Mothers do seem to do that, don't they? Romanticize their young." Raphael smiled, but it looked a little pained.

"You say that like it's a bad thing."

"It's just an amusing thing that we do as a society, give our children names at birth when we have no idea who they'll become," he responded.

I cocked my head at his statement, the takeoff completely forgotten. "I've never really thought about that."

"I've shown you mine, now you show me yours," he said.

"What?"

"Your name. I don't believe I've gotten that yet."

"Dahlia," I answered, a faint flush rising on my cheeks. For some reason, it seemed intimate to give him my name, even though that was the normal thing that people did.

"Any story behind that?"

"My mum was a romantic as well," I said with a laugh. "She grew up on a farm in Lacock…that's a blink and miss town in southern England if you didn't know…and evidently there were flowers everywhere. Dahlias." I shrugged. "It's not a very interesting story."

"I like it," he answered, and I realized that he was still touching my arm.

He must have realized the same thing because he withdrew his hand, reluctantly it seemed. Or I was probably imagining that.

"Oh, look, we're in the air," he announced, turning his head to try and see out the window.

The plane had leveled, and I'd escaped the usual fifteen minutes of terror. "Thank you for the distraction," I smiled.

He laughed, and I about died from the sound of it.

The next hour passed quickly. We talked about football—European football, that is—and I found out that he actually knew a little about the game.

"Chelsea till I die," I argued with a laugh as he tried to convince me that Real Madrid was where my heart should lie.

"You'll have to go to a Giants game," he told me. "I have season tickets in a suite."

My heart fluttered...it almost sounded like he was planning...a date.

Which would have been a dream—if I wasn't about to be a married woman.

"Did I say something wrong?" he asked.

I just shook my head, my stomach clenching. I was good at that, disassociating so I could forget hard truths.

But they were always waiting for me.

"No, sometimes I do that, get lost in my head," I answered sheepishly.

"So, is there a boyfriend back home?" he asked. I fiddled with the blanket that one of the flight attendants had just dropped off.

"Why do you ask?" I answered.

"Ahh, so there is someone special. I knew an English rose like you wouldn't be unattached." His hand was touching my arm again, and I swear I was feeling drunk from it.

English rose. I'd heard that a lot, that my name should have been Rose instead of Dahlia. I was delicate looking, with blonde hair and blue eyes, and lips that were cartoonishly large in my opinion. I had similar coloring to Raphael, but somehow my features didn't add up to the brilliant package that he was blessed with.

I'd secretly always liked my name, even if it didn't fit my appearance. Dahlias were unexpected. They came in so many different colors and sizes that half the time the gardener had no idea what was going to spring up when they planted one. People would probably find a lot of things surprising about me if they could see behind the mask I perpetually wore.

I thought about his statement...that I had someone special.

I most assuredly did not. A future mafia boss and a Uni boy-child most assuredly did not count as special.

"There's no one, actually," I said defensively, as if I was trying to convince myself. "You?"

The cabin lights dimmed just then. The flight was a red-eye. We'd land around 4:00 pm in New York with the time change, so I assumed that most of the passengers were going to sleep.

"I'm excruciatingly single," he announced.

"Excruciatingly? Not a fan of playing the field, then?"

He smirked as if he knew a joke I wasn't in on.

"I have a difficult time forming attachments. Or maybe the right girl just hasn't come around yet."

The way he said it was like he was hinting that he thought I could be the right girl.

Which obviously was just my wistful, wishful thinking since he didn't even know me.

He didn't seem to care that I was tongue-tied. "Are you tired, or do you want to watch a movie? This barrier goes down all the way. It's usually reserved for couples so they can have little rooms to themselves on the flight. We could watch a movie until they bring by some food."

I flushed, hoping that the dim lighting of the cabin hid my blush at least a little bit.

Was I going to do this? This was decidedly very non-good girl behavior.

"I'm just going to use the loo, and then that sounds lovely," I told him, getting up from my seat and trying to hide the fact that my hands were shaking. I also needed a minute to get over the fact I'd actually just said something as asinine like "that sounds lovely" to the hottest man I'd ever seen.

"Have fun in the "loo"," he teased, and I flushed more, remembering that Americans used terms like restroom and bathroom.

I rolled my eyes and hurried away.

THREE

Most of the first-class seat pods had their privacy walls up as I walked to the restroom at the front of the plane. The flight attendant who'd been enthralled with Raphael earlier shot me an annoyed look as we passed each other. I'm sure she was on her way over to try and get his attention with me out of my seat.

I opened the door to the loo and then slipped inside, grimacing at how small the space was. It didn't smell too bad yet this early in the flight, but by the end, I'm sure it would reek. I shivered just thinking about all the germs. I carefully put a paper toilet cover on the seat and then lowered my trousers and used the restroom.

How did people have sex in these tiny things? I tried to imagine the mechanics of it. Just thinking of how many surfaces you would have to touch with your nether-regions exposed made me want to gag.

Of course, thinking about the mile-high club, made me think of Raphael and the vibes he was definitely sending my way.

At least I thought he was sending me vibes. Did he usually caress strangers' arms and make every excuse to touch them? Was that the weird thing he did?

I didn't think so.

I was a virgin. It was a miracle, really. But *he* had been careful to leave that since a mafia princess's virginity was basically the holy grail.

He'd just taken everything else from me. My arse. My mouth. My soul.

Before this deal was made, I probably would have been given to someone high ranking in The Firm. And all hell would have broken loose if, on my wedding night, there wasn't blood. I didn't know what Lucian's opinion of my virginity was, but I guessed that a woman's "virtue" was probably looked at the same way in every mafia organization.

I felt for the slightly ridged skin on my hip and ached for a blade. Just a small cut would do. Just something to take off the edge, so I didn't have all this pent-up craziness inside of me when I went back to my seat.

I sighed as I stood up, realizing I'd been in here for a long time. Raphael was probably thinking that I was taking a shit, and that was the last thing I wanted.

I washed my hands in the sink and splashed some water on my face, trying not to grimace at my reflection. It had been raining in London and at the boarding school for what seemed like months, and I looked pale and gaunt in the mirror. It had been hard to eat once I'd found out the news, and the weeks with little to no food showed.

I wandered back to my seat, surprised when there was no

sign of the flight attendant lurking around Raphael's seat. He shot me a grin that sent lightning bolts through me, all thoughts of my need for a sharp blade dissipating in the brilliance of his smile.

I slid into my seat, noting that someone had been by for at least a moment while I was up. There was a food tray on a fold-out table that connected with the wall in front of my seat. I put up my privacy wall, so I was shielded from the aisle, and then lifted my lid to examine the goods.

"It's good," Raphael commented, gesturing with a fork to the steak, potatoes, and salad in front of me. "I got the same thing. You never know on flights what the food will be like, but I'm actually impressed."

"I love steak. I get it every chance I get," I told him, greedily cutting into my food. Maybe he had magical powers, because I was suddenly starving. I took a big bite and tried not to moan too loudly...it really was good.

It must have been louder than I wanted though, because when I looked up from my plate to ask him if he'd seen any movies he wanted to watch from the choices available on the seat televisions, he was staring at me hungrily, like he was a lion and I was the lamb he was about to devour. I shivered under the weight of his stare, a million ideas in my head, and none of them good. My gaze flicked to where he'd also put up the privacy screen, effectively cocooning us in our own private bubble.

I focused my eyes back on my food, trying to calm my racing thoughts.

"So what do you like to do for fun when you're not cheering on terrible football teams and eating steak," Raphael teased, trying to break the sudden tension—sexual tension—that was thick in our little room.

I bit my lip as I tried to think of what to say. I always froze on these types of questions. My real answers felt a bit too close to that scene in Jim Carrey's *The Grinch* where he talked about "wallowing in despair." You couldn't tell a perfect stranger that most of your days were just about surviving. I finally settled on something I was interested in, if only for the protection that it gave me.

"Martial arts. My brother taught me jiu-jitsu, and we used to spar all the time," I told him, my mind filled with memories of the long sessions when I was home on holiday when I'd find my brother working out and I would convince him to teach me things.

Raphael looked surprised at my answer, and he did that sexy lip rub again as he looked me over, like he was seeing me differently.

He was trying to picture an "English rose" fighting. I inwardly smirked, thinking about what his face would look like if he saw me throw a two-hundred-and-fifty-pound man to the ground. I'd done it before.

Too bad it had never done any good against *him*.

Stop thinking about that.

As if my mind had summoned it, my phone chose that moment to buzz, alerting me that the plane wifi did in fact work and that I'd gotten a text message. I left Raphael to his thoughts as I bent over and grabbed my phone.

I immediately wished I hadn't.

Be good, little Dahlia, the text read from an unknown number. My insides froze and my breathing sped up. Because even if I didn't recognize the number, I knew who it was from.

Him.

Bitter hate and shame wound their way around my vital organs, squeezing my heart until it felt like I was going to die.

He was always going to be there, wasn't he? He would always be the ghostly specter haunting my every step. There wasn't a place I could go in this world where he wouldn't find me. I'd tried to change my number multiple times, telling my mum that I was being bullied at school. But somehow, he always discovered my new number. I would get texts from him unexpectedly, like he didn't want to establish any pattern so that I was always on my guard.

I clenched my hands so tightly I could feel my nails cutting into my skin. It wasn't a razor, but it was something.

I suddenly had the urge to do something crazy, something life-ruining, just so I could forget for at least a moment.

"Do you want to fuck?" I blurted out as I powered off my phone and tossed it into my bag.

"Pardon?" Raphael responded with a surprised, choked laugh. "You're going to need to repeat that because I feel like I just stepped into the fantasy playing out in my head, and I'm not sure if this is actually happening or not."

I laughed, really liking that he'd been imagining something like this happening with me.

"Do you want to fuck?" I repeated, facing him and hoping I looked confident. "We're clearly attracted to each other, and we're both available." I glanced at the screen. "And we've got six hours left. I'm not really in the mood for a movie…are you?"

"Definitely not in the mood for a movie," he said eagerly as he pressed the Do Not Disturb button.

My heart was racing as the center partition went all the way down. Raphael pressed a button and his chair began to flatten out. I did the same for mine until we were basically sitting on a full-size bed.

I didn't know what to do after that. Did I whip off my shirt and my trousers and plop down on the bed? Did I leap over and try to kiss him? Anything with Leo had been done while out with friends, fumbling around in shadowed corners and during movies.

And I obviously didn't count things with—*don't think about that.*

"Breathe," he murmured softly, looking amused at my awkwardness.

I almost blurted out I'd never done anything like this before…but I didn't want him to read more into that statement… like that I'd never done it at all.

My thoughts cut off when he wrapped an arm around me and pulled me close to him.

"Angel," he murmured, softly touching the skin on my face as he stared at me intensely like he was memorizing every freckle on my face.

"I think that's my line," I whispered, right before his lips closed over mine, cutting off whatever ridiculous comment I was about to add. My mouth immediately opened for him, and his tongue dipped in sweetly, shallowly…like he just wanted to tease me. He pulled away and I felt lightheaded, drunk with the sudden flush of arousal coursing through my body.

And I was desperate for more.

He studied me again for what felt like an eternity before he leaned in slowly, his soft lips just barely grazing mine—once, twice—then closing over mine in a hot, wet kiss like none I'd ever experienced before. His tongue slid into my mouth again, and at first, he took his time, tasting me, exploring. That just lasted a second though, because then he was fucking my mouth with his tongue—deep, long licks that resonated straight to my core.

He dominated me with that kiss. And I loved it. It felt freeing to have him take control. You would think that I would hate that kind of thing, but with someone I was choosing to let touch me... it felt...perfect.

Raphael broke away, his mouth moving to my ear.

"This fucking shirt, showing every inch of your perfect, fucking tits," he growled. "I've wanted to fuck you since the moment I saw you bent over in that dreadful store, rifling through the rack of t-shirts."

"The Union Jack just does it for you, then?" I said breathlessly. I was swooning, totally shocked by the dirtiness coming from his mouth.

He fisted my hair, angling my head as he began devouring my mouth once again. His other hand moved to my lower back as he yanked me closer and my breasts smashed against his hard chest. A low moan escaped me as I sucked on his delving tongue with a desperate hunger that should have scared me.

Groaning, he pulled me closer until the upper half of our bodies were as close together as you could get. Some small part of me was still vaguely aware we were on an airplane with very thin walls separating us from tons of people, but it was hard to care.

Not when it felt this good.

Raphael slowly lowered me down to the makeshift bed, the hand on my back moving dangerously to the little patch of scars hidden on my hip. I moved my hips, changing the trajectory of his hand, and I breathed a little sigh of relief when he bypassed the scarred skin.

I didn't want to have him asking any questions.

His other hand slid to my breast, and I sighed in relief because they were fucking aching for his touch.

Raphael lounged next to me, half of his body covering mine as his hands explored my still-clothed body. His lips trailed down my neck, his warm tongue licking along my pulse point.

"Raphael," I murmured.

His hand slid from where it had been touching my thigh down in between my legs. He palmed my core, pressing the seam of my trousers against my clit perfectly. "Tell me what feels good," he ordered, gently rubbing my clit until he found just the right amount of pressure. His other hand began to pinch and tug at my nipple through my thin bra and t-shirt until I was writhing shamelessly, softly whimpering as the sharp sting of pleasure shot fireworks through my entire body.

"So fucking responsive," he murmured. A desperate hunger built, growing, raging through me. I couldn't stop the low moan that slipped out of me as his talented fingers continued to press and rub, my insides coiling tight. "Sexiest fucking thing I've ever seen," he growled.

I didn't respond. I was too busy concentrating on my impending building orgasm.

He moved until he was on top of me, and my legs automatically wrapped around him as he moved me into place. Another moan escaped my lips when he pressed his body against mine, the hard, long outline of his cock rubbing against the seam of my trousers.

It didn't take long until I was cumming, one hand over my mouth to keep us undiscovered.

Although really...this had to happen quite often in these things, right?

We were both breathing heavily when he pulled away from me and kneeled at my feet. He began to take off my shoes, and the gesture meant more to me than it should have. I mean, he was about to get lucky, but the thing was…people didn't really do things for me in my life.

This was nice.

He pulled off my socks next, and then he began to unbutton my trousers and pull down the zipper. My heart began to flutter as I lifted my hips and helped him as he tucked his fingers inside the waistband and slowly pulled them off of me until I was left in my shirt and my knickers.

And then he began to unbutton his freaking shirt.

I didn't know how something like that could be the most excruciating form of foreplay, but watching him undo those buttons had me panting and working on orgasm number two. My mouth dropped open when he finally revealed his whole chest.

It was official. I was sleeping and having the best dream ever because men who looked like that…they didn't exist.

He was flawless, lean flesh over hard muscle. Every muscle was built to perfection, a homage to the human form. If he had lived in Ancient Greece, artists would have lined up in the streets to carve his image.

There was an actual eight-pack there. I swore I'd read some-where that it wasn't possible, but whoever had written that was wrong—because it was right in front of me. And he had the V, those lines that ran along guys' hips that seemed more fantasy than reality that disappeared into his dress pants. And those tattoos…under his shirt he was hiding an ink covered canvas.

I really wanted to lick him. Would that be weird?

Or maybe just worship him.

Both could work.

"You're perfect," I blurted out, and he chuckled sexily, obviously used to hearing that all the time.

Raphael slowly slid his hands up my legs and under my shirt. I lifted up so that he could take my Union Jack shirt off, which I was framing after this, because it obviously was good luck.

And then, with the ease of a man who'd had far more practice than I wanted to think about, he slid his arm under my back, unclasped my bra, and removed it.

I shivered under his gaze, tiny goosebumps pricking up all over my skin. I'd never felt so…seen? Was that the right word? He was seeing everything.

"You are a fucking angel," he growled almost reverently. "I could spend days on this body."

I wanted to blurt out that he was free to keep me, but I managed to hold that little bit of craziness in.

Raphael leaned down and captured the sensitive flesh of my nipple, suckling on it until I was arching my back and writhing in desperation. He moved to my other nipple, doing the same exact thing.

I whimpered and then slapped a hand over my mouth to hide the sound.

"Fuck, I'm tempted to just see how loud I can make you scream," he said in a hoarse voice as he lifted up from my breast and began to trail one of his hands in between my legs until it was rubbing up and down the edge of my knickers. He suddenly jerked the material to the side and slipped one of his fingers inside until he was trailing it along my embarrassingly wet center.

"So wet. I bet you have a pretty pussy. Don't you, little angel?" I swore I gushed right then at his dirty words.

I was mindless as I rubbed against his finger, desperate for him to penetrate and give me what I wanted. He continued to tease me until I was so out of my mind with desire that I was tempted to punch him.

"Tell me you want me to finger fuck you," he ordered, and I gushed yet again, bringing another sexy, naughty smile to his face.

"Yes. Do it," I begged.

"Ask me nicely, little angel."

I groaned. "Please finger fuck me, Raphael," I begged again, breathlessly, out of my mind with lust.

Had I somehow healed myself, or did he just have magical powers that were allowing me just to let go and not freeze at every touch thinking of *him*?

He bit his lip, his golden hair falling in his face…and then he shoved two fingers deep inside my aching core.

"Fuck," I moaned…definitely too loud. I tangled my hands into his hair and pulled him up so that I could kiss him again as his fingers moved in and out of me. I lost my breath as he worked a third finger inside me.

"You're so fucking tight. Can't wait to sink into your cunt."

Using the heel of his hand, he massaged my clit with each thrust of his fingers. I was writhing under him, my hands trailing over as much of his perfect body as I could touch.

I was sure I was going to taste blood any minute with how hard I was biting my lip to stop from screaming out.

"That's it, angel. Give it to me," he said in a raspy voice.

His lips fell on mine again, but I was so mindless from his fingers that I didn't kiss him back.

He fisted my hair with his free hand. "Kiss me," he ordered before his mouth was on mine again. He fucked my mouth the same way that he was fucking me with his fingers.

He owned me in that moment. I was pretty sure he could have asked me to do anything, and I would have done it.

"Give it to me, Dahlia. Give me what I want and cum again."

I whimpered as my body obeyed him and I fell over the edge once again.

"Yes. Fuck. You're perfect. Squeeze my fingers."

I looked up through hazy eyes and saw that he was staring at his fingers inside of me.

It was so hot.

"I have to fuck you now," he said, looking up at me, his eyes wild and out of control.

His movements lacked his previous finesse as he practically tore off his trousers in his haste to get undressed.

And then my knickers were gone, ripped right off.

I froze for a second as I lay there. This was about to happen. Was I really doing this? There wasn't any going back. This could ruin everything.

His text flashed through my mind, along with a million other scenes I wished I could forget.

Fuck yes, I was doing this.

"Ready?" he asked as he pulled out a condom I hadn't seen him reach for, and he tore off the wrapper.

Oh, there was his dick…and it was huge. And pretty.

Was that a thing? Pretty dicks? He grabbed his dick and slid his hand up and down. My mouth was actually watering from watching a bead of cum leak out of the tip.

I watched in awe as he rolled on the condom. And then he slid between my legs, his weight comforting as he braced on one forearm as his other hand slid slowly up my chest until it was at the base of my neck, rubbing along my racing pulse.

"Is this okay?" he asked, and I felt something warm grow inside of me.

He rubbed his cock through my folds until I nodded. He was probably going to notice when he pushed in. I just hoped that it didn't freak him out too much.

Raphael pushed in slowly, not looking at all surprised when he hit my barrier. He had to realize what it was, right?

I opened my mouth to explain…but then something that looked a bit like possession flashed in his gaze and he suddenly pushed all the way in, pushing past my virginity so hard that a sharp gasp rushed out of me.

After pushing in, he held still for a moment, his lips descending on mine as his tongue intertwined with mine sensually. Then he pulled back, his eyes closing in ecstasy at the slow glide.

I was still slightly out of breath from the whole losing my virginity thing, but as he began to move in and out, stretching me open, filling me completely, the sore ache transformed into something more…something delicious.

"Fuck, you're just as tight as I thought," he groaned filthily as he began to slam in and out of me. I felt possessed by him. Like for the first time in my life I was doing exactly what I was meant to do. Not just something that someone else wanted from me, but what I wanted.

His soft kisses across my face were at odds with the way he was taking my body, and as his lips dragged against my skin, a tear slid down my face.

Raphael just kissed the tear away. "You're fucking exquisite. Every inch of you," he murmured as he angled his hips, hitting some other place inside of me that felt incredible.

He continued to move his hips, changing angles until he hit a spot that literally made my eyes roll back.

Raphael chuckled and repeated the move, hitting the spot over and over again until I felt like I was going to scream.

"You're perfect. Absolutely perfect," he breathed, and I inwardly winced despite the pleasure he was giving me—because if he only knew.

I was consumed by him, his smoky orange scent surrounding me. I was going to have to find out what cologne he used, because I was pretty sure that I could get myself off in the future just from smelling it.

My nails dragged down his back as he began to move faster, and he groaned in greedy pleasure. Raphael's face was strained as he kissed me fiercely, his tongue licking hungrily in me as he moved relentlessly, hitting that perfect spot with each impact.

I felt it then, another orgasm. Was I really going to have three? This man was an actual god. My chin lifted up, and I closed my eyes as I came and I convulsed around his cock. I gritted my teeth, trying to hold in my scream.

"Should we go for another one? Get this whole plane to hear you, to know what I can do to you?"

I was mindless with pleasure, and it just continued when his finger reached down and pressed perfectly on my clit, setting off yet another orgasm.

This was insane. I guess if my life was going to end after this, this was for sure the way to go.

He whispered a parade of dirty words as he continued to fuck me, chasing after his own pleasure now. He finally groaned... loudly, as he came, his thrusts slowing as he pressed his forehead against mine and our breath mingled together.

He stayed there, inside of me, his arms beside my head as we stared at each other. Finally, he broke the way too intimate silence. "Fuck, that was unbelievable," he said with a breathless chuckle as he gave me another soft kiss.

"Excuse me, everything okay in there?" came a knock just outside my privacy wall, and I froze, staring at Raphael in horror. He just laughed and pulled himself up and removed the condom before beginning to get dressed.

I immediately missed his warmth.

"Everything's good," I called out. "Just a funny movie," I continued, because I was nothing if not ridiculous.

I breathed a sigh of relief when I didn't hear anything else, although I was going to make sure that I didn't lock eyes with any of the flight attendants when I left.

I got dressed, my core already starting to ache, and then I hopped back into the little bed, and Raphael crawled in it with me.

He held me in his arms for the rest of the flight. We talked about everything and nothing. Our favorite movies, our favorite books, even our favorite colors. My mind was filled with images of me running off with him and living happily ever after. Obviously, I was high on endorphins or something because my mind was totally free of any of my usual dark, morose thoughts.

Raphael never made one mention of the fact that he'd just taken my virginity even though he'd obviously noticed.

So I didn't bring it up either.

FOUR

R eality hit, in the form of the captain announcing we were on our final descent. In just a few minutes, my lifelong prison sentence would begin.

Or maybe I'd just be thrown out into the street once my new fiancé found out that I wasn't untouched.

"Everything alright?" Raphael asked as we situated our chairs upright once again and I lowered the privacy barriers, making sure not to look out into the aisle just in case there were any judgmental or knowing looks.

"Yep," I whispered, those fireworks from before bursting inside me once again.

"Isn't she beautiful?" he said, and I looked over and realized that he was gesturing outside the window where you could see bits and pieces of New York.

I smiled and nodded, lost for words at the moment. He didn't say anything about my silence.

The plane landed.

And then it was time to meet my destiny. Or my ending. I guess that remained to be seen.

"So, this was fun," I said awkwardly as we stood up to walk off the plane. Because what else was I supposed to say?

"You can at least let me walk you to the baggage claim before you toss me to the curb," he joked, sticking his tongue out at me and lifting my spirits just a bit.

Until I remembered that was where someone from the Rossi organization would be meeting me.

He could at least walk near me though, right? No harm in that. I could pretend he was a friend and there to give me moral support.

"Of course," I finally said, and he gave me a brilliant grin as we walked out of the plane, neither of us missing the jealous, loathing look from the flight attendant who'd been after Raphael earlier.

"Hope I don't ever run into her again," I breathed as we set off down the gangway.

The airport was packed, just like Heathrow had been. A million people frantically trying to get to their destination. I felt numb as I walked, grateful that Raphael was obviously reading my mood and not saying anything.

I kind of felt bad; he was going to think I was upset about the whole sex thing.

No. He knew he was good. I didn't have to worry about that.

We made it to the escalator that led down to the baggage area and I stopped, my heart thumping so rapidly I was afraid I was going to have a heart attack.

"Dahlia?" Raphael pressed, his warmth surrounding my back.

"Just preparing myself," I said a bit hysterically before I finally stepped onto the escalator.

There was a pair of stern, sharply dressed men waiting near the bottom, and I didn't even need the sign they were holding to know they were there for me.

They nodded at me as soon as I stepped off, obviously knowing what I looked like.

"The car's outside," one of them said.

I nodded, my voice feeling broken. I turned around to at least wave goodbye to Raphael, but he was nowhere to be found.

My heart clenched at his abrupt departure. But maybe that was better. No awkward goodbyes, just longing memories to deal with, and no dead bodies if Lucian happened to see him.

"Where's Lucian?" I asked as I followed them out the door. They somehow already had all of my bags so at least I didn't have to bother with that.

"He's waiting in the car," one of them gruffly replied, and a cold sweat broke out on my forehead. I couldn't help but give one last longing look behind me as we stepped through the sliding glass doors outside.

But there was still no sign of him.

Turning my attention to the street, I saw a Bentley with blacked-out windows waiting by the curb. I knew immediately it was Lucian's. At least he had good taste in cars.

As we approached the car, the back door opened and out stepped…fuck.

My fiancé was not an old man. He was sin incarnate actually.

Maybe that was worse.

He was a direct contrast from the perfect specimen I'd just been with—a dark, beautiful angel to Raphael's light.

My brain short-circuited a bit just staring at him. He was tall —huge, in fact—with broad shoulders and beyond impressive muscles that you could see even with him wearing a pristine suit.

He gracefully stalked towards me, every inch of him a predator. Fuck me. He was...gorgeous. Was there something in the New York air? Was everyone going to resemble some kind of movie star? He had wavy, overgrown black hair that fell into his light green eyes, and the perfect amount of dark stubble accentuated his chiseled face.

"Dahlia," he said in a smooth voice as he picked up my hand and brushed a kiss across it, ink spilling out under his cuffs.

"Lucian," I answered in a choked voice as he examined my features. And I could tell just by looking at him that he was thoroughly unimpressed.

Well then.

His eyes flicked from my face to somewhere behind me as I heard footsteps approaching.

"Flight go smoothly?" Lucian asked.

I turned around to see who he was talking to, and my breath left me in a harsh rush because standing right there, a cocky smirk on his face...was Raphael.

"You've met my brother, Raphael," Lucian said, gesturing to where Raphael stood. "I sent him to be your escort on your flight," he continued with a casual head nod to Raphael for a job well done—like he hadn't just rocked my world.

Shock reverberated through me, and I began to feel a little light-headed.

I'd just given my virginity to my fiancé's brother.

Lucian turned back towards the car, and Raphael chose that moment to lean in close to me. "Half-brother, if that helps," he whispered in my ear with a smirk.

I schooled my features, determined not to show the hurt and anger coursing through me.

My mind was a jumbled, distraught mess as I thought about

everything we'd talked about on the plane...everything we'd done. And worst of all, he'd fucked me even knowing what it would mean when Lucian found out.

He was a snake.

Lucian slid into the Bentley while another man dressed in a sharp suit took my purse out of my hands and rifled through it, for reasons I was unsure of. I didn't have it in me to start a fight though.

I haltingly went to get into the car, but I couldn't help but say one more thing to Raphael.

"Was any of it real?" I murmured, so quietly there was no way anyone but him could hear me. There was an ache tearing at my chest as I waited for him to answer.

"Not a single second of it," he whispered back before he winked at me and strode off towards another waiting car, whistling a cheerful song that I knew would star in some of my nightmares.

FIVE

I slid into the Bentley, my mind a jumbled mess as I tried to wrap my head around what had just happened. I needed a release. When my thoughts got like this, there was only one thing that helped. Just one tiny cut…

"Something wrong?" Lucian asked from beside me, bringing me out of my head and into the realization that I was now sitting in a car with my future husband.

"Nothing. Just a long flight," I said, hopefully nonchalantly, turning my head to really look at him close up.

He was typing something on his phone, seeming to not be flustered at all about the fact that he was meeting his future wife.

I didn't know how it was possible to feel anguish and lust at the same time, but I couldn't help it as I stared at him. His energy was palpable, filling the whole cab of the car, almost like electric sparks jumping across my skin.

What should I say? He wasn't saying anything, so should I be quiet? Or should I try and get to know him?

"How was the flight?" he finally asked in a cool voice, still not tearing his eyes away from his phone.

A cold sweat broke out across my chest, and my heart was going a million miles an hour. Did he suspect something? There was no way that Raphael would have said something, unless he wanted to get shot.

I mean, there was no way Lucian could know, right?

"It was fine," I said calmly, really proud of myself that my voice hadn't come out in a squeak.

I wrung my hands, the adrenaline spike and the long flight showing themselves in my beyond exhausted body.

"So, ummm. When's our wedding?" I asked him, needing some sort of conversation because the silence was deafening. My mum was extremely vague with any details about the marriage, as was my brother. So I was going into this completely blind.

As shown by the way I'd fucked my future brother-in-law unknowingly just a few hours ago.

With that thought, I shifted, an ache in between my legs that had me wanting to cry, if I could cry…not because of the pain but because of the constant reminder it was about what happened.

"In a week," he responded calmly.

"A—week," I stammered.

That finally got his attention.

"Do you have a problem with that?" he asked coldly.

Okay, so my future husband was an arse, good to know. "It's just sudden, that's all. I thought—I thought maybe there would be time to get to know one another before the wedding."

"I know everything I need to know about you," he answered, before going back to his phone.

What the hell did that mean?

Alright, so I wasn't going to be asking any more questions.

I put my hands in my lap and squeezed them again, needing that sharp prick of pain to ground me. Unable to look at him anymore, I stared out the window at the teeming streets. We were passing a row of reddish-brown row homes, and I stared at them interestedly.

At least I had a new city to explore. If my marriage was as unhappy as I thought it was going to be, I could just spend my days walking around. I put my forehead against the cool glass, wondering how I had gotten here.

The row homes soon gave way to metal skyscrapers. People were milling about on the sidewalk like swarms of ants, so many it gave me anxiety to look at them. There were a lot of people in London, but I'd become accustomed to the quiet of the little town where my boarding school had been.

At least it would be easy to blend in here. At school, there had always been whispers about who I was and what my family did. There were too many people in a city like this to stand out.

Or so I thought…

Traffic was horrendous, and I was feeling a bit nauseous from all the stop-and-go.

"Is it always like this?" I blurted out, beginning to feel a little green. How long had it been since I'd eaten?

"Yes," he answered succinctly, and then he reached down beside him and grabbed a bag, which he then threw at me.

I was actually hoping to throw up now…and I was going to make sure I completely missed the barf bag and it ended up all over his perfect, shiny dress shoes.

Right before I was about to get sick, the Bentley pulled to the side of the road. Peering out my window, I saw a massive revolving door with two men in grey uniforms standing just outside them. Beyond the revolving door, I could see some kind of decadent lobby.

"Where are we?" I asked Lucian, turning my head and catching him staring at me with a disgusted look on his face.

Ok, I mean, I didn't compare to his beauty, or Raphael's for that matter...but come on, I wasn't hideous. He was looking at me like he'd stepped in shit.

"Home," he answered with no emotion in his voice. "Feel free to get out."

"Um—are you coming in?"

"No," he answered just as my door was opened by one of the uniformed men and a hand was extended to help me out.

"I have work to do. Get out," he said, his tone brokering no room for argument.

"Excuse me, you can't just—" before I could get my full sentence out, I was practically yanked out of the car and the door was slammed behind me. I glared at the man that had just pulled me from the car. If my brother were here, he would have lost his arm. I was tempted to punch him, but then I heard the car pulling away.

I watched in disbelief as the Bentley drove off, Lucian not even sparing me a backward glance.

People on the sidewalk shot me curious glances as they passed by, and I pointedly looked at the ground. My bags were on the sidewalk next to me, including my purse. Glad they decided that my tampons and lipstick weren't a threat to my big bad fiancé.

I gave myself a moment to have a pity party and then decided to go inside.

When I looked up, the doormen were back at their posts.

Were they not going to help with my bags? And how the fuck was I supposed to figure out where Lucian lived?

"Um, excuse me. Could I trouble you for a bit of help?" I asked, trying to keep my tone polite.

The doormen stared straight ahead as if they were guards at Buckingham Palace.

"Okay then," I muttered, plotting their deaths in my head…if I did that sort of thing.

I stacked my smaller suitcases on top of the larger ones and then attempted to awkwardly start pulling them towards the door. One of the suitcases immediately fell off. I was just lucky it didn't fly open with the impact.

A piece of hair fell in my face, and I frustratedly blew it out of the way.

"Bollocks," I muttered, stacking the fallen suitcase on top again and starting the process all over again.

I made it about halfway to the doors before another one fell.

This same scenario happened twice more before I made it to the doors.

The doormen were still silent, bored-looking sentries.

I'm sure that if anyone was paying attention, it was most likely extremely comical watching me get that luggage through those revolving doors.

I know I would have been laughing if I could see myself. However, since it was happening to me, I was decidedly not laughing.

Fuck Lucian. Fuck this stupid city. Fuck my family for sending me here. Oh, and fuck Raphael. Especially him.

I eventually made it through the doors where a luxurious lobby stretched out in front of me. It had white marble floors with gold flecks, and ebony black walls. The lighting was gold and muted, making everything feel expensive and imposing. I noted cameras up on the walls, enough that every inch of the lobby was being monitored. I'm sure there had been a camera recording the walk of shame I'd just experienced as well. Someone was getting first-class entertainment in a security office somewhere.

There was a man behind a black podium off to the side of the room and at least six pristinely polished gold elevators in the back of the lobby. Very uncomfortable and expensive-looking black sofas were set up in the middle of the room with a gleaming gold coffee table in the middle of them. Everything was stark and modern, and so not my taste, but I had to admit it looked nice.

At least Lucian hadn't dropped me off at a crack house or something. And based on what I'd seen of him so far, I wouldn't have put it past him.

"Hello," I called to the man standing behind the podium. The man was dressed in a well-fitted black suit with a blindingly white dress shirt underneath. He was older, with grey streaks in his chestnut brown hair and skin that was timeworn. His light grey eyes were sharp though, examining me closely as if I was a potential threat.

"Ciao, signora," he finally answered after he apparently had decided I wasn't going to do any harm.

Italian. I could have guessed that.

"Do you think you could help me? Lucian Rossi just dropped me off...I'm supposed to be staying at his flat."

"His flat?" he asked, clearly confused.

"Sorry, I've just come from England if you hadn't guessed. I meant his home? Or apartment. I have no idea what he lives in."

"Ah, yes. Mr. Rossi instructed me to take you to his pent-house," he said, reaching under his podium and revealing a key.

"Perfect," I replied in relief as I wiped some sweat from my forehead. I mean, I was in good shape, but not *lug five thousand stone around* good shape, which was what my suitcases felt like they weighed.

"Of course, signora," he replied easily like he hadn't just watched me almost die pulling my bags into the lobby, and honestly, I thought I was only exaggerating a little bit.

The man turned to the wall next to him and pressed a button. A panel slid open, revealing a row of gold luggage carts.

Those really could have come in handy ten minutes ago.

He pulled one of the carts out of the closet and then pressed the button again to close the panel. Then he pulled the cart over to my luggage and started loading it onto the cart, making it look far easier than I had.

"This way please," he said smoothly as he grabbed the cart and began pushing it towards the elevators. I followed him, feeling tired enough to fall asleep on the floor right then.

The man put his hand up to a panel on the wall and a green light pulsed beneath it. Immediately one of the elevators slid open.

That was nifty. "Will that scanner thing recognize my hand?" I asked as I followed him onto the elevator.

"That's up to Mr. Rossi," he answered.

"Okay then…"

I watched as he waved his hand in front of a screen on the wall. The screen lit up. "Thyrus," he murmured, and the elevator immediately began to ascend.

I didn't bother asking him what Thyrus meant.

"How many floors are in this building?" I asked, seeing that there weren't any buttons in the elevator, just that screen that had now gone black.

"Forty floors," he answered. I waited, just in case he was going to offer something else up. But of course, he didn't.

"I'm Dahlia by the way," I finally said as we rode up the elevator.

"I know, signora."

"Right, of course you would know that," I said awkwardly. "And your name is?"

He paused, as if he was debating whether he was allowed to answer. "Lorenzo," he finally said.

"It's nice to meet you, Lorenzo," I told him, and I saw a ghost of a smile on his lips.

"You as well, signora."

The elevator began to slow and then it came to a stop. My stomach churned, realizing that I was about to step into my new home. Or at least I thought it was my new home. It's not like Lucian had been verbose in his description of my new life.

The doors slid open and Lorenzo gestured for me to walk out first.

"Thank you," I murmured, my attention solely focused on the view in front of me.

The elevators opened into an enormous room. Ahead of me was a sunken living room. The walls on the far side of the living room were completely made of glass, and they extended at least twenty feet high. It felt like all of New York was stretched out in front of me. I tore my gaze away from the incredible view, noting the black leather sectional, the glass coffee table with gold accents, the sleek black floor lamps, and the enormous television set up on one of the walls. On the other wall was a black marble-

70

looking bar with enough bottles of alcohol to keep someone drunk their whole life.

Evidently, whoever decorated downstairs had decorated up here as well. There was a lot of black.

I looked back when I heard the elevator doors and watched as Lorenzo disappeared from sight.

He'd just left me here without so much as a goodbye.

Everyone was so friendly here. Seriously top-notch hospitality so far in New York.

Not.

Bloody Americans.

The weight of everything that had happened so far on this journey, and the reality of being in a foreign place without one single soul seemingly willing to help me, hit me then. I sank to my knees, my whole body trembling as a panic attack began to build.

I bit my lip, hating how weak I was. My heart was pounding so loudly in my chest that it felt like it was filling the whole room. I could feel my shirt sticking to me as sweat broke out all over my body. My breaths raced as I fell apart.

I abruptly stood up and stumbled down the long hallway to the left, letting out a strangled sound when I finally found the kitchen. I was only faintly aware of the black marbled countertops and the sleek black cabinets; I was focused on one thing: the block of knives sitting on the counter.

I grabbed one of the smaller knives, my hand still shaking as I held it. I lifted my shirt up with my other hand, revealing the spot on my hip that held my dirty little secret, my patch of scars that had been my salvation since I was ten and discovered that pain could heal.

I carefully slid the knife across my skin, relishing the pain and the crimson drops of blood that trailed from my cut. My panic attack began to recede as if it was exiting my body through my blood. Relief. Blessed relief.

"Fuck," I muttered when I realized I hadn't even cleaned the knife. Amateur hour over here.

I put my hand on the cut to make sure that none of the blood ended up dripping on the, you guessed it, black marble floor, and then I walked over to search for a paper towel. There weren't any on the counters, but I eventually found some in the cabinet under the sink. At least there was one thing in the kitchen organization that made sense.

Of note, the paper towels were white, I'm sure a blight on the decorator's reputation.

I pressed one of the paper towels on my cut, enjoying the sting of pain. Then I carefully cleaned the knife in the sink and put it away before walking back down the massive hallway and then down the steps into the living room, where I made my way into the bar.

"This should do the trick," I whispered to myself as I grabbed a bottle of vodka and carefully trickled some of it onto my cut, trying my best not to get any on the floor. It stung even more, and I grinned, I'm sure a bit crazily. I would usually put a bandage on it now, but finding a first aid kit in this place was probably a task I wasn't up for.

I threw the bloody, vodka-soaked paper towel into a sleek gold trashcan and then walked over to the enormous sofa that probably could have seated at least fifteen people. It was literally the largest sofa I'd ever seen. But I guess it had to be large to match this ridiculously enormous living room.

And Lucian's probable ego.

Before I sat down on it, I decided to try and find the loo. Errr...bathroom.

Nature was calling.

The first door I opened was completely empty. Just a big empty black room. Door number two unveiled a moody-looking movie room complete with a screen that filled up the entire wall. The sofas in this room were set on three different levels so you would never have your view blocked, and they looked very squishy and comfortable. I could see myself spending a lot of time in there.

But that would be later...after the bathroom.

Door number three held a bedroom. A messy bedroom. There were clothes strewn all over the room, along with some empty boxes. There was a king-size metal-framed bed on the center wall that could sleep at least five people. I think I recalled reading something about how small European beds were compared to American beds, and this was proof. It was enormous. The bed was unmade with black silk sheets that honestly made you think of sweaty sex—although I couldn't quite pinpoint why. Maybe it was something I'd seen in the *Fifty Shades of Grey* movies. Pretty sure the guy in that had black silk sheets.

My gaze darted around the room, taking stock of everything I saw until I came across a pair of inside-out boxer briefs on the floor. There was a crusty white stain on them that I suspected was dried semen. I blushed for some inane reason like someone was watching me.

Wet dream perhaps?

I quickly closed the door and started back down the hall.

Whose bedroom was that, I wondered? Just from meeting Lucian for that small amount of time, I knew if I saw his room, it would be perfectly neat. The bed was most likely made with military precision even if he had his staff do it. I assumed he had staff—most rich men did.

My thoughts were cut off when I opened yet another door and finally found a bathroom. The walls were dark in there as well, but a dark, forest green color rather than black. There was a black marble sink with grey veining throughout it. And there was the toilet...

After I relieved myself...and made use of the fancy bidet, I stumbled to the sink to wash my hands.

"Fuck," I whispered when I saw how awful I looked. My hair was a mess. I swore I'd at least patted it down before getting off the plane. But it looked like I'd been fucked and then fallen into a bird's nest where I'd been pecked to death. I was deathly pale, and my makeup was smeared around my eyes, making me look like a deranged raccoon. I was also still wearing my Union Jack shirt, of course, still a size too small. Which was always going to remind me of Raphael from this time forward, and thus I was going to cut it up in a million pieces and then burn it as soon as I got the chance.

I was honestly surprised that Lucian even let me in the car looking like this.

It wasn't quite the impression I'd intended when I got dressed that morning—or yesterday morning at this point. Who knew what time it was right now. It was still light outside when I'd started my search for the loo.

What I did know was that I needed some sleep. I felt and looked like the walking dead at the moment. I checked under the sink to see if there were any band-aids for my cut, but of course there weren't any. Because that would have been too easy, and my life was nothing if not the opposite of easy.

After I exited the bathroom, I looked down the hallway and saw at least five more doors, as well as another hallway that veered to the right. I wondered which door was my bedroom—if I even had a bedroom.

I was too tired to search for it at that moment. I wandered back down the hall and down the steps that led into the living room where the sofa was calling my name.

I threw myself down on it, thinking that it was actually a lot more comfortable than it looked. My finger absentmindedly rubbed against my cut, making sure that the continuous sting of pain kept me grounded.

The silence in the place…was unnerving.

I'd always been one that preferred to be by myself. It was hard to keep a mask up all the time, to hide how dark I was inside when everyone always expected me to be the epitome of a good girl, a good daughter, a good sister…just good.

But right now, the silence felt like too much. At least out on the busy street, trying to lug a million stone of luggage, I was distracted from the new life I'd found myself in. Now it felt…excruciating.

I pressed on my cut harder. I could do this. I'd gotten away from *him*. This was a new start.

There was a black decorative fur throw on the sofa, and I tugged it off the back where it had been expertly placed and threw it over my body as I tried to get comfortable.

I pulled out my phone, breathing a sigh of relief when I didn't see any more texts from *him*. It was six o'clock. What time was that in England? I did a quick google search. Five hours. That wasn't too bad. Mum was probably in bed already, needing to get her beauty rest. But Church and Benny were for sure up.

I made it, I typed out.

His response was instantaneous. *Killed anyone yet, little sis?*

I snorted. Only he would say that. Or Danny, I guess. I had yet in my life to kill someone, although I didn't think that was a huge accomplishment. Maybe in my family it was. My mum had probably never even held a gun though, let alone killed someone before.

So far so good, I typed out. *Give the bastards hell*, he responded back.

I cringed at that, thinking of how little hell I'd given so far. I'd been tricked by Raphael, compromised the whole treaty by giving away my virginity, and I'd let Lucian literally kick me out of the car.

I had given no hell.

At least there was still time.

There was also another text from Leo. *Call me. Please.*

My finger hovered over the keys, tempted to just type back. I hadn't been in love with Leo, far from it. But I was comfortable with him. He'd been a convenient distraction.

No. It had to be a clean break. I couldn't string him along just for a momentary spot of comfort.

I set my phone down with a sigh and sunk farther into the sofa.

I would just close my eyes for a moment...and then I'd get up and try to find my room—if there was one.

Just for a moment...

SIX

Boom!

I sat up with a start when the sound of glass shattering echoed through the room. My heart was racing a million miles a minute as I tried to figure out what had just happened…until I heard the sound of a girl giggling and the low murmur of a guy's voice.

Someone was here. Or should I say someones?

I waited for a moment, trying to make out what was being said or seeing if I could recognize the man's voice. But there were just a lot of whispers. Until I had a thought, a weird dread growing in my stomach that I couldn't understand.

What if Lucian had just come home…with another woman.

I mean, I had just lost my virginity to his half-brother on a plane, but the idea of him bringing a woman home on my first night burned. Irrational fury burst inside of me, and I sprung from the sofa, almost tripping over the throw blanket I'd somehow managed to wrap around my legs and falling headfirst into the glass coffee table.

"Bollocks," I murmured, before shaking off the blanket and storming towards the voices to do...I don't know what.

They weren't right by the door, but when I turned to my right, in the hallway I'd ventured down before was...not Lucian.

A man I hadn't seen before was leaning against the wall, his eyes closed, soft, sexual groans coming from his full lips as he massaged the head of a girl.

Who was on her knees...sucking the biggest cock I'd ever seen. I mean, to be fair, I hadn't seen that many cocks. And I'd thought Raphael's was huge...but this, this was a monster cock.

I stared at it for a second in shock before the man noticed me standing there.

"What—" he said, whipping his dick out of the girl's mouth, revealing even more inches. Wow. I mean, props to that girl for fitting that much in her mouth. He was swinging an elephant down there. I doubt I'd be able to get one-fourth of it inside of me.

The extremely hot guy shot me a cocky grin, letting his monster cock hang out a bit for my viewing pleasure, I assumed, before he tucked it back in. He must have had magic trousers, honestly, to fit that thing in there, and for some reason, it was the sight of the outline of his cock down his trousers that made me blush over seeing him get a blowie. The man was definitely a shower, not a grower.

"Um—sorry about this," I stuttered as I finally came to my senses that I was just staring at them. I began to back away with my hands up in the air, I'm sure looking crazy.

"Who are you?" the man said, cocking his head as his gaze

went lazily down my body like he had all the time in the world, and I hadn't just caught him in a compromising position.

"Dahlia," I answered awkwardly, trying to keep my gaze averted from the girl, the very pretty girl…who was still on her knees and glaring at me like she'd very much like to get back to work…on the monster dick.

It actually wasn't that hard to not look at her, because the man…was fantastic to look at.

I mean, really…Did Lucian only surround himself with gorgeous men? I assumed this was another guy also in the Rossi Mafia, or Lucian was a lot more lax in the security department than I'd thought, since this man had waltzed in and felt comfortable enough to be serviced in the hallway.

He was tan…and tall…and fit, with hair the color of rich chocolate with streaks of gold throughout. If those highlights were natural, which I suspected they were, every girl in the world was going to be envious. His hair was long, long enough to be pulled back into a haphazard bun in the back of his head. Tendrils of hair had fallen into his face, and for some reason, the effect was devastating.

His eyes were also brown, but not dull looking at all, because even standing a few feet away from him, I could see a ring of gold around his iris. Dragging my gaze away from his eyes to skim the rest of his face, I realized that his nose and mouth were familiar. And I knew exactly where I'd seen them before.

Lucian.

This guy was definitely related to my future husband.

How disappointing. He was probably an arsehole too.

Something in his golden gaze sparked when he heard my name…he was obviously familiar with it.

"Dahlia," he repeated, something in his tone sensual, like he was savoring the sound of my name.

My cheeks flushed again as they had the annoying habit of doing.

The girl shifted in place and made a slight coughing sound. I assumed it was to try and get the man's attention, which, strangely, was still attached to me.

His gaze darted back down to her, and he looked surprised to see her still there, as if he'd forgotten she was here at all.

"It's been fun, doll," he said. "But it's time to go." I felt like those words coming out of almost any other man's mouth would have been highly insulting. But for some reason, they sounded completely charming coming from him.

What a gift.

She looked dazed at his words, and a bit confused as she gracefully stood up from her knees.

I was jealous she could move like that. I'd probably have fallen over trying to get up, right into his monster dick.

The image flashed through my head, and strangely...I was a bit turned on.

What the fuck was wrong with me?

I watched, a little bit amused and a little bit horrified, as he patted her on the back like she was his mate and hadn't just been...taking care of him.

"Thank you," the girl said meaningfully. And my jaw dropped as I surveyed the guy once more, wondering if he had some kind of magical power. She'd just thanked him for the opportunity to give him a blow job and then be sent away.

That was a special talent.

"No problem," he responded, shooting her a wink. She went to the elevator doors without a word, turning her head to blow him a kiss before stepping inside. "Call me?" she pleaded as the doors began to close. He just smiled at her in response, a swoon-worthy smile I had to admit, but a definite "no" to her question.

And then he turned his attention back to me.

GABRIEL

I was obsessive.

And compulsive.

I'd been diagnosed with OCD when I was four and the nanny caught me hoarding toys and food and other people's belongings. I would get fascinated with toys or belongings that kids in my preschool class had and would have to have them. I'd steal them from the kids, or just straight up take them, and then I'd hoard "my treasures" in my closet...where my nanny eventually found them when she was looking for dirty laundry.

My father didn't care when the nanny told him. I mean, shit, a crucial element of a mafia man was knowing how to steal, so she'd gotten my mother's permission and taken me to a doctor where I'd received a formal diagnosis.

I wasn't a clean freak, and I didn't steal my friends' belongings anymore...at least not that often. But what I did do was obsess over people. Women, to be more specific.

The parade of women that I'd supposedly "fallen" in love with over the years was a source of unending amusement to my brothers. I would see someone across the room, and just like a fairytale, I'd be a goner, completely obsessed over the girl. I'd get her to fall in love with me...quickly, until she was just as obsessed with me as I was with her...usually even more so. It was pretty easy when you looked like me, talked like me, and were a key member of the Cosa Nostra.

I'd wine and dine them, then fuck them until they saw stars, and the obsession would usually last for a few weeks, maybe a few months even. And then I'd wake up one day, usually with them in my bed, and the obsession would be gone.

I'd kick them out and that would be that...until I saw my next girl.

I supposed I should have felt bad about all the ruined, broken-hearted girls I'd left around the city...and country. But I'd never really gone for that whole guilt-ridden thing. My disorder was a part of me; why should I feel shame for it? If God had wanted me to be different, he would have made me different.

At least that's what I told the priest in confession every month.

Not sure that he bought it, but I couldn't care less.

Plus, the girls got a lot out of it. Fantastic sex, for one. I mean, they'd never get sex like that again, or probably find someone with as big of a dick as me who actually knew how to use it. And I gave them tons of gifts, treated them like they were the center of the world. They got into the best parties, wore the best clothes, and ate at the most exclusive restaurants in the world.

I mean, what girl could ask for more.

A flash of annoyance burst inside of me when I thought about the teary-eyed, insane women who followed me around, crashed parties, and sent me letters after it was finished. But I pushed that away. It didn't matter.

I loved the initial rush of falling in love. I loved love. Raphael and Lucian seemed to get off on telling me that I wasn't really in love, but honestly, what the fuck would they know about being in love? The two of them wouldn't know the feeling if it kicked them in the head and licked their nutsacks.

Whatever they said about it just being chemicals in my brain acting up, I didn't care. I got the biggest high from it. I would keep on falling in love forever if I had any say about it.

I winked at the girl in the elevator, her name fading from my mind. Genevieve. Persephone? No, that was some Greek goddess, wasn't it? Definitely not that girl's name. I probably should have felt shame that I'd been with that girl for three-ish weeks and she was already fading from memory, but again, I didn't operate like that.

And who was that girl, when I had this exquisite creature in front of me?

Dahlia. Was it strange that I wanted to roll in her name, wrap it up around me, tattoo it on my skin?

A little voice inside my head reminded me that she was my brother's fiancée, the key to ending the decades-long war we'd had.

But I pushed that nosy fucker away.

Dahlia was mine.

She was standing there in a pair of dark, tight jeans that showed off her toned legs. I kind of wanted to ask her to turn around so I could see her ass. I'm sure it was as sweet as the rest of her. And her shirt…was that the British flag? I wasn't really up on my geography or World History, but I was pretty sure that's what it was. As ridiculous as it was, I kind of wanted to frame it. The way it showcased the hottest pair of tits I'd ever seen was a glory to behold. I kind of wanted to find the factory that had made it, buy it, and then just have her wear those shirts for the rest of our lives.

Except she'd look much better with it off, wouldn't she?

Her hair was a mess, a glorious mess. It was gold, almost like Raphael's, but obviously way better. Would it be weird if I asked to cut off a piece to keep? Hmm. Maybe I should wait until after a few dates before I did that. Her eyes were what really took the cake, though. They were a stunning shade of light blue, like a sky on a cloudless summer day.

She was perfect, absolutely perfect.

"I'm sorry, what's your name?" she asked, crinkling her nose a bit in a fucking cute way.

"Gabriel. Gabriel Rossi," I responded.

"Are you…" she asked hesitantly.

"Lucian's brother? Yes. I'm obviously the best of the Rossi men, though. The best in all the ways that count." I watched in amusement as she flushed, her gaze flicking to my dick that I knew was showing through my pants. I was kind of glad she'd seen it in all of its glory. It was quite the way to meet someone, definitely a way to make sure that she couldn't forget me.

Although we could have done without the whole dick-sucking thing.

"Dahlia Butcher," I said slowly, savoring her name on my lips once again. "I have to say, it's nice to finally meet you. The anticipation has been killing me."

She bit her lip, obviously nervous.

I looked around, kind of expecting Lucian to pop out at any moment. I knew I wouldn't be able to leave her alone for too long.

"Did you just arrive?" I asked when I noticed her bags lying against the wall in the entryway.

"It's been a few hours now," she said softly, crossing her arms in front of her in a way that only made her tits jut out more.

I wanted to pull her top up over her breasts and suck on what

I was sure would be pretty pink nipples. I was getting hard just thinking about it.

As if she could read my mind, her eyes briefly darted to my dick again. Her face flushed and she looked away.

Well, that was good. She was at least attracted to my dick. I could work with that.

"Have you eaten anything?" I asked, walking close to her and pressing my hand on her lower back as I began to move her towards the kitchen.

"Not since the airplane," she said softly. "I—well, no one showed me around, so I haven't been quite sure what to do." A bit of anger threaded through her words and it just made me harder.

Wait a minute. "Lucian didn't take you up here? Show you around?" I asked, practically seething at the thought. If Lucian wanted to make it easy for me to move in on her, he was doing a bang-up job. Her body was trembling under my touch in either fury or exhaustion...or maybe a mix of both.

She gave me a look, studying my face as if she wasn't sure what she could say or not. Good girl. You needed to be careful in our world. I'm sure she'd learned that growing up in "The Firm". But she needed to be even more on her guard here. I'd heard about her brothers. They used their fists more than their brains. There was no one I trusted in our world, no one but my brothers. And even they were manipulative, savage creatures most of the time. They would tell you one thing and then do the exact opposite if it suited them.

But she didn't need to have her guard up with me. I thought she was incredible, the girl of my dreams. I'd always be on her side. I'd always protect her.

"Hey, I'm sorry for what happened. If I'd been here, I would have punched Lucian for you."

A little smile peeked through, and I was immediately obsessed with the idea of seeing more of it, of making her smile as much as I possibly could.

I led her over to one of the sleek black barstools that surrounded the massive marble island in our fucking pretentious apartment and helped her sit down.

She eyed me warily as if she didn't know what to think about what was going on. I didn't blame her. I mean, she had walked in on me getting a blowjob from another chick. But that was in the past. If I'd known she existed, there would have never been another girl. She would have always been my world.

After I got her situated, I strode over to the built-in refrigerator and started pulling out ingredients, stopping to take a peek at her every so often because I couldn't handle going too long without seeing her face. I felt like I had a whole life without her to make up for. It was like I'd been in purgatory all this time, and now that I'd found her, I'd been brought into the light.

Yeah, I was a cheesy motherfucker, but she just did something to me.

After I got out everything I needed to make spicy rigatoni, it suddenly hit me, I didn't even know if she liked spicy food. What if she had an allergy?

"Shit. I'm making spicy rigatoni. It's my specialty. Do you like spicy things? Do you like Italian? Do you have any allergies?" I fired off the questions to her, desperate to know everything I could about her.

A giggle slipped from her mouth, and she looked kind of shocked about it. "Um, I love pasta. I haven't had spicy rigatoni, but I love spicy anything. And I'm only allergic to beets."

"You're allergic to beets?" I asked quizzically, already planning on searching all the cabinets and refrigerators in the place to make sure there wasn't a beet to be found.

"Yes. I break out in hives. We found out at a fancy party my parents were throwing. I had giant red welts all over me in the middle of the party after I happened to eat a beet salad. It was embarrassing at seven years old," she told me, again looking surprised, like she couldn't believe she offered me anything about herself.

"Alright, no beets. I think we'll be safe with this dish, then. Absolutely no beets involved."

Another smile. Fuck. I wanted to grab my phone and start snapping pictures. *Down boy, we don't want to scare her off*, I told myself.

"Are—you allergic to anything?" she asked after I'd started cooking. My back was to her as I filled a pot with water and placed it on the stove.

I smiled to myself as I threw some olive oil and a handful of salt into the water and set it on high. She wanted to get to know me. I liked that. I'd tell her anything she wanted to know.

"Absolutely nothing. I'm a human garbage can, I'm afraid. I can eat everything, and I do… quite often."

I turned back towards her and started to chop some garlic and some shallots for the sauce.

"You're quite adept at that," she commented as I expertly minced the garlic into tiny pieces. Fuck, I loved that proper British accent of hers. It was so fucking sexy. My new favorite sound in the world.

"Hmmm, I love to cook," I mused as I worked on the shallots, adjusting myself behind the marble because I was so hard it was starting to hurt. I wondered if this was going to be my perpetual state of being from now on. Just walking around stiff as a board and desperate to fuck her. "I've taken a bunch of cooking classes. And it's the way I relax at the end of the day. Do you like to cook?" I kept my voice casual, trying to play it off like I wasn't obsessed with the idea of finding everything out about her that I could.

She laughed and I leaned forward, drawn to it like a moth to a flame. My list was already adding up, things I wanted to see her do. Smile, laugh, show me her boobs.

"I'm one of those people that would probably burn a pot of water. If that's possible," she said, cocking her head as she stared at the pot of water that was just starting to boil. "I can make passable tea, I suppose. Which is probably a good thing since I doubt anyone here knows how to make a proper cup."

Note to self, research everything I could about making a proper cup of British tea so she never had to do it herself.

"What kind of tea do you like?" I asked as I pulled out some rigatoni I'd had shipped straight from my favorite restaurant in Italy. I poured it into the water and gave it a good stir. Usually I would make my own pasta, but I kind of wanted to get done cooking as soon as possible so she could eat, and I could give her all of my attention.

"You know, it's funny. I'm not marrying you, but you've asked me more questions in the last fifteen minutes than my fiancé asked during the over-an-hour-long car ride."

I held in my grin until I wasn't facing her again. Lucian was such an asshole. It was perfect.

"Oh? Lucian didn't have anything to say?"

"Apparently not," she huffed. I heard her shift in her seat as I added some salted butter into another pan and began to melt it. "He—seemed unhappy about the situation," she said tentatively.

I thought about what I should say. Lucian had been pretty quiet about the whole arranged marriage thing. Raphael and I hadn't been present when the contract was signed. But once he'd come home, Lucian hadn't so much as flinched when it had been revealed everyone would basically be trading their daughters in exchange for peace. I'd been horrified on behalf of Lucian...and my little sister.

I couldn't imagine being forced to marry some random girl. What if she was hideous? But Lucian, he'd agreed to it immediately. As the oldest brother and the future boss of the Cosa Nostra, he took his role seriously. Too seriously, if you asked me.

But right now, I was more jealous than I'd ever thought possible that he was getting to marry Dahlia. He was the luckiest bastard in the world as far as I was concerned. But as long as her heart belonged to me, I could deal with him getting to marry her. She'd still carry the same last name as me.

"Gabriel?" she asked questioningly. I tossed the garlic and the shallots into the butter to soften and added some chilis and some salt and pepper before speaking.

"He's very focused on his position," I said carefully. "Right now, he's the underboss for my father. Lucian has a lot of responsibility. I'm sure...things will warm up between you two," I continued. Over my dead body.

And that was as much as I really wanted to talk about Lucian.

Her stomach all of a sudden let out the loudest growl I think I'd ever heard. I turned to look at her, and she had an appalled look on her face like she wanted to go run and hide.

It was fucking cute.

"Glad you're hungry," I said with a wink, and something inside of me growled in satisfaction when a beautiful blush appeared on her cheeks.

I made a mental note to add lots of winks to my game card in the battle to get Dahlia's heart.

The pasta was almost perfect, so I gave it another hard stir before I grabbed some vodka from the cabinet and poured a shot in the sauce before adding heavy cream, tomato paste, and freshly grated parmesan. Then I took some of the pasta water, which anyone with Italian ancestry knew was the secret ingredient, and I poured some of it into the sauce.

Fucking perfect.

I heard the barstool move, and I quickly turned around, scared that she was leaving. Instead, I watched as she walked sexily over to where I was standing and looked at the sauce. Sexiest walk I'd ever seen.

This is what I meant by the high of falling in love. Except this high was nothing I'd ever experienced. It was like I was having an out-of-body experience, and I hadn't even slept with her yet. I could only imagine how good that was going to be.

"This smells amazing," she said breathily, and I got a little entranced watching her cute pink tongue peek out of her mouth and lick that fucking sinful bottom lip of hers.

I could think of a lot better uses for that tongue. And that mouth, for that matter. I groaned when she bent over to get closer to the sauce, showcasing the heart-shaped ass of my dreams.

I angled my body away and subtly adjusted myself, because this was fucking agony. Not able to help myself, I scooped up some of the sauce onto my wooden spoon and brought it to her mouth. Dahlia went to take the spoon, obviously uneasy about having me spoon feed her, but I decided to push her just a little bit more.

"Taste it," I practically growled, and she blinked at me shyly before opening up her mouth and letting me slide the spoon in.

As soon as the sauce hit her tongue, her eyes were closing, and a little moan escaped her mouth.

That's what I'd been going for. My sauce was fucking awesome.

She swallowed, and for just a second, I let myself have the image of her on her knees in front of me...swallowing something else.

"It's incredible. Better than anything I've ever had, even in Italy," she said, and I knew she meant it. I felt like preening like a fucking rooster at the praise. A million other recipes flashed through my mind, but of course that evolved into spreading her out on the island and eating *her,* and I had to cut off that line of thought.

I could tell it was going to be hard to keep focused around her.

"Go sit down and I'll get us some bowls," I said, unable to stop myself from patting her on that perfect ass.

She let out a little squeak that was beyond fucking adorable and practically sprinted back to her seat.

I hummed a little Taylor Swift as I drained the pasta and then mixed the noodles in with the sauce. Then I spooned huge heaps of it into bowls and sprinkled more grated parmesan and some crushed red pepper onto the top.

"Bon Appetit, my lady," I crooned as I set down the steaming dish in front of her.

She swooned for a moment before carefully schooling her face. I wanted to tear off the calm mask she wore, because that's what it was. I couldn't wait to see what Dahlia was like underneath. And I meant I wanted underneath in all the different ways.

"I thought the Cosa Nostra was Italian," she teased as she

spooned a big bite of the rigatoni into her mouth and moaned again.

I bit my lip as she continued to torture me.

"I'm an equal opportunist when it comes to different cultures," I responded, making sure to give her another wink just so I could see that blush again.

It was the best dinner that I could ever remember. I poured her some Pinot Noir from Raphael's collection, because he might have been a psycho, but his wine collection was next level. As soon as the alcohol kicked in, she relaxed and let down her defenses. She told me about her boarding school and a little bit about her life in London. I gobbled up every scrap she gave me like a dog begging under the table.

I was already plotting out the rest of the night, and how I could keep her with me.

DAHLIA

Gabriel was amazing...and terrible all at once. He was the most charming man I'd ever met, immediately casting a spell over me.

And the way that he looked at me. Like he was enthralled and absolutely convinced I was the most interesting girl in the world. No one had ever looked at me like that.

Not even Raphael, a little voice whispered, and every time I heard that warning, I tried to shore up my defenses.

But it was fucking hard against Gabriel's pure exuberance. He casually touched me whenever he could. I tried to ignore it— I'd already probably ruined my life with one stranger today—but it was difficult.

I'd never met anyone so…alive. He was like an extremely hot puppy, completely focused on giving me attention…and affection.

The offer was there. So tangible I could practically taste the sex in the air. I wasn't sure how I'd gone from being a virgin at the beginning of the trip to having images of hot sex on the floor…or on the kitchen counter, but it was kind of hard not to.

I didn't know what was wrong with the Rossi brothers. I'd never heard of a mafia man wanting to share unless it was a whore they'd bought for the night.

Is that what they thought of me? I was a whore that they would pass around? Or was this some kind of game, a twisted form of sibling rivalry to see who could destroy the future boss's wife first?

"What did you just think about?" he asked me, standing way too close as his gaze danced all over my face.

"It's just been an interesting day," I told him, itching for a blade once again to help with my complicated thoughts. "I'm getting a bit tired."

"Fuck, of course you are," he said worriedly, like he couldn't believe that he hadn't thought of it first. He also looked disappointed.

"Let's get you to your room," he said, unnecessarily reaching for my hand as he helped me out of my chair.

The problem was, he didn't let go of my hand as he began to pull me out of the kitchen, leaving a huge mess behind us. And I didn't know how to politely pull away.

"Um, should we clean the kitchen first?" I asked as we turned the corner and went back down the hallway I had briefly explored when I'd been looking for the bathroom.

"Nope. Emilia will be here first thing in the morning, and this place will be spick and span before you even get up for breakfast."

"Emilia?" I asked, ignoring the fact that I didn't like the sound of another woman's name coming from his lips.

"She's the woman in charge of keeping us all in line. She's worked for the family since before I was born." He looked back at me over his shoulder, still holding my hand. "She's going to loooove having you around. She's been missing my sister like crazy. She cleans both here and at our father's place."

His sister. For a second there, I'd forgotten I wasn't the only woman in this mess. That there were five other women in the same situation as me. I'd never met them, and I wasn't sure that I ever would. But I felt some kind of solidarity with them. Like we were united in a sort of sisterhood. We'd all been sold, like property…like we were nothing. My gut clenched just thinking about the unfairness of it all.

"Where does your father live?" I asked, trying to distract myself.

"My father lives on the other side of Manhattan, in the same brownstone that we grew up in," he said stiffly, and there was no missing the edge to his voice at the mention of his father.

Gabriel stopped at a door a few doors farther than I'd ventured and he opened it up. "Fuck," he said, letting go of my hand and trying to close the door before I could follow him in.

"What is it?" I asked. I pushed on the door and then stopped abruptly when I slowly looked around the room and saw that it was…piled with junk. There were some broken chairs, boxes, stacks of books…what looked like sacks of clothing. Most importantly was the fact that there was no bed—no furniture of any kind.

"Was this supposed to be my room?" I asked, a sinking

feeling in my gut. I'd been looking forward to having a space I could escape to after such a long day, and of course they'd made sure that wasn't going to happen for me.

"Maybe they've got you set up in the other guest room," he said with a frown, leading me to the door next to that room.

That one was completely empty.

"There must have been a mix-up in the directions with the staff," Gabriel said hurriedly, something that looked like irritation burning in his gaze. He ushered me out of the room with a hand far too low on my back, and then he pulled out his cell phone and started to furiously type someone a message.

I rubbed my hands down my face. That nap had barely taken the edge off of the utter exhaustion I was experiencing.

Gabriel pocketed his phone and then reached his hand towards me, gently moving a piece of hair out of my face.

Why was that move so fucking sexy to me?

"How about this—let's get in my room. You can use my shower, get changed into something comfortable, and just sleep in my bed...with me somewhere else, obviously." He got a mischievous, sexy look on his face. "Unless you wanted to have a sleepover."

I rolled my eyes and snorted as he led me back down the hallway and into the messy room that I'd discovered earlier. After showing me the huge connected bathroom that featured the tub of my dreams, he left the room briefly, only to return with all of my bags.

"I wonder where the rest of my things are? They were sent ahead of me," I mused.

"I'll find them, don't worry. I'll take care of everything," he said, a bit mysteriously as he gently closed the door and left me to take a shower.

I walked into the bathroom, admiring how sleek and fancy everything looked. My mum liked things extravagant, but that often meant gold brocade and statues of angels. Although I wasn't a fan of the all black, it did look nice.

The shower could hold at least six people, and I quickly turned it on, making sure not to look in the mirror as I stripped off my clothes. I'm sure my reflection had gotten even worse as I'd grown more tired.

After grabbing the shampoo and conditioner I'd packed, I stepped into the shower, breathing a sigh of relief as the piping hot water pounded on my skin from directly above, and directly in front of me. Steam rose around me as I leaned my head against the black marble in front of me. What a fucking day.

I felt like I'd honestly lived at least four lifetimes since I'd left England. Not to mention I was still aching between my legs as a continuous reminder of my mistake with Raphael.

No, not a mistake. I'd very purposefully done it, either as a fuck you against *him*, or a fuck you against Lucian and this treaty. Maybe it was a fuck you to both.

I still needed to decide if I was going to try and fake the whole virginity thing or just let the pieces fall where they may. I'd heard stories of other mafia princesses carrying a packet of ketchup with them to bed, or even red paint in some cases. But that all seemed a bit ridiculous. Girls these days lost their hymen with tampons for God's sake.

My impression of Lucian was also that he wasn't someone easily fooled, so schemes like that would probably not work.

I'd think about it later when it didn't feel like my brain was going to ooze out of my skull.

I washed myself, my fingers dancing over the bundle of scars that marred the small patch of skin on my hip. The wound from today looked like it was already healing well, and I pressed on it until a tiny drop of blood came out and then was washed away. My muscles relaxed at the prick of pain.

I stood in that shower so long that I actually drifted to sleep briefly, which I hadn't known I was capable of doing. Usually I needed perfect conditions, a dark room with the closet doors open and the closet light on, a noisemaker, and a sleeping pill.

Finally deciding I'd been in there long enough, I turned off the water, impressed with the water heater's capability in the place. It was still as piping hot when I turned it off as it had been when I'd gotten in.

There was a towel hung up on a warming rack, and I frowned at it. Had it been there before? Or had Gabriel come in and put it there? Surely I would have noticed if that had happened.

Was it a little bit wrong of me that I didn't particularly object to Gabriel walking in on me in the shower?

I shook the thought away. What the fuck was wrong with me?

I sighed as I wrapped the warm, fluffy towel around me. I guess if I was going to be in prison for the rest of my life, at least it was a gilded one.

I peeked out the bathroom door to make sure Gabriel wasn't in his room, and when I saw that it was empty, I walked into the bedroom and rifled through my suitcase until I found some sleeping clothes. This one was a pink satin material comprised of shorts and a spaghetti strap top with a built-in bra. I'd bought all new sleeping things for my trip here. I wanted a fresh start in everything.

I brushed out my hair, and then made sure to go through my nighttime skin routine even though I was exhausted. From the time I could talk, it felt like my mum had pressed into my brain the importance of skincare. And even though I was twenty, with no wrinkles to be found in the immediate future, my mum always made sure I had a cabinet of skincare products to use day and night.

I would have to figure out how to order all of that myself now, wouldn't I?

The idea gave me a strange wave of melancholy. It was an interesting thing about human nature, how you could miss something and be glad that you had left it…all at the same time.

After finishing up getting ready for bed, I cast a glance at the ginormous bed in the room. It was still unmade with his sheets. Sheets that he had slept in, sheets that he'd probably bonked other girls in.

The thought made me a bit sick. I definitely needed to change the sheets if I was going to sleep in there. I had an aversion to other people's bodily fluids.

Although you sure had been lusting after Raphael's, a nasty inner voice reminded me.

I shivered, trying not to think about how absurdly sexy that bead of pre-cum on his perfect dick had been. How much I'd wanted to lick it.

I walked out of the room and down the hallway towards the media room where I heard noise. The door was wide open, but the room was dim when I peered in, the only light coming from the huge screen where Thor and Iron Man were running towards a burning building.

"Gabriel?" I asked hesitantly. I really didn't want to walk in on Lucian…or Raphael.

I breathed a sigh of relief when Gabriel stood up from where he'd been lounging on the sofa, and he started towards me.

Except, holy fuck, he was shirtless, wearing nothing but a

pair of low-slung grey sweatpants that showed the outline of everything...and I mean everything.

With his monster dick, it was pure sin for him to wear something like that.

My brain turned into a puddle of mush. His body...I mean, the big man upstairs either thought I'd been very good...or very bad based on the sight in front of me. Gabriel's body should be illegal. His broad planes of muscle tapered down to a trim waist. He was a bit leaner than Raphael had been, but no less sexy. The ridges and valleys of his abdominal muscles were perfectly outlined, and I found myself seeing my second set of the elusive eight-pack. He only had a sprinkling of hair on his chest, and it led down to a V and a happy trail that made me want to drool. And his tattoos. They were everywhere. His chest and arms were a work of art. There was an intricate crest in the middle of his chest with a skull and a crown. The words "loyalty, honor, family," were engraved under the crest. I wondered if every Cosa Nostra man had that tattoo. I hadn't remembered Raphael having one that looked like that, but I hadn't got a chance to look closely. Gabriel's other tattoos were more random. There was a rose, and a lion, and a compass...I even spotted a butterfly. I could probably spend hours going through his tattoos.

"Want a closer look?" he purred, and I quickly averted my gaze from his chest back to his face, garnering a sexy chuckle from him.

I guess at least I was going to have man candy to look at in this place. I wasn't sure if that was a good or bad thing.

I wondered what Lucian looked like without a shirt. The thought hit me and I inwardly grimaced, even though I knew it was going to be an impressive sight. His muscles had been outlined even through the suit he'd been wearing earlier.

Gabriel's hair was wet, and I realized that he must have taken a shower somewhere else while I was taking a shower.

Gabriel stalked towards me like a panther, his gaze lazy as he took his time looking me up and down. His gaze was like a caress, and it sent a wave of heat through me. My nipples stood at attention the longer he stared.

"Is that what you sleep in?" he finally asked gruffly after we both had eye-fucked each other for way too long.

I felt naked now after the way he was looking at me, and it felt like I needed to go throw on a sweatshirt or something.

"Umm, yes," I answered, shifting awkwardly. His gaze tracked the movement intensely, and I felt like he was paying close enough attention to me that he could probably hear the rapid pace of my heart. "I was wondering, do you have a new set of sheets that I could use?"

"Fuck. I should have done that while you were showering," he said, again seeming to be strangely upset with himself that he hadn't anticipated my every need.

It was honestly endearing, and an unfamiliar warmth flickered in my chest

You can't trust any of them, that inner voice reminded me. *Think about what happened today. Don't be a fool.*

The words pounded through my head, and I worked to push the warm feeling out of my chest. *Fool me once, shame on you. Fool me twice, shame on me.* The rhyme darted through my mind.

My parents had been neglectful in a lot of ways growing up, but they hadn't raised a fool. And I wasn't about to start acting like one, any more than I already had.

Gabriel brushed past me as he moved down the hallway. The

sight from the back was just as good as the front, his shapely arse outlined perfectly…muscular and bitable.

Okay, weirdo.

He stopped in front of yet another door I hadn't opened and winked at me over his shoulder, like he'd known exactly what I'd been looking at. And, of course, I blushed. I'd like to see any woman act cool in the face of that wink. He opened it up, and I saw a bunch of what looked like cleaning supplies. I assumed that was where the staff kept their supplies. He looked at me with a little chagrin on his face.

"I'm not exactly sure where clean sheets would be."

I snorted. "I'll just fall asleep on the sofa in the media room," I told him.

"Afraid you'll catch cooties in my sheets, Dahlia? Don't want to smell like me?" he teased, sticking out his tongue at me. How did he make even that seem hot?

I just blushed in response, not wanting to offend him, but also, the idea of smelling like him was not quite as distasteful as it should have been. "It's just…um. I assume there's been girls in there…and that's…um, not exactly hygienic?" I ended my word vomit in a question like an idiot, but he looked horrified.

"Oh, I've never had a girl in that bed. Ever," he told me emphatically, taking a step towards me like he wanted to touch me. He bit his cheek and stepped back to where he'd been standing.

I was a little shocked by his statement. "You brought that girl home to sleep with her, did you not? Was that not going to happen in your bed?"

Now he was the one who was blushing. He glanced up at the ceiling like he couldn't look at me while he answered my question. "We have a room for that sort of thing," he finally said.

"That's why there are only those two empty rooms as options for you to stay."

"Oh," I responded, not really knowing what to say to that. I'd just met the man and felt like I knew way too much, and had seen too much, involving his sex life.

"I'll just set you up in the media room, and I'll make sure your room is sorted out first thing in the morning," he promised. He hesitated for a second before he grabbed my hand and pulled me into the media room. My whole hand tingled like he was shooting electricity into me with his touch.

There were a bunch of throw blankets all over the sofas, and he immediately went to work gathering a bunch of them and stacking a few of the squishy-looking throw pillows together until he'd set up a pretty comfy looking bed for me.

It was amusing, and a little hot, watching him work because from what I knew of *made men*, they weren't usually so helpful... Every mafia man I'd ever known had two things they were focused on: the "organization" and themselves. And here this mafia man was, fluffing my pillows.

"Will this work alright?" he asked eagerly, and that warmth in my chest that I was desperately trying to keep at bay, struck up again.

"It's great. Thank you," I told him. I brushed past him to get onto the sofa, wishing he'd put on a shirt because it was really distracting. I sunk down onto the sofa and sighed, it was actually really comfortable.

He stood there awkwardly, and suddenly...I didn't want him to leave. I'd thought I wanted to be alone but facing the night in this new place seemed daunting.

"Want to finish this movie? Although, I'm warning you right now, I'll definitely fall asleep," I told him. Gabriel jumped into action like I'd made his life. He settled at my feet, picking them up and placing them in his lap.

I blamed my tiredness for the fact that I didn't pull away even though it was highly inappropriate. Gabriel picked up a remote and pulled up a screen that had what looked like every movie on earth.

"Let's see if there's anything you want to watch more than the *Avengers*."

"Is there any movie you don't own?" I gasped.

Gabriel chuckled, his thumb dancing across my skin and driving me crazy. "Lucian is a bit of a cinephile. He has some sort of supplier that gets him every movie before they even come out. I don't think there's a movie he's seen that he hasn't loved."

Gabriel's voice was so fond when he told the story about Lucian, and I wondered what kind of relationship he had with him. Because while he was mentioning Lucian, his hands were actually massaging my feet.

It kind of felt like an out-of-body experience because I'd just met this man, and after being betrayed by his one brother, and humiliated by his other brother, I was now letting him massage my feet of all things.

I'd clearly left my brain back in England.

"So what movie would you pick if you had every movie at your disposal?" he asked, as his hands continued to work magic on me. What could those hands do on other parts of my body?

Bad Dahlia.

"*Wedding Crashers*," I blurted out, the decision easy.

"Have you seen it before?" Gabriel asked with an amused chuckle.

"At least a million times," I admitted. "But I love it every time just as much."

"Alright," he said easily. "*Wedding Crashers* it is."

He turned it on, and I snuggled into my pillow, both of us chuckling a few times at Vince Vaughn and Owen Wilson's antics. Gabriel never took my feet from his lap, and I never pulled them away.

And somehow, exhaustion took over and I was pulled into dreamland, just like that.

My last thought...I could still feel Raphael in between my legs.

SEVEN

I woke up the next day to a heavenly smell. It took me a moment to remember where I was and what I was doing on the sofa.

Right. I was in New York City. About to be married.

Dread pricked at my skin as I pushed the blankets off of me, and I sat up, realizing that I'd slept through the night.

For as long as I could remember, I'd woken up throughout the night, my senses on high alert like *he* was suddenly going to appear in my room. And yet, my first night a continent away from him, and I'd slept like a baby.

A major perk to this whole "being shipped away against my will" situation.

I glanced to the other side of the sofa where there were pillows stacked up and a pile of blankets. Had Gabriel slept there the whole night? I didn't know what to think about that.

I got up from the sofa and walked out to the hallway, taking a moment to use the loo in the hall bath before I ventured hesitantly towards the kitchen, where the delicious smell was coming from.

Gabriel was still shirtless, and still ridiculously good-looking. He was standing in front of the stovetop, his arms extended so that every muscle in his shoulders, arms, and back stood out in stark relief. I stood there for a second, just looking at him… because what else could you do?

"Sleep well?" he asked casually, and I jumped, completely embarrassed he'd known I was standing there the whole time, just eye-fucking him.

"Very well, thank you," I answered, walking over to see what he was cooking. There were actually several things—eggs, bacon and sausage…pancakes. I faintly noticed that there was no sign of the dishes and food from last night. Maybe the staff was actually comprised of house elves or fairies who cleaned in the middle of the night while you were sleeping.

"It's not a traditional English Breakfast, but we're very much against baked beans in this house," he teased, beginning to plate up the food.

"I happen to feel the same way about baked beans," I responded with a laugh.

He set the plates down in front of the stools at the table where two glasses of orange juice already sat.

"You're going to spoil me."

"I intend to," he murmured softly. Like last night, his gaze felt like a physical touch. I could *feel* him, like his hands were sweeping over me. Was it a Rossi thing, this ability to make me burn just from a look?

A pang of longing hits me then. Why couldn't Gabriel be who I was marrying? If this was real, his sweetness and caring…

combined with his looks, I'd have been the luckiest girl in the world. I'd have run down that aisle.

What kind of torture was it going to be instead to walk towards Lucian when I knew someone like Gabriel existed?

Whispered dirty words and lips tangled together flashed through my mind. I shoveled food into my mouth in an effort to push those thoughts away.

We ate breakfast mostly in silence, something I was grateful for.

"Well, doesn't this look cozy," a familiar voice purred from behind us. I froze. It was Raphael.

Gabriel continued to chew before he answered. "Good morning to you too, brother."

I didn't look back at him. I was frozen in place, my whole body attuned to his presence.

I could feel those beautiful eyes of his, drilling into me. His footsteps seemed to fill the room as he walked around the island until he was standing in front of both of us, a familiar smirk on his beautiful face.

I'd half convinced myself that I was never going to see him again. Yet here he was.

He was just as beautiful as he'd been yesterday, practically taking my breath away. It was really a shame that the ugliness that lived inside of him wasn't visible on the outside.

"Hello, Dahlia."

I clenched the bottom of my chair to stop myself from doing something drastic like throwing my juice glass at him. I'm sure that would catch Gabriel's suspicion.

Just by the way he'd said my name, I knew he was picturing me naked.

Prick.

"Hello, Raphael," I answered, proud of how steady my voice came out.

"I'm sorry you had to deal with this asshole your whole flight," said Gabriel as he stood up and grabbed both of our plates. "I would have gone, but Lucian was insistent that Raphael go get you. He probably thought my charm would be too much for you." And there was that wink again. Seriously, having the attention of both of these men on me was way too much.

"Oh, I don't know, Gabey. Maybe Lucian didn't think that he'd be able to drag you out of Francesca's bed. Wasn't that the name of the girl from last week?" Raphael's voice was mocking, obviously intended to embarrass rather than tease.

Francesca. I guess I had a name now for the girl who'd been "helping" Gabriel out yesterday.

Gabriel froze in front of the sink where he'd been placing our dishes while I studied Raphael while his attention was elsewhere.

He was a master con artist, he had to be. There was absolutely no trace of the man I'd met yesterday. I wondered if it had been his plan all along to seduce me, or if he'd just smelled the pathetic all over me and gone in for the kill.

Either way, I hated him.

He was going out of his way to stir up trouble right now, and I didn't understand why. What exactly had I done for him to want to torture me like this?

Maybe I was really bad at sex and he was taking it out on me now.

"Is there a particular reason that you decided to grace us with your presence, Rafe? I noticed you never came home last night. Whose bed were you in?" Gabriel's voice sounded perfectly calm, but the tension between him and Raphael was clear.

I wanted to excuse myself and go hide somewhere, but I didn't have anywhere to hide.

"Some of us have to work every once in a while. I was down at the warehouse; someone was trying to poach one of our fighters."

I perked up at the mention of mafia business. When I'd been home, my brothers and my father were always busy with The Firm, getting called away at all hours of the night and day to handle issues. The fact that Gabriel was able to stay at home the entire night was impressive considering what I knew about mafia business.

Wait a second…something struck me right then. Something I should have already thought of, but dread was literally curling in my chest.

"You live here?" I asked, unable to mask the horror in my voice.

Gabriel snorted while Raphael just looked pleased as could be. "Wow, he must have been himself on the plane and not bothered with any niceties. I can tell you already like him as much as the rest of us do."

Raphael stared at me, playing with his bottom lip again with his thumb in a way that reminded me far too much of how he'd been on the flight.

"Yes, Dahlia, please tell Gabriel just how horrible I was on the flight."

"He was way worse than I thought he'd be," I finally said, enjoying the flash of annoyance in Raphael's gaze at my innuendo, even though he had to know that it was a lie.

He was freaking incredible in bed.

"Well, as nice as it is to see you, big brother, is there a reason you're hovering in the kitchen?"

I watched them interact, trying to see any resemblance. Besides both being absolutely gorgeous specimens, I didn't really see any similarities with the exception that they both held this air of confidence that you didn't see very often. They were both very much Alpha males, although Gabriel had obviously shown me a sweet side.

"His highness has called for us," Raphael said, sounding disgusted at the idea.

I was realizing quickly that the relationship between the three of them was...complicated, to say the least.

"I'll throw on some clothes," Gabriel said with a sigh, shooting me an apologetic look like I'd actually expected him to keep me occupied all day. He squeezed my hand as he passed by, and I almost ran after him when I realized that I was alone with Raphael.

Raphael was whistling as he leaned against the counter and scrolled through his phone. It was that same tune from yesterday, and it succeeded in bringing me back to the disgust...and pain I'd felt at the big reveal.

"Trying to bed all of us before the big day, little angel?" Raphael commented calmly, and I flinched at the insinuation, or maybe I was flinching because he was hitting a little bit too close to home.

"Are you going to tell him?" I asked, digging my nails into my hands until I broke the skin.

He smirked. "I don't have a death wish, Dahlia. But I think the bigger question is, are you going to tell him? And if you're not, how do you plan on tricking my big brother?"

I bit down on my lip. "That was out of character for me. I was —running from some demons in my head, I suppose. And it went too far." I wasn't sure why I was telling him that, but a part of me wanted him to understand that I wasn't just some foolish girl who'd destroy myself for no reason. "I think the bigger question actually is, if you knew who I was the whole time, why did you do it?"

He walked towards me until he was standing just an inch away, so close I was sure he could hear my heart trying to pound its way out of my chest. He leaned towards my ear, and a shiver crept down my spine.

"Some people do things because they just like to see the world burn, little angel. And I happen to be one of them."

With that shocking statement, he brushed past me and left the room, leaving me a shaking wreck where I stood.

LUCIAN

I'd been sitting on this couch in silence for twenty fucking minutes. My father had about one more minute before I forgot about the fact that he was the "Capo," and told him to fuck off.

He'd been doing that more and more lately, trying to test just how far my allegiance went. Carlo Rossi was only in his fifties, but for a mafia man, that was practically a lifetime. As he'd gotten older, he'd gotten more and more suspicious of threats designed to take him out.

And it was clear, based on his recent behavior, that I had made it somehow on his list of suspicion.

Like he could read my mind, he opened his mouth right as I was about to stand up.

"One of our shipments disappeared at the docks," he

commented, pulling up some footage on the screen on the wall that showed one of our cameras at the dock.

"What did they take?" I asked, my annoyance growing as I saw a moving van pull up to the docks, and our dockworkers load several crates into the back even though they must have known it wasn't our truck.

Honor, Loyalty, Family. There was nothing that quite got my bloodlust going than being betrayed by one of our own.

About five minutes in, one of the idiots remembered there were cameras watching everything. Someone with a hood covering his face fired a gun towards the camera, and the picture disappeared.

"What did they take?" I repeated coldly, already plotting what I was going to do to every single one of our dock crew.

"Weapons. AR-15s. They had cost us a pretty penny, but we were set to make a good profit." My father went off on some Italian tangent, and I stood there, ignoring the urge to roll my eyes. My thoughts briefly went to the changes I would make once I was Capo, plans that relied less on weapons and more on corporate takeovers.

"What else was on the boat?" I asked, remembering all the other crates that would have been on that shipment.

My father shifted in his seat, his face remaining stoic but for a slight tic in his eye that I marked as his tell long ago. "Just odds and ends. Some equipment for the fight coming up, a few cases of alcohol, those sort of things."

He was lying, and now I wanted to get down to the dock and start "questioning" everyone even more. Carlo Rossi was a liar and manipulator, and I'd learned to do the same at his knee.

But at some point, the student had become the master, and it was only a matter of time before my father realized that.

"Boy, are you listening to me?" Carlo snapped.

"Of course." Just another example of an attempt to get under my skin. But the thing was, as much as my father thought he knew about me, what he didn't know about me was far more. I was an impenetrable void, and no matter what he did or said, he'd never make a dent.

"You'll take care of it?" he asked, his attention already somewhere else as he typed out a message on my phone.

"Right away." I headed to the door, not surprised at least to see what looked like two Eastern European whores waiting in the hallway. They already looked like they'd been sampling some of product, and it was probably good for them, knowing what my father most likely had planned for them.

Bile clogged my throat just thinking about some of the scenes I'd walked into over the years. I was all for experimenting sexually, and to each his own, but the last thing I wanted to see was a pair of emaciated hookers taking turns eating my father's ass and fucking him with a giant dildo. I'd thought about pouring bleach over my eyes after that one.

I still might.

Shaking the image out of my head, I picked up my phone to call Raphael. "Get Gabriel and be ready in fifteen. And make sure the cleaning crew is on call," I ordered, not bothering to listen for a response before I hung up.

I strode out of the building and out to where Riccardo was waiting with the car, regretting the car choice the second I slid in. Fuck. I should have told him to bring something else, anything else. The Bentley had always been my favorite car, but now…it reminded me of her.

I swore that if I inhaled too deeply, I'd still catch her scent—

coconut and vanilla mixed with something that was just her. I'd gotten hard the second her scent had hit me.

And that was a problem. A big problem.

I would have preferred if my future wife had been hideous. Someone I could easily ignore. I could throw her in one of the country estates and ignore her until I was forced to fuck her a few times to get a legitimate heir.

I could still do that with Dahlia, but I knew that even out of sight, she'd haunt me.

I'd had my people collect pictures of her, because I never stepped into a situation unprepared.

And now I'd been jacking off to pictures of her for the past year.

Another man would have been a bit ashamed...I was just annoyed.

Seeing her in person had just made it worse. She'd been wearing that hideous outfit, her hair looking like she'd lost a street fight with a cat, and I'd still wanted her.

Dahlia Butcher had also looked far too innocent and fragile. I'd break her, destroy her, cut off the angel wings I swore she'd been wearing when she'd stepped out of the airport.

I'd spit her out until she had nothing left to give and I'd still ask for more.

When I said I was an impenetrable void, I meant it. I'd ask for more while giving nothing in return.

She'd looked at me with such hope when she'd first seen me. And if I knew anything about hope, it was that it needed to be destroyed immediately.

We stopped in front of the building, and Raphael and Gabriel immediately strode to the car. Answering an email, because I never allowed myself idle time, I wondered what she'd do all day up there alone. I'd specifically instructed the staff to make no preparations for her ahead of time, trying to make sure she knew from the beginning just how unwelcome she was. Unwelcome, but necessary for the future of the Cosa Nostra.

I was tempted to check the cameras up there that not even my brothers knew about, but I pushed the thought away. The thing about addiction was that if you let it in once, it was almost impossible to stop the floodgates. And I never let myself get addicted.

Something told me that if I got even just one taste of Dahlia, it would be too much.

My brothers got in and nodded to me. I signaled for Riccardo to get going and then turned my attention to them.

"How did it go at 11th Street last night?"

Raphael smirked, I'm sure reliving whatever fucked up shit he'd done to the people who'd been going after our best fighter. Fucking psycho.

"Everything's taken care of. No one will be going after our fighters any time soon unless they have a death wish."

I didn't bother asking if he'd disposed of the bodies yet. I'd been in his "lair" enough to know he had plenty of tools…and a tub full of acid, to get the job done.

"So what exactly was so important that you dragged us out this morning?" Gabriel pressed. I frowned as I turned my attention to my pouting little brother.

Gabriel didn't pout. He was perpetually happy, like a golden retriever. Unlike a golden retriever, he could change into a monster when needed, but even when doing his work, he was usually so fucking happy that it made me sick.

Gabriel hadn't realized this yet, and Raphael and I had for some reason done our best to shield him from the truth, but a mafia man didn't get to be happy. Life in general wasn't meant to be happy.

The fact that he hadn't discovered that truth was either a testament to my job as a brother, or he was being willfully ignorant.

"Is there a reason you're sulking, Gabriel?"

Raphael snorted. "He has a new little crush."

I rolled my eyes, so far back I was surprised I couldn't see behind me. "Francesca didn't last long. I thought you said she was the best fuck you'd had in years."

Gabriel fucking blushed. What the fuck was going on?

"Yeah, Gabriel, who's the latest love of your life?" Raphael teased, except there was a thread of malice in his voice that was impossible to miss.

"Shut the fuck up, Raphael," Gabriel said, his tone completely serious.

Raphael opened his mouth to speak, but before he could say anything else, Gabriel reared back and punched him right in the mouth, blood spewing all over the car.

"Cazzo," hissed Raphael, although knowing him, he was probably getting off on the pain.

I stared at them both like they'd lost their minds, and then I shook my head. We had work to do.

"If you two are done playing, we need to go over what's been going on," I told them in a tone that brokered no argument.

Gabriel shot Raphael one more death glare and then turned his attention back to me. Raphael was wiping the blood off his face, but I knew he was listening.

"There's footage of shipments being stolen from the dock. It happened two nights ago. Our workers transferred crates of our newest gun shipment into unmarked vans. And they looked to have done it willingly."

Raphael and Gabriel exchanged glances. They knew what that meant. There would be a lot of deaths today. Transporting shipments had a very specific process with specific people that picked up the shipments from the docks.

"Why are we just finding out now?" Gabriel asked with a frown.

It was just one of the many questions I had about what had happened the other night. If my father had that footage, why had he waited until today to have me handle it? There was also the fact that my father hadn't said anything about our regular transport crew not showing up...so what had happened to them?

"Carlo," I answered simply, and they both nodded their heads, knowing what that meant. Little made sense lately when it came to him, and we seemed to always be cleaning up his messes.

Even Raphael's work last night had been because security had let the leader of a local gang into one of the fights, someone who had been trying to encroach in our fighting ring...something that would normally have never happened.

"So, what's the plan, oh Captain, my Captain," said Raphael, blood dribbling down his chin all over his shirt. Even with his angelic appearance, he looked crazy right now. I was tempted to punch Raphael myself when he used that tone with me, but I knew it wouldn't do any good.

I'd known there was something off about Raphael from almost the moment I'd met him. His mother had dropped him off on our doorstep as a seven-year-old, the byproduct of one of my father's many indiscretions. The only one that I knew of that produced a child, however.

He'd been gaunt and quiet, and at first, I'd thought he was going to be my best friend because we both had that haunted look in our eyes.

But he'd wanted nothing to do with me.

I'd caught him experimenting with dead animals on many occasions, and I was never quite sure if he'd found them dead or killed them himself. When my little sister's tabby cat, Mr. Buttons, turned up dead and in his room, that question had been answered for me. My father had taken his sadistic, psychopathic personality and molded him into a killing machine.

Raphael didn't care about anything or anyone, and I thought it was only because he hated our father as much or maybe more than I did that he did anything I asked him to do.

Someday he was going to stab me in the back.

And someday I'd have to kill him.

Luckily, today was not that day.

"The same crew that was working that night should be on day duty today. I have Thomas and his crew ready to step in while we "talk" to the other workers."

"Excellent," said Raphael, that crazy glint visible in his eyes that he always got when he was getting ready to kill someone.

"Anything else planned for today?" Gabriel asked, so casually that it was clearly fake.

Eager to get back to the new girl. This must be the early stage of his infatuation. I'd have to get an investigator to find out who she was so I could keep an eye on the situation. Gabriel was smart and usually cunning, but he tended to lose his head around these girls. And they in turn definitely lost their head around him. I'd had to pay off...or get rid of, way too many of his exes who couldn't take no for an answer.

Hopefully this wasn't another one. I was a bit busy at the moment.

The air was charged with anticipation as we turned right and the dock area was spread out in front of us. Lorenzo parked the car in my usual spot. I wasn't trying to sneak up on them. I wanted them to see me coming.

The chase was always one of the best parts.

I checked to make sure that my gun was ready and my silencer was on. Normally, I wouldn't have cared if everyone heard the shots, but we were doing this in the middle of the day. I had most of the NYPD in my pocket, but sometimes the more straight-laced ones decided to play hero and drive by the docks.

I didn't feel like dealing with that today.

While Gabriel checked his gun, Raphael opened a compartment under the seat and pulled out his trusty metal baseball bat that he'd carefully wrapped in barbed wire. That had been his weapon of choice ever since Negan had introduced the world to "Lucille" on *The Walking Dead*. Gabriel and I hadn't even asked when he'd appeared in the kitchen with the bat one morning and spent the next few hours wrapping and rewrapping barbed wire around it. He'd left bloody fingerprints all over from cutting himself so many times. Raphael's bat was named Scarlett, in case you were wondering.

We were used to him being batshit crazy.

Plus, there was nothing quite like him hitting someone in the head and seeing chunks of flesh fly through the air. As long as they didn't land on me.

Maybe I was a little bit batshit crazy as well.

We walked towards the dock, Raphael whistling some idiotic tune that made me want to choke him.

"Can you at least find a new song?" Gabriel complained, for probably the millionth time in our lives.

"I know what I like," Raphael said simply, and I was struck by the truth in that statement. Raphael did know what he liked, and once he found something, he was unwavering in his devotion to it. He'd decided when he was ten that caviar was the food of rich people, and since he was "a rich person now," he'd decided that he had to have it.

All these years later, he still ate caviar as an afternoon snack…every single day.

I saw the resignation in Aldo's eyes as we came around the corner to where he'd been stacking some crates in preparation for the next night's shipment.

Maybe I wasn't going to get the chase I wanted.

The rest of his crew were all there as well, and they went silent as they watched us approach.

"I wasn't expecting to see you here today," Aldo said after we stopped a few feet away from him. It was impressive, really; there was only a slight edge of panic to his voice.

Let's see if that lasted.

"I was planning on stopping by next week, but a little birdie told me there'd been an issue here two nights ago. I told the bird there was no way that something could have happened, and you wouldn't have let me know." I began taking slow steps towards him, watching as his face turned white as a sheet. "But you know what that little birdie did?"

Silence.

"Why don't you take a guess, Aldo."

He wasn't running yet, and I would have admired his bravery…if he hadn't stabbed the famiglia in the back.

He gulped. "I—I don't know, sir. I haven't noticed anything

out of the ordinary." He looked around him to where the rest of his crew was quivering in their boots.

I stopped an inch away from him, my six-foot-four body towering over him and forcing Aldo to look up to meet my eyes.

"The little birdie showed me a video. A video that showed all of you loading some of *my* guns into a truck that wasn't mine."

Aldo was practically hyperventilating at this point, beads of sweat dripping down his face. The sour stench of fear was wafting off him.

A loud whacking sound suddenly filled the air. An inhuman scream was abruptly cut off by another whack that ended with a squelching sound.

I turned around to see Raphael twirling the bat around in the air; a body with splatters of goo for a head was on the ground next to him.

Sighing, I gave him a pointed look as Aldo had a heart attack in front of me.

"I was tired of you playing with your food," Raphael said with a yawn, chunks of what I was pretty sure were brain matter dripping off his bat.

This was when the running began. The other men tried to take off and I let Raphael and Gabriel deal with them.

My target was Aldo, who'd just sprinted away towards where the warehouses began. I took my time, following close enough behind him that I could force him in the direction I wanted. He thought he knew the area better than I did since he'd been working the docks for the last five years.

He was wrong.

Aldo turned left in what an hour ago would have been an outlet that led to the busy fish market, only to find a huge storage container now blocking the way.

He was looking around in terror when I made my appearance.

"Tell me, Aldo, what did they offer you to betray us?" I asked calmly.

"Please—I needed the money," he stuttered.

"Isn't that how the story always is? Except, I've been very clear about what my men should do if they're having money problems, haven't I?"

I was every inch the predator as I stalked towards him.

"I—should have come to you. It was a mistake. Please," he begged.

But it fell on deaf ears. When I was still a few steps away, a wet stain began to spread on his crotch as he pissed himself.

I grabbed him by the throat. "Who offered you the money, Aldo?"

"They'll kill me if I told you," he choked out as my grip tightened, not even trying to escape.

"You'll die either way."

Tears were streaming down his face, combining with his rancid sweat until his whole face was wet.

It wasn't a good look. I squeezed tighter until he was turning a nice shade of blue. There, that was better.

"It was the Hawks," he garbled out.

"Mmmh, of course it was," I mused, thinking about the Buffalo gang that for some reason had decided to start testing the limits of our control over this city. I'd be taking care of that problem very soon. But there was one more thing that I wanted from Aldo before he died.

"Tell me, Aldo, what else was on that ship?" I asked as I brushed the tip of my gun down his face with my free hand.

He just shook his head as he turned even more blue. Tucking the gun into my suit jacket, I grabbed his right hand

and pulled his fingers back until four of them cracked and broke.

He tried to scream, but it came out as a squeak with how hard I was squeezing.

"Want to try again? I know you'd much prefer your death to be quick. Since I'm short on time today, I'd have to hand you over to Raphael if I don't get what I want right now.

At that, he did begin to squirm, and I was honestly a little bit offended. He seemed more scared of Raphael than he was of me.

Really, though, that was a mistake--Raphael had been born crazy, but me...I was made that way.

And that made a huge difference.

"He doesn't want you to know." I was really starting to lose my patience.

"Who doesn't want me to know?" This time, I grabbed his right arm and quickly broke his elbow. He managed to stay conscious...but just barely.

"Raphael," I barked, knowing he and Gabriel would be close by now.

"I'm sorry," he whimpered, and all of a sudden he was shaking in my grip, foam bubbling out of his mouth as blood poured from his nose and eyes.

What the fuck? I dropped him in disgust right as Raphael and Gabriel rounded the corner.

"You rang, Master?" Raphael purred, and I snarled at him, too annoyed to put up with his crap.

"Did you leave any of the others alive?" I barked as they eyed the dead body at my feet in interest.

"I believe one of your marching orders was "kill the rest," Gabriel said dryly. "The cleaning crew is already on their way here to take care of everything."

Raphael squatted down and pulled a leather glove out of his back pocket. After sliding it on, he pried Aldo's mouth open and rubbed some of the foam onto his glove. "A cyanide capsule. He must have had a false tooth," he commented. "I'm a bit impressed. I wouldn't have thought the old dog had it in him."

I kicked the body, enraged. "There's no one left to question about that shipment. I know Carlo's hiding something."

Raphael and Gabriel stayed quiet, watching me carefully…I supposed just in case I attacked.

"We're done here," I growled, spitting on the body just because and then striding away. "You'll have to get one of the drivers to pick you up," I called over my shoulder.

"And why would that be?" Gabriel snapped.

I turned to look at them. "I have a flight to catch. Someone should probably tell my fiancée I've decided to delay the wedding for two weeks."

There was grumbling behind me, but I didn't bother worrying about it.

A visit to an old friend in Dallas was on the agenda.

I'm going to find out what you're hiding, Father, I silently promised.

I didn't admit to myself that I was also trying to avoid *her*.

EIGHT

DAHLIA

I didn't know what to do with myself now that Gabriel wasn't here. I couldn't even put my things away because I didn't have furniture…or a room. I also couldn't figure out how to put on a movie in the media room because the remote looked like it belonged to a spaceship.

I thought for a moment about going out to explore the city on my own, but considering I didn't know if I could find this place again if I left, I decided to stay put for now.

So here I was sitting in the massive living room, back on the enormous black sofa, playing Candy Crush on my cell phone.

The front elevators dinged. I didn't think that Gabriel…or Raphael would be back so soon. And heaven forbid that Lucian showed up.

Although just thinking about Lucian not being here last night sent me down a rabbit hole of wondering where exactly he had slept last night.

Not that I cared.

A stout, tiny woman with silver-streaked black hair hustled into view. "Oh," she cried when she saw me, putting her hand over her heart like my presence had given her a heart attack.

"Hi," I said awkwardly, standing up from the sofa and smoothing down the imaginary wrinkles on my outfit. One of the lessons from my mum that continued to live rent-free in my head, was the concept that a lady dressed to impress. I sincerely believed that my mum got up every day and dressed like she was going to meet Queen Elizabeth herself.

I didn't go so far as to dress for the queen. But I was dressed in a sharp pair of tan trousers and a cream blouse, this one bless-edly without any stains…yet.

But that was probably because I'd felt too awkward to try and cook anything in the kitchen since the guys had left.

"Aren't you a pretty thing, sweetheart," she cooed as she hustled towards me. She was dressed in a blue linen dress with a frilly white apron tied in front of it. I wasn't sure if it was a uniform or her personal style, but she looked like a grandma. The kind who baked chocolate chip cookies with you in the kitchen and gave warm hugs.

"Are you with Gabriel, dearie? I think the boy will be out for the afternoon, but I can whip something up for you in the kitchen if you'd like."

She hustled towards the kitchen like it had already been decided, leaving me a little bit shell-shocked by her cheerfulness and energy. I also couldn't help but smirk at her calling him a "boy." Gabriel was a lot of things, but a boy was not one of them. I probably should have spoken up that I wasn't one of Gabriel's random girls—by now I knew there'd been a lot—but for some reason, I didn't correct her.

Instead, I found myself following her into the kitchen, drawn to her energy…and maybe attracted to the chance to not be alone.

It wasn't until I sat down that I realized that not only had I not corrected her about who I was, but in general, I hadn't said a word to her yet. "I'm sorry, I didn't catch your name," I offered, watching as she bustled around the kitchen, as familiar with it as if it was her own.

She paused at my question, maybe debating whether she wanted one of Gabriel's random hookups to know her name.

"Emilia Bianchi, dearie, and based on your accent, I'm thinking that you might welcome a cup of tea."

I sat up straighter in my chair. "That sounds wonderful," I breathed. Maybe it seemed a bit stereotypical, but I absolutely loved tea. I actually hated coffee. The only reason that I'd been drinking it at the airport was because I couldn't find a store that sold it besides a chain. Every good British citizen knew that tea from a chain was akin to piss water.

And no, I wasn't exaggerating.

I watched a little bit in awe as she pulled a teapot—black, of course--out of the cupboard above the stovetop and filled it with filtered water. Then she got out a sleek metal box and set it in front of me, opening it up to reveal rows and rows of high-end tea options.

I'd hit the jackpot.

I chose an Earl Gray, and she put the box away before grabbing the tea package out of my hands.

"Thank you. I'd been desperate for a cup, but I wasn't sure where everything was."

I watched, a little in love with her, as she put the teabag into the mug and then poured the boiling water on top of it. Then she hustled to the fridge and got out some lemons and milk and offered them to me. "Do you want any sugar, dear?" she asked, already grabbing some out of another cabinet.

I made mental notes of where everything was. As good of a cook as Gabriel seemed to be, I'd seen him rummaging through the cabinets for things, obviously not cooking in this kitchen very much.

"You know how to make a proper cuppa," I told her as I put two spoonfuls of sugar into my tea before adding a dash of milk.

"I went to England ten years ago with my husband Ned, God rest his soul, and the hotel we were staying at had the most darling restaurant where they offered a specialty tea hour. I signed us up, much to Ned's chagrin, and halfway through, I was demanding that the waiter teach me how to make a "proper cuppa" as you call it. I haven't gotten much use of it since the boys all seem to live on black coffee, so this is a nice treat." She laughed, and I fell a bit more in love with her because when she laughed, it was with her whole body. She shook as her laughter rang through the air.

I took a sip of my drink, sighing with relief as the hot liquid slid down my throat. It tasted almost as good as one that I made myself.

I may have been a bit addicted.

She took a rag out of a drawer and wet it before beginning to wipe down the counter. I winced when I saw all the remnants of breakfast that were still scattered around the kitchen. Instead of feeling sorry for myself on the sofa, I probably should have come in here and cleaned up after they'd left. I needed as many people around here as possible to like me.

"So, how long have you and Gabriel been seeing each

other?" she asked casually as she continued to wipe down the counters.

I froze in my seat, taking a sip of my tea to give me a second. "I'm not with Gabriel," I finally said quietly.

She looked up at my response in confusion. "Oh, dearie, I just assumed…"

I held up my hand. "I should have corrected you, but to be honest, I'm still trying to wrap my head around the whole situation."

"What situation?" she asked, stopping her movements and staring at me, concerned.

"I'm Lucian's fiancée, Dahlia."

Emilia went completely still, all the color draining from her face.

I set my teacup down, worried she was going to have a heart attack.

"You weren't supposed to come for weeks. Lucian said he would let us know when to start getting ready. You poor thing. We have nothing done. Your room's not ready. You didn't have a meal waiting for you…" She was pacing back and forth, completely flustered. "When did you get here? I left yesterday at five o'clock and no one had said a word."

Of course Lucian hadn't told the staff I was coming. Bastard.

But her reaction did make me feel a bit better. I'd assumed that everyone just hated me, but that was clearly not the case based on Emilia's reaction.

"I got here after that. Please don't worry. It's not a big deal," I told her, trying to calm her down.

"Oh dearie, it is a big deal, but I'll fix everything. Poor Lucian's been so busy with work, it must have just slipped his mind," she said, clearly blind when it came to my future husband.

I'd known Lucian for two seconds and already knew he wasn't the kind of guy to let anything "slip his mind." This had definitely all been very purposeful.

But I had to admit, it hadn't been all bad…Gabriel's face flashed through my mind.

"Everything will be done today. No matter what it takes!" she exclaimed, putting up her pointer finger like she was willing it to be done. "Now, you stay right there. I'll be back to fix you some lunch in just a few minutes. I have some phone calls to make." She hustled out of the kitchen, clearly a woman on a mission, before I had a chance to say anything else.

If I learned anything today, it was that Emilia Bianchi was a force to be reckoned with, and when she decided that something needed to be done, it was done.

In just a few hours, one of the guest rooms had been completely cleaned out. Furniture had been moved in, and the room and connecting bathroom had been expertly decorated by a designer Emilia seemed to have procured out of thin air. She'd brought in three women who had organized my belongings, including the ones that had been sent ahead and had been waiting in a closet in the lobby apparently…and my clothes had even been hung up and organized by color.

While doing that, Emilia had somehow managed to make me the best chicken salad sandwich I'd ever eaten, along with home-made sweet potato fries, and she'd made a list of all my favorite foods and had them delivered. Even my toiletries had been stocked in my bathroom and upgraded, I noticed, as she'd seen fit.

I could only imagine if someone like Emilia was elected leader of a country; she'd have all of society's problems solved in a day.

"Now, here's your key to the penthouse, your card for the swimming pool on the fourth floor, and the number for the driving service. Anywhere you want to go, you call that number and a driver will be sent..." She hesitated for a moment. "Just make sure that Lucian knows where you're going so the proper security can be put into place."

I cringed at the thought of having to basically ask permission from Lucian to move about the city. I wouldn't argue about security though, even though they would report everything back to Lucian, like my security detail in London had reported everything to my brothers and father.

Well...almost everything.

"Is there anything else you need before I leave?" she asked, and I shook my head.

"You've been amazing. This is all more than I expected." I gestured to the room around us that now looked fit for a queen. Or should I say *principessa*?

Gag.

"Alright, dearie, I work five days a week, so I'll be off tomorrow. I've sent a text to your phone already so you have my number, and please text or call if you need anything. I'll make sure it's done. I've had my fair share of calls at midnight from the boys," she chortled.

I once again hid my smile at her calling them "boys" and waved goodbye before closing the bedroom door after her.

And then it was just me.

I looked around my room. It really was beautiful...and it wasn't black. I wondered if Lucian was going to have a panic attack when he saw it. If he even saw it. How often was he actually at the penthouse? I had a suspicion he was avoiding me, but maybe he really was that busy.

My bedding was a pale pink color with silver, dark pink, and white pillows stacked on top. The dressers and nightstands were white, and there was a white armchair in the corner with a pale pink decorative pillow that matched the bedding perfectly. It was girly and lovely...but it didn't quite feel like me.

I wasn't sure what did.

There was a knock on the door, and I tensed.

"Who is it?" I asked, like any good mafia daughter would do.

"It's me." Gabriel's voice came through the door and sent tingles down my spine which definitely should not have been there.

"Come in," I called, suddenly nervous.

And there he was, looking like every woman's wet dream.

"Hi," he breathed, his eyes devouring me like they'd had the habit of doing since he'd first set eyes on me. It was a heady feeling, to feel like I was the only thing he saw in the world.

"How was work?" My voice had a squeak to it as I spoke, and he shot me a cocky grin, clearly loving that he had that effect on me.

"Hmm. The usual," he answered vaguely. I wondered if his usual was the same as my family's. Blood, bodies...sometimes a little bit of betrayal.

"So, I wanted to let you know that Lucian had business that called him away for a few weeks. The wedding will have to be delayed."

Relief spread through my veins...but strangely, so did a little bit of hurt. Had the other women been as completely rejected by their new fiancé's as I was?

Or was that just a special thing that only applied to me?

"Oh?" I responded, proud that my voice was calm. "He couldn't tell me that himself?"

"I'm sorry," Gabriel finally said, apologizing for Lucian. But he didn't look sorry at all. He took a few steps towards me until he was standing just a few inches away, towering over me. He tilted up my chin with one finger so that I was looking up at him, while his other hand stroked the side of my arm, goosebumps cascading across my skin from his touch. His gaze was molten with want.

I should have pulled away.

But I didn't.

"You haven't been out in the city yet. Care to change that, bellissima?"

Any words got choked in my throat as his gaze dipped to my lips, and his tongue slid out to lick his bottom lip, like he was imagining our lips colliding right that very second.

So I just nodded.

Gabriel's eyes lit up like I'd just told him Father Christmas was real.

"Let me just change," I whispered, practically whimpering as my heart hammered in my chest. He reached out and pulled me closer, so close that I could feel how hard he was. He stared into my eyes, and he leaned forward like he was about to kiss me…

"See you in a few," Gabriel murmured gruffly as he reluctantly stepped away from me.

There was longing in his eyes as he looked back at me over his shoulder before leaving and closing the door behind him.

My legs felt weak as I dragged myself to the closet to find something to wear.

The closet was enormous, and I noticed that there was a rack filled with clothes that I hadn't brought with me. Glancing at some of the labels, I decided I wasn't just falling in love with Emilia Bianchi—I was in love with her. She was a goddess.

There were a few white dresses hanging on the rack with a note in sprawling cursive that said: "For the Engagement Dinner." The reminder was like a splash of cold water, completely extinguishing the heat inside of me from my encounter with Gabriel.

Engagement. This was certainly not what I'd imagined my engagement would look like. I'd always known that as a daughter in The Firm, my life was not my own, but I had still dreamed.

My hand automatically went to my patch of scars where my cut was still healing, and I felt my usual craving for a bit of pain.

No, I don't need it. I had two weeks. I would be fine.

I'd survived much worse.

I looked at my phone, seeing I had a missed call. There was also a text, from Benny, that said I should call him on Church's phone.

I took a deep breath, thinking I'd better let someone in my family know that there'd been a change in plans.

Not that any of them were planning on going to the wedding. I dialed Church's number.

"Hey," Benny answered, sounding a little out of breath. I could only imagine what he was up to. He'd recently been let out of prison early for "good behavior" and had this whole takeover plan going to kick out our other brother, Danny, from running the show. I supported him, of course; Benny was a million times better than Danny. Danny was a fuck up in all the ways that counted.

But it would be interesting if he could pull it all off.

"Lucian's delayed the wedding by two weeks," I told him, getting straight to the point. I set my phone down and put it on speaker so I could start to undress.

I realized I had no idea what Gabriel meant by going out in the city, but he seemed to be a bit of a pampered superstar-type guy. I doubt we'd be hiking in Central Park.

If that was a thing that you could actually do? I'd need to look into that.

"That fucker better not be pulling out. The last thing I need right now is to have to come to New York and kill someone." I heard a banging sound in the background followed by a thump.

"I don't think you need to worry about that," I said with a small laugh, trying to picture Lucian and Benny up against each other. I honestly didn't know who would win. And my brother was a beast, so that was saying something.

I rummaged through my clothes before deciding to see what else Emilia had found me other than the engagement dresses.

"How are you?" Benny asked after a long pause.

I hummed, rolling my eyes at the sentiment even though he obviously couldn't see me.

"Since when have you cared about that?" I finally answered, trying not to sound petulant. It's not like he'd been walking the streets the last eight years. But before he'd gone to prison, he'd moved out as soon as my father had died. And then it had just been my mum and me in that quiet house with its hidden horrors.

"Dahlia." He sighed, and I wasn't sure if he was frustrated with me…or with himself.

I squeezed my eyes shut, trying to get a hold of the sudden wave of emotion.

"I'll make sure the wedding goes through," I finally said stiffly, before hanging up the phone.

I stood there for a moment collecting myself, and then I began to look through dresses again, needing a distraction.

A dress covered in pink and purple flowers caught my eye. It had a white background, Emilia seemed to have a theme, but the flowers all over were the centerpiece of the dress. It was gorgeous—and spaghetti strap, so it would work well in the heat that I knew was waiting for me outside. The front of the dress dipped down so I'd be showing a bit of cleavage, and the skirt fell to right above my knees.

Perfect.

I changed to a strapless bra because, again, Rosemary Butcher had imprinted on me how to be a lady. And then I slid on the dress.

It was made of a silky fabric and was cool and smooth against my skin. I loved it.

Running a brush through my hair, I called it good and left the closet, grabbing a pair of Steve Madden sandals that I knew were comfortable on the way out.

I walked into the hallway and saw Gabriel standing there, dressed in a pair of tan shorts and a navy blue v neck top that showcased his muscles perfectly. There were aviators hooked on the collar. He probably had a flock of women out there in the city, just waiting for him to walk outside of this place so they could see him.

He looked like sin.

Like my downfall.

He took his time taking me in, heat in his gaze as his eyes

trailed across my skin, starting at my legs and moving up in that lazy way of his that made me feel like he'd undressed me by the time he was done.

"Bellissima," he murmured, and everything in me seemed to light on fire.

He reached out his hand with a smile, and I took it even knowing the consequences.

I took it even knowing what would happen.

I took it even knowing where the path would lead me.

And that's how I fell in love with Gabriel Rossi.

NINE

GABRIEL

I was pretty sure this was the most perfect day in the whole history of days. I'd started our little field trip taking her to the "Top of The Rock" so she could look out on the city… and that's where I'd discovered that Dahlia was terrified of heights.

She held on to me with a remarkably fierce grip as she inched towards the walls so she could look out.

I loved every minute of it.

The Top of The Rock was a tourist trap if there ever was one, but she was loving it. And I had the urge to take her to every corny touristy thing in the city. Hell, I just knew that someday soon I'd be on a fucking boat taking her to see the Statue of Liberty…our yacht, of course. I shivered just thinking of taking a ferry with all the sheep.

And fuck, after that I'd probably find myself in Times Square too, and riding in a carriage around Central Park.

What the fuck was happening to me?

The answer to that came quickly as I watched her, entranced.

The sun was shining down on her hair, making it appear even more golden than usual. With the brisk wind that was always up here, she looked like some kind of ethereal creature. One that I badly wanted to bring to hell with me.

My chest tightened as a random thought passed through my mind. How good she would look standing next to Lucian, the light to his dark. I was making plans—plans for how I could keep her. But there was nothing I could do to stave off the inevitability of that wedding.

"You're beautiful," I told her, because how could I not? Every time I looked at her, there was something about her that I liked more. The light dusting of freckles across her cheeks. The way she scrunched up her nose when she was thinking.

The sound of her laugh.

And that dress. It was driving me crazy. When she'd stepped out of her room, I hadn't been ready for that much smooth skin. I'd been hard since the second she'd appeared.

It was torture to look and not touch…much.

I was the kind of guy who'd always believed in instant gratification, and the whole "teenage dream" thing she had going was really testing me.

"We're so flipping high up," she told me with a small gasp as she made it to the wall and warily looked over the edge, still holding on to me tightly.

Or maybe I was the one holding on to her. I couldn't seem to let her go.

146

She leaned forward, and her dress slid up her thighs a bit, and of course, my gaze got stuck on that area, just imagining if I could pull it up higher.

I bet she was probably wearing lacy panties; she seemed the type.

She turned to face me, catching me checking her out. I was rewarded with a faint blush. Fuck. I loved that she blushed. City girls were so full of themselves, so confident that you would think they were hot shit.

Dahlia didn't know that she could own any room she walked into if she wanted.

"Okay, how much of this city do you and your brothers own?" she asked with a sly grin.

Hmm. So she'd identified me as the weak link for getting information.

"Would you believe me if I said all of it but Hell's Kitchen?" I told her, backing her up against the glass until I was pressed against her. She glanced behind her nervously, before turning back to me.

"If this glass breaks and I fall to my death, I'm going to make sure I come back from the afterlife and kill you myself," she said, but there was no menace in her voice, only arousal. Her breath was coming out in gasps, and every time she breathed out, her soft tits were pressed against me even more. I couldn't help but moan, and I knew she heard it, because her breath hitched and her eyes widened.

"You didn't answer my question."

"I think I shouldn't believe a word that comes out of your mouth, but for this, you're probably telling the truth." Her gaze was dancing around my face, getting caught on my lips. I could lean in right now, kiss her like I wanted until she was begging me to drag her somewhere and fuck her.

Fuck.

"I'll never lie to you," I told her, the words almost unrecognizable as they left my mouth.

I lied. A lot. Part of my job with the Cosa Nostra was to charm and wheel and deal and generally get people to do what I wanted, and to give me what I wanted. We owned almost half of New York's real estate, thanks to my silver tongue.

I lied, and I was good at it.

But as soon as my promise came out of my mouth, I knew I would keep it. I'd never lie to her.

No matter what.

"Okay," she breathed, biting at her lush, bottom lip. I randomly noted her lips were the color of cherries, and I could tell she didn't have any lipstick on.

And now I was hungry.

And definitely not for food. I stepped away and pushed a hand through my hair, watching as her eyes followed the movement and she admired my biceps.

Because I was evidently turning into a fucking saint, I withstood the urge to flex or rip off my shirt so she could look at me like she had the other day.

It was like she'd been born to entice me...to tempt me. Everything about her was my favorite thing.

I cleared my throat. "Should we go get something to eat?" I asked, watching obsessively as she tangled her fingers in her hair.

"I'm starving," she answered with a wink as she brushed past me, leaving me panting after her like a dog.

The restaurant was about ten blocks away, and normally I'd be in a car with Riccardo, or one of our drivers, enjoying the air conditioning as I headed to dinner...but Dahlia wanted to see everything.

And at this point, I was pretty sure I'd do whatever she asked.

Although a funny thing happened as we walked the streets, while she pointed at shops and people rushing by. Our path took us past where a lot of the Broadway shows were, and I listened as she talked about the London shows she'd seen.

"I'm desperate to see Hamilton, though. I had strep throat when I had tickets, and then they were all sold out, so I missed the show."

I made a mental note to pick up Hamilton tickets...as soon as possible. Tomorrow in fact.

"Your brothers didn't threaten people and get you some?" I asked, frowning. From what I'd heard about the Butcher twins, from our interactions with The Firm in the past, they took what they wanted.

"Well, my brothers moved out when my dad died...I guess it's been about ten years now," she mused as she watched someone wearing an American flag around his waist...just an American flag. "And then, well, I'm sure you heard that Benny went to prison."

"You have another brother, Denny or something?" I asked gently. Lucian had a file ten inches thick on "The Firm," but I'd never listened closely when he'd talked about them.

I was regretting it now, now that I wished I knew everything about her so that she'd never have the look she had on her face right now.

She laughed bitterly, and I hated the sound. "Getting me tickets to Hamilton would literally be the last thing that *Danny* would ever do. He's only cared about himself since the moment he was born. Not that I was there, but Benny always says that, and I believe him a hundred percent."

"So it was just your mother and you?"

She nodded, a darkness growing in her gaze. "Just my mum and me." Dahlia's cheek pulsed in anger, and I wondered what she was thinking about. When she saw me watching her, she schooled her features and then pointedly looked away from me, like she was revealing too much. "I was at my boarding school most of the time though. And there were plenty of people there," she eventually added after we'd walked a block...as if she was trying to keep me distracted.

"Anyone you keep in touch with?" I asked the question casually, but I was 100% planning on finding that file and reading every fucking thing I could about Dahlia's life. Had her school been coed...or just girls? Did she have someone that she'd left back there? The idea made my chest burn. Which was ironic since she was about to have a very big someone in her life in two weeks.

She shrugged her shoulders, obviously not wanting to answer my question. Which only made me more antsy.

I didn't press her anymore on any of that. I only wanted her to have good feelings when it came to me, and trying to get her to open up when she didn't want to wasn't the way to do that.

One thing was clear though.

My little Dahlia had been lonely. I could hear it in her voice, the longing she'd had for years to have someone care about her.

I couldn't wait for the day that I could tell her that she'd never have to be lonely again. That I would always be there for her from now on.

If I did it right now, she would run away screaming.

I put my arm around her waist and pulled her close, tucking her in tightly against me. She didn't push away...in fact, she seemed to cuddle in closer.

This was a good sign. If I'd managed to make her this comfortable, this fast, just think of what I could do with two weeks.

"Here it is," I told her, pointing to the discreet sign that said *Smoke*. It was one of my favorite steakhouses in the city, the kind of exclusive place that you didn't get into until you were someone...or you knew someone.

Obviously, I was the former.

Not only was the sign discreet, but there was graffiti all over the outside, ensuring that most people's attention would skip right over it, thinking it was rundown. The windows were also blacked out, so you couldn't see inside.

She tilted her head, taking it in with a fucking cute confused look on her face.

"Are you sure they're open?"

"Trust me. The food's amazing," I told her as I led her forward. I stuttered to a halt right as we got to the door, a thought hitting me. "You're not vegetarian, are you?"

"Definitely not," she responded indignantly, like I'd offended her with my question.

"Perfect." I moved my arm so that my hand was just resting on her lower back, and I ushered her inside. The first door led to a small entryway with plain black carpet and dark grey walls. There was another blacked-out door in front of us, and I led her through it.

"This is unexpected," she murmured as we entered a lavish open lobby area with red brick floors, cream walls, and an ornate old-fashioned bar straight ahead. Rows of every expensive alcohol you could imagine were placed in neat, straight lines on the shelves. Men and women dressed in all kinds of finery were milling around, waiting for their table or sitting at the bar in the black velvet high-backed chairs, sipping on their specialty cocktails.

A woman dressed in a black cocktail dress was standing behind a glossy, wooden stand, and her eyes widened the moment she saw me.

"Mr. Rossi," she gasped. "We didn't know you'd be in." Her gaze flicked to my hand which was now wrapped around Dahlia's waist.

"I'm sure you'll have no problem finding us a table." She nodded and practically ran off into the dimly lit seating area behind her. I'm sure that the patrons she was about to kick out of the best table in the restaurant were going to be furious.

Poor things. Not.

"Where should we go if there's a long wait?" Dahlia asked, furtively looking around at the crowded room. Everyone was staring at us while trying to look like they weren't staring at us.

Fucking sheep.

"We'll get in," I said confidently, shooting a glare at a man nearby who was staring intently at Dahlia's perfect ass. We were dressed far more casually than anyone in here, but Dahlia outshined everyone.

A few moments later, a red-faced man in a tuxedo came storming in from the dining room, dragging a much younger woman wearing what looked like a diamond-encrusted scarf as a dress. The mayor. How lovely. I loved when I could kill two birds with one stone—remind the mayor exactly what his place was in this city...and eat my favorite food.

"I can't fucking believe this," the mayor spat, glaring at anyone he passed. "You people have lost your fucking mind!"

"Donovan," I said in a mild voice, before he could make a bigger scene.

His face went a putrid grey color when he saw me, like just the sight of me made him physically ill.

I heard Dahlia's soft intake of breath as she watched interestedly as he physically cowered in front of us.

"It—it's really good to see you, Mr. Rossi," he stuttered, and only because I was a freaking boss was I able to keep my face stoic instead of laughing my head off at this sixty-year-old man shaking like a leaf in front of me.

"A pleasure as always," I answered with a nod.

He moved like a much younger man as he dragged the girl after him like his ass had caught fire.

"Who was that?" Dahlia asked as she watched him run out the door.

"The mayor."

"Oh," she said, her mouth adorably gaping open in shock. Then she shook her head in mock disgust. "Mafia men."

I just chuckled and kissed the top of her head as the hostess hustled over to us. "Your table's ready. I'm so sorry for the wait."

Dahlia waited until the hostess had turned back around before looking up at me and rolling her eyes.

Fuck. I really wanted to kiss her.

The seating in the dining area was mostly made up of elaborately carved black wooden booths with black velvet cushions. Everything was black and grey...designed to look like smoke, obviously.

I nodded in greeting as we passed much of the who's who in New York.

"I saw that woman in a movie," Dahlia remarked calmly as we went by a particularly famous actress…that I'd fucked several times in the past.

I ushered Dahlia forward, not wanting the actress to try and talk to me. She'd been particularly clingy when I'd decided we were done.

We made it to our booth, and we slid into our seats. I regretted sitting across from her immediately because it meant I couldn't touch her.

A waiter in a pressed white dress shirt, black pinstripe suit vest, and black dress pants appeared a second later, pouring us water and handing us our menus. He was smart. He only gazed briefly at Dahlia as he went through the specials. "I would suggest a Merlot or a Cabernet Sauvignon, sir."

"A few bottles of the Château Pétrus," I told him, and he nodded and rushed off.

"A few bottles? You trying to get me drunk?" Dahlia remarked as she picked up her menu.

"Mmmh, undecided."

She laughed, looking almost surprised at the sound. She flipped through the pages slowly before looking back up. "You know, I was kind of expecting Italian."

"Stereotyping's a very dangerous thing, Dahlia," I answered with a wink. "I'm pretty sure the chef would shoot both of us if you tried to order anything but meat."

"Good thing I love meat," she quipped, and being the dirty bastard that I was, my dick immediately started growing in my pants just thinking about her handling my…meat.

The waiter arrived with the wine just as I was about to lose my head and pounce on her. He presented the bottle to me. 2005, one of my favorite vintages. After I nodded, he poured a taste in my wine glass and handed it to me. Dahlia watched me intently as I swirled the liquid around in my glass a few times before inhaling the strong, heady scent. I took a sip. Fuck, that was good.

After getting my approval, he poured us both a glass, and then we ordered our steaks. Filet mignon for her and a Japanese Kobe steak for me. The chef would know to bring every side the restaurant offered to our table.

She picked up her wine glass and took a sip before her face scrunched up in disgust. When she noticed me watching her, she tried to school her face.

I lifted an eyebrow. "You don't like wine."

She bit her lip, fiddling with the tablecloth. "It's fine. I mean, fuck, it's more than fine."

I snapped my fingers, and the waiter appeared a second later. "Get her a cocktail, something fruity," I ordered.

But she was shaking her head. "Single malt scotch, actually," she said with a blush.

Fuck, I somehow got even harder under the table. I usually ordered Château Pétrus because it made the girls go crazy, but I guess I should have guessed that Dahlia wouldn't be like other girls.

The waiter nodded, and what seemed like a second later, he was back with her drink. She sipped at it, closing her eyes in pleasure as she swallowed. Her eyes were sparkling in satisfaction when she opened them back up, and I got a little lost staring at her.

"So, Gabriel, tell me. When you're not busy with Lucian, or getting blow jobs in the hallway, what do you like to do?"

I coughed up my wine in shock because she brought *that* up so casually. She smiled widely as she watched me.

"Hmm. There's not much time left between those two things," I teased. "But I do spend a lot of time cooking…and then I spend a lot of time running or at the gym working it off."

Those were the basic things I told everyone, though, and I suddenly had the violent urge to tell her more.

"I also—draw," I admitted. I didn't know why I told her that. It's not like I was any good. I had notebooks stacked a mile high in my closet though, filled with random drawings and thoughts in my head. Maybe it had something to do with my OCD, but…

"Your tattoos," she breathed, leaning forward and putting her breasts on display.

I didn't know what was torturing me more, the breathy interest in her voice or those fucking amazing tits.

"Yeah, I designed all of them," I admitted with a shrug.

"They're amazing."

I smiled, for some reason uncomfortable with the praise.

The food arrived soon after that, and we enjoyed our dinner as I peppered her with questions. Some she had no problem answering, but others—like talking about her childhood—she was purposefully vague.

That was alright, though. Someday we'd know so much about each other that I'd know what she was going to say before she opened her mouth.

Was it weird that I loved watching her eat? I'd actually always hated the sound of people chewing and the weird way their mouths moved, but somehow, she managed to make even that sexy as fuck.

Crazy thoughts like that dominated my head throughout

dinner as I tried to get as much information out of her as possible.

She sipped at her drink, growing more relaxed as the night went on, and I took every chance I could get to touch her hands...kick her feet gently under the table like an irrational school boy...just be close to her.

Bernard Dubois, the main chef of the restaurant and an old friend of mine, stopped by to check on how we'd liked the food. Of course, he immediately fell under Dahlia's spell as she raved about it, and it was honestly all I could do not to stab him with my fucking fork. He was just lucky that my steak knife had already been taken away.

He was also lucky that the food had been particularly good tonight and I was feeling too full and lazy to pull my pistol out.

When she smiled at him a little too much, I actually growled, and they both looked at me in alarm. I was the easy-going Rossi, and sometimes people forgot I had teeth just as sharp as my brothers.

Bernard excused himself shortly after that.

We finished dessert, the best damn creme brûlée in the fucking city, and then we headed out. I pointedly ignored the people trying to get my attention as we walked by.

It was past ten as we stepped out into the night air, but the city was still alive. I'd always liked that about New York. There was a frenetic energy here, like the city as a whole had gotten ahold of Adderall and was never going to fall asleep.

My hand slipped into hers easily, like it was always supposed to fit perfectly in mine. Riccardo was waiting outside because I wasn't going to walk thirty fucking blocks to get back to the penthouse. It was one thing to walk from the Rockefeller Center in broad daylight, but I knew what hid in the dark corners of this city, and I wasn't going to put Dahlia at risk. Ever.

She fell asleep on my shoulder in the car, and I ignored the pointed looks that Riccardo was giving me through his rearview mirror as I kept a hold of her hand the entire ride home.

My dreams of carrying her upstairs were dashed when she woke up right when Riccardo stopped in front of our building.

Dahlia wiped her mouth, glancing at my shirt worriedly, like she was afraid she'd drooled.

Don't worry, sweetheart. I'd think even that was cute.

Lorenzo, who was still manning the lobby, nodded at me as I walked by, and then we were in the elevator, headed upstairs.

"I don't want the night to end," I admitted to her in a low voice. She didn't answer, just stared at me searchingly until the door opened to the penthouse.

"Thank you for tonight, Gabriel," she told me as soon as we stepped out. She was retreating back into her shell. I hated that.

I wanted to follow her into the room, slide off that dress that had been tempting me beyond measure all night, and place my lips on every inch of her delectable body.

I wanted her so badly that my hands were actually shaking from the strain of not reaching out to her and pulling her into my arms.

"Goodnight, bellissima," I murmured instead, brushing a kiss against her forehead and watching in delight as a blush filled her cheeks.

"I'm going to figure out what that means. I know Google can translate things," she responded with a huff.

"Good," I told her, before shooting her a wink and walking away towards my bedroom, knowing that if I stood there any longer, I wouldn't be able to hold myself back.

I'd be taking a very long shower tonight…and spending some quality time with my hand.

Thinking of Dahlia, of course.

There was a countdown dangling over my head. Every second that passed was one second closer to when Lucian returned. I was preparing myself for the showdown, the words I would say to try and convince him that Dahlia was mine. Why did it matter what Rossi son she married? It was still tying us to The Firm and honoring the contract…right?

The thing was, I couldn't exactly remember the terms of the fucking thing. And I hadn't been able to find the file on Dahlia either, so even though she showed me glimpses of herself, I felt like I was still missing the big picture.

At first, two weeks had seemed like forever…and now it was almost gone, and I didn't know what amount of time would be long enough. Maybe there wasn't one.

The last two weeks…well, there weren't really words to describe them. When I hadn't been in meetings negotiating contracts for new businesses we were acquiring, I'd consumed every second I could with her, sleeping less and less every night, not wanting to waste my time unconscious when I could be spending it with her.

I'd taken her to Hamilton. And she'd been awestruck the entire time, staring at the performers with rapt attention until I was almost jealous of them by the time the show ended.

I'd taken her to a game in our suite at Yankee Stadium where she'd peppered me with questions about baseball.

"So you basically took cricket and Americanized it," she'd mused as she watched a player slide into second.

I'd cringed at the comparison. I mean, I guess they were a bit similar. Except, obviously we weren't trying to hit it off the ground. She'd laughed at the look on my face, and I'd fallen for her even harder.

We'd taken a carriage around Central Park, which wasn't as terrible and corny as I'd believed, and we'd had cocktails at many of the rooftop bars around the city. We'd gone to a concert in Bryant Park, and I had in fact taken her on a private boat tour around the Statue of Liberty...on my yacht.

I'd discovered New York in a way that I never had before. But I was afraid the magic of the city that I loved was now wrapped up so much in Dahlia, that if this whole thing blew up in my face, I'd never be able to look at it the same way again.

We were currently in Central Park, sitting under a tree because Dahlia had insisted she needed "some nature."

And of course, even though I hated nature, here I was, barefoot, eating a fucking hotdog from the vendor she'd spotted when we'd first walked into the park. Just hoping that I didn't end up with food poisoning.

She was fidgety and a bit agitated, leaning against me while I leaned against a tree, obviously feeling the weight of the countdown just like I was.

"Tell me about Lucian," she said quietly, and I stiffened. I hated his name passing from her lips.

When I didn't answer, she shifted off of me and turned to meet my gaze.

There was a light breeze floating through the park, and a few pieces of her hair swirled around her, giving her an almost halo effect.

"He'll be back tomorrow, right?"

I sighed and nodded. He would indeed be back tomorrow. He'd been mysteriously quiet the last two weeks, only texting or calling when I needed to update him on the outcome of my meetings. I'd asked him what he was doing, and he'd hung up on me. I hadn't bothered to ask again. Asshole.

"What do you want to know?" I finally answered.

She pulled her knees up to her chest and wrapped her arms around them.

"Will I be able to make him happy?"

Fuck. She was such a fucking sweetheart. But she didn't stand a chance. Lucian was broken in a different way from Raphael, in a way that I didn't understand. I don't think I'd seen him happy before. Ever. Even as perfect as she was, there was nothing she could do.

He'd been this serious and foreboding even as a boy.

"I don't know," I said at first, shaking my head. But then I remembered I'd promised her I wouldn't lie to her. Fuck. "But I don't think so," I reluctantly added.

She nodded, like she hadn't expected any different.

One thing that I'd noticed about Dahlia...she didn't cry. Every time I expected it to happen, she didn't shed a tear. I perversely wondered what would.

"You know, I wonder sometimes what my life could have been like if I hadn't been born a mafia princess," she spit the words out bitterly. "I wonder who I pissed off before I was born for my entire existence to be acting as nothing more than a fuck-ing, useless...pawn."

I grabbed her arms and yanked her forward, a small squeak falling from her mouth in surprise. "Your entire existence isn't just fucking that. I won't have you talking about yourself that way."

She studied my face, and I wondered—not for the first time —what did she see? Because after spending the last two weeks with her, I knew she was too good for Lucian. But I also knew she was far too good for me as well.

Dahlia gently pulled away from me and stood up, brushing off her blue sundress. I couldn't help but devour the sight of all that golden, smooth skin. I couldn't decide which thing about Dahlia I was more attracted to. Her exquisite rack? Her ass that I just wanted to grab and squeeze? Her legs? Fuck, and then her face and her hair.

I wanted it all.

My skin itched as I wrenched my gaze away from her and, for the millionth time, tried to control my aching dick.

She was quiet on the drive back, her hands firmly in her lap so I couldn't hold her hand, her attention focused out the window.

I felt like I was trapped in an hourglass just watching as the last few pieces of sand fell. She was slipping out of my grasp, already mentally moving away from me...and moving towards him.

I'd been angry at Lucian plenty, but right now, what I was feeling was more akin to hate.

The silence continued all the way up to the penthouse until I felt like I was going to lose my mind. It wasn't comfortable like it had been in the past weeks when Dahlia was lost in her head.

The silence was torture.

She opened her mouth to say something...and I broke.

I pulled her roughly against me and put an arm around her waist, pinning her soft, perfect body to mine as I fisted her hair, pulling her head back so I could finally claim her lips in a desperate, hungry kiss. My tongue dove in her mouth, fucking it deep. She tasted better than I'd even imagined, like strawberries and cream and something I couldn't quite identify, something I wanted to have over and over again. I pressed against her body, grinding myself against her so she could feel how much I wanted her. I kissed her like I owned her. Just in case this was all I ever got, I wanted her to believe that no one could ever make her feel the way I did. I wanted her to always know she was mine...even if she was his.

"Gabriel," she whimpered before tearing her lips from mine with a gasp. She pulled against my arms and I reluctantly let her go. She tore off to her room, and I followed her all the way to her door, my fists clenched in frustration.

"I'm sorry, I shouldn't have done that. But you have to know—"

"I can't fall in love with you, Gabriel," she whispered, cutting me off, and looking completely devastated.

"Dahlia," I murmured, and she winced because she could hear the ache in my voice. "If I have to, I'll love you enough for the both of us."

Her haunted eyes widened at my admission, and then she slipped into her room and closed the door without saying anything else, and despite the fact that I'd come close to dying many times before, courtesy of being a Rossi and all that entailed, this...this felt like it could end me.

I stood there for a long moment, hoping she would change her mind and come back out...or invite me in again.

But she didn't. Only silence came from her room.

I shook my head and walked towards the bar in the living room, thinking that I'd drown my sorrows. I'd made it around the corner when suddenly I found myself against the wall, a hand to my throat, and a gun pointed at my temple.

Its owner...Raphael.

He'd been a ghost for the last two weeks...I'd assumed gone on Cosa Nostra business. Figured he would turn up now.

"Little brother, what do you think Lucian is going to do when he finds out just how close you've gotten to his little flower?" Raphael hissed, his voice low, I assumed so Dahlia wouldn't hear.

I stayed perfectly still. There was no telling what Raphael would do. Raphael only held onto sanity by a thread, and you never knew what was going to tip him over the edge.

"Raphael, what are you doing?" I asked, keeping my voice calm.

He slid the gun to the front of my head until it was pressed up against my forehead, perfectly centered between my two eyes.

"Just wondering if I should end you right now so Lucian doesn't have to."

I couldn't help but roll my eyes. Drama queen.

"Nothing's happened," I told him, but I could hear the lie in my own voice.

"Is that what you call what just happened in the hallway... nothing?" Raphael's voice was mocking and cruel, but I was used to that. What I wasn't used to was Raphael giving a fuck about something.

My gut clenched, suspicion flooding my veins. "Tell me, Raphael...why do you care? Was your flight a bit more adventurous than you reported?"

His gaze hardened, and something flickered behind the cruel, crazy mask he always wore. His finger pressed against the trigger, and I braced myself for the end.

Raphael smiled and pulled the trigger.

Click.

He snorted as I let out a gasp of air, realizing his gun wasn't loaded. I pushed him away and then reared back and punched him in the gut.

"What the fuck is wrong with you?"

He bent over from the force of my hit and wheezed out a laugh. "You should have seen your face, little Gabey. I'm surprised you didn't piss your pants. What do I care if you're fucking *the boss's* future wife."

That was more in line with Raphael; he listened to Lucian and our father, but it was the way a rabid dog listened while it was still chained. You knew that the second he was released, he'd bite your face off.

My fists stayed clenched, adrenaline racing through my fucking veins. Raphael lightly rubbed where I'd punched him. "You should probably hit the weights. That was weak, even for you."

Fucker.

Raphael walked over to the bar and poured himself some vodka, throwing it back like it was water.

I followed him, needing a drink...badly. I didn't bother with a glass; I just grabbed a bottle of whiskey and walked over to the window, enjoying the burn as I swallowed a huge sip. "If this comes back on Dahlia, I'll kill you," I murmured. "That kiss was all me."

"If you're going to stab someone in the back, you're supposed to make sure you're not caught," Raphael said lightly, appearing next to me at the window.

I just huffed, taking another long draw from the bottle. I'm sure the list of things that Raphael had done to betray us was a mile long…but he was right; we'd probably never catch him in the act.

He slapped me on the shoulder, splashing some of his vodka onto my shirt as he did so. "You should probably try and get some rest, little brother. I'm sure the engagement dinner tomorrow is going to be a hell of a ride."

Raphael walked away, and I listened as his footsteps faded away before I pressed my forehead against the cool glass, wondering what the hell I was going to do.

TEN

DAHLIA

I was in the kitchen when I heard footsteps behind me. I turned, and my gaze widened when I saw that it was Lucian, looking like a dark dream. He was perhaps the best-looking man that I'd ever seen. And that was saying something since I also had Raphael and Gabriel for reference.

"It's not real, you know," Lucian said, without so much as a hello. There was a wicked smirk on his face that both infuriated me and turned me on.

"What's not real?"

"How Gabriel's acting with you."

Something jerked in my stomach.

"I don't know what you're talking about," I mumbled, hoping he couldn't hear the tremble in my voice.

"You think my men haven't told me? The movie nights, the shopping dates, the tours around New York. There's fucking

169

restaurant boxes in the fridge from the best restaurants in the city."

I shifted uneasily. "He's just being nice, just showing me around. Something you should have been doing yourself," I snapped.

Something glimmered in his eyes, something I couldn't read but was suddenly deathly afraid of.

"Gabriel has OCD, Dahlia," Lucian announced, practically crowing it as if he delighted in hurting me. Maybe he did.

My hands clenched as I dug my nails into my palms so I could hurt, something I hadn't found myself doing once in the last few weeks. OCD. I knew I'd heard of that, but I couldn't quite remember what it was.

"Obsessive-compulsive disorder. His brain literally forced him to become obsessed with you. He foolishly calls it love because he doesn't know any better. But it's not real. None of it is real. And eventually, he'll see another girl, and it will be like lightning's just struck. And he'll feel nothing for you. Can you picture that in your head, little girl? Picture having to see Gabriel every day, and him not even noticing you. You'll be like a broken toy sitting forgotten on a shelf to him. And you'll have to be reminded of what you think you've lost every day of your life because he's my brother, and he won't be going anywhere."

I was full-on trembling at this point. Lucian's words were like barbs, digging under my skin. I went over that first time that I'd met Gabriel, how easily he'd dismissed that girl. I'd assumed he'd met her in a bar and brought her home. She'd seemed to be nothing to him, practically a stranger. He'd told me himself that he called her "doll" because he couldn't remember her name.

But what if that wasn't true? What if he'd known her for

weeks...or months. She sure had looked at him like she was crazy about him.

And he had just forgotten her, moving his attention to me in a way that my greedy, lonely heart had loved.

I'm sure there'd been a tingling sensation in the back of my head, that something had seemed off to me.

But I'd ignored it. Because I wanted to. I'd wanted to latch on to the first kind person I'd met in my new life.

I'd—been a fool.

I cleared my throat, trying to get myself under control. "I don't know why you think you're warning me about this. But Gabriel and I are just friends." I tried to say it with a straight face, tried not to think about that kiss.

Lucian shook his head at me as if he was disappointed with me...or worse, as if he was pitying me.

I'd always hated pity.

"The next time he looks at you like you're the center of his universe, ask him about Victoria and Lacey and Clarissa and Mary and Genevieve and...The list is literally a mile long. My brother's the biggest whore in this city, but he'd never admit that because he genuinely thinks it's love."

"Are you done?" I spat, desperate to get a moment alone, a moment with a sharp blade and a rush of pain. Anything for me not to feel so out of control.

"Do what you want, Dahlia," Lucian said as he poured a glass of scotch from an expensive-looking glass decanter. "But don't say I didn't warn you."

I left after that, not having anything else to say, and unable to hear anything else he wanted to tell me.

I slipped into my room, careful not to slam the door, and then I slid down it until I was sitting on the floor, leaning against it.

My eyes were burning, but of course, no tears came out. Even when faced with something like this, I couldn't cry.

It would be alright. Whatever was happening with Gabriel wasn't supposed to happen in the first place. It wasn't real. I was about to be married. To the devil, apparently.

I…would be all alone in this place. Once again.

When I finally stood up, I headed towards the bathroom where my razor blade was hidden under my toothpaste.

Just a tiny cut.

The Rossis weren't worth another scar.

None of them were.

Gabriel knocked on my door an hour later, the knock eager, almost as if he couldn't bear to stay away.

Except now I knew it wasn't anything special, that he'd probably done it with every girl.

"Come in," I called, wishing the tremble in my voice would go away.

He opened the door with a huge smile on his face, his features falling when he saw I was in bed. I'd known he wanted to try and do something before Lucian got home.

Too bad for him, Lucian was already here.

"You're not ready?" he asked, softly closing the door and leaning against it, his eyes boring into me like they always did, like he was trying to read my soul.

"Yes, I'm not quite feeling up to going out. I intended to text you…and then the morning got away from me," I lied. Although maybe it wasn't a lie. I was feeling absolutely sick. And like a fool.

"Well then, we'll stay in. I'll order from that Chinese place you loved the other day. And we'll stuff our faces while we watch a movie. I got that new superhero one that's not even out in theaters yet."

It was tempting, tempting to just give in and pretend like everything was fine. I could just wait for the eventual disappointment and heartbreak when he was through with me.

But I couldn't do that.

"I'd rather be alone. I need to get ready for the party tonight," I said softly, digging my nails into my palm as my eyes burned again.

"Alright, but tomorrow...?" he asked, his voice sounding desperate.

I cleared my throat. I was tired of being so fucking weak. So fucking weak that I'd leapt headfirst into everything that he'd offered me.

That ended now.

"I don't think we should hang out anymore," I whispered.

"What?" He looked incredulous at my statement.

"I'm about to be married. And it's...not proper," I blurted out.

"When did you talk to Lucian?"

"Pardon?"

"When did you talk to my asshole brother? What did he say? It had to be this morning."

"This has nothing to do with him," I argued.

He lifted an eyebrow. "It has nothing to do with him, yet you just told me it wasn't "proper" because you're about to be his wife?" he asked, mocking my accent.

I flushed.

"I'll fix this. It's not over. It's never going to be over," he swore as he strode over to me. He lifted me up, and then he kissed me. He didn't just kiss me. He claimed me. He devastated me. He stopped my heart.

Just like he had last night.

And then as quickly and feverishly as it began, it was done. Gabriel strode out of the room without a glance back.

I sat there on my bed for hours, trying to talk myself out of jumping right back into his arms once again.

LUCIAN

"What did you say to her?" Gabriel practically screamed as he stormed into my office, the door crashing against the wall and sending one of my pictures to the ground, shattering the glass into a million pieces.

I'd liked that picture.

I sighed in exasperation and turned away from the contract I'd been reviewing. I'd known he would do this. Just like I'd known that she would want to get away from him.

She wouldn't want to be played for a fool, not any more than she already had been. She had too much pride for that.

"I'm not having this conversation if you're going to continue to yell," I told him calmly.

"What did you say to make her hate me?" he seethed, gritting his teeth as he struggled for control.

It was an interesting sight, honestly. Gabriel was the affable one in the family, the one that everyone always loved. He'd been shielded, coddled, and even though I leaned on him heavily to broker contracts and smooth tensions, he'd always been my baby brother who lived with his head in the clouds and his heart on his sleeve.

Gabriel never got mad. And right now, he seemed mad enough to try and tear my head off.

"I simply told her the truth, Gabriel."

"And what would that be, Lucian? What bullshit version of 'the truth' did you give her to not want anything to do with me?"

"You do remember you're talking about my fiancée, don't you?" I asked, something that felt alarmingly like jealousy burning in my gut. I pushed it away as quickly as I could, mentally throwing gasoline on the feeling and lighting a match.

"It's not like you didn't know what was happening, Lucian, so don't try and pull the 'wife' card now. I—I love her." His shoulders dropped as he stared at me beseechingly.

A cold feeling washed over me. And then I laughed, the sound coming out cruel even to my own ears.

"Love. Do you know how many fucking times you've told me you've been in love, Gabriel? More times than I can count. More times than I could possibly remember. You've been in love with half the country at this point."

"It's different this time. It's more. So much more than I could have comprehended. It's not just in my head. It's not because of my disorder. It's not!" Gabriel waved his arms emphatically, obviously believing every word he was spitting.

I sighed, shaking my head in disgust.

"And what happens the next time you see a girl, and you fall in love with her? You think you'll be able to keep from leaving Dahlia high and dry? It's not like you'll ever get all of her. We both know it. She'll always belong to me, even if I've been letting you borrow her." Heat rose under my stiff collar, the truth of that burning in my gut. She did belong to me. No matter what. Even if I could never really have her.

"Don't talk about her like that. Like she's one of your possessions to be bought, sold, and traded away."

I laughed.

"Don't lecture me about treating women like possessions, Gabriel. You've treated every single woman you've been in love with like a possession, casting them off when it suited you."

His cheek twitched as he gritted his teeth. His eyes were actually watering. Was he crying? He never cried over women. He never showed anything but lust, puppy dog love, and then annoyance when they didn't go away like he told them to.

Unease rippled under my skin. I cleared my throat. "Anything else, Gabriel?" I asked, wanting to be done with this.

He wiped furiously at his eyes. "I'm going to get her to trust me again. I'll show her that it's real. And then...I'm going to make her fall in love with me too. I don't fucking care what your jaded, broken soul thinks, Lucian. It only matters what *she* thinks."

The insane urge to sucker punch him in the teeth, or choke him until he turned blue dashed down my spine like fucking lightning.

I counted backwards from five, as I always did when I was tempted to lash out. "Anything else?" I said, proud of myself when it came out cool and collected, just like always.

Gabriel stormed out of the room without another word, slamming the door closed as hard as he'd banged it open.

I turned back to my contract, determined not to think about them, to think about her.

I read the contract over a hundred times. And I still didn't catch a word of it.

ELEVEN

DAHLIA

The girls that Lucian had hired to get me ready for tonight's dinner tittered around me, gossiping about their friends and going on and on about how lucky I was to be marrying Lucian, "the most eligible bachelor in the city," apparently.

I just sat there, giving one-word responses and turning my head this way and that as they did my makeup and hair. My arms were crossed in front of me so I could inconspicuously press against my fresh cut, anything to try and calm my raging nerves. My dress was hanging on a hook on the door, and my gaze kept flicking over to it.

It had been the longest day in my life. From Lucian's sudden reappearance and delightful message, to my goodbye to Gabriel; I felt like I'd been frozen in place. The girls had arrived an hour ago, and as annoying as they were, at least they'd served as a little bit of distraction from the night's events.

"Fuck, you're gorgeous," my makeup artist crowed as she dragged her brush against my cheek once more before stepping back. "Lucian is the lucky one." She eyed me hungrily, and I couldn't help but giggle. The makeup artist was evidently one of the best in the country, but I really hoped she'd done my makeup a hell of a lot differently than she'd done her own. Her hair was dyed purple and styled in a cool-looking faux hawk. Her lips were the same color as her hair, and she had sparkly green eyeshadow and long false lashes. Piercings were going up both of her ears, and she was impossibly cool...just not my style.

"Stop flirting with Lucian Rossi's girl and let's get her in front of the mirror," one of the girls said, a slight tremor in her voice as she glanced at the door like Lucian was about to storm through and shoot everyone.

I obviously barely knew him, but based on what I did know, that was probably not out of the realm of possibilities.

I stood up from my chair and they ushered me towards the floor-length mirror that hung on the wall of my room.

My jaw dropped when I looked at the stranger staring back at me in the mirror. My hair was done in loose curls with a dramatic side part that showcased the diamond drop earrings that had been delivered to my room a few hours ago. I hadn't wanted to wear them, especially since the accompanying note said *Wear these.* But after what had happened this morning, I didn't have it in me to battle against Lucian over this.

And they were absolutely stunning earrings.

My eyes were dark and dramatic, done in a classic smoky eye rather than anything vibrant. The vibrant was saved for my lips that were stained a dark, dramatic red. I looked sensual and fierce, like a woman that men would bow to.

Like I said, she looked nothing like me.

I realized that the hair and makeup team was waiting with bated breath for me to say something, and I quickly gave them a big smile I hoped looked somewhat authentic. They had done a very good job.

"You guys are incredible," I announced, and they all let out almost identical sighs of relief.

I waved goodbye to them as they packed up their stuff and left the room, and then I walked over to the shimmering white dress waiting for me. It was floor-length and dripping a mix of diamonds and sequins. It was a one-shouldered dress, with a slit on the chest and up both sides. The dress was meant to tease, to show just enough skin to leave them panting for more.

Too bad my fiancé was not the panting type. And he definitely didn't want *more*.

I forced myself not to think about what Gabriel would think when he saw me. I took a few deep breaths to try and stop the ever-present ache I'd had in my chest since this morning.

I can do this. I've been through far worse.

As if summoned by my thoughts, my phone buzzed on the chair where I'd left it. I grabbed it absentmindedly, my thoughts still focused on the dress.

I'm sure you'll look beautiful tonight.

Six innocent-sounding words.

Me, a mess on the floor at the sight of them.

How did he know what tonight was? Did he have my mum's phone bugged?

He can't touch me here, he can't touch me here. My breath came out in sharp gasps as I struggled to get a hold of myself.

Wasn't it a damn shame that the bogeyman of our pasts had such a hold on our present?

I struggled to my feet and blindly lurched forward towards the dress, knowing that I only had minutes to spare.

And the last thing I wanted was for a Rossi to see me like this.

But fuck, I didn't even have time to run into the bathroom and make a tiny cut.

I grabbed the dress and fumbled with the zipper, my breath still coming out in gasps.

After I slid it on, I reached back to try and get the zipper, but I couldn't quite reach it.

Fuck.

I'd have to use the old hanger trick.

Before I had a chance to grab the hanger the dress had been dangling on, fingertips grazed along the skin on my back.

Before I could scream, a hand clamped itself against my mouth, muffling any noise.

"Need a little help, angel?" Raphael offered smoothly from behind me, his touch sending goosebumps cascading across my skin.

That didn't help me to calm down at all, and I bit into his hand.

"Fuck," he said with a shocked laugh as he yanked his hand away, leaving the sharp tang of his blood in my mouth.

"Feisty little thing, aren't you? Gabriel would be shocked that his princess has a bite."

"Fuck you," I told him, trying to step away, but his other hand was holding on tightly to my dress, and I knew he wouldn't have a problem ripping it if I tried to get away.

He held out his bleeding hand in front of me as his other hand held me tight. "Should I drip this all over your pretty little dress, Dahlia? Get everyone really asking questions?"

"What do you want, Raphael?" My voice was filled with derision, but he just chuckled again as if my anger delighted him.

It probably did. Freaking psycho. How had he even gotten in here? I'd surely have noticed if the door had opened.

I shivered, a mix of fear and awful lust coursing through me as his fingers on his other hand continued to sensually move down my spine. My body remembered what those fingers could do, how he'd made me fall apart again and again on that flight.

There'd been a few times when I'd had breaks from my nightmares, and instead, I'd dreamt of Raphael, of what his mouth could do…of how he'd made me feel. I'd wake up aching and breathless, sweat dripping down my spine.

And I'd be disgusted every time by my traitorous body.

"Maybe I just feel like playing," he murmured as he abruptly spun us so that we were facing the mirror.

He dwarfed me in size, and I examined the outfit he'd chosen for tonight. His tuxedo coat was made of a blue velvet fabric with a black lapel, and he had a silky white dress shirt underneath it with the first few buttons undone. My eyes couldn't help but trail down to where I could see he was wearing perfectly tailored black suit pants. I had a feeling the combo would look ridiculous on anyone else, but he looked like a male model. Raphael was stupidly pretty, no one could argue about that.

But apparently Lucifer was the prettiest angel in heaven, and look what he became. Maybe Raphael should get a name change.

I glanced at my phone for the time, only to see a message from Lucian saying: *I'm waiting.*

"Have you thought about that plane ride at all, Dahlia? Have you gotten your pretty pussy off, thinking about me making you cum over and over again?"

"Of course not," I said quickly, but my chest was heaving and my goosebumps were only spreading...and arousal was thick in my voice. My body was a traitor; it seemed to go stupid over beautiful men.

Raphael was watching me in the mirror, a little smile on his face like he knew a secret I didn't. His hand that I'd bitten was now wrapped around my neck, and I knew there'd be blood on my skin that I'd need to wash off before I left the room, but at least it hadn't dripped on my dress.

His other hand began to slide my zipper up, and fuck, how was I getting as turned on by him putting my clothes on as when he'd taken them off?

My phone buzzed again, and I knew it was Lucian, most likely getting impatient as I was now bordering on late, but I was caught in Raphael's spider web, staring into his eyes through the mirror.

When he'd fully zipped up my dress, he let go of my neck, grinning crazily at the blood smeared all over my skin. It felt like he'd branded me, like the blood was seeping into my skin and leaving a mark inside of me that I'd never be able to remove.

"Enjoy your party, angel," he finally drawled before stepping away from me and leaving the room without a look back.

My legs were shaking as I smoothed down my dress and hastily reapplied the lipstick that the makeup artist had left. Then I rushed into the bathroom and grabbed a towel, carefully washing off the blood. After stepping into the sparkling white shoes that had way too high of a heel...I was ready.

I was ten minutes late when I left the room and was awarded for my tardiness with a scowl on Lucian's face.

But holy fuck. It was hard to think straight in the face of his ridiculous hotness. Seriously, what was in the Rossi water? He'd gone with a classic black tux with a black bow tie, and his dark hair was slicked back, a few curls escaping like they were making sure everyone knew this was the kind of guy who couldn't be tamed. And that scruff, seriously. It was like God had put all my favorite things into one body, and then made sure it had a rotten soul just to torture me.

A crazy surge of hormones and chemicals begged me to have him fuck me senseless, and I dug my nails into my palms to try and get rid of it.

Lucian's face was perfectly blank as his eyes roved over me. There was no hint in his body language of what he thought about how I looked.

"Let's go," he said abruptly and strode off towards the elevators.

Arsehole, I thought. I'd had so little interaction with him, yet that was the word that blared in my head every second that I was around him.

He didn't say a word to me in the elevator, and I was thinking perhaps that the elevator was cursed because its occupants always seemed to lose the ability to speak every time I was in it.

My heels clicked against the floor as I struggled to keep up with him through the lobby, and Lucian shot me a frustrated look at my slow pace.

"I'd love to see *you* wear six-inch heels," I growled, and something sparked in his gaze. "And besides, aren't you the big boss man? I don't think it's a big deal if we're a few minutes late."

Lucian huffed in annoyance. He seemed to do that a lot around me.

"I abhor being late. Remember that in the future," he said as he strode through the doors to where a Rolls Royce was waiting, leaving me in the dust.

"I abhor being late," I mimicked in my best snooty voice as I finally made it to the doors and outside.

I'd been obviously flustered the first time that I'd driven in a car with Lucian, so I hadn't really taken the time to appreciate the Bentley...but I was definitely appreciating the Rolls Royce Phantom that we would apparently be traveling in to the party.

Fun fact about me. I had a thing for cars. Leo had driven a rust orange Lamborghini, and it had turned me on every time I'd gotten in that thing.

"Are you going to keep drooling all over my car, or are you going to get in?" Lucian sighed through the open door of the car, and I reluctantly stopped eye fucking it and slid into the interior where I was surrounded by delicious smelling white leather.

Or maybe that was just him. His scent was surrounding me, leather and spice...gunpowder wrapped in exotic musk. The most delicious smell I'd ever experienced.

The car pulled away from the curb into the traffic that I was learning never stopped here. London was bustling, but it didn't feel quite as frantic as New York did.

I was feeling more and more anxious the longer we drove. Lucian was on his phone, completely ignoring my presence. I hated socializing in large groups to begin with, but being thrown in blind like I was tonight...it was beginning to make me feel crazy. My mind was whirling trying to imagine what I was going to step into.

So many people staring at me.

It was a complete recipe for disaster.

As was my habit, I dug my nails into my skin.

"What the fuck is wrong with you?" he growled. His hand shot out and grabbed mine, forcing my hand open and revealing the crescent indentions I'd been digging into my skin. His teeth clenched together as he examined my hand.

How had he even noticed me doing that? He hadn't seemed to be paying me any attention.

I huffed in exasperation. "What should I expect tonight? How many people were invited? Where is the party even at?" The questions rolled off my tongue.

He was still holding onto my one hand, and I couldn't miss the tingles going up my arm from where he was touching it.

I tried to yank my arm away, but he didn't let go. "I would have thought *The Firm* would have treated you to lots of events with the rich folks," he mocked, and I gritted my teeth, wondering if it was okay to give my fiancé a shiner before our engagement party.

"I don't know, Lucian. Everything I ever hear about Americans is how uncivilized you all are. I can't imagine it's like what I'm used to, and since I've never been engaged, maybe you could enlighten me."

He finally let go of my hand and sat back into his seat, crossing his arms in front of him in a way that stretched his coat and only accentuated the fact that he was most definitely hiding a perfect body under his clothes.

"There'll be three hundred people there. Most we hate, a few we don't, but all power players in the city. They'll kiss our ass the moment we walk through the door and then curse us the moment we leave. The party's being held at the Met because I'm a pretentious bastard that enjoys throwing my power into people's faces. We'll smile and nod, eat ridiculously overpriced food, and then I'll spin you around the dance floor so everyone thinks we're madly in love. And then we'll be done." He answered all my questions calmly and methodically, without any emotion in his voice.

It was clearly all business to him. Nothing more.

If only it could be that way for me.

"So you're not that different from The Firm after all," I commented, pretending to examine my nails while still very much aware of the apex predator sitting just inches away. "You're all a bunch of power-hungry men, growing your dick size with every life you ruin."

His hand was suddenly on my neck, squeezing until it was hard to breathe. His other hand grabbed my wrist and thrust my hand against his raging hard-on. He was huge…of course. All the Rossi men seemed to be. The better question was, why was he so fucking hard right now?

My eyes widened as my breath came out in gasps. I didn't bother trying to yank my hand away. I knew he wasn't going to kill me. He was teaching me a lesson. How very *Mafia* of him.

"As you can see, princess. I don't need any help in the dick-growing department. And what would you know about drive, hard work, and power? You're just a little girl who's been in her ivory tower her whole life looking down on everyone who's made her life so cush."

He abruptly released my neck and wrist and sat back in his seat like nothing had happened. Some of his hair had fallen into his face, the only sign of his temporary loss of control.

My hands shook as I placed them in my lap, and I wondered if I'd actually traded one devil for another.

We didn't speak to each other the rest of the way to the museum. Once it came into view, I noticed paparazzi standing at the base of the stairs, many of them looking quite disgruntled that security was preventing them from taking pictures of the glamorous, powerful New Yorkers walking up the steps. One of the security guards—a hulking beast of a man dressed in a sharply tailored suit who obviously worked for Lucian based on his menacing presence—grabbed a camera from one of the photographers and threw it on the ground, shattering it into a million pieces. The cameraman threw his arms up, shrieking something I couldn't hear through the thick glass of the car.

Didn't people usually get in trouble for that kind of stuff? Apparently not when the Rossi family was involved. Security looked over to the car and began pushing all the paparazzi down the street. Lucian didn't get out until they were all around the corner and out of sight.

"So that's how you managed to never get a picture of yourself online," I mused. "Your staff scare all the cameramen away whenever you attend an event."

"That and a team dedicated to erasing my online presence," he added nonchalantly, like that wasn't overkill.

I laughed to myself despite the awful circumstances, remembering my frantic search when I'd first found out about the treaty and my impending marriage. I'd literally spent hours and hours scouring the web to try and find a picture of him.

At least now I knew it was impossible.

"Doesn't everyone in this town already know what you look like though?"

"The only people who know what I look like are people who I want to know," he retorted.

I didn't bother asking him anymore about that.

"One thing before we go in," Lucian said suddenly, grabbing a black velvet box that I hadn't seen lying next to him. He tossed it at me, and I gave him my best annoyed look before opening it up.

I couldn't help but gasp when I saw the most enormous, and ostentatious diamond ring that I'd ever seen. And that was saying something, because my mum had been a big fan of jewelry, and my pa had spoiled her during their marriage with extremely expensive pieces that she'd worn quite often, even now that he was gone. The ring in front of me was emerald cut, and although I didn't know much about diamonds, I knew the carat count had to be completely ridiculous.

I raised an eyebrow at him. "What's this?" I asked.

Riccardo opened the door just then, and Lucian slid out of the car. He straightened up his tux and then leaned down to look at me. "What do you think it is? It's your fucking engagement ring. Now put it on and get out."

I slid the ring on and immediately hated it. Not because it wasn't absolutely gorgeous, but because the girl inside of me who had once dreamed of fairytales had imagined this whole thing so much differently. Having the ring tossed at me had definitely not been in those dreams.

Riccardo helped me exit the vehicle, and I tried to do it as gracefully as possible. Once I'd stood up and adjusted my dress, Lucian held out his arm. "Showtime," he murmured, and just the thought of the night that lay ahead of us made me want to scream.

For most of my life, I'd felt like a show pony. First parading around for my father, and then for my mum at society events. I'd always been under the microscope at school, all my classmates having heard rumors about The Firm's little princess.

It had been never-ending.

And here it was, beginning again.

I pasted on my best fake smile and took his arm, allowing him to begin leading me up the steps into the Met. We made it to the top of the stairs and through the glass doors where a crowd of elegantly dressed women and men were gathered, sipping on flutes of champagne. The crowd immediately grew silent when we walked in, and I felt the weight of their stares—hundreds of them—assessing me and tearing me apart in their heads. My fake smile faded under their scrutiny.

Lucian pulled me close and leaned in so his lips were just a hairsbreadth away from my ear. "Breathe, principessa," he murmured to me, and goosebumps trailed down my neck from the feel of his breath on my skin.

I turned to glance up at him, and he shot me a look that to anyone else would've screamed besotted fiancé. But this close to him, I could see the blankness in his eyes, the unfeelingness.

I immediately flashed him an automatic smile, desperate to get this over with as soon as possible. He brushed a soft kiss against my lips then, completely surprising me. Butterflies went crazy in my stomach at the light touch. I'd obviously assumed that I'd have to kiss him, and sleep with him at least a few times…but the kiss still caught me off guard.

The floodgates broke then, and everyone seemed to come forward at once, trying to be one of the first to congratulate us. Lucian began to lead me forward amidst all of it, deeper into the beautiful lobby, nodding and saying hello to people as we went along. They commented on how beautiful I was, and what a lucky man Lucian was to have me. And the entire time I kept that broken smile on my face, trying my best to look happy.

We walked down a set of stairs where there was an enormous room. There were fountains set up throughout it, almost like a courtyard. Round tables draped with champagne gold tablecloths were situated around the room, the cloth and the cream and gold dishes on top of the table glittering under the flickering cande-labras placed every few feet.

There were chandeliers hanging from the ceiling, and elegant greenery placed here and there that only added to the elegance.

It was gorgeous. Everything I would have picked, really. It was like whoever had designed this for Lucian had read my mind.

"This is amazing," I whispered, noticing what seemed like half an orchestra set up along the far wall, filling the room with a soft melody that fit the glamorous setting perfectly.

"Only the best for my bride," Lucian murmured sarcastically, before flashing another brilliant grin at another pompous-looking couple who was approaching us.

It seemed like there were far more than three hundred people in this room, because every time I turned around, there was another stranger hell-bent on giving us their congratulations. Lucian never let go of his proprietary grip around my waist, even after his free hand had been filled with a glass of fluted champagne.

He'd barely taken a sip of it before a debonair, familiar-looking older man approached us with a woman who I was pretty sure I'd seen in a Victoria's Secret ad plastered against him.

"Fuck," Lucian breezed, downing the rest of his entire glass of champagne in what seemed like one gulp.

"Who's that?" I asked, unease dripping down my spine. It couldn't be someone good for Lucian to seem so agitated. He was, in my experience, the epitome of "cool" at all times.

"My father," he commented dryly, before schooling his face in a look that was devoid of all emotion.

Carlo Rossi, the "Boss" of the Cosa Nostra. Gabriel had warned me about him, how he was a snake. Fuck.

Before I could ask anything else, they were in front of us.

"Son," the man said in a deep voice. Lucian nodded at him but didn't make any effort to shake his hand, or heaven forbid, give him a hug.

It would've been impossible to miss that Lucian and his father were related, just like it would've been impossible to miss that this man had created Gabriel. He was a perfect mix of the two, incredibly handsome like they were, and I felt like I was getting a glimpse into what they both would look like in thirty-five years. I didn't see any of Raphael in him, however.

Carlo turned his attention towards me, and Lucian's fingers dug into my side.

"It's nice to meet you, sir. Lucian told me so many good things about you," I said, feigning excitement.

Carlo laughed, and it sounded demonic, I'm sure sending shivers down every person's spine in the vicinity. It certainly was sending shivers down mine.

"The beautiful Dahlia. I must say, you don't disappoint," he sneered, his gaze devouring my body, and unlike when his sons did the same thing, his look only made me sick.

He held out his hand, and I felt like I had no choice but to give him mine, even as Lucian's fingers dug into my side even more.

Carlo took my hand and lifted it up to his mouth, pressing a kiss against my skin that filled me with revulsion. And I definitely noticed when he used a bit of tongue. I did my best not to shake, even though everything inside of me was telling me this man was pure evil. You couldn't show weakness in front of men like this. It only made them want to pounce.

"I hope my son's treating you as you deserve," Carlo commented, finally letting go of my hand. It was all I could do not to wipe it off on my dress. I was that desperate to get any trace of him off of me.

"Of course," I responded, giving Lucian what I hoped looked like a loving smile.

Carlo's date was very interested in Lucian, eye-fucking him the entire time, and a small part of me...a very small part, wanted to stab her with a fork from a place setting on the table next to me.

I noted that Carlo didn't bother to introduce her.

"So glad you could make it, Father," Lucian told him with derision that made my eyes widen.

I noted that there were what felt like a million pairs of eyes on the four of us. Clearly, everyone felt the need to keep their eyes on the most powerful people in the room.

It was smart of them. Because there was violence in the air surrounding them, like at any minute they could take out the guns I knew both of them were packing and shoot each other... and perhaps everyone else.

I turned into Lucian and put my hand on his chest, trying to play my part. But Lucian stiffened under my touch. His fingers on my side grew painful, and he practically threw his glass on a passing waiter's tray and grabbed my wrist that had been touching him.

I tried not to make a face, but his grip was so tight on my wrist that it would probably leave a bruise.

All the while, Carlo watched us avidly, an amused smirk on his face. His gaze caught on my ring.

"Your mother's ring, Lucian. I wouldn't have pegged you for the sentimental type."

I kept my face still, not wanting Carlo to know that I'd had no idea I was wearing a dead woman's ring.

Gabriel had told me about his mother, how she'd overdosed and died a few years ago after decades of heavy drinking and prescription drugs. It certainly didn't bode well that her ring was what Lucian had chosen to give me. From what Gabriel had mentioned, none of them had a good relationship with her... especially Raphael, an eternal reminder of her husband's infidelity.

"I thought it was a good idea to keep it in the family," Lucian answered, an undercurrent in his voice that I didn't understand. "As good as it is to see you tonight, Father, I'm afraid there are more guests I want to introduce my lovely fiancée to before dinner starts."

There was a tic in Carlo's cheek, and his eyes turned stormy and dark at Lucian's clear dismissal. He obviously hadn't missed the sarcasm in Lucian's voice, and I'm sure that *the Boss* wasn't keen on being dismissed.

But appearance was everything evidently, because he flashed us both a deceptively charming smile, wiping all traces of his underlying anger away. "Of course, son. We'll talk first thing in the morning. I'm interested to hear about your recent trip to Dallas."

I felt Lucian stiffen a bit more under my touch, but he just smiled and nodded.

"And Dahlia, I can't wait to get to know you more," Carlo continued, and the sharp taste of fear flooded my mouth at his words. If I had any say in it, I'd never see him again. If only that was up to me.

Finally, Carlo turned away, pulling the hussy he was with

behind him. Not before she flashed Lucian one more "fuck me" look over her shoulder.

As soon as his father turned his back, Lucian ripped my hand from his chest. He leaned in close, a bright smile on his face that didn't hide the menace in his gaze. "Don't ever touch me again without my permission," he growled, somehow keeping his smile even with the clear threat in his voice.

I flinched from the venom in his tone. "I'm sorry, I was just trying to play a part. I didn't know."

"Well, now you do," he said before turning to greet a group of handsome men that looked to be around Lucian's age. Gabriel had said that he was six years younger than Lucian, putting Lucian at 32. The group definitely looked like they ran in Lucian's same circle.

I noticed that Lucian had an actual genuine smile with this group, and I did my best to pay attention to their conversation after they had greeted me.

But then I saw him.

Raphael. Walking in with his arm casually around the shoulders of a beautiful brunette draped in a skin-tight blue dress. Hot jealousy exploded in my stomach as I watched him murmur something into her ear.

He'd brought a date. When I could still feel the ghost of his touch along my skin, and it felt like the blood he'd marked me with had intertwined with my own.

He'd brought a date.

My thoughts were ridiculous, because of course he brought a date. He wasn't mine, and he'd made it perfectly clear that I wasn't his.

But still...I hadn't been prepared to see him with another woman.

Lucian noticed that my attention had drifted away. "Why exactly are you staring at my brother like you want to kill him?" he purred in my ear as the group of men he'd been talking with moved away.

I stiffened, all ideas of what I should say completely slipping from my mind.

"I—I wasn't looking at him. It's just... his date's familiar to me," I told him in a rushed voice. "I was just trying to recall where I knew her from."

He laughed, and I wondered if his laughter ever came out not sounding cruel.

"I find it very hard to believe that you would recognize Raphael's date as she's one of the most famous escorts in New York City. I don't believe that Madison's managed any trips to London lately. She's kept quite busy here." His tone was mocking, the insinuation clear that he was someone who'd kept her busy as well.

It was official. I was in complete and utter hell.

And just to make matters worse, Raphael spotted us and began to lead his *lovely* date our way.

"I'm just going to use the loo," I told Lucian hurriedly, not waiting for a response before I all but ran away from him.

I'm sure it looked suspicious as fuck, but I couldn't deal with that right now.

Lucian and Raphael's voices, combined with the lilting musical voice of Raphael's date, followed me as I crossed the room, luckily spotting the signs for the bathroom before I'd had to circle the room.

I slipped into the room, relieved when it appeared to be empty, and I made my way into a stall. Only seconds after I'd sat down to pee, I heard the door to the bathroom open and the sound of heels clicking along the tiled floor. I could see them through the crack in the stall, doing their best impression of a fish as they reapplied their lipstick.

"She so fucking young, Alessandra. What was Lucian thinking? If it's an heir he's after, I would've been up for the job," one of the women began.

Her companion laughed, like she'd told a particularly funny joke.

I for one didn't think it was humorous.

"Poor thing. I'm sure she thinks he's in love with her. He's been throwing her those looks all evening. Lucian was always a little bit too good at making girls think that he was interested. She'll quickly learn that she's not up to the task of fulfilling Lucian's…particular tastes. One night with him and she'd probably run away screaming."

What the hell was she talking about? His tastes?

The other woman sighed, like she was imagining fucking Lucian right then. "I still think about that night, you know. My ass was sore for four weeks. Quite frankly, no one's ever measured up, and I'm not sure that anyone ever will. It feels like I've been ruined for sex…not that I haven't tried."

They tittered again. I was pretty sure they both had the most obnoxious laughs in the world.

"I've heard the brothers are just as good in bed," her friend commented.

"What I wouldn't give to have an hour with Raphael."

"Raphael is a bit too intense for me. I'd definitely go for Gabriel. He's such a sweetheart."

"Yeah. Until he forgets you exist. Remember poor Katrina?"

Okay, I'd officially had enough. Apparently, there wasn't

anywhere that I could escape for a moment of peace in this wretched party...not even the loo.

I flushed the toilet and their voices stopped. I heard the sound of water running, and then their hurried footsteps as they exited the bathroom.

Taking a deep breath, I left my stall and walked over to one of the many sinks to wash my hands while staring at myself in the mirror.

I can do this. I've been through worse. Anything is better than him. I chanted the words in my head because, despite everything that had happened in the last few weeks since I'd come here, it was still better than the alternative.

I was surprised at how put together I still looked. After everything that had already happened tonight, you would've thought my makeup would be smeared and my hair would be a mess.

But no. I was the perfect English rose...as always.

When I'd given myself enough of a pep talk, I stepped out of the loo, immediately spotting Lucian talking to a few couples standing near the middle of the room. Thankfully, there was no sign of Raphael and his date.

As I began walking to join him, I spotted Gabriel sitting by himself at one of the bars set up to my left.

He was all alone, no sign of a date. And I cursed myself for thinking like that.

Gabriel looked incredible. He wasn't wearing a tuxedo, just a suit. But it was tailored to perfection, and even from here, my mouth was watering just from looking at him. His tie was undone, hanging loosely around his neck, and his hair was down and hanging around his face. It was the first time I'd seen it down, and I loved it.

His glass was empty, and I watched as he signaled the bartender to pour him another. He happened to look my way right at that moment, and our eyes connected.

I hated it, but something inside of me, something that felt suspiciously like my soul…it longed for him.

His gaze roved over me, so much yearning and devotion… and heat, that if I could have cried, I would have.

He stood up from his barstool as if to come towards me, but right at that moment, I felt a hand grip my arm. I turned and saw that Lucian was beside me, not looking happy with Gabriel's and my interaction.

Lucian locked eyes with Gabriel, his gaze glimmering with anger and a warning to stay away.

Gabriel just casually flipped him off and then gave me one more meaningful stare before he sat back down and grabbed his drink.

"Everything go alright in the bathroom? You were in there for quite a long time. If I didn't know better, I would think you were avoiding me," said Lucian lightly, as if that interaction with Gabriel had never happened.

It wasn't you I was avoiding…

"Just got caught up listening to some of your old friends," I told him saucily, and once again, his eyes flickered with heat.

It almost seemed like Lucian liked when I talked back.

That was probably for the best, because his acid tongue was making it harder and harder for me to hold mine.

"Dinner's about to be served," a waiter informed us, and Lucian put his hand back around my waist and led me to a table in the center of the room.

Just what I liked when eating—a million people staring at me.

I cringed when I saw that Raphael was sitting at our table with his date, and his gaze tracked me as we walked towards him, not even trying to hide where he was looking.

And fuck, if Raphael was seated at our table, that meant...

No sooner had I sat down in the chair that Lucian had pulled out for me than Gabriel was pulling out the one on the other side of me and sitting down, his chair way too close to mine. Lucian's eyes flashed when he noted Gabriel's close proximity to me, but surprisingly, he didn't say anything. He just sat down on my other side.

It felt like I was the punchline of a joke made at my expense. Three brothers and a hooker sat at a table...

But the horror show wasn't done yet, because Carlo and his date were the last to appear, settling into seats directly across from me.

I really needed to start thinking ahead. Of course the entire Rossi family would be at the same table, even if Carlo's sons seemed to abhor him.

"Quite a party you've put together, son," Carlo commented as a waiter stopped by to fill up his wine glass.

"It's all Emilia. She seems to have gotten to know my bride quite well in my short absence." Lucian appeared to be bemused by that fact.

"Emilia put all this together?" I asked Lucian, searching for her in the room.

"She insisted on it, actually. Emilia seemed to believe that she knew exactly what you would like."

"Hmm," I commented, trying to remember if I'd said anything over the course of the last two weeks that would have hinted at my wedding style. I couldn't think of anything. I'd actually tried to not talk about the wedding at all. Regardless, a rush of warmth passed over me as I thought of Emilia caring about me enough to create all of this.

But the warmth wasn't enough to overpower the dread flickering through me as I faced a dinner with all of these people.

A delicious smelling soup was placed in front of me, but it might as well have been a bowl full of paint. I couldn't stomach even one bite. I swirled it around with my spoon while everyone talked stiltedly around me.

"Not hungry, bellissima?" Gabriel whispered to me. I could feel the weight of Carlo's, Raphael's, and Lucian's eyes on me, so I just shook my head.

"Just nerves," I murmured back to him.

"Did Emilia put together the wedding as well?" Carlo asked, while his date made goo-goo eyes at Lucian.

The wedding. In the excitement of the night—and I said that with great sarcasm—I'd forgotten that I'd been informed the wedding would take place the day after tomorrow.

And with that reminder, I no longer felt like eating. I felt like throwing up.

Dinner continued, with me cutting up my steak—my favorite food—into little pieces and moving it around my plate so it looked like I was eating.

I heard Madison's voice all too much. She seemed to have a *great* relationship with everyone but Gabriel, who basically ignored her presence despite her attempts to bring him into the conversation. But Carlo, Raphael, and Lucian all chatted with her like she was an old friend.

Gross.

When she touched Lucian's shoulder, I suddenly found myself gripping my steak knife, seconds away from leaping across Lucian and slicing her throat.

Lucian's hand was suddenly on my knee, gripping it tight. He shot me a confused look, and I dropped the knife with a too-loud clatter that drew the gaze of everyone at the table.

"Whoops," I murmured, a deep blush staining my cheeks.

And dinner continued.

Lucian's hand stayed where it was.

"So Gabriel, where's your date tonight? Unusual to see you alone," asked Carlo in between bites of steak, a smug smile on his lips.

I pointedly looked down at my plate. Lucian had cocked his head and was studying his father, like a predator did before it pounced.

"She had another date," Gabriel said lightly as he grabbed his wine glass and drained the whole thing. Lucian tensed beside me but he didn't say anything.

"Is she going to be free for your brother's wedding?" Carlo seemed to be taunting and I wondered how many eyes he had on his sons...and what he had seen over the past few weeks.

Gabriel was gripping his wine glass so hard I was shocked it hadn't shattered into a million pieces.

"Not likely," he finally answered.

I deserved a fucking medal of achievement when dessert was finally done. At one point, Carlo had literally bit into his date's— I still hadn't learned her name—neck. Right there in front of everyone.

And she had moaned, like a fucking porn star.

These people were savages, and I came from a line of people that literally embodied the word "butcher."

Gabriel had not said another word throughout dinner, somehow even quieter than me, and I hadn't thought that was possible. Every time he'd taken a bite, he'd shot me looks so full of emotion I could feel them on my skin, even when I looked away.

Carlo looked at him confused a few times, but he hadn't commented on it. I'd realized quickly that Carlo really couldn't care less about his sons. He saw them as tools, not actual people.

As the servers came by to collect the dessert plates, a chocolate cake that I again hadn't touched, Lucian put his arm around my shoulders and leaned in close.

"Time for our dance, principessa," he murmured, his chocolate and bourbon scented breath dancing across my skin.

"Dance?" I asked, looking around the room in confusion. Everyone was still seated at their tables, with a few people milling around at the multiple bar stations set up around the room.

Lucian was already standing up though as the performers switched from the Mozart it had been playing to a song that I instantly recognized even with just the orchestra accompaniment. It was "Young and Beautiful" by Lana Del Rey.

There was an open area in front of the performers that I hadn't noticed before and Lucian led me by the hand to the center of the floor.

"Am I allowed to touch you?" I murmured, a pasted smile on my lips as I was aware of a room full of eyes on us both.

Instead of answering, Lucian wrapped his arm around me and pulled me close, too close, giving me no choice but to place my hand on his shoulder while he held my other in between us. Sparks skipped across my skin from the feel of his arms around me.

He began to move, and as if I'd been born to dance with him, I melted into his movements effortlessly.

He gazed down at me, his brilliant green eyes impenetrable

as always even as he gave the crowd his best impression of a man in love.

I couldn't take it. He could look at me any other way he wanted, but not like that.

"Please don't look at me like that," I whispered to him, making sure that my pain wasn't written across my face.

"Like what, Dahlia?" he said, bemused.

"Like you're not going to spend the rest of our lives breaking my heart."

His eyes glittered as the candles flickered around us and he continued to spin me around the floor. In the muted lighting, he looked like a dream, a dark dream that a girl could spend her entire life craving…and never possess.

"At least you're prepared," he finally murmured.

Something inside me, something that felt awfully like my soul, burst into flames.

Before I could respond to him, a throat cleared nearby and I looked over to see Gabriel standing there, determination in his gaze as he studied how close Lucian was holding me.

The last notes of the song we'd just danced to faded away, and Lucian brought us to a slow stop.

"Can I help you, Gabriel?" Lucian said in a clipped voice, a smile still on his face, but his eyes telling a very different story.

"I thought I'd cut in and give Dahlia a spin."

I cringed at the way his words came out, and Lucian gave a low growl.

As if he remembered we were the center of attention, Lucian finally nodded. "Of course, brother," he said sarcastically, before finally letting go of me and stepping away.

The part of my body that always seemed to betray me, immediately missed his touch.

Gabriel didn't waste a second gathering me in his arms as the music changed to the instrumental version of "Take Me to Church" by Hosier.

He was drunk. That was obvious, holding me far too close than was acceptable at my engagement party.

"Gabriel, what are you doing?" I hissed, as I tried to put some space between us. But he didn't let me move away even an inch.

Despite how drunk he was, Gabriel was still smooth as he moved me around the dance floor. Luckily other couples had started dancing as well so we weren't the only ones, but I knew that there were still so many people watching us.

"I'm dying. You won't talk to me, you barely look at me. I knew at least in public you'd have to acknowledge me." His lips brushed against my ear as he spoke, and I shivered reflexively.

"We've said all that needs to be said. There's no good that can come from us spending time together."

His arms tightened even more, like the more I said no, the more he didn't want to let me go.

"You're all I think about, Dahlia," he said hoarsely. "It feels like I'm going to die every time he touches you."

I sighed and closed my eyes for a moment. "It's not real, Gabriel. Just as much as what you think you feel for me isn't real, it's never going to be real with Lucian either. It will just be a performance for a stage that I never wanted to be on."

"Maybe right now it is. But I can already see that you're getting under his skin. And I know from experience that once you're there, he's never going to be able to get you out."

I shook my head. "Gabriel, it's been one day. Whatever you're feeling will fade, just…you just need to stay away."

"Dahlia, the one thing that I know about my OCD is that it makes me single-mindedly focused on what I want. There's not going to be a day for the rest of our lives that I'm not going to try to get you back."

I looked up at him, his golden eyes gleaming as he stared down at me. And maybe perversely, the devotion in his gaze when he looked at me, made me feel a little bit better about the lack of devotion I would always see in Lucian's.

The song reached its crescendo, and Gabriel tipped me back, his gaze devouring my form as he did so. When he pulled me back up, and the song began to end, I smiled sadly at him.

"Gabriel, the problem is that you never had me in the first place."

I pasted on my fake smile once again as Gabriel led me to the table, and then he promptly headed towards the bar without another word, or a look back.

"Where did Lucian run off to?" I asked after I'd settled back into my seat.

Raphael was sitting back, sipping his drink, staring daggers at Gabriel as he walked away.

"It's really a funny thing. Lucian disappeared right in the middle of that *show* you just put on. And it's such an odd coincidence…but so did my date."

Fire flashed through my veins when I realized what he was insinuating…but surely. No, even Lucian wouldn't… I abruptly stood up from my chair, not even bothering to pretend to be casual about it. "I'll just be right back," I murmured.

"Not sure you want to do that, angel," Raphael called after me, but I was already on my way.

I turned down one hallway and then the next, opening random closets and finding…really interesting things.

That was definitely not the woman that guy had been with earlier.

And I'm pretty sure that guy on his knees sucking that guy's willy had a wife.

I wanted to burn my eyeballs by the time I got to the end of that hall, but I kept on, something sick in my gut pushing me forward.

I'd made it to a hall that had Egyptian artifacts when I heard soft moans, and I just knew I'd found what I was looking for.

I peeked my head around the doorway.

And I saw them.

I was so incredibly disappointed, and I didn't even know why.

Lucian was sitting on an Egyptian throne—yes, a literal throne--with his pants undone. Madison was on her knees, her hands tied behind her back with what looked like Lucian's bow tie, her head bobbing up and down on his dick.

I stood there, watching the scene for way too long, a numb sensation spreading across my skin.

And then I snapped.

My heels echoing down the hall immediately drew Lucian's gaze. He didn't show a hint of surprise, like he'd been expecting me all along and this was a show he'd wanted me to see.

"I wouldn't have expected any less from a *made man*. Wouldn't want to buck stereotypes, now would we?" I sneered.

Lucian didn't respond.

Madison's head popped up at my words, and shock marred her features. There was no guilt in her eyes, but I didn't expect that from a whore. This was par for the course with powerful men, after all. And I'm sure she was used to scenes just like this.

"Go ahead, finish him," I said coldly, not taking my eyes from Lucian's. "Make sure you give my fiancé your best work. A Rossi always deserves the best, after all."

Out of the corner of my eye, I saw her give me a quizzical look before going back to work.

I should have walked away, but Lucian and I stared at each other until he finished with an erotic moan, a slight flush to his cheeks as she sucked every last drop out of him.

Madison stood up, her hands still tied behind her back, and she flashed Lucian a seductive smile.

I reared back, just like my brother Benny had taught me, and I punched her right in the temple, grinning savagely when she collapsed to the ground, knocked out cold.

Hopefully the bitch would have a traumatic brain injury and forget how to give blow jobs.

A choked sound of shock came out of Lucian, and I locked eyes with him once more, finally letting him see the depths of my emotions—my disappointment, my anger, my hate…my jealousy. Something that looked remarkably like shame burned in his eyes as we stared at each other.

And then I ran.

I heard a loud "fuck" behind me, but I didn't turn to see what was happening. I just kept going, running through the twisting hallways until I found a door with a red exit sign on top of it.

I burst through the doors, not caring if anyone was watching me.

Right into someone's chest.

"Woah, slow down, Dahlia. What's the emergency?" Carlo purred, and I cringed as cigarette smoke curled around my head, because of course he was smoking in the lobby of the Met.

Bloody arsehole.

I tried to take a step back, but his arms had clamped around me…I was dangerously close to getting burned by his still-lit cigarette.

"I have a migraine coming on. I'm just going to slip home and get some medicine."

Carlo pulled me closer, and I did my best not to struggle. Wasn't that what they said to do with predators in the wild? Play dead. It seemed like the answer for this situation as well.

"I have some 'product.' You'd be feeling fine in no time." One of his hands had drifted down to my butt, and my plans to not react were quickly fading. My breath was starting to speed up, and the edge of my vision was beginning to close in.

In my head, I was in my bedroom, and *he* was sitting on my bed.

"Don't move, little one. I'll make you feel so good." He was *breathing heavily, his excitement evident.*

"Cazzo," I heard faintly, and I felt the sensation of falling. Then something cold and hard was against my back. I struggled to open my eyes, and when I did, I realized that I was on the ground, Carlo nowhere to be seen. Had I fainted in his arms, and he'd just left me here?

A couple stumbled out of the exit I'd taken to get out here in the first place, and their eyes widened when they saw me on the ground. I hastily struggled to my feet.

"Should we get Lucian?" the woman slurred, and I just shook my head.

"I'm fine. Just tripped," I murmured, turning and walking towards the door before Carlo popped up again…or Lucian. My whole body was shaking, and I cursed myself a million times over for fucking freezing. I knew how to defend myself, but it was as if there was a button on my back that men like Carlo… and my uncle, knew how to press.

I was a waste of space, a pathetic excuse for a person.

Weak. The word reverberated through my soul.

There was a storm coming in as I stepped out into the night air, and my hair whipped across my face as a gust of wind practically knocked me over. Raindrops began to fall as I made my way down the stairs, eventually ripping my heels off and carrying them in my hand so I could make it down without killing myself. I just tried not to think about everything on the ground I was stepping on.

The street was quieter than I was used to, probably because of the storm, but as I made it to the sidewalk, I realized I had no ID and no money.

I wanted to scream as the heavens opened up and the drops of rain turned into a torrent that had me looking like a drowned rat in seconds.

If I could have cried, this would have been the moment. I squeezed my eyes shut, willing them to come, just so that I could release some of the intensity thrashing around inside of me.

But of course, nothing came.

"Dahlia," Raphael's voice cut through the storm. He was leaning against a sleek black Bentley, his arms crossed in front of him.

I walked slowly towards him, leaves and sticks slapping against me as the storm raged.

"You wanted me to see that," I told him quietly as his blue eyes glittered under the street lights.

"Mmmh, perhaps."

"I don't know what your goal was, Raphael. I was under no illusions that Lucian and I were going to run off into the sunset together." Something struck me then. "Did you set this up? Did you bring that bitch on purpose?"

Raphael shrugged, a ghost of a grin on his beautiful face. He leaned in towards me, and I braced for the impact. "Get in the car, Dahlia," he murmured, and my whole body shuddered.

I took the out he was giving me. I couldn't take anything else tonight.

I slid into the car, taking a bit of pleasure that I was most likely ruining his leather seats thanks to the rain. Raphael got into the car and started it.

As we began to drive away, I couldn't help but look out the window to where the Met was outlined in the rain.

A man stood at the top of the stairs, the rain beating down on him, watching us leave.

And I knew, even without seeing his face, that it was Lucian.

"You should have been smarter than to run after him, Dahlia," Raphael grumbled, piercing the quiet of the car. He almost sounded like he cared.

I continued staring out the window, long after Lucian had faded from view.

"You should know by now that 'should' is a worthless word, Raphael. It's almost as worthless as hope."

He didn't say anything else after that, and as the rain hammered down on the car, I closed my eyes and made a promise to myself.

No Rossi would ever hurt me again.

TWELVE

A doorman I'd never seen before was manning the desk when we walked through the lobby of our building. It had only been a few hours since I'd left, but it felt like a lifetime had passed.

Raphael tossed him his keys with a nod, presumably to park his car in the garage to this place, which I hadn't yet seen.

"Oh, Mr. Rossi, a batch of wedding presents came in. I left them in your entrance," the doorman said nervously.

Raphael laughed, and I felt like punching the arsehole, because of course he knew that opening wedding presents would be the last thing that I wanted to do.

We were in front of the elevator, and I couldn't help but drag my hands down my face. I didn't want to go up there. It didn't matter which one of the Rossi brothers were up there, they all filled me with dread…including—and maybe especially—the one next to me.

I got into the elevator of course, because where else could I go? The penthouse was silent when we arrived, with no sign of Gabriel…or Lucian. Thank God.

There was a stack of presents sitting in the entryway, and I contemplated burning them.

"Oh, goody. Present time," Raphael drawled, kicking one so hard it soared into the living room…where the lid promptly fell off. Along with something brown.

"What is that?" I murmured, walking towards it. I stiffened as soon I made out what it actually was.

A dead frog. A dead frog that had been splayed open like we'd been forced to do in science class in secondary school.

"Don't touch it," Raphael barked, and I shot him a look… because the last thing I wanted to do was touch it.

Raphael jogged to the kitchen, and I heard the sound of a drawer opening and utensils, or something like that, clanging to the floor while he shuffled through it.

He reappeared a moment later with a pair of tongs. I made a mental note to throw those away as soon as we were done here so Emilia…or Gabriel didn't use them while cooking.

Raphael crouched down and used the tongs to push the frog back into the box and then set the box upright. "What the fuck?" he murmured as he held up a tiny, frog-sized crown.

"Please tell me this is a weird American custom that people do for impending marriages," I said lightly, even as tension curled in my gut. Raphael shot me an unamused look.

He dropped the crown back into the box and fished a scrap of paper out of the box.

The kiss didn't change the frog into a prince. The kiss killed him.

I opened my mouth, and then promptly closed it. I had no

idea what to say. All I did know was that there was a foreboding feeling sliding up my spine.

Raphael threw the note back into the box with disgust and stared at it for a minute, his thumb rubbing his bottom lip as he concentrated.

"Do you have any idea who would send something like that?" I asked hesitantly.

He scoffed at me. "We're the Cosa Nostra, Dahlia. We have a million enemies. But they don't usually send warning shots in the form of dark fairytales," he said sarcastically as he dropped the tongs he'd still been holding.

Raphael shook his head and then picked up the box before striding off towards the elevator.

"Where are you going?" I called after him.

"To kill the fool who brought this up here," he said calmly, before he stepped into the elevator.

I was 100% positive that he wasn't joking.

I didn't bother going after him. Instead, I practically ran to my room, wanting the comfort of a closed door between me and everything else. Once inside, I tore at my gown, ripping the zipper as I struggled to get out of the dress. I tossed it into my closet, determined to burn it the first chance I got. It could join my Union Jack shirt as something I would never wear again.

I was freezing from being caught out in the rain storm, so I tiredly walked to the bathroom and turned on the shower before stripping off the rest of my clothes.

When the water had warmed up, I grabbed my razor from its hiding spot and stepped in. The warm water rushed over my skin, but no matter how hot I made it, I couldn't seem to get rid of the chill inside of me.

It couldn't seem to get me clean either. I'd thought the stain on my soul couldn't spread anymore, but a few weeks with the Rossi brothers, and the blemish felt all-encompassing.

Disgusted, I scrubbed at my makeup, determined to get rid of everything from this night. My skin felt pink and raw after I finished.

Anticipation flooded my veins as I grabbed the razor and slashed at my skin, making a much bigger cut than usual.

The blood streamed down my side, turning pink as it mixed with the water. I slid down the wall of the shower until I was sitting on the ground, the water so hot that every drop burned.

I stayed there with my head between my knees, every so often fiddling with the cut so it wouldn't start to close, and I could just feel that constant pain. Not for the first time, and probably not for the last, dark thoughts flicked through my mind. Of just ending it all right here so that I wouldn't have to face another day filled with pain and another night where my demons haunted me.

The bathroom door suddenly flew open and Gabriel was standing there, a frantic look on his face.

"Fuck," he murmured as he saw me sitting there, blood-stained water on the shower floor. His eyes flicked to the razor I'd set beside me. I should have felt shame at him seeing me like this.

But I couldn't feel anything.

He grabbed a towel off the warming rack and immediately opened the shower door, cursing when he reached to turn the water off and it scalded his skin. I just looked up at him in a daze, my mind gone to the headspace that only blood loss and grief could give you.

Gabriel looked down at me sadly. "Bellissima, why?"

I just stared up at him blankly, and he bit his lip before moving towards me.

I didn't make any moves to help him as he wrapped the towel around me and lifted me gently off the floor, like I was precious.

He walked into my bedroom and sat me down on the bed, methodically drying me off, not even seeming to be affected by the fact that I was completely naked. The towels that Emilia had gotten for me were white, so of course they were blood-streaked and ruined by the time he'd gotten me dry.

Gabriel didn't seem to care, though. "Lay down, Dahlia. I need to clean this before it becomes infected."

He walked back into the bathroom and appeared with a first aid kit that I hadn't known was there.

Opening it up, he rifled through the contents until he found an alcohol swab. He grimaced when he looked down at my cut. "It may need stitches," he murmured.

"It will heal," I murmured tiredly.

He growled and ripped open the foil package before pulling out the alcohol swab, and then as softly as he could, he started cleaning the cut. My eyes closed in almost euphoria as the cut stung from the alcohol.

There was no denying it. I was extremely fucked up.

Gabriel got some Neosporin next, and he dabbed it on the large Band-Aid before covering up my wound. He'd covered all my important parts with my towel before doing this, and although a voice in my head was yelling at me to get up, get dressed, and get Gabriel the hell out of my room, I continued to lay there.

Gabriel disappeared into the bathroom, and I heard the sound of water running as he washed his hands. When he came back in, he walked into the closet, stopping in the doorway for a second to look at my ruined dress on the floor.

There were built-in drawers in the closet, and I heard him opening up a few until he found a shirt. Then he strode back into the room and lifted me up. "Put your arms out for me, bellissima," he cajoled softly as the towel slid down my body, revealing my breasts. There was a flare of heat in his gaze this time, and his breathing stuttered as he glanced at them, but then he ripped his eyes away, and he quickly pulled my shirt on.

"Whose fucking shirt is this?" he abruptly snapped, taking a step back and frowning at what I was wearing.

I looked down and my eyes widened. It was a replica of the Union Jack shirt that I'd bought at the airport, but it was multiple sizes bigger.

Was it Raphael's? How did it get in my drawers?

Gabriel gritted his teeth and shook his head, but didn't say anything more about it. I could tell he wanted to rip it off me, but instead, he slid me over to the top of the bed so that I was on my pillows, and pulled the blanket over me.

He got up from the bed and strode over to the light switch.

"No!" I practically screamed, causing him to jump. "They need to be left on," I told him without explanation.

In the weeks that I'd spent with him, I'd done a good job of hiding the darkness inside of me. Tonight he was getting a crash course in the Dahlia horror show.

Gabriel didn't ask for an explanation; he just walked back over to the bed and sat down next to me, grabbing one of my hands in between his own large ones.

"How often do you do that?" he asked hesitantly.

I closed my eyes, unwilling to look at him if he was going to make me talk about this.

"As often as I can," I finally admitted. "Why did you come into my room?"

"I heard the water running for hours, I was afraid you'd passed out in there or something," he haltingly explained, but at the moment, I wouldn't have cared if he'd walked in for no reason.

"Don't tell anyone," I whispered.

Gabriel sighed deeply, and I felt his hands softly stroking my face. "Go to sleep, *amore mio*," he whispered.

And quicker than I would've thought possible, I did.

"Has anyone told you what a pretty little girl you are, Dahlia?" His hand slid up my leg, and my whole body trembled in fear.

Thirteen

My nightmares violently shook me awake, and I sat up in bed with a gasp as images that I tried so hard to forget slowly faded away.

It was light outside, and a quick look at my phone told me that it was almost noon.

I was exhausted, though. The kind of exhaustion that sleep couldn't take away, no matter how much you got.

I groaned as everything from the night before came roaring back.

Gabriel picking me up out of the shower, him cleaning off my wound. Dressing me...I should've felt deeply ashamed about all of that, but honestly, there was a little bit of relief that there was one person in the world who knew my shameful secret. Even if he never looked at me the same again, at least I wouldn't have to carry that secret alone anymore. I had enough of those.

My stomach growled, and I reluctantly slid out of bed, the ache in my hip reminding me how far I'd gone last night.

It wasn't until I was in the bathroom, washing my face, that I remembered what I was wearing.

Maybe the maids had confused the shirt for mine since it clearly had a British flag on it? Even if it was several sizes bigger than the rest of my clothes…

Not wanting to think about it anymore, I hurried into the closet and grabbed some clothes, deciding on a pair of black leggings and a dark blue oversized sweater that slid off my shoulder and was extremely comfortable.

Please God, let Lucian be gone already.

Taking a deep breath, I walked over to my door and opened it.

Oh goodie. Another day.

RAPHAEL

I was sitting at the dining room table, poring over some dreadfully boring reports, when Gabriel strode into the room.

"Can I help you, little brother?" I drawled. He looked surprisingly awake this morning despite the fact that he had consumed more liquor than half of New York at the party last night.

Gabriel marched towards me, his face perfectly blank. I went to ask another question, but then his fist was pounding my face, his knuckles splitting my top lip open so blood dripped all over the reports I'd been trying to read.

Awesome. Now I wouldn't have to read them.

Licking some of the blood off my lip, I raised an eyebrow. "It's a little early for foreplay, Gabey. Wouldn't you say?"

Gabriel just growled and reared back to throw another punch.

I flew up out of my seat and caught his fist in the air before he could break my fucking nose. Wouldn't want to mar my beautiful face with a broken nose.

I pushed Gabriel back. I was starting to get pissed now.

"What the fuck is wrong with the two of you?" Lucian barked.

Gabriel and I both looked to the doorway where Lucian was standing, glaring at us. Unlike Gabriel and myself, who looked as fresh as daisies this morning, Lucian looked like he'd been ridden hard and put away wet. He had deep circles under his eyes, and the poor excuse for scruff that he kept on his face was longer than usual. He was still dressed in his perfectly pressed suit, though. He had to keep the 'prick' image, after all.

I took a step back and leaned against the wall, crossing my arms in front of me and making sure I had a clear view of both of them. "I'd love to know that too, Lucifer—I mean Lucian. Gabey over here decided to attack me out of the blue." I shook my head. "Just look at what he did with your financial reports," I scoffed in mock horror as I waved at the table in front of me.

A vein in Lucian's head throbbed, and I snickered as Gabriel shot me another dark look.

"I don't have time for this," Lucian hissed. "There was another shipment stolen from one of the docks. It's a little suspicious how we had two crews defecting within the last month."

"What did they steal this time?" Gabriel asked, pulling back his hair and putting it in one of those metrosexual bun things that always seem to drive the girls crazy.

"A shipment of SoC chips this time. In the shipping ledger, it shows that there were other 'products' on board, but it doesn't name what they are. Those disappeared as well, judging by the fact that I only have half a shipment in our warehouse right now." Lucian shook his head in frustration. "Get your shit together and be ready in ten to head out."

"Sorry, *master*, but you're stuck with just Gabey today. I'm afraid, I'm busy."

Lucian looked at me like I'd lost my mind; Gabriel was giving me an almost identical look. "Please tell me, Raphael, what do you have to do that's more important than this?"

I shrugged "I got a thing."

"A thing," Lucian repeated slowly.

He stared at me intently like he was trying to pull my layers back. It was a fruitless pastime that he engaged in quite regularly, but unfortunately for my dear brother, my skin was impenetrable.

"Whatever," Lucian abruptly snapped. He turned his attention to Gabriel. "Get ready to go, and put something on other than the lumberjack meets *Yellowstone* look you have going there." Lucian prowled out of the room. I pitied whatever servant he ran into next. They'd probably get their head cut off.

Mmmh, maybe I should go watch.

"What's wrong with what I'm wearing? This shirt was three thousand dollars?" Gabriel whined, examining the plaid monstrosity that he was wearing over his leather pants and combat boots.

I shook my head. "A suit, Gabriel. He wants you to wear a suit." I waved my hand at him in annoyance. "Now please, leave me in peace and go obey your master while I attempt to fix these reports that you ruined."

I was definitely not going to be fixing the reports.

Gabriel huffed and then stepped towards me again. I readied myself for another fight, although I was tempted to knock him out this time.

"Stay away from her," Gabriel growled.

It didn't take a rocket scientist to know who the *her* was he was talking about.

Dahlia, the girl I couldn't seem to get out of my head.

An image of her standing in the rain last night filled my thoughts, her white dress plastered against her body, outlining her form perfectly, and calling to mind what laid under that dress. Every curve of her body was carved into my brain, but the darkness I saw in her eyes last night...It was attempting to carve itself into my heart.

And we couldn't have that, not with what I was planning.

"Pray tell, little brother. What did I do to little Miss Dahlia?"

"I know you stuck your shirt in her drawers."

I snorted, shaking my head. I'd almost forgotten that I put it in there. I traded a pair of her underwear for a shirt that I knew would mean a lot to her. Just because I was fair like that, of course.

"What shirt exactly are you talking about? I can't quite recall," I teased.

Gabriel was looking at me like he wanted to kill me, and the feeling was mutual lately. He'd always been the brother that I got along better with, his easy-going nature smoothing over my psychotic one. Recently—Recently, I'd been thinking of creative ways to torture him.

"What's going on?" Dahlia asked as she appeared in the doorway. She pulled at the edge of her blue sweater, the color of it accentuating her eyes as she glanced between us. I studied the sweater, perplexed. It was a sweater, and yet somehow the sight of her shoulder peeking out from it, showcasing all of that creamy skin... it made me hard. I recalled how easily her skin had been marked by my teeth and my tongue. Something inside of me hated that any marks I'd given her had long since faded away...

All the anger had fled from Gabriel's features. I've never witnessed someone look at another human being like they were missing half of their soul before, but if I could describe Gabriel's face at that moment, that would be it.

"Bellissima, how are you feeling this morning?" he asked. There was a hidden meaning in his words, and her head ducked away from him like she couldn't bear to look him in the eyes.

Interesting. What had I missed? Also, enough with the "bellissima" shit, like Gabriel had just come from a lifetime walking the streets of Florence.

Besides, she wasn't "bellissima." She was an angel. Mine.

"Fine. Better, I guess," she told him, still not meeting his gaze. Or mine for that matter. Every word she gave me was a miracle these days, not that I should expect any different...Not that I deserved any different.

"I heard yelling as I was coming out of my bedroom. Is everything okay?"

Gabriel shot me a look. "Everything's fine. I was just lecturing my brother...on his shirt collection."

Dahlia couldn't help but meet my gaze then; she knew exactly what he was talking about.

"Was any of it real?" Her words that day echoed in my head.

"Well then," Dahlia said, as she wrapped her arms in front of her, and pushed on that spot on her hip like she always did. I didn't remember anything being on her hip during that flight, but with the dim lighting and how fucking amazing she'd been in bed, I could have missed something. "I'll just leave you two to discuss...his shirt collection."

And then she disappeared from sight.

Gabriel deflated like her absence had taken away his air. He began to leave the room as well.

"Oh, and Gabriel," I began.

He looked back at me.

"If I were you, I'd watch my back on the job today. After your dance last night, Lucian might want to get rid of some extra bullets."

Gabriel just rolled his eyes before exiting the room.

I was tempted to go to the kitchen and antagonize Dahlia into talking to me some more. But instead, I waited for my brothers to leave before I went to the elevator myself and took it down to the basement where we kept some of our...more interesting rooms.

I walked down the dimly lit hallway, stopping in front of the metal door at the end and keying in my passcode. The lock released, and I stepped inside where I had the "doorman" from last night trussed up like a Thanksgiving turkey on my long metal table.

He began to struggle when he saw me, and I just smiled. Although my brothers and I took the hiring in our building very seriously, sometimes people slipped through the cracks.

He was one of them.

I'd intended to just find out last night where he'd gotten the package and torture him a bit to remind him of the importance of his job, but I'd found out quickly that Alex had been hired by my father to "keep an eye on us."

And that just wouldn't do.

Carlo might technically be "the boss", but at this point, there was so much directed by the three of us in the organization that he might as well be useless.

In the last couple of years, he'd been catching onto that, and one of his ways to counteract the inevitable conclusion of his authority was to try and spy on us.

I was pretty sure that I'd gotten everything I needed from Alex last night. Carlo may have been able to pay people, but he'd never been good at securing loyalty, not like Lucian, I grudgingly admitted.

But with a little bit of work, Alex could be the perfect little gift to send my father to remind him the end was coming. Preferably at my hands.

Alex's eyes widened. At least the eyeball he had widened. The other socket didn't have an eyeball anymore, so it wasn't that useful.

"I hope you had a restful night," I chirped cheerfully as I arranged my tools on the stainless steel counter. Maybe I was a tad OCD myself, but I did like a neat and tidy torture room.

Alex gave a muffled groan under his gag, but I ignored him as I flipped on my favorite NSYNC song and finally decided on the potato peeler that worked remarkably well on skin as my tool of choice.

'90s boy bands just did it for me.

I walked over to the table and looked down at Alex. "Let's have some fun, shall we?"

Dahlia

I had the place to myself for most of the day, with the exception of Emilia who was bustling around, on and off the phone the whole day while she finalized last-minute wedding details.

She'd wanted to go over them with me, but after last night, I found myself not caring about one single detail of the wedding.

She'd given me a disapproving look when I'd said I wanted to be surprised, because obviously, that was a lie, but she hadn't challenged me.

I was playing a game on my phone when a text from Leo came in:

Please call me. We need to talk.

Right at that moment, my phone buzzed, showing that he was trying to call.

I rolled my eyes and rejected the call before finally deciding just to block the poor guy's number. Hopefully, without any access, he would get over me soon.

A knock sounded on the door. "Who is it?" I called, hoping it wasn't one of the guys. Although I wasn't too sure how into knocking they were based on what I'd seen so far...

"It's me, deary," Emilia answered through the door.

"Come in," I told her, dropping my phone on the bed and standing up.

She had a long black garment bag with her, and I wasn't so sure I should've let her in.

"Now I know you said you wanted to be surprised, but you at least need to try the dress on so I can get some last-minute tailoring done if need be," she cajoled.

I sighed and nodded, and she clapped her hands excitedly despite my less than enthusiastic response.

Emilia hung the dress up on the top of my closet door and then slowly unzipped the bag. White lace peeked through the opening.

"Lucian had this specially rush ordered for you the day you arrived," she cooed. I lifted an eyebrow at that. I assumed that was just Emilia once again trying to give "her boys" more credit than they deserved, if they deserved any credit at all.

I'd been determined to hate the dress, but as soon as she unveiled the entire gown, I couldn't help but fall in love. It had an ivory satin bodice that narrowed at the waist. The body of the dress was ivory and satin with soft pleats that unfolded to the floor. Above the cinched bodice there was lace in a delicate flowery pattern that extended down the sleeves as well. It was beautiful.

"There are sixty buttons on the back of this thing, so it'll take me a minute to get you cinched up. "

I nodded but didn't say anything, still admiring the dress. I slid off my shirt and padded into the closet to grab a strapless bra as bra straps would show through the thin lace that went up over the shoulders. When I came out, Emilia was standing with the dress open so I could simply step into it, bouncing around on her toes like a giddy schoolgirl. I stepped into the dress, my skin tingling. Emilia then helped me pull it up, and I slid my arms through the lace sleeves. She immediately went to work on the sixty buttons while I stood there admiring the dress.

"There," she said excitedly, wiping her brow from her efforts. "I think it fits perfectly. We won't need any tailoring. What do you think?" she asked excitedly.

"I don't think I could have dreamed of a more beautiful dress," I said honestly.

She went on and on about features of the dress, like how the lace had been made in France, and how I looked like a storybook princess.

"Now, you have a cathedral train for the ceremony in the cathedral, and then there will be a much shorter veil for you to use for the reception, but you can always take it off at that point if you wish."

"The cathedral?" I asked absentmindedly.

"Yes, St. Patrick's Cathedral. Every member of the Rossi family has been married there for the last hundred years."

It was a little humorous to me that I was going to be married in a Catholic Church after all the work King Henry VIII had done to eradicate Catholicism from England so he could divorce his wife.

She cleared her throat, and her cheeks blushed. "I also took the liberty of getting you some La Perla lingerie for your wedding night. I hope you don't think I overstepped, but I got several sets for you to choose from." I wanted to die of embarrassment thinking of wearing something she'd picked out for my wedding night.

Which presented me with another problem—the whole virginity thing.

Right now, I was planning on going with the whole tampon ripped my hymen excuse. If I decided that wouldn't work, I was just planning on getting as trashed as possible at the reception so he wouldn't want to linger.

If I had my way though, there wasn't going to be an after-party tomorrow. I could still see his huge dick sliding in and out of that bitch's mouth.

I didn't know if there would be enough condoms in the world to layer on that thing in order for me to ever feel comfortable putting it inside of me.

I got itchy just thinking about it.

"I was sad to hear that none of your family would be able to make it, even with the wedding being pushed back a few weeks," she commented as she began the task of undoing all the buttons.

My heart clenched, and I sighed. I hadn't expected any of them to come, at least not my brothers with everything a bit crazy in their world, but a part of me had hoped that my mum would have made the trip for her only daughter.

But she'd told me on the phone there was a huge charity gala that she was in charge of and she "just couldn't miss it."

It wasn't a surprise, but seeing at least one familiar face in the crowd tomorrow would've been comforting.

Emilia finally finished with the buttons, and I slid the dress off my shoulders and down my body before carefully stepping out of it.

It really was a beautiful dress fit for a storybook princess.

Too bad I was as far from that as I could be.

FOURTEEN

I hadn't slept for more than an hour during the night, and it felt like there was a ticking bomb inside me, counting down the moment when my life ended. Of course, it had technically ended the second the plane had touched down in this city, but this felt more final…more irreversible.

The ceremony wasn't starting until six that night, but I got out of bed early anyway and trudged into the bathroom to wash my face. I cringed when I looked at myself in the mirror. There were deep, dark circles under my eyes. The raccoon look was back in full force, and I looked more animal than human at the moment. My skin was pale and blotchy, and despite the fact that I'd taken a shower the night before, my hair looked stringy and greasy. This must've been what desperation looked like.

No sooner had I finished washing my face than there was a knock on the door.

"Come in," I said, not really caring at this point who it was.

Emilia burst through the door with a huge smile on her face, carrying a tray loaded down with my favorite breakfast foods. Over the past couple of weeks, she had peppered me about my likes and dislikes, and the Eggs Benedict with hand-carved honey-baked ham with the eggs cooked all the way through told me she'd been listening. There was a bowl of strawberries and cream to the side, and she'd poured my orange juice into a fancy decanter that I hadn't noticed in the kitchen before.

She set the tray on the bed and clapped her hands together like I'd learned she had a habit of doing when she was excited about something. And lately, Emilia always seemed to be excited about something.

"Eat up, dearie. You need your strength today," she crooned.

I sat down on the bed and looked at the tray of food, not sure that I could eat a bite. Emilia chattered away about what the schedule would look like today—apparently, I had a million different appointments to look forward to. Luckily for me, everyone was coming here so I wouldn't have to leave my room if I didn't want to. The plan was for me to get ready at the penthouse, and then to be driven to the front of the Cathedral to make a dramatic entrance …like I was Princess Kate herself.

I picked at my food, only stuffing bites in my mouth when she pressed me to eat more. My mouth was so dry from my nerves that the food, which normally would have tasted amazing, might as well have been cardboard for how much I got out of it.

My first appointment came an hour later. Emilia had somehow procured a white silk robe with the word 'Bride' written on the back in cursive like I was some kind of Instagram blogger having my dream wedding. I was expecting her to have hired bridesmaids who would be popping through the door at any minute.

I wondered what it said about my life that even if I was back home in England, I wouldn't have a single mate to invite to stand by my side.

Two women arrived, dressed in plain gray uniforms. They set up a massage table right in my bedroom and encouraged me to strip down so they could start. The massage felt amazing; they were clearly very talented, but I didn't think there was any relaxation method that existed in the world that could cure the jittery nerves running haywire through my veins.

After the massage, I took a bath that Emilia had filled with an assortment of scented oils and who knows what else to wash off the massage oil and "make my skin look like a million bucks." A facial followed the bath. I didn't think there was a way to resurrect my face, but the woman must have had magical powers because when she finished, my face was glowing. No sign of the raccoon drug addict look I'd been sporting that morning.

Nails were next. My toes and fingers were painted a soft color that was actually titled 'blushing bride'. I had a brief break for lunch where Emilia tried to stuff salad down my throat. All she was able to get me to eat was one solitary lettuce leaf and a cup of chamomile tea, but with the way I was feeling—like I was going to throw up everywhere—she should have called that a victory.

The same makeup and hair team that had attended to me before my engagement party arrived then. Although they encouraged me to pull my hair up in an elegant bun, I decided on a similar look as my engagement party—classic Hollywood curls with a softer part than I'd worn the other night. The flirty makeup artist told me she was doing a lighter look today as instructed by Mr. Rossi, and I just rolled my eyes, wondering if there was enough money in the world for me to convince her to give me a goth look for the wedding.

I giggled just thinking about it...which probably had the whole glam squad thinking I was a bit nuts.

Which I probably was at this point.

The big reveal of my final look probably would've made a normal girl cry, but I just stared at the beautiful creature in the mirror, wishing there was a way to trade places with her.

The whole team left after that, all of them obviously disappointed with my muted reaction, and Emilia left the room to give me a moment alone.

I was wearing a white, lacy, satin lingerie set under my robe, complete with thigh highs—I'd reluctantly gotten over the fact that Emilia had picked them out, and I examined myself in the mirror, noting that I'd lost weight over the last few days.

I continued to stare into the mirror, my breath beginning to come out in gasps, and I knew that a panic attack was imminent.

My hands shook as I grabbed my phone and dialed Church, hoping that Benny would be nearby and could talk.

"Dahlia?" Church's concerned voice sounded through the line, and I drew in a shuddering breath. After Benny had been sent away, Church had been there for Mum and me, continuing on with my fighting lessons and being a sympathetic ear.

"Hi, is Benny there?" I asked, trying to keep the panic out of my voice.

"Yep, he's—" There were sounds of scuffling and then Benny's voice replaced Church's. "What's wrong?"

"I don't know if I can do this," I told him shakily. "My wedding dress is right here, and it's almost time to go, and I just want to run. Tell me I can run, Benny..."

"I'll fly out there right now and end this whole thing if you want me to...but are you sure?"

I squeezed my eyes closed, knowing what he was really

asking. Was I ready to smash the treaty into pieces and put everyone's life at risk, including my own? Benny didn't even have control yet. He'd be waging war on two fronts if I walked away.

I hated having to be the martyr. I'd been born to be sold, my fate decided for me before my life could even really begin.

"No. I'm not sure. Just a bit of cold feet, big brother. I'm sorry I said anything," I told him softly.

Part of me wanted him to say, "fuck it," and just tell me to run anyway. But I knew he wouldn't.

There was too much at stake for that.

"Dahlia...I'm sorry," he murmured, and I knew he meant it.

"Promise me it will turn out alright in the end," I whispered. As a little girl, one of my weird quirks had been to get people to make promises to me all the time. *Promise me we'll have a tea party. Promise me I'll get that dress. Promise me you'll come back.* I'd done it for anything and everything until I realized that no one around me ever kept their promises.

"I promise, Dahlia," Benny said, more emotion in his voice than I'd thought him capable of.

"I'll talk to you later?"

"Whenever you need to," Benny promised.

And then I hung up.

I wondered if a part of me had still been holding on to the hope that this was just temporary. Because after the conversation with Benny, it felt like a cord had been cut, like my life in England had never existed.

Was there any place in this world where I could have been happy?

I was losing control and the seconds were ticking by. The sound was so loud in my head, I thought for a moment that Emilia had set up a loud clock in my room just to drive me mad.

Needing to get a hold of myself, I rushed to the bathroom and grabbed my replacement blade that I'd hidden yesterday.

My other one had disappeared with Gabriel.

I wandered into my bedroom, staring at the razor and wondering what I could get away with after the deep cut I'd made the other night. At this point, I had scars on top of scars on my hip.

I stopped in front of the mirror, my hands trembling as I held the sharp blade in my hand, and when I went to make a cut, I dropped the razor to the floor.

Evidently, that was enough to send me over the edge. I fell to my knees, my fingers digging into the carpet as I tried to stop the pain and fear rolling over my body in waves. I gasped, the ability to breathe disappearing.

I kneeled there, my whole body shaking, for what seemed like forever, and when I finally picked up the razor and stood up in front of the mirror, Raphael was standing there behind me.

I stared at him through the reflection as his hand began to trail up my right arm until he was holding my neck…just like he had the other night. He flexed his hand, tightening his hold, and a part of me wanted him just to keep squeezing, to keep going until I was gone. His thumb fluttered over my racing pulse.

"You're a beautiful mess, angel." His voice was low and raspy, and he pressed closer to me, lining our bodies up so there wasn't a piece of me that wasn't enveloped by him. His warmth bled into my icy skin. Raphael's other hand grabbed my hip, digging into the scars and the still-healing cut, the spark of pain tasting so sweet.

I could feel his thick length through his black dress pants, pressing against my arse, and there was a fierce, raw hunger in his gaze, like he saw the darkness inside of me and it made him

242

want me all the more. His eyes were a wild blue right now, gleaming with unspoken words, as he continued to grip my neck while he began a slow, steady grind against me. I felt pinned, trapped...owned.

"Raphael," I tried to object, but it didn't come out with quite the force that I'd intended. Instead, my voice came out breathy, slightly high-pitched...needy.

My eyes danced all over his reflection. He was so fucking beautiful, and my gaze followed the line of his arm, obsessing over his flexing forearms as his hand gripped my hip. His other hand was still wrapped around my throat, and it did something to me to see it there, the edge of a tattoo peeking out from the sleeve of his suit coat. I perversely felt threatened and protected, all at once.

It only made it worse to know that I knew what he looked like underneath.

I knew what I was missing out on.

I couldn't help but push back into him, cushioning his huge dick into the cleft of my arse, the pressure rubbing my thong against my clit and driving me insane. We both groaned almost in tandem as I moved.

I didn't recognize myself; this greedy, flushed, beautiful woman in the mirror bore no resemblance to the scared, quiet little mouse I was most of the time.

His greedy hand moved away from his hold on my hip. He glided it up my sides, to my left breast. There was worship in his touch, even while it was rough. He went to work massaging my breast, kneading it almost brutally, his rough fingers rubbing over my nipple, making it pebble and making me moan once again.

Desperate hunger pumped through me, and I writhed against

him, rubbing my arse even harder against his dick, as the front of my thong continued to rub against my clit.

"Yes," I groaned. My eyes closed, and I arched into his touch as he continued to cup and squeeze my breast.

"Open your fucking eyes, angel," he growled harshly. His heavy breaths filled the entire room.

I couldn't help but obey, once again taking in the image of us in the mirror. He was so much bigger than I was, his perfect, hard angles pressed against my soft curves. His large hand completely enveloped my throat, his big body pressed in behind me. He was magnificent. I was almost stunned by how sexy he was. A walking wet dream in the form of a golden god.

"Your body is fucking perfect. I've never seen anything like it. Look at it. Your sweet, tight fucking pussy. That ass I'm going to bite someday...those fucking incredible tits." His hand moved away from my breast briefly to trail it down my side. Goosebumps sprang up under his touch. "You're so soft, little angel..." His hand went back to work on my breast, teasing my nipple, and I gasped. "So responsive," he breathed as he got rougher.

The sharp sting of pain/pleasure was what I needed. Everything tightened and warmed at once, and I was shocked when a small orgasm pulsed through me, gentle spasms overtaking my body just from what he was doing.

The pleasure was, of course, followed by shame.

"Good girl," he murmured, and whereas the term usually made me sick, I found myself preening under his praise.

"Want me to help you get out of your head, little angel?"

I couldn't even respond; my chest was heaving from the arousal still sparking through my body. Raphael gently reached for my hand, unclenching my hand where I'd been squeezing the razor.

Fear, and another flash of arousal pulsed through me.

He took the razor and began to trace it softly down in between the valley of my breasts, down towards my stomach where he circled my belly button. His touch was so soft that it didn't leave a mark, but I could still feel the faint scratch of pain.

"Raphael," I moaned. I was practically gushing at this point. If there hadn't been anything else that proved how messed up I was, this would've done it.

"Keep rubbing against my dick, and I'll just cum in my pants. I won't change, and you'll know while you walk down that aisle that I still have cum all over me from what you did to me."

"Fuck." My pussy gushed at his words. I hadn't even realized I was still writhing against him. All I knew was that white-hot heat was shooting up my spine, and I let my head fall back against his muscled chest, my hips shifting, seeking more friction.

"Stop," he ordered. "Let me take care of you."

I wasn't quite sure what he meant until he dragged the razor over to my patch of scars.

I froze, my gaze locked on his hand in the mirror.

"Is this what you need, little angel? Is this what you need to put on that ice queen mask you show the world every day?"

"Yes," I whispered. His hot tongue glided over the outer shell of my ear. "Please."

"Please what? Please fuck you? Please give you pain? I can still remember how tight you were when I stretched you over my cock. Nothing's ever fit me so perfectly."

His grip around my neck tightened, and I was getting a light-headed feeling that only added to the arousal.

I watched in the mirror as he slid the razor across my skin, blood instantly dripping down onto the delicate white lace of the lingerie. "Was that what you wanted, Dahlia?"

"More," I begged. He'd only made a small cut; surely one more wouldn't be so bad.

He pressed the blade against my skin again, on top of a scar that was already there, and he followed the white line of it exactly, until the white was completely taken over by red. The blood droplets fell through the lace of my knickers, streaking down my leg until they hit my thigh high.

"We'll do one more. There are three of us, after all," he murmured.

My mind was too high to ask him what he meant. All I could do was watch in the mirror as he gave me another release, pain to keep me centered through this day. After he made the third cut, he dropped the razor, his fingers pressing into the cuts, smearing the blood all over my skin.

I shivered as I watched him wipe his thumb through my bloody cuts, and then lift it up to his mouth, locking eyes with me as his tongue slid along the skin, making sure to get every drop of the blood off.

Fuck.

Maybe I was turning into a vampire because that was the fucking hottest thing I'd ever seen.

His hand loosened around my neck, and he slid his fingers down and circled each nipple through my thin bra. His other hand went back to the blood on my hip, smearing it even more across my skin.

"I don't want you to wash it off or change, little angel," he breathed. "Can you do that for me? I want our little secret to be hidden under that pristine white dress today as you walk down the aisle. And when my brother fucks you tonight, I want him to know someone else has been here."

We were still standing in front of the mirror. My lips were parted, my eyes bright and alive. His gaze was hooded, a faint blush to his cheeks. His lips made a torturous assault down my neck and across my shoulder, his eyes still locked on mine. He pressed one last kiss against my skin, and then he abruptly released me and left the room.

I trembled as I dragged my fingers through the cuts, in disbelief that that happened. I finally glanced at my phone and promptly hissed. Only five minutes until Emilia was going to be back, and here I was looking like an extra in the *Corpse Bride*. Or maybe *Bride of Chucky* was more accurate.

I ran into the bathroom and grabbed a wet washcloth and some alcohol swabs, hurrying to clean the cuts, and hoping they would scab over before tonight. There was no way Lucian wouldn't notice though. I'd just have to come up with an excuse.

After taking care of the blood on my skin, I walked back into my bedroom to change my lingerie. Blood was actually fairly easy to get out of material with cold water, and there was only a little bit of red on my lace thong. My thigh-high, however, was completely stained with streaks of watery blood, and I hastily took both of them off and replaced them with another identical set. It was like Emilia had seen this moment coming. I cringed at the thought of anyone witnessing what had just happened.

Even if it had been hot as fuck.

I moved to shimmy my knickers down, but something made me pause.

And when Emilia came into the room a few minutes later, I was still wearing the bloodstained knickers...just as Raphael had requested.

What I had learned over the last few weeks was that every single person who lived in this place was sick, including me. And I was beginning to doubt that I'd been made into this. Instead, it was feeling like I'd been born that way all along.

The drive to the Cathedral seemed to take forever. Emilia was sitting next to me in the vintage cream-colored Bentley she'd arranged for the occasion, happily chattering away, saying inane things like this was going to be the "best day of my life." I wasn't sure what fantasy world she lived in, but I'd honestly like to go there someday. It sounded awesome.

My eyes widened as a towering Gothic cathedral made an appearance straight ahead, hidden among the skyscrapers that engulfed it. It looked out of place there, like it belonged in another time, and it was huge, taking up an entire city block. The doors were flanked by towers with spires that stretched into the sky. As we got closer, I saw enormous bronze doors in the front of it. There were gates set up from the entrance to the street, and curious passersby were taking pictures of the building and asking questions to the security stationed outside of the gates.

"Isn't it lovely?" Emilia gushed.

"Yes," I breathed. What was that quote by Virgil? *The descent into hell is easy.* It should have said, the descent into hell is beautiful. That would have been much more accurate for my situation.

We had just pulled up to the front of the Cathedral when a swarm of foreboding men dressed in black suits came streaming out of the intimidating front doors. I watched with a frown as they spread out across the property.

Riccardo, who was driving us, held his phone up to his ear. "Yes sir? Yes. Right away." After he set the phone down, he pulled forward before turning right so that we were on the side of the Cathedral.

"What's going on?" I asked. "I thought I was supposed to come in from the main entrance?"

"Change of plans. The ceremony's been delayed for a little bit while Mr. Rossi looks into something. You're going to wait inside one of the rooms until then. Boss doesn't want you waiting in the car."

Going to look into something?

I opened my mouth to press Riccardo for more questions, but Emilia tapped on my arm, shaking her head when I glanced over at her.

I shut my mouth.

Riccardo stopped the car and then rushed around to help me out. The train on my dress was eight feet long, and although it was bustled on a hook on the back of my dress, it still swept the ground. Emilia got out of the car on the other side and hustled over to me, picking up the back of my dress like she was my lady in waiting. Riccardo shut the car door, and then led us towards a nondescript door directly ahead of us. All the while eyeing his surroundings suspiciously like someone was going to jump out of the bushes at any moment and keeping his hand under his jacket where I knew he had a gun stowed.

I was wearing a dreamy pair of Louis Vuitton Follies Strassita heels, and I struggled to walk on the uneven ground. Riccardo finally extended his arm and helped me get to the door.

Once inside, my heels echoed along the marble floor. We were alone in the hallway, but I could hear the faint sound of an organ and violin playing from somewhere nearby. The lighting was dim, and that, combined with the hundred plus years old walls around me gave an eerie feel to the place.

Riccardo seemed to know exactly where to go, and after a few turns, he stopped in front of an intricate wooden door. He pulled a key from his pocket—because why wouldn't he have a key to the rooms in the most famous cathedral in New York—and opened it up to reveal a nondescript room.

"Wait in here and I'll be back to collect you in just a little while," Riccardo directed. Emilia moved to walk into the room with me, but Riccardo stopped her. "Mr. Rossi needs to talk to you," he murmured, and Emilia shot me a comforting smile and stepped away from the door.

As soon as I walked in, Riccardo was closing me in, and I heard the click of the lock engage.

I went to the door and tried the knob, thinking it would have a way to unlock from the inside, but somehow there was no way to do it.

Sighing, I walked over to a chair and sat down, making sure to hold up my train so it didn't drag on the ground.

I'd been sitting there for only a minute when I heard the sound of wood scraping against stone. My jaw dropped when I looked behind me and saw fucking Leo stepping through a hidden passageway into the room.

I scrambled to my feet. "Leo, what are you doing?" I gasped.

His chocolate brown eyes glimmered as he took me in. I took a step backward.

Leo was handsome enough. Dirty blonde hair that he always had perfectly styled and a great smile complete with straight white teeth. But after seeing the Rossi brothers, he was like watered-down milk. He completely paled in comparison.

Leo had been my secret. I'd sneak out to see him or

bribe my security team not to say anything when he showed up to places I was at. He'd been easy-going, someone who went with the flow, and he'd always seemed to be totally fine that we weren't serious, and that he was my dirty little secret.

Although calling him a dirty little secret seemed laughable now that Raphael was in the picture.

I'd told him we were done, not giving him any details about my arranged marriage, and thought that was that. I'd been surprised when he'd even bothered trying to text and call, because we'd never been like that.

To say I was in shock seeing him in New York City, on my wedding day, was an understatement.

"You've somehow gotten even prettier," he murmured, taking a step towards me.

I held up my hands in front of me.

"Leo, you need to leave right now. You do not want my fiancé to catch you here."

I was annoyed and freaked out, but I didn't want him to die. Which would probably happen if any of the Rossi brothers found him here.

"I came to get you out of here. I called in a fake bomb threat to buy us some time. But we need to leave right now."

His offer would have been compelling if not for the crazy I saw bleeding from his eyeballs—crazy I had somehow missed while I was with him in England.

"Thanks for the offer, but I'm good," I told him, lying of course.

He looked at me incredulously. "You're going to marry Lucian Rossi? I've looked into him, Dahlia. He's a bad man."

A laugh slipped out and his gaze darkened. "How did you

even find out I was marrying Lucian? And if you think he's a bad man, why the hell did you come here?"

Leo took another step towards me. "I thought I could just bide my time and you'd eventually come around to the idea of me and you. But then you just ended it. I know they must be forcing you to do this, Dahlia. I can save you."

I backed up until I hit the wall behind me and had nowhere else to go. My hands were trembling. I could do this. This was not a big deal. I would just kick his arse.

That would have been all well and good if I didn't have a giant Achilles heel in the form of freezing every time a man threatened me.

He was standing right in front of me now. "Dahlia. We have to leave—right now."

Before I could say anything, his lips were on mine, his arms pinning me against the wall. I tried to pull myself away, but just like with Carlo, I couldn't move as the harsh wave of a panic attack hit me.

I turned my head towards the door…and locked eyes with a shocked looking Lucian, who was standing there, peering into the room through the now cracked door.

He saw me then. Saw my fear and my patheticness. I let him see how this kiss was making me bleed, ripping open the wounds that were already inside of me.

And I saw the yearning in his soul. A deep yearning for me… like I held his future in my hands and he was just waiting for me to destroy it.

A second later, the door was wrenched all the way open and Leo was ripped off of me and a knife plunged directly into his neck.

"You'd dare to fucking touch what's mine?" he roared as

blood sprayed out of the wound, all over my dress. He must have gotten him right in the artery. I watched in shock as blood continued to gush out. I watched until the light in Leo's eyes was completely gone.

Lucian kicked him to the side and prowled over to me, somehow not a speck of blood on his fitted black tuxedo. His hair had fallen into his face, and all the vulnerability I'd seen in the doorway completely gone, replaced by a fierceness as he pinned me to the wall by my neck, squeezing much harder than Raphael had just a few hours earlier.

What was it with every fucking man in my life pushing me against walls?

"Is this the part where you kill me?" I choked out as I held Lucian's gaze which was filled with a dark possessiveness that sent shivers ricocheting over my skin.

His chest was heaving up and down as he took the knife and trailed it gently down my face...not so different from what his brother had done just a few hours before.

"I would sooner die than hurt you," he confessed softly, like I was a priest absolving him of his sins. "But if you ever let another man touch you again, there isn't a place they could hide in this world. I will hunt them down to the ends of the earth, and every scream they give me will belong to you."

For a girl that had never been wanted for a single day in her entire life, his crazy words were like a drug, tugging at something deep inside of me.

And like a drug, after the high, I would come crashing down...never to be okay again.

"I've thought about nothing but fucking shoving my cock into your tight little pussy since the moment I saw you exit the airport doors. I'm going to fuck you until you're so sore you can't breathe without remembering who's been inside you," he whispered thickly.

My eyes widened at his admission, and my insides caught fire. "I wouldn't have guessed that based on your little detour at our engagement party," I snapped sarcastically, doing my best to keep the disgusting arousal out of my voice.

He ignored me and leaned forward until his forehead was against mine.

"Tell me, principessa, will your blood stain my sheets tonight and prove to me you're untouched?"

"The only blood that's going to be staining those sheets is the blood spewing from your dick when I stab you for daring to touch me," I growled as I lifted my hand and tried to slap him in the face.

He dropped the knife and caught my wrist in an iron grip before I could make contact. Our eyes clashed against each other until he released my neck with a snarl.

"We'll fucking see about that." Lucian tugged me forward by my wrist and wrenched me towards the door. I tried to struggle against him, but he was holding on too tight, so tight that it felt like the bones in my wrist would be snapped.

He dragged me down a long hallway until an arched doorway appeared in front of us. I could see a priest in a long green robe with golden stitching standing on an elevated platform.

"What are you doing?" I hissed.

I was covered in blood and he was about to drag me out into the cathedral in front of all the guests? Someone in that crowd was bound to have snuck a phone in. I could only imagine the headlines. There was no way his tech people would be able to stop it.

He didn't answer me, he just pulled me forward, clearly gone mad. A loud murmur spread throughout the crowd as we came into view. Lucian didn't acknowledge them, and he didn't stop walking until we were standing in front of a horrified-looking priest. Raphael and Gabriel were waiting to the right of the altar, and they both stepped forward like they were prepared to rip me out of his grasp.

"Take another step and I'll kill you both," Lucian snapped at them as he pulled out a gun from under his tuxedo coat. They froze, twin looks of fury on their faces.

The crowd's murmurs were more like a roar now, and I heard the sound of pounding footsteps, most likely belonging to fleeing guests. Although I suspected most would stay for the show. I couldn't look away from Lucian to see, he was too out of control. I didn't know what he would do next.

"Lucian—"

"Father Sullivan, if you don't fucking marry us right now, I'm going to burn this whole fucking building down."

The poor priest looked like he was about to have a heart attack. He was shaking so bad that his tall hat kept falling off his head. "Okay," he said in a panicked voice. "Dominus vobiscum—"

"Just the Rite of Marriage," Lucian ordered, and the priest jumped at the interruption.

The priest nodded. "Dearly Beloved," he began.

The next thirty minutes would undoubtedly be carved into my head for the rest of my life. I had no idea what a Catholic ceremony was usually like, but being asked if I'd come there to enter into marriage "without coercion, freely, and wholeheart-edly" while I was standing there with blood all over my dress and a madman with a gun holding onto my wrist so tight that bruises were forming was…unbelievable, unimaginable? I didn't know the right word to describe it.

When it came time for the vows, I thought I was doing a great job in not scoffing when Lucian vowed to be faithful. But then I hesitated for half a second, and evidently, that was half a second too long for Lucian because he lifted his gun and pointed it at the priest's head. I'm sure the poor man had peed his pants by now. "You'd better cooperate, sweetheart, or his brain matter's going to be all over the altar," he said calmly, like he hadn't lost his goddamn mind.

"Yes…I do!" I practically screamed.

When it came time for us to exchange rings, my hand was shaking so hard that Lucian had to briefly let go of my other wrist to grab my hand and slide the wedding band on. Then he took my engagement ring out of his pocket, something I didn't know he had, and he slid it on top of the band.

"Dahlia, receive this ring as a sign of my love and fidelity. In the name of the Father, and of the Son, and of the Holy Spirit."

It seemed…wrong to be swearing things you didn't mean in the name of God right after you'd threatened to destroy his house…but what did I know?

Emilia had given me Lucian's ring earlier, before all hell had broken loose, and I was surprised to find it still tucked into the tiny slit sewn into the dress. I slid it onto Lucian's tattooed finger and made the mistake of looking up at him. His eyes looked soft…almost warm. The violence inside me stilled for just a moment as I got caught by his stare.

The ceremony continued on, the priest talking so fast his words were a little hard to make out. "Amen," he said with a relieved gasp, sweat dripping down his face.

Lucian abruptly tugged me to him, and his mouth collided

with mine, our bodies flush as his tongue licked deep into my mouth. My knees got weak as he took something from me I didn't think I could ever get back. Time stopped. The guests faded away. No one else existed but me and him.

I could feel his hard length against me, and it was all I could do not to move against the psychopath.

Lucian kissed me like he never wanted to stop. Like he couldn't get enough.

And I was right there with him.

That kiss destroyed me.

That kiss remade me.

That kiss…may have been the end of me.

FIFTEEN

LUCIAN

I'd officially lost it. I'd always known it would happen eventually. But I didn't know that it would be caused by *her*.

I'd already been on edge coming into this day thanks to the shipments disappearing, the men that were betraying me, and the warehouses that were missing guns. The envelope that had been waiting for me in the dressing room of the Cathedral stating there were bombs placed around the whole building, had only made it worse.

After my men had searched everywhere and found nothing, I'd been furious that someone had dared to mess with me on my wedding day. I was a ticking bomb, waiting to explode.

I could use all of those things as excuses for what happened in that room, but the truth was that when I saw him kissing her, it was like a haze of red descended on my vision. Any sane

259

reasoning had completely left the building, and all there was left in my head was a voice screaming and demanding that he die.

I'd meant what I said to her. She was mine. I hadn't realized it until that moment. And now that I had, anyone who thought differently was going to die.

No one talked back to me, especially a little slip of a woman with curves that could kill and an accent that drove me insane. When she'd talked back to me, I'd gotten so hard that I felt a little lightheaded. The urge to claim her became too strong to be argued against.

I was pleading temporary insanity. Wasn't that what men usually claimed when they killed their wife and their wife's lover after they came home early and found them in bed together? I had no desire to kill Dahlia, but insanity was the only word to describe me stabbing that idiot in the throat, and then dragging her to the front of the Cathedral in front of all our guests, covered in blood. My team would already be working themselves to death to suppress any of that coming out, but right now, as I dragged her down the aisle, the gasping crowd of sheep around us…after a kiss that sent shockwaves down my spine—I couldn't care less.

She was mine. And no one, no matter how hard they tried, could change that.

I'd make sure of it.

Riccardo was waiting with our Bentley out front, the one that Dahlia had pinned on her fucking wedding board my investigators had found when looking into her. I practically threw Dahlia into the car, and then stepped in after her. Something inside me tightened as I watched her wince as she gingerly rubbed at the wrist I'd kept hold of during the entire ceremony, like I was afraid she'd run away.

After today, Dahlia probably was a flight risk.

But there wasn't any place on earth she could hide from me.

I pulled on my bow tie until it was undone and just hanging around my neck, and then I popped open the first two buttons of my shirt.

"Riccardo, turn on the fucking air conditioning," I ordered. It was a million degrees in here. It had felt that way since I'd walked into that room.

I lounged back against my seat, not able to take my eyes off of Dahlia who was steadfastly staring at her lap while she fiddled with her blood-stained dress.

Now that I had a moment to think about it, I was regretting marrying her with another man's blood on her. The thought made me perversely jealous because I was obviously a sick fuck.

"Is the reception still happening or do you plan on murdering someone else?" Dahlia asked me as she finally turned my way, crossing her arms in front of her.

"Who said that the two of those things were mutually exclusive?" I asked dryly, and she rolled her eyes.

"Well, are you at least going to let me change? Or will all the guests be wearing blood tonight so I don't have to worry about it?"

I'd always thought that I liked subservient women—timid things that kept their mouths shut or wrapped around my cock, and did exactly what I wanted. But there was something about Dahlia's mouth. Even if she wasn't wrapped in the most delicious-looking package I'd ever seen, that mouth would have had me hard as a rock. I never knew what she was going to say next. She was a strange mix of brave and insecure, both of them somehow intertwined. Half the time I said something to her, I was just trying to provoke her into snapping at me.

It was my favorite form of torture. Probably healthier than most of the activities that I got up to, though.

"I believe that Emilia has another dress for you to change into," I finally told her when I realized that she was crossing her arms in front of her to try and hide the fact that her hands were shaking.

The ceremony was a blur, honestly. It was hard for me to even look at it from her perspective. All that really stood out to me was that kiss. Logically, I knew that I'd just put her through a wedding ceremony that might be seen in some kind of horror movie, but as I took in the sight of her finger wearing *my* ring, all I could feel was satisfaction.

The only downside about it was that somewhere in Dahlia's mind, I knew there was a ledger loaded down with all of my sins, and the list was so long even in the short time that I'd known her, I wasn't sure if I could ever clear it.

With the exception of one week of my life, I had always 'made' my life happen. I'd never 'let' it happen to me. This would be no different.

If I had to make Dahlia love me, I would. The obsession that was beginning to live inside of me couldn't be experienced alone. It definitely wasn't love. It was the kind of obsession that destroyed lives, torched buildings, and ended empires. She would feel this way about me too; there was no other option.

Suddenly, I needed to know something. I leaned forward, and she jumped at my movement. "Did you love him?" I demanded.

She stared at me for what seemed like forever, clearly debating what to say.

"No, Lucian," she said softly in a defeated voice that I immediately hated. "I'm not even capable of loving myself."

I sat back against my seat again with a small frown, my mind whirling.

I knew a lot about Dahlia. I'd started collecting information about her years ago after the treaty had been signed and she was still a little girl. I knew the places that she went, her favorite hobbies, that she loved Cadbury bars. I had a dossier about a mile long on her brothers, and her father when he'd been alive. I knew what her grades were in school, what extracurriculars she participated in, and I'd had my team hack into all of the secret Pinterest boards she had online showing her favorite things.

I knew a lot about her, so when she made comments like that, or when I caught her unaware and saw the pain she was holding, I didn't understand it.

I knew it wasn't because of her dad. From the reports I'd gotten, he hadn't been abusive, just cold and aloof, and they hadn't had any relationship to write home about since she'd just been a girl when he died. It could perhaps have been because of her brother Danny, but anything I'd read about him said they rarely talked, and Danny didn't care about anyone besides himself. Her other brother was in prison, or maybe he'd just been released, and her mother was a society debutante who treated Dahlia like a pet goldfish she only needed to feed once in a while.

Nothing that I'd read explained *her*.

I had secrets—a million of them, in fact. I was messed up in ways that prevented me from ever being happy, but the things that had created that in me couldn't be what she'd experienced. There was too much goodness in her.

I pushed that particular puzzle out of my mind for now as we approached the Plaza Hotel where our reception was being held.

Maybe now that I owned her, I could get through the night like a normal person.

Yes, I was laughing at the thought as well.

We pulled up in front where there was already staff waiting to escort us in. I got out and Dahlia reluctantly took my extended hand so I could help her. The employees looked nervous when they saw Dahlia's dress, but I knew they'd be discreet about it.

I was a majority owner in the hotel, and they'd heard enough stories about me to be wary.

They didn't want to die.

We got inside the hotel, and Emilia was there, immediately hovering over Dahlia like a worried mother hen. Now that I'd gotten over the shock of how quickly Emilia had fallen for Dahlia, I was appreciating it. Emilia had been the one constant in my life since I was a little boy, and something told me that Dahlia was just as in need of something like that as I had been when Emilia had first been hired.

Emilia began to guide Dahlia to the elevators where she would go up to her room to change and get her makeup and hair retouched since I'd basically ravaged her, but I suddenly wasn't so keen on being separated from her.

I grabbed her hand before she could get any farther, and she looked at me, rebellion and a little fear gleaming in her gaze.

"Kiss me," I demanded. She bit her bottom lip, her eyes darting over to where employees weren't hiding the fact that they were staring at us. Before she could think any harder about it, I grabbed her and pulled her towards me, one hand wrapping around her waist and the other fisting in her hair. My mouth descended on hers. I was rough. I wasn't capable of anything else. My tongue thrust in time with the image in my head of me fucking her a million different ways. A whimper spilled out of her as my lips closed around her tongue, sucking eagerly.

Emilia loudly clearing her throat managed to break the spell. She tried to look angry at me, but there was an excited gleam in her eyes that told me she was happy I was getting on with my wife.

If that's what you could call it.

Emilia was a little blind when it came to me. I knew she was non-plussed about the blood all over Dahlia's dress, and the scene at the ceremony. She'd cleaned up enough blood on my clothes to be used to it by now.

I'd had a plan for Dahlia. I was going to put her up in a house far away after the wedding and ignore her, except for when I tried to get her pregnant.

All that had disappeared as soon as I'd set eyes on her.

I'd been furious when Gabriel had cut in at the engagement party, knowing that I wouldn't make a scene, although that probably wasn't wise of him in retrospect since I'd had no problem making a scene at a much bigger event today.

I'd been enraged that I even cared.

Madison had been an easy way to let out some of that fury and annoy Raphael.

I've always been a big fan of multi-tasking.

But the only reason I'd even been able to cum was because I was staring at Dahlia.

I'd regretted only a few things in my life, but watching her run away after that scene was one of them.

"Stay out of trouble," I murmured to Dahlia, reluctantly letting her go.

She shot me a perturbed look that was lessened by the fact that her pupils were dilated and there was a flush to her cheeks.

She was aroused.

I'd never seen anything more beautiful in my whole fucking life.

And that was a problem, because one thing that I was good at —maybe the thing I was best at—was breaking beautiful things.

"What the fuck was that about?" Gabriel hissed as I walked into the room set aside for me to get ready. Without warning, he slammed me against the wall. Immediately, my hackles rose, and I pushed him back.

"You really want to fight on my wedding day, little brother?" I taunted. Gabriel lurched forward and slammed a fist into my gut. A gasp fell out of my mouth, and I gritted my teeth at the pain.

Deciding I'd had enough, I put a fist in his gut and then threw him to the ground before putting my shoe on his throat and pressing down...hard.

Gabriel was a force to be reckoned with, but he'd never had anything on Raphael and me when it came to fighting.

"I feel like I've been having this conversation a lot with you lately, Gabriel. You want to tell me what you're so upset about?" I pressed down harder with my foot to put more pressure on his throat so it would begin to hurt, and he would get the message that I wasn't going to be messed with today...and then I stepped back.

I crossed my arms in front of me and stared down at him, still very much aware of Raphael to the left of me who was leaning against the wall, his face perfectly blank. I never knew what that psychopath was going to do. He shouldn't be upset about the ceremony though. I would have thought he'd be impressed at my loss of control. It seemed like he could barely stand Dahlia and marrying someone in a dress soaked with the blood of a fresh kill was something I would've put money on him doing rather than anyone else.

"How could you fucking do that to Dahlia? Do you have any idea what a mess you've made? Our men were literally having to pat every guest down and destroy everyone's phone that they found."

"I got that all taken care of already," I said with a yawn, bored with the conversation.

Gabriel threw up his hands in disgust. "Whose blood was that? What the hell happened in there? What made you lose your mind?"

"I walked in on Dahlia kissing another man," I said through gritted teeth.

Gabriel stiffened and betrayal bleached through his features. I grimaced at the sight. I needed to have my assistant line up a new round of girls that he could get interested in. This obsession with Dahlia had been going on far too long.

"She was kissing another man?"

I turned towards Raphael, confused about the malice in his voice. I waved my hand in the air. "It was an ex-boyfriend or something. I don't think that *she* kissed him. I think he was forcing himself on her, and when I walked in and saw it, I just lost my head. I stabbed the motherfucker without asking any questions, and the blood happened to get all of her dress. Everything else is kind of a blur after that," I said with a careless shrug that intentionally left out that moment when I was frozen in the doorway and she'd fucking looked right into my soul. "Not that I need to explain myself to either of you," I growled.

Abruptly, a small brown moving box skittered across the floor, stopping a few feet away from where I was standing.

I looked at Raphael, annoyed he'd just kicked something at me. "What is this?" I asked exasperatedly.

"Open it up," Raphael challenged.

I sighed and squatted down to undo the panels of the box before slamming them closed as a disgusting smell assaulted my senses. "What the fuck?"

I reluctantly lifted up the panels again, knowing that I needed to see what was inside. Gabriel cursed when the box revealed a rotten apple. But not just a rotten apple, an apple that was covered in maggots and who knows what else, crawling in and out of it. I didn't know that an apple could smell like this, and maybe it was the maggots' fault, but the smell was almost as bad as a rotting corpse.

And I'd had a lot of experience with those. I slammed the panels shut once more when I saw a cockroach had made its way almost to the top.

"You want to explain?" I asked, stepping away from the box like it could contaminate me.

"Read this," he said, walking forward and thrusting the note in my hand instead of just explaining himself.

I frowned as I examined the note. It was comprised of letters that had been cut out of a magazine or something similar.

Here in the forest dark and deep, I'll offer her eternal sleep.

"I'm not getting it. Our enemies are sending us rotten apples now?"

"Snow White," Gabriel said quietly, his face scrunched up in concentration. "I think it's referencing Snow White."

I shook my head. "I'm pretty sure it's from a song or something like that."

"No, he's right," sighed Raphael. "Whoever sent this has a thing for fairytales, and they're not happy about your nuptials based on the other box Dahlia and I discovered the night of the engagement party."

"What was in the other box?"

"A dead frog…with a crown," Raphael said nonchalantly.

"You'll have to catch me up, brothers. Seems I didn't have as much time as the two of you growing up to make sure that I was up to date on fairytales."

"The Frog Prince," Gabriel threw out in disgust. Raphael nodded.

"It was mixed in with some of the other wedding presents that you'd been receiving. Which, by the way, props to people who would send you gifts. I wonder if there's some kind of reference book out there entitled, "What To Get the Mafia Man Who Just Might Kill You.""

"I think I've told you this before, but you're not very funny," I told Raphael, rolling my eyes like an insolent teenager. "But what I'd really like to know is why wasn't I informed about the first box?"

Raphael's gaze hardened. "At the time, I probably thought you were too busy getting your dick wet with my date."

"Oh, are we calling the whore 'your date'"now?" Gabriel drawled slowly.

Before Raphael could pull out a knife and gut one of us, I put my hands up. "Focus!"

"Obviously, your highness, I thought it was some kind of joke. I even tortured the fool who'd brought the box up to the suite only to find out he'd been planted by our father. I thought that was the end."

"That was 'your thing' you were doing yesterday, wasn't it?" I asked incredulously.

Raphael just shrugged his shoulders.

"So, Carlo sent the box?"

"Does that sound like something our father would even have enough brain cells to do? I don't know who did it. I just happened to find out the doorman was a mole while trying to investigate it."

I pulled out the knife that I'd gotten back from Riccardo after he'd cleaned up the dead guy at the Cathedral. "Raphael, I'm not sure why I have to say this, but if you ever fucking hide something about my wife from me again. I will kill you."

Raphael was non-plussed from my threat, and he just looked at me with a smirk.

"Of course, *master*."

I kicked the box back towards Raphael. "Take care of that," I ordered before walking over to the mirror on the wall and adjusting my cufflinks. The bow tie wasn't going back on. I was a mafia man, not a stuffed penguin. I ran a hand through my hair, not caring in the least bit that it was all over the place, and then strode towards the door.

"Be down right after you get rid of that box. I want extra eyes in the room," I said before leaving.

"Valentina is going to be so mad she missed all of this," I heard Gabriel murmur to Raphael as I left the room.

I ignored him. Dahlia was waiting for me.

Sixteen

DAHLIA

"Presenting for the first time, Mr. And Mrs. Rossi," a voice blared right before the doors were opened to reveal the grand ballroom where the reception was being held.

I was holding on to Lucian's arm, ready to get this over with, in a new dress with no blood on it that was beautiful but didn't compare to my original one.

"A little corny for a big, strong mafia man, don't you think?" I whispered to him as we both pasted on smiles and walked into the gorgeous room amongst applause. I'd had a video saved on my computer back home of a wedding reception where they'd done that. I'd always thought it was adorable. Corny but cute for what was supposed to be the most romantic day of your life.

Obviously, it was none of those things in the current circumstances.

Lucian just shot me his typical amused look that was far too sexy.

We hate him. Let's not forget that, I reminded myself.

I'd been terrified during the ceremony, sure that he was going to start killing everyone around us, and me, with how absolutely insane he was acting. I'd also been humiliated. I had enough social anxiety that for something that outrageous to occur in front of a large group of people—it was a lot for me.

The blood itself...not such a big deal. I was a Butcher, after all. I'd seen plenty of that thanks to my dad, brothers, and Church.

Lucian seemed to be back to normal now, or what I thought was normal for him. Mr. Cool and Collected and In Charge.

Something must have been wrong with me because the terror had somehow faded. In its place was...resignation.

Lucian was acting as he had at the engagement dinner before he'd had his dick sucked—smiling and nodding at everyone while holding me tight. He caressed my skin every chance he got and pressed soft kisses against my cheek...and occasionally my lips.

Like he was actually happy about this marriage.

He was so good at pretending that...it almost felt real.

"Remind me why we have to play pretend when all of these people know you could kill them in an instant if you wanted to?"

He shot me another amused look and then leaned in close, so for anyone watching us, it would look like he was just whispering something sweet in my ear. "Most of the people in this room are power players in the city, as you know. They're always watching us for a weakness. I like to keep them guessing. They'll think I'm obsessed with you after the rather interesting ceremony, and they'll think we must have had some sort of lover's

spat, so if we're suddenly acting like everything's fine here…"
He gave me a wink that sent a lick of heat flaring through my insides.

"So at the next event, should I expect to be completely ignored…you know, to keep them guessing?"

He shrugged and turned his attention away from me to greet the next group of people who were desperate to give us their congratulations, so desperate that after Lucian had waved a gun around in a church, and I'd shown up looking like a character from The Walking Dead, they were still here trying to lick Lucian's arse.

And the show went on…

My stomach was churning with anxiety as we waited for the photographer to okay us to go outside where the guests were waiting with sparklers—another thing I'd always wanted at my wedding. Emilia was magical.

In just a few moments though, we'd be alone in the car, headed back…to wherever Lucian had chosen for us to spend the night. The penthouse, I guessed.

And then it would be time.

If Lucian acted that way today just from seeing a guy kiss me, a kiss that I hadn't wanted any part of, how was he going to act if he believed tonight that I'd been with someone else?

I'd never be able to admit it was Raphael. I hated the guy, but I definitely didn't want him dead.

Well, maybe a little dead. But definitely not the "all the way" kind of dead that Lucian seemed to be fond of.

The photographer gave us the thumbs up, and the grand

double doors were opened in front of us to reveal an aisle covered in white flower petals with the guests lined up on each side holding sparklers that I knew would look amazing in any photos. We were just beginning to walk down the aisle to everyone's fake cheers when fireworks started to go off in the sky above us.

"I thought fireworks were illegal in New York City?" I gasped, imagining one of the skyscrapers catching on fire.

"Nothing's illegal in this city with the right amount of money," he commented.

I looked over at him and realized that he wasn't looking at the fireworks; he was watching me with a soft, almost fond smile.

Painful shivers drifted across my skin. I hadn't seen this smile of his before. It should never be allowed to see the light of day. It was absolutely heart-twisting. Women all over the world would be stripping naked and begging him to take them if they caught sight of it.

I snapped my gaze forward as Lucian chuckled, like he could read everything in my fucking mind. He led me down the aisle as sparks of color exploded in the sky above us and sparklers lit our way to the street.

When we got to the end, Lucian took me in his arms. "Have to give the people what they want," he murmured, like he was a king and all the wedding guests were his subjects—which maybe wasn't that far off.

Lucian bent me backward with one hand on my lower back and the other hand tangled in my hair. His lips claimed mine in a lush, wet kiss as the crowd cheered us on. His tongue slid into my mouth with slow, lazy sweeps. The world around us blurred.

It was just us here, two pinpricks of light that would eventually explode and burn everyone around us.

Warmth flooded my insides...and my knickers. He was a fucking amazing kisser.

Maybe "crazed psychopath" and "kissed like a god" went hand in hand in America.

Lucian lifted me up and we just stared at each other, something passing between us.

Nothing groundbreaking enough to erase being dragged to an altar in a bloody dress though.

I ripped my gaze from his.

Lucian just gave me an infuriating smirk and opened the car door for us to get in. I got in, but something pushed me to take one last look behind me.

When I did, I immediately regretted it.

Gabriel's brilliant golden eyes were locked on mine, pain slicing across his features, and suddenly there was a lump in my throat that I couldn't swallow, and all the air in my lungs was pushed out. I gave him a sad smile, a silent offering of consolation for his hurt.

I felt it too.

It's amazing how someone can walk into your life for just a moment, yet leave a scar that will take a lifetime to heal.

Lucian glances over his shoulder to see who I was looking at, and suddenly he was the green-eyed monster of jealousy. He practically threw himself into the car, all traces of our levity gone, like a candle that's been snuffed out by the wind.

The car took off, the crowd soon faded from view, replaced by the normal hum of New York traffic. Lucian was staring out the window and his silence was unnerving. He slid a knife out of his pocket and flipped it open and shut repeatedly. I watched his movements, the sight somehow mesmerizing to observe.

"Are you trying to make me into a monster?" he finally asked hoarsely.

I gulped. "What do you mean?"

He continued to stare out the window, flicking that knife open, shut, open, shut. "There will come a day that you push me too far. And I'll do something we won't be able to come back from. What you saw today was just a taste, an appetizer if you will, of what happens when I lose hold of my humanity."

He finally turned to look at me.

"Don't fuck my brothers, Dahlia. You won't like what happens," he warned in a muted voice.

"Noted," I murmured after a long minute.

Because what I could say?

I already had.

We were back in the penthouse, and I was officially freaking out.

I didn't want to do this.

Not at all.

There was a runaway thump battering against my ribcage, and I felt like I might throw up. The three glasses of champagne hadn't made a dent to calm the storm warping its way through me.

I stood awkwardly in the entryway of the penthouse, resisting the urge not to bolt. That would only provoke the beast. A predator always wanted you more if you ran.

It seemed like he was thriving on the buildup. The more time that passed, the more my breathing felt suspended in place.

"Are you ready for me, principessa?" he murmured, the warm caress of his breath falling over me.

I wished I could tell him that it was never my goal to be a "principessa." I'd never even wanted to be a queen.

I'd only ever wanted to be free.

"We're going into my room now." He slid my hair over to one shoulder, and then placed his hand on my lower back, so low he was almost gripping my arse.

I let him lead me towards the hallway opposite the one that led to my room.

It was a death march, the cruel, cold beat of a drum thrumming in my ears with every step that I took.

Lucian opened his door to reveal a massive bedroom, almost twice the size of my own, which was already humongous. Unlike Gabriel's room, which always looked lived in and messy, there was no sign that anyone lived in this room. Sure, there was furniture, but the bed was made with crisp corners, there were no clothes in the room, and not a single personal effect to be found. There were no photo frames, no trinkets. Nothing.

I looked back at him to see what he was doing and saw that he was leaning against the door he'd closed behind us, just watching me: tall and perfectly still, brooding with a clenched jaw.

I quickly turned away.

The focal point of the room, besides the massive bed in the center that had tall bedposts that nearly reached the ceiling, was the harrowing painting that took up almost the entire wall. I recognized it immediately. We'd learned about it in Art History. It was the bottom portion of a painting by Jan Van Eyck, appropriately called *The Last Judgment*. In the painting, there's a winged, grinning skeleton that roosts over hell, where the devil lords over the damned, splitting them at the seams and swallowing them whole.

It's not a picture I would ever pick for a bedroom, and it only adds to my unease. It was impossible to miss the darkness in Lucian, but looking at his choice of artwork made me wonder just how far down that darkness went. I walked deeper into the room, noting the doorway where I could see a bathroom covered in black marble. I didn't see a tub in there. Not that I would ever think of Lucian as the kind of guy who regularly took baths. The thought almost made me laugh.

Almost.

What was supposed to happen now? Was he going to kiss me? Was he going to bend me over the bed and do a slam-bam, thank you ma'am kind of thing, and he'd just hope that I'd get pregnant right away?

Not that that was going to happen.

Before I'd left England, I'd slipped away from security and secretly gotten a birth control implant. I was twenty years old and nowhere near ready for children.

If I'd ever be.

I'd have to tell Lucian eventually, but that was definitely not going to be a conversation for tonight.

It had been so easy with Raphael, like two sparks coming together to become an inferno. This felt like I was waiting on the chopping block, the guillotine blade above my head. I was just waiting for the blade to drop and end me.

"You're trembling, principessa," he murmured, and I almost shivered as he finally broke the silence he'd been torturing me with. He slowly dragged his fingers across my skin. Goosebumps sprang up under his touch. The sound of our breathing filled the room.

I'll say one thing for Lucian's bedroom skills...he certainly knew how to build anticipation.

The dress I changed into at the hotel was silk with a bateau neckline that wrapped around my neck and was kept in place by a single button. His fingers ran through my hair once before he piled my curls into one hand and unsnapped the button with the other. Then he released my hair to fall in waves around me. The front of the dress immediately fell forward, revealing my see-through lacy white bra as the dress got caught around my waist where a zipper held it up. Lucian made no move to undo the zipper. Instead, he slowly walked around me, his gaze eating me up. His eyes darkened to a dangerous green. I had the urge to try and cover myself up, but he must have read my mind.

"Don't hide what's mine," he ordered in a silky voice that would destroy the knickers of anyone who heard it.

He licked his lips, and I could feel it as if his mouth was on my ear biting a path down my neck.

He prowled towards me until we were just inches apart. His hands slid down my arms and then he pulled my arms behind my back and held my wrists in place with one hand, making it impossible to touch him. He hovered in front of my lips for a moment, but he didn't kiss me. Instead, he pulled my hair with his free hand, baring my neck to his mouth, teeth, and tongue as he trailed a path down to my breasts. I arched towards him obscenely. My nipples pebbled beneath the lace of my bra, and I couldn't stop myself from letting out a moan. It was a desperate, bleating sound that ripped from my lungs and seemed to echo around the room.

He took pity on me and his head finally dipped to my nipple. Taking me into his mouth through the thin lace of my bra, he teased with his tongue and bit down. Hard. Only releasing me when I gasped. He did it again, and this time I went a little wild, pulling at his hold on my wrists and bucking my hips in desperation for some kind of friction to calm the pulse between my thighs. It had started as a slow flutter the moment when he touched me, but it built into a steady cadence. I hovered in a place between pleasure and pain as he sucked my nipple so far into his mouth, I could feel it in my clitoris.

I was mindless with need.

And my bra wasn't even off yet.

He went back and forth between my breasts, torturing them until he finally reached back and undid the clasp to my bra. And then his lips were right back on my chest, as he tugged and bit the sensitive peaks. I was writhing, desperate to touch him, and for him to touch me in the place I needed him the most.

But his grip on my wrists was firm, practiced, not slipping for one moment even though the black of his pupils were blurring into the green with a need so powerful it was scaring me.

Everything he was doing was magnified in my aching core. I climbed higher, faster, and I threw my head back in ecstasy.

His control finally snapped, and with a growl, he literally tore the dress off of me, the ripping sound reverberating through my skin as I stood there in nothing but my pair of lacy white knickers--already soaked once today with my cum and...blood thanks to Raphael—my thigh highs, and my heels.

The lighting was dim in here, though. So, unless he was looking for it, it wouldn't even be noticeable.

Lucian was still fully dressed in his tuxedo, and I was salivating just thinking about what's underneath that suit.

Even though I hated him. And he's insane.

"Stop thinking," he murmured as he pulled his already undone bow tie from his neck and used it to quickly and smoothly tie my hands together behind me so that he didn't have to hold my wrists anymore.

He really was going to keep me tied up for this. I tried to move my wrists, but he'd tied the bow tie so tightly that I couldn't move an inch.

I waited for fear to simmer in my stomach at being tied up. But there was nothing other than the ever-present ache in my core.

Satisfied I wouldn't be able to get free, Lucian took a step back, and his eyes sparked like fire as he took in my body with a calculated assessment. "I need one thing from you," he said roughly.

And my eyes widened, wondering what it could be. "What's that?" I asked in a breathy whisper.

"Your trust."

My insides shuttered, because what he was asking was impossible. How he could think I would trust him after what he'd done in the little time that I knew him...I didn't understand.

He stepped towards me again, took my chin, and gently lifted it so I was forced to look up at him.

"From now on, I'll always be honest with you, and I expect the same from you." The sincerity in his gaze...was maddening, dangerous. It stormed the walls around my heart I was doing my best to fortify.

I couldn't respond. I could sense that trust and honesty wasn't all he wanted...he was hungry for far more than that.

He wanted my truth, the dark secrets of my soul that I didn't think I could ever tell.

My heart stumbled over the prospect, and I got lost in a tunnel, overwhelmed by the thought of it. My secrets were insurmountable. The most recent ones involving his brothers...

Lucian must have known that I couldn't answer right then, because suddenly he was against me, taking my mouth with a repressed aggression that spoke to the extreme control he'd shown up to that point. One hand snared my nape and the other gripped my waist to pull me into him. The desperate lashes of his tongue tried to claim me as his. I groaned against him, pulling at my bindings in frustration. I ground into his hard ridge as his hand moved from my hip, down to the edge of my thigh high.

"Fuck," he growled, as he dragged his mouth from mine. He looked down and we both watched as he slid his fingers towards my knicker line. The evidence of my arousal was stained on my white satin knickers. I buried my head against his hard chest and breathed in, trying to get myself under control. But every breath I took was torture as I gulped in his leather, spice, and gunpowder musk. It only made my clit throb harder.

I whimpered when his thumb finally slipped under my knickers to find my swollen, aching clit.

"Lucian," I murmured as I lifted my head and arched my back, a slave to the sensations coursing through my body.

His eyes flared at the sound of his name, and he bit his stupid lip again, only fanning the flames inside me.

"Do you want me to touch you, principessa?"

He didn't wait for me to answer, and I groaned as he rolled his thumb in expert circles.

I was ashamed to admit that in that moment, I couldn't have said no if I tried. He had me under some kind of spell. He was wrapping me up in knots at his touch, and I was afraid I'd never be able to get them undone.

He removed his hand and I cried out, panic shooting through me as I hung so close to the edge that I thought I might die.

Okay, that was a little dramatic…but still.

Abruptly, he picked me up in a cradle hold and carried me to his enormous bed. I made sure not to look at his creepy painting above me as he set me down. He gently and efficiently untied my wrists and then laid me down on my back before tying my wrists together above me with his bow tie, tying them to a metal hoop that was bizarrely in the center of the headboard. I tried to move my arms but, once again, he'd tied me in a way that was impossible to escape from.

But there was still no twinge of fear.

My gaze flicked to the bedposts in front of me...noticing how steady they looked and that they also had hoops and hooks in multiple places.

Oh fuck. This was some kind of bondage bed. I wasn't even sure what the word for it was.

"Wait," I cried out, but he just laid a gentle kiss on my lips before I could say anything else. Somehow it worked to effectively shut me up.

He got off the bed and stood at my feet. Dark, mesmerizing lust rolled off him while his gaze drifted all over my body. Finally, our eyes met; his were hot and tempting, and I wasn't sure if I'd ever wanted something more.

How the fuck had this happened?

He's a monster. Remember that?

Lucian put one knee on the bed, and he pressed his lips to my ankle. He began to kiss and lick his way up until he was groaning, sucking, and tasting my inner thighs as he spread my legs wide.

"So fucking beautiful. You can't even be real, Dahlia." He whispered my name reverently, licking my slit through my knickers. A cry broke free as my head slammed into the mattress.

I squeezed my eyes closed as shockwaves reverberated through my body.

He sucked my clit through the lace, lapping and teasing with his tongue and then teeth. I bucked against his mouth with a groan. Each lick peeled back a layer, leaving me free of everything. I was bare.

I lost the ability to speak. I could only watch and feel and breathe through the pulsing ache in my core while he kissed me everywhere, my knickers long gone. Every time I got close to exploding, he stopped, edging me over and over again until my entire body was shaking.

"Please," I begged, desperate for a push off the cliff he was holding me hostage on. His answer was to slide a thick finger inside my welcoming body. Just the thought of that tattooed finger inside of me made me hot. I moaned—loudly.

Somewhere in the house I heard the sound of crashing glass, but I couldn't find it in me to be concerned...or care that someone else was here. My desire was skyrocketing, the friction of his finger along with his mouth shooting me so high it felt like I could touch the stars. I bucked against him, the dance becoming frantic.

"I—" He plunged two fingers into me again and again while his tongue flicked and rolled...and finally...he shot me beyond the brink. I exploded, screaming out in awe as the crescendo washed over me violently. Waves of pleasure crashed through my entire body, and my back arched as his mouth and fingers continued their magic, pushing my orgasm on and on.

"Please," I choked out hoarsely when the sensations became too much.

He shot up, his mouth latching onto mine so I could taste

myself on his tongue. I never knew I'd be into it, but it just sent my body into hyperdrive.

I was desperate for more.

I bit down on his bottom lip, sucking on it, a mimicry of what he'd just done to me. He growled, and I pressed down harder until I could taste blood.

"Fuck, fuck, fuck," he hissed.

His fingers began to play with the tight peaks of my nipples, and I released his lip as a cry slipped from my lips.

He laughed at my desperation, the fucking bastard, and began to move down my body, pressing soft kisses as he did until he was once again standing at the bottom of the bed.

There was nothing quite like being tied to a headboard in only a pair of thigh highs to make a girl feel vulnerable.

He slowly began to unbutton his shirt, never taking his eyes from mine. Each button showed a bit more of his delicious, tan, tattoo-covered skin, and I was suddenly famished to taste it.

A shiver passed through me, and I whimpered.

And then he froze, like the sound had triggered something in him. His face was suddenly drowning in sorrow, his hands hanging limply at his sides. His skin paled and his breath was coming out in gasps like the oxygen in the room had suddenly disappeared. "Look at what I did to you," he said in a horrified voice. "I'm so fucking sorry."

"What? What do you mean…"

He began to back away, ghosts in his eyes as he stared at me, like he wasn't seeing me there anymore…but something else.

"Lucian," I cried, confusion crashing over me in waves.

Then he was gone, out the door without another word, slamming it so hard behind him that everything in the room vibrated. My chest was heaving, beads of sweat dotting my skin.

And my hands were still tied above my head.

I tried to struggle against them, pulling in desperation, but the tie he'd made didn't loosen even a little.

He had to be coming back. Surely he wasn't going to leave me like this. Right?

But he never returned.

And finally, I passed out, delirious from the day, the orgasm, and struggling to get out of my bindings.

I woke up when the monsters got too loud. Muted sunlight was streaming through the window, and it took a minute for everything to come back to me. I was in Lucian's room. Our room. It took me a minute to realize that I wasn't alone anymore...and that Lucian was asleep beside me.

He was still in his tuxedo pants and his white dress shirt from the wedding, but the dress shirt was undone so every perfect bump and ridge of his tattooed chest and abdomen was visible. He looked like a completely different person lying there, the intoxicating, terrifying alpha energy wiped away, leaving an angel there you could fall in love with.

I hated him. The feeling was burrowing into my soul, creating a black cage around my heart so that he couldn't get in. He'd left me here all night, my hands tied above my head, the blood draining from my limbs until my arms had started to tingle...and then they'd eventually grown numb. I'd had to sit up to try and stop the ache, and then somehow, I'd finally fallen asleep, dreaming about familiar shadows hiding in the corner of the room before slowly approaching my bed. Once they got there, they'd...

I shook my head. I needed to get untied, get off this fucking bed, and then run away so far that he'd never find me.

A moan cut through the silence of the room, dragging my attention back to where my husband lay on the other side of the bed. My husband. Who knew the taste of that word on my tongue would make me want to puke?

Lucian cast out another moan, this one so erotic it made my knickers wet, which said a lot because I was literally in the most unsexy situation possible at this point. Lucian's tattoo-kissed hands grabbed onto the blanket underneath him as he moved against the bed sensually...like he was being fucked. It felt like I was watching a live porno.

Until the moans abruptly cut off. "Please, no. Fuck. Please. It hurts," he whimpered, followed by another erotic moan.

My stomach hurt as I watched Lucian, not sure what to do. He wasn't just trapped in a nightmare—he was trapped in the past. I knew from firsthand experience that it was dangerous to wake someone up from that. Our housekeeper had once tried to rouse me from one of my nightmares, and I'd woken up with my hands around her throat.

"Lucian," I said softly but urgently, hoping I could wake him up that way. His whimpers had turned into screams intermixed with the sound of pleasure. Unwillingly, some of that cage I'd spent the whole night building up started to melt as I wondered whether Lucian might have more similarities to me than I'd thought.

Abruptly, his moans escalated as he gripped his cock through his trousers and came, a dark, wet spot appearing in the front of his pants. He sat up with a gasp, his chest heaving and tremors shooting through his body.

"Fuck," he murmured before putting his hands in his hair and pulling, like he could somehow eject the gross slime that dreams like that always left—like a tangible coating on your insides—out of his body.

"Lucian," I murmured in a voice I didn't recognize, a voice dripping with pain and sympathy.

His whole body stiffened, and he dropped his hands from his hair as his breathing escalated. He scrambled off the bed like he'd been shot at. He stood there staring at the wall until, finally, his gaze turned towards me, shame and fury fighting for equal footing in his gaze.

I had the insane urge to open my mouth and let my story free. To tell him that I understood the pain and embarrassment that came when your body betrayed you at the hands of monsters.

I'd cum every single time.

"Lucian, I—" I began. "You were crying out in your sleep. I tried to wake you—" My words trailed off when I saw how pale he'd gotten, like his soul had slipped back to the hell it had come from. Before I could try and finish my sentence, he lunged at his lamp on the nightstand, the only thing in this room breakable, yanked the cord out from the plug, and threw the lamp against the wall where it shattered into a million pieces.

I trembled in fear, very much aware of my fragile position, but he didn't take a step towards me.

He just pointed a tattooed finger at me with a look that had me wishing for a place to hide. "You didn't see anything," he hissed, demons lying in wait in his words.

My heart got cold. There'd only been one person that I'd ever wished pain on, so it had felt sick to even have these thoughts. But I'd had a moment of hope, that maybe I didn't have to be so alone with the burdens that I carried carved into my skin. That maybe I could find a safe place to rest with someone who would understand my secret shame.

The perverse hope dissolved, and it was replaced with loneliness far stronger than any I'd already experienced once I'd set foot into this horrible place.

Lucian disappeared out the door once more, leaving me alone in the bed. Again.

But his nightmares seemed to linger in the room long after he'd left, combining with my own monsters and leaving me wondering if anything would ever be the same again.

LUCIAN

Gabriel was standing in the hallway as I staggered out of my room like I was wounded. Before he could say anything, I leaned over and threw up all over the floor. I felt like I'd been stripped, a knife slicing off my skin so that you could see everything that lay underneath. My mind was a jumbled mess of shame, familiar cravings for death that always followed the dreams coursing through me. My emotions were all amplified a million times over by the fact that she'd seen it.

I hadn't been able to look her in the eyes when I'd first woken up and realized not only where I was...but who was by me. I had finally turned towards her, expecting to see disgust. But instead, I'd seen something even worse. Pity.

It had almost been enough to destroy me.

She had been lying there, stretched out like an offering from the gods. And with the sun caressing her skin from the window on the other side of the room, she looked like pale sunshine, like the light you saw when the sun was peeking through the clouds.

I hadn't meant to end up in that bed. When I'd left her last night, I'd left the building, knowing I couldn't withstand the temptation to go back to her if I was in the same city block. It hadn't seemed possible to get far enough away to withstand her pull.

So, I'd gotten drunk, far drunker than I'd ever let myself get since I'd become fully aware of the position of power I held and the danger it presented. I faintly remembered Riccardo and one of my bodyguards hauling me out of the bar and into the car, and then after that...My drunk aspirations must've had a one-track mind and I'd ended up in there. With her. At least I hoped that I'd made it in there by myself. If Riccardo and Edward had seen her like that, I'd have to kill them.

"Lucian? Where's Dahlia?" Gabriel growled as I fell apart in front of him in a way that I'd never allowed before. Normally after a nightmare, I could regroup in my bathroom, throw up a couple hundred times, and then turn on the water in my shower to a scalding temperature so that it could burn off the remnants of my dreams.

But *she* was in there. I wasn't sure that I'd ever be able to face her again. My past was buried so deep that there wasn't a single person on earth who could find it. I'd made sure of that a long time ago.

But a few hours with her, and suddenly my weaknesses were out in the world. Just the thought made me throw up again.

"Lucian, fuck!" Gabriel hissed. "Did you drown yourself in the liquor cabinet? I thought you'd been in there with Dahlia?" Even in my current state—a hangover headache threatening to dislodge my brain and ooze out of my ears, and shame curdling in my stomach—I could hear the note of hope in his voice. I knew what he was thinking. He was thinking he had a chance.

And in that moment, I wasn't sure he was wrong.

Dahlia was always going to be mine, but I could never have her, not in the way I wanted. When I'd seen her tied up, light bruises and marks that I left already all over her body, it felt like I'd soiled an angel, like I was actively chopping at her wings with a hacksaw, preventing her from ever going to heaven. I couldn't have sex like a normal person, and I couldn't have her. Ever.

"Go help her, Gabriel," I said in a broken, gravelly voice. He eyed me cautiously, obviously wondering if it was some kind of trap.

But it wasn't a trap. It was the realization that my stained soul was never going to be good enough for her. Dahlia would be my wife in name only, and that started right now. "You'll need some scissors," I told him, long overdue panic threading its way through me as I realized she'd been tied up like that the whole night.

Fuck. I was a bastard.

"Go to her," I repeated again, urgency in my voice, and then I lurched towards the elevator, desperate to get away from there.

She'd *seen* me.

GABRIEL

There was something to be said for the mental clarity that came with trauma. I'd been protected for most of my life, the blood and gore of our family never reaching below the skin. My eyes didn't hold the haunted secrets that both Lucian's and Raphael's did.

So as I watched Lucian marry my soulmate at gunpoint, my body hadn't known how to handle what I was experiencing.

I'd been frozen, feeling like I was having an out-of-body experience as I watched the ceremony, and then wishing I could rip my eyes into shreds when he kissed her.

Watching my brother in the hallway now, falling apart in a way that I could never have even imagined, was terrifying. Except, like the bastard I was, it was hard to give any thought to what had put him in that state…once I'd read the hidden meaning in his words. He hadn't been with her last night and it almost seemed like…I was being given permission to have her in the way that I'd been craving since the moment I'd seen her.

I didn't bother asking if he needed help as he lurched his way to the elevator, purple bags under his eyes, his face a ghastly almost green color, liquor and vomit saturating the air around him—I was just thinking about her.

I burst through the door, expecting her to be walking around, or in the bathroom.

My heart lurched when I saw her lying there, every dip and curve of her body visible to me. I was suddenly rock hard, the desperate urge to take her almost overwhelming under my skin.

And then she fucking whimpered, and it wasn't a whimper of lust…all I could hear was pain. Belatedly, my gaze skipped up her arms to where she was tied to a ring in the headboard. I immediately cursed and rushed towards the bed, pulling out the knife I always kept in my pocket and hacking at the ties until she was loose.

Her whole body shuddered, and after I helped her out of the rest of the binding, she whimpered, and I went to work rubbing at her wrists and upper arms. How long had he kept her like that?

And why? I mean, I hadn't expected him to go full BDSM on his wedding night...

I wanted to kill him. But that could come later, after I took care of her.

Besides, judging how my brother had looked a moment ago, he was in a personal hell already, so I didn't have to worry about sending him there.

I tried to keep my eyes on her face. But fuck, I wasn't a saint. Far from it.

I'd spent every night thinking about her body after I'd gotten her out of the shower. Even though I'd been practically blinded by the pain she was emanating.

There was no doubt about it, though. She had a body built for sin, and as she struggled off the bed, I about came in my pants with the way her hips flared out from that little waist. And those tits. Fuck.

This wasn't the time. Obviously. There was an air of defeat about her and I hated it. Especially knowing that she already had demons inside of her that I was desperate to fix.

The fact that she was standing there in nothing but a pair of thigh highs must have hit her, because a soft expletive fell from her lips and she practically dove for the bathroom like it held the keys to her salvation. The backside was just as good as the front. And I was obviously insane because all I wanted to do was drag her ass back to the bed and then take her over and over and over again.

I jumped off the bed, giving it a disgusted look like it was the problem in all of this. And then I crept to the door of the bathroom like a demented stalker, listening to see if she needed me. I heard the sound of water running, but no tears. I guessed that was a good thing.

But I didn't want her cutting herself again. Whatever I did, I was determined to somehow make her so happy that she'd never want to do that again.

The shower was turned on, and I was tempted to go running to get my bath products because I knew she'd have to use Lucian's. And then she'd be drenched in his scent for the rest of the day. A cold knot formed in my stomach just thinking about it. I was jealous; jealous of him, jealous of the life she'd had before me, jealous that she'd ever existed without me when she was now my entire world and I just wanted to be hers.

I was turning into a psycho, and obviously, we already had enough of those in this family.

I waited outside for what seemed like hours before I heard the shower turn off. A few moments later, the door opened and she came out with a towel that showcased those legs that seemed to go on forever despite her diminutive size. Her skin was red, almost raw-looking, like she'd tried to scrape it off.

She looked surprised to see me there, and for a second, she stood there and let me in, another little peek at the soul I was obsessed with.

I saw it then, just like I had the other night when I'd found her in the shower after I'd been hovering by her door like an idiot and realized that the shower had been on for far too long.

Beyond the light blue that reminded me of cloudless skies was a storm. A storm filled with pain and despair unlike anything I'd seen before. I wanted to run over to her, take her in my arms, hold her until it didn't hurt…but I knew I couldn't.

When she yanked her gaze away, it was like a string snapped

between us. Without another look at me, she walked past, heading for the door.

Desperation flooded me. Like if I didn't tell her right then and there how I felt, I might die. Like if she placed one foot out the door, she'd slip through my fingers and I'd never be able to reach for her again.

I didn't care that we were in Lucian's room. She had to know that someone was here for her, that someone would do anything in the world to make her happy.

"Dahlia," I began, and I wasn't ashamed at the longing in my voice. She stopped in the doorway but didn't look back. "I—."

"Don't," she said softly before I could say it. "Don't say it when his scent is still coating my skin, and I can still feel his touch. Say it someday when it will save me," she murmured.

And then she disappeared down the hall, and I was left wondering when that time would come.

SEVENTEEN

LUCIAN

"I t was quite the show you put on," my father announced the second he stepped into the room, uninvited of course.

I schooled my face, not wanting to show how annoyed I was that he'd shown up.

Especially because of what was in the basement, currently being worked over by Raphael. In the weeks since the wedding, I hadn't stepped foot back in the penthouse, preferring to stay in the bedroom attached to my office at Rossi Inc., our front for our more legal ventures.

Carlo smiled sharply at me, showing his teeth in a way that was supposed to be intimidating and predatory, but had long since lost its power over me in any way. I was just counting down the days until his life of binging on drugs, alcohol, and expensive whores caught up to him. I didn't think that any of the other organizations involved in the treaty were like this, a figurehead in place for the boss. Maybe a different man would have just gotten it over with and ended his life for him, but there was something about patricide that had never sat well with me.

There had been an event almost every single day. Men disappearing, shipments of weapons gone, police showing up where they shouldn't because of tips from an unknown player.

Everything was small, like a fly settling on a horse and annoying it. But with the way it had been ramping up, it was only a matter of time before whoever they were escalated things to the point where it would hurt.

I doubted that the men tied up in the basement were anyone super important, but they'd clearly been the leaders of the crew that we'd recently taken out. I was hoping that they would know *something*.

"I'm glad you enjoyed it," I responded evenly, which only made Carlo's jaw clench. "What brings you to the office today?"

"I tried to access one of the Bermuda accounts, and I got a notice it had been closed. Would you know anything about that?"

I crossed my arms in front of me. "I didn't know that was an account you used," I told him placidly, a blatant lie. "I moved some money around for some different investments recently. It could have happened then."

"And you didn't think to ask me before doing that, son?" His voice was deadly, the sharp blade of a razor before it cut into your skin.

Now my jaw was clenching. Carlo, for the most part, left me to run things as I saw fit. That included money since he was the worst financial handler I'd ever seen. Before I'd started getting involved on this side of things, he'd almost run several of our companies into the ground. Now, under my leadership, we were flourishing. Our coffers were fuller than ever, and our portfolio expanded so that we had a foot in anything making money in this city.

I gave Carlo a report of things every week, that I knew he only half paid attention to. But when I noticed large sums of money being taken out of that account, I'd taken the liberty of closing it and moving the money elsewhere. *That* I hadn't told him.

"I'm sure it was in one of those reports. There's plenty of money in all your other accounts for you to take from." And he didn't have problems doing that. I almost wept every month when I saw the long list of charges on his accounts that I oversaw.

"Do I need to remind you–" he began right as Raphael showed up in the doorway, blood splattered all over the front of him.

Carlo stopped and raised an eyebrow when he saw Raphael's state.

"Have something fun in the basement?" he asked me, his attention temporarily diverted.

Besides blow and whores, my father loved a good torture session.

Carlo addressed the question to me. He rarely talked to Raphael if he could help it. It was something I didn't understand, but since Raphael seemed to be perfectly okay with that, I'd never stepped in.

"A few things," I answered, resigned that Carlo would, unfortunately, be involved in this. Which ordinarily would've been all right—he was very creative in his torture techniques—but since my father was near the top of my list of suspects who were organizing the attacks, I wasn't keen on him being involved.

The three of us walked over to the private elevator in my

office and took it forty floors down to where our basement was set up for these kinds of things. We had rooms like this in almost all of the basements of our residences and other important buildings. This one was a little more in-depth, with prison cells lining both walls as we walked down the hallway, and guards in place to watch over the cells when they were full of people waiting to be "questioned."

We walked into the room where three men were bound and gagged. The room stunk of piss and burnt flesh, and I noted that one of the men was now missing a hand. Raphael had cauterized the stump to keep it from bleeding out.

He didn't seem to have done much work on the other two, which would give Carlo a chance to play.

Carlo went over to one of the drawers that lined the wall and pulled out a pair of medical gloves from it. He had something against getting blood on his hands, something that amused me and my brothers to no end. At this point, his palms were definitely stained red with all the sins he'd committed.

"Now tell me what we're looking for, boys," he said as he smiled scarily at the terrified men.

Raphael was leaning against the wall, watching his father with boredom and more than a little distaste.

Same, brother.

"We found these men pouring gasoline around one of the warehouses. There was ten million dollars worth of products in them."

Carlo nodded, seeming nonplussed about the whole thing. He whistled creepily as he grabbed a machete and suddenly whirled towards one of the prisoners, slicing into his leg. A mind-numbing scream filled the air.

Blood was everywhere; he'd clearly hit an artery, and now the guy was bleeding out fast.

"Fuck," I swore as I moved to the prisoner. I put pressure on the wound, so it wasn't bleeding quite as badly. I also kept one eye on my father, not putting it past him to put that same machete in my back.

"Who sent you to the warehouse?" I growled. Snot and tears were running down the guy's face as he sobbed. I sighed, knowing we wouldn't get anything out of the guy. I didn't think whoever was orchestrating these attacks was a fool. And only a fool would put a sniveling idiot in a place of leadership.

"I don't know," he sobbed. "Please, my family—" Before he could say anything else, Carlo used the machete to chop right into the guy's throat, using so much force, it cut all the way through.

I shook my head but didn't say anything. I wouldn't have gotten anything out of the guy anyway.

Somehow, among all of the blood and the smells that would've had most men craving the grave, Dahlia flickered through my mind. Had she said anything to anyone? What was she thinking? I got nauseous just thinking about that morning. I'd found myself throwing up multiple times a day, unable to stop obsessing about it. But I'd also found myself jacking off multiple times a day at the image engraved in my head of her spread out on my bed, her hands tied above her, her face flushed, the breath leaving her chest in gasps...the way her eyes had begged me to fuck her.

Just the image was enough to make me get hard, and one thing I didn't do in this room was get hard...so this was a first for me.

"Lucian?" Raphael called, and I turned to look at him. He

nodded his head at Carlo, who was eyeing the next prisoner like a butcher with a new load of fat cattle in front of him.

This was a fucking disaster.

"Father, why don't you let me take this one?" I tried to say it deferentially, but the words just sounded hollow. We both knew that I'd lost respect for him a long time ago.

"You're too soft on them, son. If they don't bleed, they don't talk."

"At least try to not hit anything vital with the next one," Raphael drawled, and Carlo whirled around to give him a look of loathing.

Raphael smiled, like he was just waiting for Carlo to attack. I guess Carlo wasn't as much of a fool as I thought he was, because after giving his psycho son one more glare, he turned back to the prisoners.

The next thirty minutes were a complete waste of my time. Carlo didn't fail to hit every vital organ that he could, and I found myself playing doctor throughout the next man's "session" as I tried to keep him alive long enough to answer questions.

The third man kept eyeing Raphael nervously, even with Carlo standing there with a mallet and a meat cleaver, because apparently, he'd thought that the machete wasn't sharp enough.

"What are you looking at, worm?" Carlo hissed, obviously perturbed that the guy was more scared of someone in the back of the room than him.

"Maybe you're losing your touch, Father," Raphael taunted. I shot him a look that told him to shut the fuck up, wondering what his game was today. Carlo was going red in the face, and I wasn't sure who he was going to attack next, the prisoner or Raphael.

"Been a while since I taught you some respect," growled Carlos, and honestly, it was getting a little embarrassing at this point because I didn't think that Raphael had the same issues with patricide as I did.

When Raphael just stood there with a little smirk, Carlo whirled back towards the prisoner and began hacking at the man mercilessly, until chunks of flesh flew everywhere.

Cazzo. Thank fuck for the cleanup crew.

I shook my head in disappointment at how little information we'd gotten. I thought I'd at least be able to get the name of people in the next level up from this crew.

Carlo tossed down his weapons finally with a loud *clank* on the floor. He looked a little like that girl from that movie where the pig's blood was dropped on her. I didn't think there was a part of him that wasn't covered in red.

I glanced down at my clothes. I didn't look much better.

Looking back, I saw that Raphael had left the room, content with the carnage he'd created.

Fucker.

I had a migraine forming behind my eyes.

Everything was a fucking train wreck. Everything.

And in the midst of all the bullshit I was dealing with, I still couldn't stop thinking about *her*.

Eighteen

DAHLIA

I couldn't do it. I couldn't stay in this place for one more second. At least in England, I'd had a schedule, a purpose in life. Go to school, get good grades, make your mum happy. There had always been something to do.

Since that fateful morning, I hadn't done anything. Emilia came every day, but she rarely had time for much conversation with everything that she had to do directing the household. I learned from her that the Rossis had several residences, and she was in charge of them all. I couldn't even cook, because she or Gabriel made sure that there were meals ready at all times during the day.

I felt like I binge-watched every show on earth, and even movies in that nice theater room had lost their appeal. Gabriel had shown me the state-of-the-art gym on their floor, but there was only so much running I could do, and even pounding away at the weight bags couldn't get rid of the restlessness inside of me. I'd tried to leave multiple times, but there was now security posted downstairs outside the elevator, and they'd quickly "escorted" me back up every time.

With my "issues", I needed to keep busy, and this was not it. Lucian hadn't so much as shown his face around the penthouse, and I saw Raphael for just seconds every day as he rushed out, always busy. Gabriel had done his best to spend time with me, but I was pretty sure that Lucian was just thinking of ways to keep him out of the penthouse, because Gabriel had meetings all day and would come home late at night, long after dinner, looking completely wiped out. He would try to watch a movie with me, but he would fall asleep within five seconds.

The worst thing, though, was the text messages. *He* was sending multiple ones from different numbers every day. I blocked every single number. I tried to keep my phone off as much as possible, but it didn't seem like I could escape from the graphic messages he'd send that told me exactly what he was going to do to me when he saw me again.

I needed a new phone, but that would require having access to money. And since Lucian wouldn't respond to any text messages or phone calls, I hadn't been able to get a hold of that yet. My mum hadn't been answering her phone, but I'd felt awkward anyway asking her for money now that I was married. I would've asked Benny, but he was lost in the wind, sending me short texts from Church's phone that he'd "talk to me soon," but was in the middle of "something."

So like I said, I was to the point that if I stayed in this place for one more second...I was going to go crazy.

I cornered Emilia in the kitchen after another sleepless night.

"Does Lucian have an office?" I asked, cringing at the terseness in my tone. She stopped wiping down the counter and glanced at me, a frown line on her forehead and her lips pursed.

"Yes?" she answered slowly. Obviously, I was going to have to work to get anything out of her.

"I need a phone, and I need to talk to him about something important."

"You can talk to me, dearie. And I'll work right away on getting you a phone."

I wanted to hit myself up the side of the head. Of course Emilia would be able to get the phone. But also, I felt completely ridiculous that I had to depend on the house manager for that, that I had no access to bank accounts or anything else. It's not like I was going to go crazy spending Lucian's money. Since I wasn't allowed out of the house, I didn't have a lot of options.

"It's really important that I talk to him," I pleaded. It was a good thing Emilia had a soft spot for me, because her shoulders drooped, and she sighed.

"I'll get Riccardo to take you to his office. But don't go anywhere without Riccardo. It will be my head if something happens to you."

I wanted to scoff at the idea that Lucian would care if anything happened to me, but then I remembered standing in the doorway, and the way that Gabriel had looked at me, and the way that Raphael had stared at me through the mirror.

Perhaps there were a few people that would miss me.

"Thank you," I said with a relieved sigh.

Working her magic, Emilia had Riccardo in the entryway within five minutes. He tipped his head to me, silent as always, and I followed him into the elevator and down into the lobby before walking outside. I noted that Riccardo kept one hand on his gun, and his eyes were flitting everywhere constantly like someone was going to attack us at any minute.

I got into the car, this one a Rolls-Royce Wraith that made me a little wet as I slid across the leather.

I seriously needed to see the garage where they stored all of these cars. I'd probably have an orgasm right there. Who needed a dick?

We drove through the city, and of course, Riccardo didn't say anything.

But that didn't matter to me, because at least I was out of that place. I rolled down the window a little bit to let the hot breeze in, feeling like I could breathe easier just having it rush across my face.

We drove for about fifteen minutes before we stopped in front of a skyscraper that was almost as tall as the Empire State building. I gaped up at it. "This is where Lucian's offices are?"

Riccardo nodded. "Rossi Inc. owns the entire building," he explained proudly. That might've been the most words he'd ever said to me. What was the occasion?

There was a hulking, meaty-looking man dressed in a charcoal suit waiting outside of the building, and as soon as Riccardo was next to me and we were walking towards the doors, he nodded to us and headed for the car, getting in and driving away. I assumed to park it somewhere.

We walked through a dramatic-looking lobby with a ceiling at least three stories tall, and I realized how underdressed I was. Everyone here was dressed like they were ready to conquer the corporate world. And here I was dressed in my usual uniform of black leggings and an oversized sweater. I had put on a spaghetti strap shirt underneath the sweater though...since it was scorching hot outside.

I probably needed to reassess my wardrobe now that I wasn't in the frigid England temperatures.

As we walked through the lobby, it was almost like the Red Sea parting, with people taking one look at Riccardo and hastily walking away. He didn't look that intimidating to me, but what did I know?

We got into the elevator with a nod from the guard standing outside of them. "What floor does he work on?"

Riccardo pressed the top button and I internally rolled my eyes. Because really, what other floor would Lucian be on?

Storm clouds were building in my stomach as the elevator ascended.

Why was I doing this again? Just thinking about that look in Lucian's eyes the last time I'd seen him made me shiver. Fuck, what was I thinking?

Oh yeah, that I couldn't take being a prisoner for one more day.

I took a deep breath. I could do this. He was the one who had a problem.

Plus, he owed me a shit ton of apologies. The least of which was for keeping me chained up, almost completely naked, for an entire night. I was just glad that I hadn't had a panic attack.

People looked at us curiously as we walked out of the elevator. This office was of course…mostly black. In a cool gold contemporary font, Rossi Inc. was scrawled onto the wall behind the giant receptionist desk straight ahead of us that had six attractive women manning it.

Again, I was cursing myself for not having dressed up at least a little bit. What was that saying? That you got more flies with honey? In this case, the honey would have meant me not looking like a drowned rat.

The girls' eyes widened when they saw Riccardo, and they were immediately standing up and racing around the desk, asking if he needed a drink. I didn't miss the hearts in their eyes as they gazed at him, seemingly completely unaware I existed.

I gave him a considering once over. I guess he was good-looking. It's just that when you compared him to Lucian, Raphael, and Gabriel, Riccardo was like a flashlight trying to compete with the sun.

It just couldn't be done.

Riccardo remained completely professional, brushing off the girls and telling them tersely he needed to speak to Lucian.

They nodded eagerly as we took a left to where glass offices were lined along the walls, with communal desks grouped around the main area. It was only as we turned that the girls finally seemed to notice me, and their frenzied whispers followed us down the hall.

I soon forgot all about them when we stopped outside a corner office with frosted windows everywhere so you couldn't see inside.

I could hear muffled voices coming from within, and I was tempted to tell Riccardo we could just forget the whole thing and leave. Riccardo gave one solid knock on the door though, and Lucian's familiar voice bellowed for him to enter.

"Riccardo, I didn't expect—" Lucian's sentence completely stopped as I entered the room. He went stiff in his seat, his entire body laced with tension like I was someone dangerous.

"Bellissima, what are you doing here?" Gabriel asked, and I turned and saw that he was lounging in a black leather chair off to my side. My cheeks burned at the intense, possessive way Gabriel was looking at me, desperation and affection coming off him in waves.

It was the complete opposite of the way Lucian was looking at me. Like I was a bomb about to go off.

"I need money," I blurted out, immediately blushing. I'd been trying to come up with a script, and that was definitely not what I intended to lead with. "I mean—I need to be able to do something. I need to be able to leave the penthouse and live a life. You can't trap me there," I said resolutely.

Lucian's fingers were laced in front of him, his gaze caught on the slip of skin showing where my too big of a sweater had fallen from my shoulder. I wiped at the skin just in case I had something there, and that seemed to bring him back to life.

"Please tell me, Dahlia, what would a pampered princess like yourself want to do in her free time?" he drawled.

My bottom lip quivered, but of course there wouldn't be any tears. It was just another way that we'd been betrayed by every single person who had signed that contract so many years ago. I was sure that every single one of the women that had been traded like cattle for peace had things they wanted to do in life. So the fact that he had the audacity to mock the idea that I could want to do more than sit alone on the sofa in front of the TV, was absolutely infuriating.

"I wanted to be a veterinarian," I told him, holding my head high. "I was good at school, straight A's across the board. I would've gone to college if not for this. If I could just try to enroll in—"

"Absolutely not," Lucian cut in.

"And why not?" I retorted angrily.

"Do you know what a security nightmare that is? Having to have men constantly screening a campus for threats. Every single one of my enemies would love to get a piece of you."

I flushed when his gaze slowly dipped down my body. Fucking betrayal. My hormones did it to me every time.

"I could volunteer. I could get a job in a library or something. That's quiet and out of the way. Then I'd just be in one place."

Lucian was already shaking his head.

"Please." I hated him in this moment. I hated him for everything else that he'd done too. But the fact that I had to beg like a dog for the right to live made my insides burn.

"You need to leave," Lucian ordered, grabbing a pen and looking down at the papers scattered all over his desk. I wanted to stay and fight, but Gabriel was shaking his head discreetly. "I'll talk to him," he mouthed, and for a second the sun peeked through the storm clouds inside me.

Sometimes, despite what I knew about Gabriel, it seemed real.

I still felt dejected as I followed Riccardo out, Gabriel notwithstanding. Lucian, of course, didn't bother saying goodbye, not that I expected anything different from him.

Sweat was trickling down my back as Riccardo led me back through the building with what felt like a thousand eyes watching us as we walked. I always got hot when I was frustrated, and I absentmindedly slipped off my sweater to wrap it around my waist.

That was better.

We had made it to the elevators when I heard Gabriel's voice behind me. I turned to look at him questioningly.

"I convinced him that you should be able to at least volunteer at this animal shelter that my friend runs a couple of blocks from the penthouse. After things calm down, I think we can get you signed up for classes."

"Really? You were able to convince him of that?" My heart

was fluttering, this time not from nerves. It wasn't everything that I'd been asking for, but at least it was something. And maybe in the future...

If Lucian and I were going to be married in name only, I had to build a life for myself, and hopefully, this was the first step.

Gabriel's face appeared conflicted for a moment, but then he smiled.

"Want to start today?" he asked.

"Seriously? I would love that." It was all I could do not to run at him and leap into his arms, but with all the eyes watching us, I didn't think that would be wise.

Gabriel went down with us in the elevator to where the car was ready and waiting outside. It was amazing how smoothly the Rossi's life was run.

"I met Megan at one of those charity auctions where people purchase a date with a guy," Gabriel told me as we drove. "The organizers of the event thought they would make it special by having us walk out with dogs in hopes that the dogs would be adopted once we were picked for a date. Megan's the owner of the shelter we're headed to, and she had heard about me and thought that it would be hilarious for me to walk down the stage with a Chihuahua. The little shit barked the entire time that I was walking and had everyone in tears from laughing." He tapped his chin, his eyes sparkling with amusement at the memory. "You had to take the dog with you on the date, and it was a complete nightmare the entire time, which was really convenient since the woman who'd bought me was seventy-five years old and was trying to seduce me the entire time."

I giggled, and his eyes lit up like I'd given him a gift. I was beginning to think that I'd never laugh again, and yet here I was.

Gabriel seemed to have a gift for that. He was a silver lining among the dark clouds.

"So you and Megan became friends?" I tried to keep my voice nonchalant, but the smirk on Gabriel's face said he knew why I was asking.

"Just friends," he said with a wink, and something in my stomach settled. "Bellissima, if I didn't know better, I would say that you sound jealous."

I blushed and bit my bottom lip, but didn't answer him. Thankfully, before he could say anything else, we pulled in front of a nondescript three-story brown building. There was a large plaque above the door that read *New York's Animal Haven*.

Haven, I liked that word. I was hopeful that maybe this place could become a little haven for me, although I was trying to not get my hopes up. As we got out of the car and began to walk towards the door, Gabriel grabbed my hand. I should have pulled away, but there were a lot of things that I should've done differently since leaving London.

I kept my hand in his.

The musty scent of animals washed over us as we walked through the door. There was a small desk setup with a teenage girl seated behind it. She looked up as we walked in and squealed in excitement when she saw Gabriel. She flew around the desk and gave him a huge hug. "You haven't been here in forever. I was beginning to think that you'd forgotten about us," she exclaimed. She was a cute girl, with dark brown hair that she wore in a long braid down her back, and bright blue eyes that she couldn't take off Gabriel.

Looked like Gabriel had another admirer. He laughed and rubbed the top of her head, messing up her hair and causing her to loosen up the octopus hold she'd had around his waist so she could try and fix her hair.

"Now, how could I forget about you, Shelby Ray?" he said with a wink. I felt like I was watching a younger version of myself, because her face turned the same shade as a tomato.

I was pretty sure my face did that as well any time Gabriel Rossi flirted with me.

Shelby's attention flicked to me. "Is this your girlfriend?" she asked excitedly. "You've never brought a girl with you before."

Gabriel squeezed my hand, and a shadow blocked his smile. "She's a good friend," he answered, a little sadly.

I was happy that he hadn't told the truth. I don't know if I could deal with Gabriel introducing me as his sister-in-law.

A pretty woman who looked to be in her mid forties appeared in an entryway to the left of us. Her eyes sparkled when she saw Gabriel.

"Well, hello there, stranger," she said in a low voice. Unlike Shelby, who'd taken a minute to remove her gaze from Gabriel's perfect face, she immediately turned her attention to me. "And who do we have here?" she asked appraisingly.

"I'm Dahlia," I said, extending my hand. She shook my hand in a firm handshake.

"My, you're a doll. And that accent. I think I'm in love already," she cooed.

"Megan, stop flirting with the new volunteer I brought you," said Gabriel, clearly amused.

"You're interested in helping out?" Megan's eyes were glowing with excitement.

I nodded. "If you'll have me," I answered, looking to Gabriel for permission. But he was already nodding in agreement.

Shelby barged into the conversation. "We're always looking

for volunteers. We never have enough people. This is great!"

"When can you start?" Megan asked.

It's not like I was dressed fancy or anything, a fact I was now grateful for. "Can I start now?" I asked hesitantly.

Megan let out a whoop and nodded her head, looking much younger in that moment than the lines on her face suggested.

"Can I join you ladies?" Gabriel asked, and the three of us both stared at the very expensive-looking suit he was wearing.

"It's going to be a little messy in there," Megan began, but Gabriel was already taking off his suit coat, revealing a white shirt that showcased every delicious muscle in his arms. I was pretty sure Megan was a lesbian, and she was still drooling…as was Shelby…as was I.

We couldn't be blamed though. Gabriel was just too perfect.

Danger. Warning sign. Do not pass go. Alarms blared in my head as Gabriel took my hand again and we followed Megan through the doorway. I waved at Shelby Ray, who had to stay at the desk, and coughed out a laugh when I saw that she was totally checking out Gabriel's arse.

Excitement flitted through my veins as Megan began to show us around. It was loud back here. The dogs were barking, cats were meowing, and some birds in metal birdcages were definitely cussing us out.

I couldn't help but laugh when Megan stopped to feed one of the brightly colored parrots a treat and it promptly told her to "fuck off."

Megan looked back at us with a grin. "You can see why we're having trouble finding him a home," she said with a mock sigh. "Although he does liven up the place. It just gets a little dicey when we have younger volunteers and they go home knowing a whole new vocabulary."

I laughed again, and Gabriel let go of my hand and put his arm around my waist, pulling me towards him as he brushed a kiss across my head.

Megan was eyeing us knowingly, so I did my best to avoid her gaze.

She began the tour again, explaining some of the duties that we'd be helping out with—duties that included scooping up dog poop in the kennels and in the huge backyard area that was full of animals running around.

"How in the world did you find this much open land in New York City?" I gasped as I looked around a yard that must've been at least half an acre.

She pointed a thumb at Gabriel. "It's all thanks to Casanova here. This place used to have a tiny strip back here that could barely hold two animals at a time. He bought the building behind us, and the building next to that, and he had them demolished so that we could have this open area."

I looked up at Gabriel, who was now blushing, and I'm sure there were stars in my eyes.

I had thought that I had gotten to know Gabriel pretty well over those two weeks when we had spent every second together, but I was realizing now that we'd just touched the surface. There was so much more to Gabriel, and that was definitely a problem. Because the surface level information had been pretty great already, so this side of him…this side of him was devastating.

And dangerous.

After Megan had shown us the whole place, she gave us bags of food and instructed us to start feeding the animals. "Feel free to open the cages when you feed them and give them some love. It's hard for me to get to all of them in a day with everything else that needs to be done, so they'll go crazy over it."

I nodded happily and began to do just that. It was a good thing that I had a lot of extra time, because with how slow I was going while playing with the animals, I would probably need a ten-hour shift to actually get a lot of things done.

I'd always loved animals. I had a pet rabbit named Nibbles when I was a child. He had slept in a cage by my bed, and I'd let him out whenever I was in my room. One day I'd come into my room and saw Nibbles lying on my floor, all of his feet cut off and laid beside him. It had been a warning from *him*, what would happen if I ever said anything.

"Dahlia?" Gabriel asked, concerned. He crouched down next to me and tipped up my chin to look at him. "What were you thinking just then? Your face got scary pale, and you're trembling."

I forced a smile on my face, stroking the downy fur of the cat in my lap. "Just a memory, nothing major," I lied.

It was actually easy to shake off the memory in that place though as we went through the animals, giving them love. It was also hilarious, because I suspected that Gabriel had never actually held an animal before in his life. I had to tell him how to do it with each animal, and he looked delightfully awkward every time he held one.

There was one dog in particular that completely melted my heart. He was adorably ugly. His hair stuck up all over the place, a mottled gray color. Most people would probably just walk on by, but he looked so sad staring at me through the cage, not even lifting his head when I poured the food into his food bowl...I couldn't help but lift him out. He trembled under my touch and whined softly, looking up at me with soulful brown eyes that you couldn't help but fall in love with.

"He's...interesting looking," Gabriel chuckled, joining me and scratching the top of the dog's head.

The dog nuzzled into my arms. "You are a precious baby, do you know that? Such a good puppy." I grinned, belatedly realizing how ridiculous I sounded. I glanced up at Gabriel, thinking that he'd be laughing at me, but instead, it was heat that I saw in his gaze.

This was ridiculous. I was in the middle of a dog shelter, and arousal was licking my insides. I gulped and turned my attention back to the dog, reluctantly putting him back. "I'll see you soon, buddy," I whispered to him, and the dog stared at me lovingly. That was what you had to love about animals—they loved you without reason, unconditionally. You couldn't find that anywhere else.

We stayed there for hours. Megan was in and out of the area where we were working, telling us funny stories about some of the pets. And yes, we did scoop a lot of poop. As we left the animal shelter with promises to come back the next day, I couldn't remember when I'd felt that happy.

"You're glowing, bellissima," he murmured once we were back in the car, his thumb softly stroking my hand.

I leaned back against my seat, a small smile on my lips. "Thank you. That was...perfect."

Gabriel was watching me avidly. "Thank you for giving me that."

I cocked my head. "Giving you what?"

"A piece of you," he answered.

I sighed and snuggled into the soft leather of my seat.

Spending this much time with Gabriel was going to either heal me...or kill me.

And I was betting it would be the latter.

NINETEEN

The next week, I walked through the elevator doors into the penthouse, content and exhausted. I was loving my work at the shelter. Megan and Shelby Ray were fast becoming my good friends, and I didn't think there was anything better than getting to work with the animals.

It definitely wasn't glamorous work—I did not smell good right now—but I didn't care. I was actually…happy, something that I didn't think I'd ever be in this city.

Gabriel came every chance that he could, but that wasn't very often since there continued to be trouble. I hadn't gotten many details; I only knew that things, and people, were disappearing. It was stressing them all out.

I heard the sound of raised voices in the living room, and I hesitantly walked that way, wondering what was happening. When I got to the entrance of the living room, I saw that Lucian and Raphael were arguing. As soon as I came into view, their shouts abruptly cut off.

"What's going on?" I asked, eyeing them suspiciously. Lucian had still been ignoring me. I don't know that I'd exchanged more than two words with him since that scene in his office where I'd demanded to get out of the penthouse. I hated to admit it, but my heart rate kicked up just being in the same room as him. Every time I saw him, I was still stunned by his beauty, his body, and just how crazily sexy he was. Raphael standing next to him was almost too much for my traitorous body to handle. They were like two sides of a coin—one dark, one light—both cut from the same cloth…total bastards.

"We got another box from your admirer," Raphael said, gesturing toward the box that was sitting on the coffee table. His voice was calm, but there was tension all over his angelic features.

"You think these are aimed at me?" I asked, dread crawling across my skin even though I'd already started to suspect that.

"I certainly wasn't receiving gifts like these before you came around, principessa," Lucian tossed at me sarcastically.

My face flushed with annoyance.

Resisting the urge to bite his head off, or start throwing knives, I walked toward the box.

"Dahlia, I don't think—" Lucian began. But I just ignored him, my fingers trembling as I lifted the lid and promptly gagged.

In the box was a long golden braid, which might not have been that bad…if there hadn't still been a human scalp attached to the hair. I couldn't comprehend the pain that the poor woman experienced while this happened. I was shivering as I spotted a note next to the braid. I had just gone to reach for it when Lucian grabbed onto my wrist before I could touch it. I looked up at him questioningly, definitely not thinking about the last time he'd grabbed my wrist...

"Use these," he demanded, handing me a pair of kitchen tongs that had been on the sofa. "We're going to check for fingerprints, and I don't want anyone else's on them."

Oh, that made sense. They didn't bother stopping me this time as I carefully picked up the note with the tongs. The note read:

Rapunzel, Rapunzel, let down your hair. Or I'll...cut it all off.

Well, that didn't seem quite as foreboding as the others, but this was definitely the worst package we'd received so far. Gabriel had told me about the rotten apple one.

I wrapped my arms around myself, my mind churning as I thought about who this could be.

My thoughts immediately flicked to *him*, but this didn't seem like his style. I couldn't think about the possibility that he'd followed me to New York. My mind wasn't strong enough to be able to deal with that.

"This bastard's going to die." Lucian's voice was a sexy growl with an underlying intensity that was as alarming as it was comforting.

"Where did you find the box? Did one of the doormen bring it up here again?" They both went eerily silent, and dread trickled up my spine. "The person was in here, wasn't he?" I whispered shakily.

Whoever had done this had gotten in our flat.

"Don't we have security? How the fuck did they get in here?" My voice was practically a shriek, my fingers pressing into my patch of scars. It wasn't giving me enough pain though. I hadn't cut myself since the day of the wedding, and that cut had long since healed.

I hated this place. Looking around it now, it felt like monsters could be hiding in all the corners. And they seemed far scarier than the two monsters standing in front of me.

"We're doubling up security. There will be a top-of-the-line fingerprint and retina scanner to get up here from now on that will only be keyed to the four of us and the staff that we trust," Lucian said...almost soothingly.

I nodded, trying to find some reassurance in that, but it was quickly becoming clear that there were some holes in the Cosa Nostra organization. And whoever was hiding in those holes was definitely not someone I wanted to meet.

"Raphael, I have a few more things we need to talk about," Lucian threw at Raphael, walking towards the office without checking to see if he was following him, and of course not offering me a backward glance.

I looked over at Raphael, and he was staring at Lucian's back, something calculating in his gaze. After a second, he seemed to remember that I was still standing there and his attention went back to me.

The intensity of his stare made me fidget. He stared at me like he was imagining me naked...and he knew exactly what I looked like.

"I haven't seen you very much," I told him, a little squeak in my voice.

A smirk lit up Raphael's face at my awkwardness, that sexy, mischievous look that drove me nuts.

He began to walk in the direction that Lucian had headed. "Oh, but I've seen you, angel," he said mysteriously, and then he disappeared around the corner.

RAPHAEL

It was nice to have some idea of who to kill. Riccardo had accessed the cameras across the street that were pointed directly at our building. Usually we made sure that they weren't on for obvious reasons, but when the first package had arrived, I'd directed our tech guys to turn them back on for some extra security. It had been useful since our first pass through the lobby footage hadn't shown anything suspicious. We'd been able to track the bastard from when he'd gotten out of a black BMW with a dead man's license plate, all the way through the lobby.

The man had been sharply dressed in a suit, fitting right in with our usual guests. He'd been carrying the box that had been left in the entrance of the penthouse. It had taken a few hours, but our tech team had realized that someone had done something to the screens in the security room so that the footage was running on a loop, showing a scene from earlier in the day. But the cameras themselves, they still had the unaltered footage from the day.

After that, we could track him in the lobby and see how he'd waved at Lorenzo. Lorenzo, of course, being the good employee that he was, had immediately waved him over, pushing his suit coat back so the man could see his gun. We hadn't been able to hear the conversation, but Lorenzo had picked up the phone at his station and called someone.

Whatever the person on the phone had said, it was enough for him to release the man without checking his box and allow him to walk back towards the elevators. The elevator camera recorded him for just a split second until someone had hacked into the camera and put up a video of an empty car. The camera had flickered for a split second, but our security team was trained to watch for signs of hacking, and they'd completely missed it.

Whoever we were fighting had cut through our top-of-the-line security measures like they were butter.

There were so many things that had gone wrong across the board with our security that I was looking forward to killing every single one of them.

The weird thing was that the cameras in the penthouse, which were hardwired so they couldn't be hacked, showed that the man had stepped out of the elevator and looked around with a creepy grin on his face, and then he'd dropped the box on the floor and went back down. Emilia had walked out of the kitchen right as the doors were closing, and she'd completely missed him, only seeing the box.

"Did Lorenzo say who he'd talked to on the phone?" I asked Lucian, who was staring out the window, looking at the cityscape. For someone who didn't know him, they would think he looked relaxed. But seeing as I'd had ample time to study and learn all his mannerisms, I could see the stress layered on his shoulders.

Sure enough, a moment later, he picked up a crystal vase and launched it at the TV on the wall, completely destroying both.

"That bad?"

He glared at me, his patience running thin. The sight made me deliriously happy because of what was underlying his dark mood. It didn't have much to do with the security breach, or that his empire was being threatened...it had to do with *her*.

He hadn't fucked Dahlia yet. I knew that because he could barely look at her without going white as a sheet, and she looked just as frustrated every time she glanced at him. Plus, I'd obviously had first-hand experience with what a man looked like after being inside Dahlia, and Lucian was not it.

I probably had a Joker's grin on my face, but he was blind like always when it came to me.

"Lorenzo said that he dialed my cell phone, and someone that sounded exactly like me picked up the phone and approved the visitor. He said that I had told him that I was looking at the cameras right then, and that he was a business associate I'd invited over to meet my new wife." Lucian's jaw twitched, and I was pretty sure there was a vein popping out of his forehead. Dude needed a Xanax or something.

I probably would have made fun of him more, but this lapse in security was bothering me too.

Not because I was worried about myself, though. I dared anyone to try and fuck and with me.

But because of her.

Dahlia was ruining everything.

I'd never been like my brother Gabriel, who was in and out of his latest obsession at all times. I didn't get obsessed with anyone, because I didn't care about anyone. The only emotions that I really ever felt were hate and anger.

Until her.

I'd been watching her, every second that I could. I would sneak into her bedroom at night, watching her chest rise and fall, just needing to assure myself that she was there. I bugged her phone so that when she was away from the penthouse, I could listen to her talk.

When I saw the world, I saw black fumes that killed everything they touched. And then she stormed into my life and became an opportunity that I thought I couldn't pass up.

But somewhere along the way, I'd gotten addicted to her

shade of sunshine. Somewhere along the way, I'd gotten addicted to her laugh, her smile, the darkness in her gaze that made me wonder if she could understand mine.

And under the current circumstances, that was about as inconvenient as you could get. Before I met her, I'd only fucked for a release. Their faces, and certainly their names, forgotten the moment we were done.

The plane ride was supposed to be a game, a way to get back at my asshole brother who destroyed everything that he touched.

So why did it seem like *I* was suddenly the game?

I hadn't ever been as turned on as I was standing behind her, watching that bloodstained angel in the mirror. I'd stolen her bloody thigh-high that I knew she wouldn't leave on despite my instructions, and they were now covered in my cum.

The problem for Dahlia was that I didn't want to love her. I didn't want to make her happy. I just wanted to wrap her so tightly under my skin that she couldn't breathe unless I let her. I wanted to hurt her, to ruin her. I wanted her angel blue eyes shiny with tears.

I wanted to own her in a way that I'd never owned anything else.

It was just a bonus that by ruining her, I would also ruin him.

"You need to start working with her in the gym," Lucian ordered. It never entered into his mind that the last thing he should want was to have me in close proximity to his wife. "I think she has some fighting skills—she at least knows how to throw a punch. But that's not enough. Things are just going to escalate...and I want her to be prepared." I could see the yearning in his gaze. I'd never met someone who was such a fucking masochist.

"How long do you think you're going to be able to keep up

the iceman routine?" I asked casually, examining the blood that I needed to get out from under my fingernails. Wouldn't want to get sloppy.

"What are you talking about?"

"I just would've assumed that you would be the one training her. It's a funny thing, you and Dahlia don't seem to be enjoying your little honeymoon period..." No sooner had I said that than he was slamming me against the wall, his hand wrapped around my throat and rage drenching his skin. "I'd be very careful if I were you, brother. She's the only woman I would kill for, and you wouldn't want to be on the receiving end of that."

I let out a choked laugh and winked at him, and he punched me in the fucking face, right in the eye. Blood dripped from my split eyebrow, trailing down my face until it hit my lips and I could lick it off savagely.

Lucian shook his head in disgust. "You're a fucking lunatic," he muttered, releasing my throat. I just smirked at him again.

"I'll train your little *principessa*," I said sarcastically. "I'm sure she needs all the help she can get."

He growled at me like a caged animal and prowled away.

Time to have some fun. It would be nice to be able to watch her face-to-face, instead of from the shadows.

DAHLIA

I was lying in my bed, caught between the dream world and the real one, in that space you exist in when you're just starting to wake up. Something soft was dancing over my skin, and I moaned softly at the sensation.

Until I woke up enough to realize that the "something" was someone's fingers.

I shrieked and sat up, my pulse racing. I moved to jump out of the bed, and a pair of strong arms wrapped around me and held me down.

The world started to darken as panic coursed through my body, and I was flipped to my back.

"Dahlia," a voice barked, and the edge of violence in his tone pushed away some of the anxiety enough to realize that it was Raphael hovering over me.

"What are you doing here?" I gasped hoarsely. He just grinned at me, a golden tendril falling in his face.

"What was that?"

"What was what?"

"You just freaked out way more than was called for," he commented, raising an eyebrow.

I wanted to scratch off his face. The arsehole. I tried to push him off and sit up, but he easily maneuvered me onto my back, pulling my knees up so that my feet were flat on the bed. His large, hard body covered mine as he settled between my legs, caging me between his strong, tattooed forearms. I could feel his hard cock pressing against me.

"What's it feel like, Dahlia? Knowing that I could do anything I wanted to you right now." His voice was dark with sharp edges, and my breath came out in gasps, like I was forgetting how to breathe. His hands closed around my wrists, and he pulled them together so he could secure them with one hand.

Raphael leaned forward, and his breath tickled my skin. There was plenty of fear flooding my body, but perversely, there was also plenty of lust.

"Anything I wanted," he murmured. His eyes were dark,

determined…crazy. He let go of my hands to lift my legs above his shoulders. I felt paralyzed, a butterfly caught in a spider's web, just watching its impending death approach.

He held my gaze, then he abruptly bit the skin on my inner thigh, a sharp sting flooding me as my core gushed. Because if there was one thing that I knew I loved, it was pain mixed with pleasure. Raphael lifted my arse up and pressed his nose against my weeping sex, nothing between his lips but my paper-thin knickers. Served me right for not wearing sweats to bed, but it had been so fucking hot in my room I'd just put on a t-shirt over my knickers last night before climbing in.

Filthy, obscene noises vibrated from his chest as he scraped his light stubble across my inner thighs, rubbing it deliberately across my clit. Part of me just wanted to say "fuck it" and demand that he make me cum. Thankfully, the rational part of my brain came through. Without warning, I locked my legs around his neck and twisted so that he was thrown off me and I was now on top.

He looked shocked, but his pupils were so blown out from arousal you could barely see the ring of light blue that normally surrounded them.

"I could get used to this position, angel."

I scrambled off of him as fast as I could, my body feeling so hot and flushed that I would've thought I had a fever in any other circumstance.

I really wanted someone to explain to me how the devil could look so fucking sexy. He was on his side now, his arm under his head, propping it up. His hair was everywhere like I'd been pulling at it as he slid into me. The sun coming in from the window was kissing his skin, and that arrogant look on his face that spoke true possession…the package was all too much.

I really needed to figure out a way to get another lock for my door. Although, was there a lock in existence that the criminals in this house wouldn't be able to get through?

Belatedly I realized that he was dressed in a white t-shirt and a pair of loose workout shorts. I'd never seen him in anything so casual.

My jaw literally dropped as he moved to his back and pushed his shorts down to reveal his beautiful, hard cock.

I watched as if in a trance as his thumb and his finger circled the base. He was biting his bottom lip, pure sex in his gaze, as he began to stroke himself.

His strokes were slow... measured. Glistening cum was dripping down the swollen head, and my eyes devoured the rigid veins standing out on his length. His heated eyes were focused on me, watching me watch him. His strokes began to speed up, and I hated that my mouth was actually watering, desperate to lick up all of his cum.

"Fuck," I murmured, getting ahold of my senses and running into the closet. The temptation to put my hands down my pants and touch myself was overwhelming. I could just picture in my head that thick cock stretching me. Even in the closet, I could hear the sounds of his soft gasps as he continued to take care of himself...on my bed. I was going to have to burn my sheets after this. Maybe my bed too.

A low, sexy groan found me in the closet as he came. I felt like I was underwater, drowning in lust. My spank bank had certainly just been filled, probably for the rest of my life.

This was certainly not how I'd expected the morning to go.

What was happening? The lines were becoming so blurred. Between Lucian not wanting anything to do with me, Gabriel trying to be my Prince Charming, and Raphael trying to kill me with temptation, my head was spinning. Raphael suddenly appeared in the doorway, leaning against it, his cheeks flushed, and his gaze satisfied.

He still had a tent in his shorts.

"Get dressed, buttercup. You're with me today."

My eyes widened. "What's that supposed to mean?" I asked, my voice definitely coming out panicked.

"His lordship has demanded that I work you out a little bit." The innuendo was so thick it was almost laughable, or at least it would've been if my knickers weren't soaking wet.

This was a lot for me to handle. Every single thing about Raphael was designed to push me to the edge.

"I'm good working myself out," I answered, very much aware of my own response. His eyes glimmered in amusement.

"I'm going to teach you some self-defense skills. Make sure that when the next big and bad comes after us, you can fuck him up until we get there."

"Oh," I said, thinking about it. It had been a while since I'd done any training like that. Church had sparred with me as often as he could once Benny had gone to prison. But I doubted Raphael remembered me talking about that on the plane.

This could be fun.

"I'll be right out," I told him. He, of course, didn't move an inch.

I scoffed and turned away, lifting my shirt up slowly, smiling to myself when I heard his low growl.

I reached into my drawer and pulled out a sports bra. I had it halfway on when suddenly he was there, standing right behind me, his hands slowly trailing down my stomach. My arms were caught in my sports bra, and I hadn't pulled it over my breasts yet which meant that I was just hanging out.

This is what I got for playing with fire.

His hands trailed up my skin, and then he was palming my breasts, his thumbs swiping over my pert nipples. Everything in my body was clenching.

And then he abruptly released me, striding out of the closet and leaving me a shaking mess.

"See you in the gym in ten, angel," he murmured huskily, and then he was gone.

I couldn't help it. I'd think about everything that had just happened in a little while, I was sure. Shame and confusion pulsed through me, but right now, I needed a release. I was going to jump him if I stepped one foot into that gym. I pulled my knickers away from my body and slipped my finger over my soaked core. I circled my finger around my clit, gasping with how swollen and tender it felt. I closed my eyes, picturing him on the bed, and sharp pleasure sparked through me at the image. My finger slipped through my folds, and I pushed two fingertips inside, desperately wishing I had something more substantial. I pushed in deeper, working my fingers in and out of my sex, my other hand coming up to grip my breasts, my fingers trying to mimic Raphael's touch. My hips were moving, desperately seeking friction. And right there in the closet, I brought myself to orgasm thinking about my brother-in-law.

How was this my fucking life?

I quickly pulled on my sports bra and changed my soaked knickers, my body still strung so tight with lust that I could've easily gone for a second one. Thankfully, I was able to have a little bit of self-control and continue getting dressed.

Pulling on some spandex shorts and a loose tee, I went to the bathroom and splashed water on my face until it felt like I was in danger of waterboarding myself.

As the lust faded, fury and shame replaced it. Obviously, I could've stopped what happened, but I hated the games he was playing, and the way my body so desperately wanted to play them with him.

My father had women on the side. It was the mafia man's way, after all. My mum had turned a blind eye to it. They had seemed happy enough when they were together, but I wanted nothing to do with that type of relationship.

Of course, that was just wishful thinking. Lucian's face as he came in that whore's mouth popped in my head. He was probably fucking a different girl every night.

He certainly wasn't getting anything from me.

But here I was, not any better.

I'd never had any intention of playing the domicile mafia wife who looked the other way at my husband's indiscretions. But I'd also never thought I'd be the one with the indiscretions.

That look in Lucian's eyes when he'd told me he couldn't do this...

This was a total clusterfuck. When did I become this person? One moment I was a virgin, and the next I was getting myself off in the closet.

I lifted my head up from the sink and looked in the mirror, surprised at the way my eyes were sparkling, blush in my cheeks. I looked alive. That was rare.

I was tempted to grab my razor, but I knew if I took too long, Raphael would be back in here, and I didn't want a repeat of the last time he'd caught me.

Let's just say that anything that included Raphael in my bedroom was a terrible, terrible idea.

I headed across the hall, through another long hallway where the gym was kept. I stopped short when I got to the doorway and saw Raphael doing pull-ups on a metal bar, his shirt tucked into the back of his pants, his muscles straining and clenching. Lust pooled in my belly as I took in his perfect body. I already needed a new pair of knickers. This wasn't off to a great start.

It was official. He was trying to kill me. At this point, I almost wanted Lucian to walk in and just put me out of my misery.

Okay. I had self-control. I could do this. I just needed to picture him on the sidewalk at the airport that day as he'd walked away from me. The image was so real I could hear his demonic whistling echoing in my ears.

And just like that, the lust disappeared.

No problem.

Raphael finished his pull-ups and dropped down from the bar easily, not out of breath at all.

"Get on the treadmill for a minute and warm up, and then we'll stretch before you begin," he ordered. The demand in his voice was offset by the way his gaze was dancing all over my body, and I shook my head in annoyance before trotting over to one of the treadmills.

If Raphael wanted to play games, then I'd play them. I put the treadmill on a low setting, not wanting him to know that I could literally almost full out sprint for miles and miles without getting tired. After fifteen minutes, he came up beside me and motioned for me to turn off the treadmill. I pretended to be out of breath as the tread slowed down, and I stepped off, putting my hands on my knees.

"Looks like we have a lot of work to do on your conditioning," Raphael commented as he walked over to the large mat in the corner. I followed him and began to stretch. There were long mirrors on all the walls, and I kept one eye on him as I bent over to stretch out my right leg.

I heard a tsking sound and then Raphael was next to me. "Give me your hands," he commanded, and I looked up at him questioningly. He held out his hands, insistent, and I reluctantly reached up. He closed his fingers around my wrists and pulled me towards him.

And then there was no way around it. Raphael did his best to break me. Oh, he stretched me out good, but along the way his hands slid along my muscles, my curves, over my breasts, my core, as he stretched me in a million different positions. He didn't say a word. The only sound in the room was our heavy breathing. My body was completely flushed with arousal, and I was doing my best not to moan.

When he finished, I was certainly stretched out, my muscles warm and ready for anything, but especially for him to throw me to the ground and fuck me in a million different positions.

Airport, Dahlia. Remember the airport, I reminded myself as he stood up and walked over to a shelf where several boxing gloves were stacked.

"Let's practice some punching."

I nodded, rolling my neck to get out some of the tension.

I let him help me put the gloves on since, obviously, he thought that I had no idea what I was doing.

He took a stance in front of me, and I deliberately put my hands in all the wrong positions. Surprisingly, he didn't act frustrated at all. Instead, he used the moment to touch me again and move my arms to their proper place. Fuck, maybe my plan wasn't the best one after all.

"You want to turn your whole body into the punch," he explained, as he slowly moved his body to show me. "Especially for a girl; you need to use your whole body instead of just your arms to punch as you're not going to have as much power in your arms when you come up against a guy. Let's work on a few combinations."

He began to lead me through some punch combos, and I followed along like I'd never heard any of this before in my life. When he started lecturing about the correct breathing technique though, I definitely began to daydream.

"Am I boring you?" he snapped, annoyed. Of course he was. I bit my tongue and reluctantly nodded, and started paying attention again.

"I think I'm ready to try some of this for real," I suggested.

Raphael looked unsure of my request. "Maybe we should just focus on fundamentals today."

"No, let's do it."

He rolled his eyes and then walked across the room, over to the ring that was in another corner. This gym was huge, literally everything that you could ever want.

"You want to put some headgear on?" I asked casually.

He didn't try to hide his chuckle. "I think I'll be okay."

I shrugged and heaved myself over the ropes, trying to descend into that headspace that Benny and Church had ingrained in my head, when nothing else mattered but the kill.

One of the biggest shames of my life was not being able to defend myself when it mattered, but at least I could do it in here.

I started out slow, throwing a few jabs that Raphael easily avoided. He shouted out things for me to try, and I played along until I was sure that I'd gotten him right where I wanted.

I feigned towards his chin and then landed a blow on Raphael's ribs. 'A spark of surprise lit up his blue gaze.

"Nice shot, angel."

I nodded, and then before he could say anything, I launched a follow-up, a hook to Raphael's cheekbone.

"Fuck," he hissed as he rubbed his face. He looked confused for a moment, and then his eyes lit up like I'd just shown him his favorite dirty fantasy. "Oh, Dahlia. This is going to be good. Maybe instead of 'angel', I should be calling you 'little liar'."

"I did tell you on the plane this was one of my hobbies," I reminded him.

"I'd obviously forgotten," he chuckled.

I grinned savagely, and then we actually began to spar. At first, he was still holding back, but as time went on, he stopped pulling punches. I was able to block most of his hits, but there were definitely some that got through, and after thirty minutes, my ribs were aching and I could taste blood in my mouth. He rushed me and I swayed back and then came at him with a swift punch straight to his body, catching him off-balance enough that I could follow it up with an uppercut to his jaw.

And just like he'd instructed, I made sure to put my whole body into it.

His head snapped back, and he fell to his knees, a dazed look in his eyes as he collapsed to the mat, I'm sure seeing stars.

I watched him, savoring the sight for a moment.

But then he abruptly pounced at me, scooping me up and laying me down on the floor before I could do anything. His hands slid along my shorts and then up underneath my shirt.

I panted as I laid there, my core absolutely flooding as I took in his sculpted chest. There was a sheen of sweat on his skin that only further highlighted every muscle.

"I'm not fucking playing around anymore. I have to get inside you." His voice had a desperate edge to it that I'd never quite heard before.

"Going to own you, angel. There's not a place on your body that my cock, my fingers…my tongue isn't going to touch."

I was a quivering mess under his words. My body was literally aching as my legs fell shamelessly open.

His lips caught mine in a kiss that sent sparks shooting across my heart, jumpstarting it to life. His tongue slid into my mouth, hot and wet. Tasting, then devouring. Aggressive, deep licks like he was imagining himself fucking me right that minute. And I could feel every one of those licks in my aching insides.

A whimper slipped out of me, and I found myself sucking eagerly on his tongue. I gripped his hair, mindless in need as I tried to pull him against me.

A deep groan came from his chest as he deepened the kiss, cradling my head in his hand and holding me in place as he devoured my mouth. His other hand stroked my thigh and hips, kneading my breasts possessively like he owned me. Everything in me was clenching; the tension building between us with nothing more than the deep thrust of his tongue, and those hands that weren't leaving any part of me untouched. My fingers dug into his shoulder so violently that I was sure I'd leave marks. Just the thought of marking this delicious bastard had arousal heating my blood almost to a boiling point.

A throat cleared nearby, and both of us froze. Something glimmered in Raphael's eyes as he looked up towards the doorway to the room.

I didn't need to look up to see who it was. I knew it was Lucian by the overwhelming energy filling the room, an energy that sent electric sparks hissing against my skin that only added to the tension swirling inside of me.

Raphael slid off me easily and stood up. "Hello, brother," he gloated.

I took a deep breath and then stumbled to my feet, finally looking over to where Lucian was leaning against the wall. How long had he been there? How much had he seen before deciding to let us know he was there?

I expected to see the fury in Lucian's gaze. But what I didn't expect, was to see the dark hunger. To see the way his huge package was tenting his tailored suit pants. To see the way his chest was rising and falling rapidly, and the slight flush to his cheeks.

He was turned on. Not just turned on, he was wildly aroused from watching me with Raphael.

That was…unexpected.

Lucian's gaze shot fire at me, like he was trying to hold himself back from grabbing me and taking me for himself.

His gaze finally flicked away from me and moved on to his brother. Raphael was standing there, his body rigid, like he was waiting for Lucian to attack.

Lucian slowly began to walk towards us, the silence unnerving.

I wasn't sure what to say. He'd told me he didn't want me. He wouldn't go near me. I thought I'd feel some kind of shame, but there was nothing. Lucian took out his gun from where he'd had it tucked in his pants, and without warning shot at Raphael. The bullet grazed his leg, and the sound echoed around the room and rang in my ear.

"Fuck," Raphael roared.

"Lucian." My voice came out in a hoarse whisper, my eyes wide with what had just happened. He turned towards me, the gun still in his hand.

"I told you I couldn't be what you needed," he finally said. "So, you can have my brothers." He stalked out of the room, and all the adrenaline seemed to leave my body with him.

I fell to my arse, my mind in a fog, not quite comprehending what had just happened.

I finally looked over at Raphael who was examining the gash in his skin where the bullet had grazed by and embedded into something behind us.

"Well, that went well," he said lightly.

"He missed you on purpose."

Raphael nodded. His face looked conflicted, and emotions that I couldn't name whirled in his eyes. I hopped to my feet and hurried out of the room, Raphael making no attempt to stop me.

Lucian was standing in the entryway in front of the elevators when I made it to that point, and our eyes locked.

Hot jealousy that he'd hid in the gym was visible in that moment, the tension rolling off of him so tangible I could taste it. He grabbed me and pulled me towards him until my breasts were crushed against his hard chest.

"This is mine," he growled suddenly, reaching his hand between our bodies and rubbing my clit feverishly, quickly finding the right amount of pressure. His other fingers were pinching and tugging at my nipple roughly, and soon I was writhing against him shamelessly, mewling as the sharp mix of pain and pleasure shot to my core. His talented fingers continued to press and rub, and finally my pussy clenched and pulsed as I came wildly.

I whimpered again, so caught off-balance with what had happened. He leaned in close, so close that his lips danced across my skin. "No matter what you do, I'll always own you. Don't ever forget that."

He released me then, and I almost collapsed to the floor, my legs feeling like rubber after my orgasm. Lucian strode towards the elevator and quickly disappeared behind the doors.

Everything was a blur as I made it to my room and heaved myself onto my bed, tightly grasping my pillow that I belatedly realized smelled like Raphael.

It felt like I was bracing for the impact. I was standing on a cliff, and they were all trying to push me over the edge. And I knew that when I eventually fell over, none of them were going to be there to save me.

TWENTY

LUCIAN

"**F**uck," Gabriel hissed as he turned on the kitchen light and saw me sitting at the bar, holding a bottle of scotch.
He eyed the bottle. "Rough night?"

I shrugged, intent on being the ultimate morose bastard. I just needed a minute, one fucking minute away from the sudden chaos that my life had become.

Everywhere I turned, there was something else to deal with. The strikes on our supply chain were increasing. The whole group of men that I would've sworn on my life were loyal to me had disappeared in the wind. My father was showing up at my office almost daily. And I'd been fucking nothing but my hand since my wedding night. Not to mention that I'd given my brothers the green light to fuck the woman I wanted more than anything.

I took another giant swig of my drink, savoring the burn.

What I really needed was a line of coke and three whores willing to do whatever I wanted for five days straight.

My body went mutinous just at the thought of me betraying Dahlia. She was like an infection, slowly spreading through my insides, transforming me into someone I didn't recognize. Someone weak. Someone who could lose the empire that my family had spent the last hundred years building.

Gabriel slid a plate of food towards me that I hadn't even realized he was heating up.

"Eat. You look like the walking dead. When was the last time you did anything to take care of yourself?"

I searched Gabriel's eyes for any hidden agenda, but all I saw bleeding out of them was concern.

My shoulders dropped as a little bit of the tension I was carrying leaked out of me, like air out of a balloon.

"I don't know," I muttered. I reached for the fork that he'd just set beside my plate, and as I moved, I felt the back seams of my suit ripping.

Perfect.

"Cazzo," I muttered as I slipped off the jacket to look at it. In the absence of any…outlets, and the absence of sleep, I'd been working out in the early morning for hours, and all of my suits were beginning to get tight with the new muscles that I'd been packing on.

"You're beginning to look like the 'He-Man'," Gabriel teased, and I rolled my eyes. I attempted to eat a few bites of the food that Emilia had prepared earlier for us to warm up, but it might as well have been sawdust. I finally just set my fork down.

"How is she?" The words slipped from my mouth, a chaos of emotions writhing inside me. My world was burning around me, yet the only thing that I seemed to be able to focus on was her.

Was she happy? Was she eating? Did she need anything? We hadn't had any more surprise deliveries thanks to the overhaul and security, but I still found myself checking the cameras in this place multiple times throughout the day to see what she was doing. And to see who she was with…

Gabriel didn't have to ask me who I was talking about. His obsession seemed to have leaked into me, and now it was raging in both of us. No end in sight.

"She seems okay. Maybe a little quieter than usual. She's still liking working at the shelter. They can make her laugh." I read the hidden meaning in his words. Laughter was something that I definitely didn't bring her.

"That's good," I said, pushing my plate away and going back to my liquor bottle.

Gabriel shifted uneasily and I sighed. I braced myself for whatever he was going to say.

"You should tell her, Lucian."

I gritted my teeth, knowing exactly what he was talking about. To delay the conversation, I threw back the bottle and drank enough that my eyes watered. "It wouldn't make a difference."

"Cazzo, Lucian. You don't think she would care that it was your idea for her to work at the shelter in the first place? That you were the one who arranged that wedding? That all the things that have been delivered to her room have been things that you've picked out based on things you've found out about her? You fucking idiot." He threw up his hands in disgust. "Of course that would matter to her."

I was already shaking my head before he finished. He didn't understand. "I walked into the gym last week. Raphael was all over Dahlia."

My dick was hard just thinking about it. The fucking traitor. I'd watched for far too long, resisting the urge to strip and join them, and to sandwich Dahlia in between us as we worked together to make her scream.

"He was all over her? Like how?" Gabriel's tense voice cut into the porn that was streaming in my head.

"What do you think? He was seconds away from stripping her bare and fucking her right there on the floor," I hissed. Gabriel was shaking, gritting his teeth. "Why does that upset you? I'm sure you've been close as well. Or have you already crossed that line? I know our father didn't teach us to share, but it seems like that's the direction we're heading with this clusterfuck."

"The better question is, why doesn't that upset you, Lucian?"

I stiffened in my seat. Maybe my enemies would label me some kind of cuckold, but in my head, it didn't feel like that. It felt like because of *my* demons, I had nothing to offer Dahlia, especially not in a sexual way. How would she feel if I told her that I wanted to tie up her arms and legs and gag her? Blindfold her and stuff a huge dildo up her ass while I fucked her. And no matter what I did to her, she'd never be able to touch me.

She was too good for that. Too good for me. There was nothing that I could do to change.

I was willing to do whatever it took to make her happy, even if it felt like I'd been doused in gasoline and set on fire.

"I don't understand," Gabriel said shaking his head. "You've fucked a million women. Now you can't?"

I was silent. We might've been brothers, but there was so much that he didn't know, so much that I'd shielded him from.

He pushed his hand through his hair anxiously. "I don't know what you're not telling me, brother. But I do know that if you change your mind, it'll be too late. I won't be able to let her go."

That truth hovered in the air, and I suspected if Raphael was actually honest that she wasn't just a game in a way to hurt me, he'd feel the same way.

"It's not going to happen," I said, grabbing my bottle and wandering back towards my bedroom where I'd probably spend the rest of the night drinking alone in the dark before I gave up on sleeping and worked off the alcohol in the gym.

Fuck my life.

DAHLIA

He was holding me down. A dirty sock was stuffed in my mouth as his fingers trailed over my skin.

"No. Please. Just kill me," I shrieked.

"Dahlia," an urgent voice ripped through the darkness, and my uncle froze like he could hear the voice too.

"Dahlia. Wake up!" The dream vanished just as I was hauled into a pair of strong arms. Lucian's scent invaded my senses, pushing away the disgust and leaving only…him. I was trembling in his arms, the nightmare trying to suck me back in. His hands were stroking my hair, and he was pressing kisses to my forehead.

"You're safe. Nothing's ever going to happen to you. It's okay, sweetheart," he murmured.

"It always seems so real," I whispered, and I must've been screaming in my sleep because my voice felt scratchy, and it hurt to talk.

"I've got you," he murmured soothingly. I was fully in his lap, his arms enveloping me, making me truly feel safe. The worst thing about what happened was that I'd had years of abuse, and then I'd had nightmares almost every night since then, like the abuse had never stopped. I felt like he was always going to have a hold on me. Always.

I didn't know if I could live with that.

After who knows how long, when my shaking had eased a bit, Lucian lifted me off his lap and settled me into my pillows. The lamp on the far side of my room was on, but it was dim. And the little bit of light made his eyes glimmer like stars above me as he stared. His thumb was softly rubbing my cheek, and I leaned into the feeling of it, needing it to ground me. Because if I got hold of a razor right now, I didn't know that there would be a part of my body that was untouched.

"Are you going to be okay?" he asked as he moved to get off the bed.

"Stay," I murmured, desperation thick in my voice. The word hung between us, and I felt frozen in place as I waited to see what he would do.

To my surprise, he nodded and then moved so that he was lying behind me. He slipped his arm under my head so I was using him as a pillow, and he slid towards me until our bodies were plastered together. It felt like a dream, because Lucian didn't make me feel safe. Lucian didn't make me feel like I wasn't alone, and that he'd slay anyone who tried to hurt me. Lucian wasn't the prince in my happily ever after.

But right now, he felt like all of those things. And I don't know why I did it. I don't know if it was because the dream was even worse than normal and I felt like throwing up. But I did it. I opened my mouth, and I told him my truth.

"My uncle began sneaking into my room when I was a little girl. He would hide in all different sorts of places, getting off on my terror. The first place he hid was my closet, the proverbial bogeyman. At first, he was just coming to the edge of my bed, and he would stroke my hair. And then it escalated from there. Until he knew my body far better than I knew it."

Lucian was stiff as a board behind me. I could feel the slight tremble he was trying to hold back. But he didn't say anything, he just let me keep talking.

"He told me he would kill everyone in my family, and at first I didn't believe him. I thought I could get help. But then things started to happen. He cut off the feet of my favorite pet bunny, left him there on the floor to bleed everywhere. And no matter how much the maids tried to scrub at the stain, it never went away. My favorite nanny disappeared after I tried to scream when he was doing something particularly terrible to me. And so I stopped trying to tell anyone. Not that I thought anyone would believe me. He was my father's brother, his best friend. It only all ended when my brothers kicked him out of The Firm, not because they knew he'd hurt me, but because they thought he was creepy and that he would probably try for my father's spot after he died. It's been years now, but every night when I close my eyes, he's still there. I feel like he'll always be there."

"What happened to him?" I heard the promise of death in Lucian's voice. If only it was that easy. "Sometimes when I was around London, I'd think that I saw him, but when I looked closer, he was never there. He texts me awful things from all different numbers, even today. I only got the texts to stop recently because Emilia got me that new phone. But I'm sure, somehow, they'll start again."

"Over my dead body," he growled, and his chest rattled against me, his promise of vengeance soothing to my soul.

I was tempted to ask him for his story, since there was obviously one based on what I'd seen that night. But he didn't offer anything to me. He just kept his arms around me, and his fingers softly stroked the skin that was showing where my shirt had pulled up from my sleep shorts. The sound of his breathing was like Ambien, and I felt myself being pulled back under, even though that was the last place I ever wanted to be.

"In your dreams, do you ever win?" he suddenly whispered.

My eyes flew open at his question. "Never. The monster always wins." He didn't say anything after that, and I drifted off into a dreamless sleep where I felt the presence of someone watching over me and keeping me safe all night.

When I woke up, he was gone. I hadn't expected anything different.

But something had changed last night. By trusting Lucian with my secret, I'd given him a piece of my soul. And I wondered, what was he going to do with it?

TWENTY-ONE

Someone in the house had been leaving me gifts. One day, there was a vase of bright pink dahlias waiting for me on my nightstand when I walked in. Another day, there was a box of chocolates from the chocolate shop in Paris that I was obsessed with, but certainly had never told anyone in this house about. Another day, there was a beautiful bright blue cocktail dress and a pair of sparkly silver Christian Louboutin shoes that I'd been looking at just the other day online and I'd saved to my wish list on Pinterest.

I'd mentioned it to Emilia, but she'd just gotten a little secretive look on her face and refused to give me any information.

I'd just stepped into my room after a day at the shelter, a little sad because my favorite dog, the ugly one, had been adopted, and there was a robin egg blue colored box lying on my bed.

Tiffany's.

I was some kind of shameless hussy as I practically ran to the bed and tore off the white ribbon, and then the lid, to reveal the most gorgeous diamond tennis bracelet I'd ever seen. I gently touched the diamonds, ridiculously giddy. My family had been wealthy. But beyond designer clothes for special events, I'd never been given anything expensive, certainly not like this.

I held the bracelet to my chest, fully aware that I was acting ridiculous. But. I. Did. Not. Care.

I really needed to figure out who was leaving me these gifts though. It was kind of weird that there were potentially three men doing it. Well, I really couldn't picture Raphael doing anything like this. He was more likely to catch an exotic animal and have it stuffed and left in my bedroom to scare the living shit out of me than he was to buy me jewelry. Or maybe a head. I could see him leaving that too.

"That's a pretty bracelet," a familiar voice drifted in from the doorway. I stiffened, the voice making me physically nauseous. I took a steadying breath and tried to school my face so that he couldn't read the panic and disgust that would normally be there.

Carlo was leaning against the doorway, looking like an extra from "Scarface" with his slicked-back black hair and his pinstripe suit. All he was missing was a machine gun.

"Carlo," I said with a nod, sliding off my bed in a way that I hoped looked casual. "I haven't seen you since the wedding."

"I've been trying to set up a dinner so I could get to know my new daughter-in-law better, but Lucian said you've been a very busy girl."

"Yes. It's been a whirlwind since the wedding." I flashed him a polite smile, trying to figure out how we could move this conversation somewhere else besides my bedroom. This room was the only safe space I had in this house. I didn't want him tainting it. Carlo didn't seem to get the memo. His imposing hulk

358

took up the whole doorway, and unless I wanted to try and push by him, I was stuck.

"I was actually just on my way out," I finally said.

But he still didn't move, and little bits of fear began trickling into my bloodstream.

There was no one else here. Emilia had just left for the day, and I hadn't seen any of the guys around. There'd been a fire at one of the warehouses, and Gabriel had said they'd lost half of everything inside as he was hustling out of the penthouse.

"Maybe we could set up that dinner for another day." I was proud that my voice wasn't shaking. Carlo took a step into the room, and then another. And I watched as he closed the door behind him.

Was this really happening?

"Please. I think it's best if you leave," I told him firmly. But he just shook his head and chuckled like we were in on a joke together.

"You know, my son really got lucky. You're beautiful, Dahlia, but I'm sure you know that. A rare, untainted, natural beauty that we don't see around here very often." He took another step towards me, and even though I was trying to look like I wasn't scared, I couldn't help but take a step back. His grin widened, predatory looking, like the cat who was about to pounce on the canary.

"I highly doubt that Lucian's been satisfying you. It takes a real man to do that."

I didn't say anything. My eyes darted around for my phone, but it was on my nightstand, several feet away.

I started to try to form a plan for how I'd get over there and grab it, but he was taking another step forward.

No, this was not going to happen. I didn't need any more

chapters to my story on sexual assault. The book was full enough, thank you very much.

I pretended to look towards the phone, hoping Carlo would follow my gaze, and sure enough, he did. "I don't think that you'll be needing—"

I darted towards the bathroom. There was a lock on it. It would at least buy me a spare second.

But Carlo was too fast. He grabbed my arm and yanked me forward, popping my left arm out of the socket and sending a blinding rush of pain through my body.

"Please." I choked out as I tried to struggle against him. One more yank on my arm had a tight scream ripping from my lips. But at least the stab of pain distracted me for a moment when his filthy hand started to massage my breast.

"I think that fire's going to keep my sons very busy. Plenty of time for us to get to know each other properly," he hissed, the evil in his soul leaking out of his eyes. I tried to knee him in the balls, but he moved at the last second, laughing as he threw me to the ground. My arm was hanging by my side, useless, and all I could do was try and kick at him as I tried to crawl away.

"There's nowhere to go. Now let me show you how a real man fucks." He put his hand on my throat, and unlike when Lucian and Raphael had done it, there was definitely no flash of pleasure, only the hope that he would choke me hard enough that I could pass out before he started.

He fumbled with his other hand on my shirt, finally just yanking hard enough that the thin cotton ripped open, show-casing my lace-clad chest.

"I bet you wore this just for me, didn't you, Dahlia? You're a good little slut, aren't you?" I tried to struggle, but his knees were on my thighs, holding me down. I was trying my best to keep the panic from taking over. I'd been taught ways to try and get out of the situation, but it was no use; the black haze began to descend on my vision, and I started to hyperventilate as he pulled down my bra and put his nasty tongue all over my nipple.

I was losing grasp on reality, and so when I heard a loud roar nearby, I thought that it was all in my head.

Carlo's weight on my body suddenly disappeared, and I was able to breathe again. I blearily tried to get hold of my surroundings, and like a shock to the heart, I sat straight up when I saw a crazed-looking Lucian leaning over Carlo and beating the ever-loving shit out of him. Carlo reared back and punched his son in the mouth. Blood sprayed everywhere as Lucian's lip split open. I gasped in horror as he stumbled back, looking dazed. But before Carlo could stumble to his feet, Lucian had pulled out his gun and had it against Carlo's forehead, his chest heaving as blood ran down his chin.

"Lucian," Carlo said sternly, as if he was in control of the situation. "Let's not be too hasty. I was just having fun with your whore."

"You're going to die, you fucking bastard, and just in case no one's told you yet, there's no such thing as heaven."

A single shot reverberated through the room, and I was frozen in place as Carlo fell backward. At the last second, Lucian had moved his gun, and the bullet had gone right into Carlo's chest. Blood was gurgling out as he laid there, and he must've hit something vital, because Carlo wasn't moving, his eyes blank and unseeing as they stared up towards the ceiling.

He was dead.

And then there was just the sound of our sharp gasps around us as we stared at the body.

Lucian had just killed his father…for me.

"What the fuck did you do?" said Raphael from the doorway, in the scariest voice I think I'd ever heard. Raphael was standing there, his face drained of color, a gun clenched in his hand.

I was a bit confused, because from what I'd seen, Raphael had hated his father. So why did he look like Lucian had just destroyed his entire world?

Lucian didn't acknowledge his brother. He rushed towards me, sinking to his knees beside me.

"Principessa, where are you hurt?" he stammered. Lucian held himself back, like I was going to fall apart if he touched my skin.

But weirdly, all the fear had leaked out of me. There was a buzzing sound in my ears as I stared at him in shock.

He'd come for me. He killed the monster. He'd killed his own flesh and blood to save me.

Before I could say anything, Raphael lunged at Lucian, grabbing him by the hair and slamming him against the wall so hard he must've seen stars.

"It was supposed to be me. I was the one who was supposed to kill him. You couldn't even give me this one thing," Raphael whispered hoarsely.

Broken. That was the only word I could use to describe what I was seeing right now. Raphael wasn't a frayed edge, he was a sharp tear.

Tears were streaming down his cheeks as he slammed Lucian against the wall once more and then stumbled backward, his hands tearing at his hair as he sank to his knees just a few feet away from me, and then he began to rock back and forth.

Lucian was staggering as he slid down the wall until he was seated on the floor, blood trickling now from not only his lip, but also from a cut on his forehead. He stared at Raphael blankly.

I wasn't sure who to go to—Lucian with his definite concussion, or Raphael.

And fuck, my arm was hurting so bad.

Lucian didn't look like he was going to die, so I stumbled to my feet and took a tentative step towards Raphael, the same way I would approach a wounded animal I'd found in the middle of the woods.

"Rafe," the nickname slipped out, and Raphael tensed for a minute before continuing to grip at his hair and rock back and forth while wracking sobs tore through his entire body.

I looked at Lucian to see if he had any advice for me, but his eyes were closed, and his face was in his hands.

I took a few more steps until I was standing in front of Raphael, and then I gingerly knelt down in front of him. I didn't try to touch him yet. Some types of pain had to be wrenched out of you, like poison from a snake bite.

Gabriel was suddenly in the doorway, and I watched as his jaw dropped as he surveyed the scene, his eyes getting caught on my shirt that was torn open.

He opened his mouth, and then promptly closed it, I'm sure not knowing what to say.

I fell back, my arm on fire, when Raphael suddenly leapt to his feet, looking dazed and confused, like he was the one with a head injury.

Lucian lifted his head. "Raphael," he croaked.

"I fucking hate you," Raphael growled. And then he rushed from the room, pushing Gabriel roughly as he passed.

I winced, and Gabriel let out a growl, a second later at my side.

"What happened?" he asked as he carefully examined my shoulder.

"Your father happened," I told him softly, trying to breathe through the pain while he carefully moved my shoulder around. Without warning, he popped it back in, and a scream tore from my throat.

"A little warning next time."

Gabriel shook his head, no hint of humor in his gold eyes.

I was shaking, and I felt lightheaded, that feeling that came when you dropped down from a rush of adrenaline.

Gabriel gathered me in his arms, and I snuggled against his chest, soaking up his touch and not caring that Lucian was in the room. I needed this. I needed this desperately.

He stroked my hair softly as I shook against him. "You're safe now, bellissima," he whispered comfortingly. The slow rise and fall of his chest was like a drug, and I moved in closer.

"Did he—" Gabriel's voice broke off.

He didn't need to finish the sentence. I knew what he was asking.

"No. Lucian got here just in time."

The temptation was there, to blame myself and wonder what I'd done that all these arseholes came for me. I did my best to push the dark thoughts away. There was nothing in me that wanted anything to do with Carlo; that wanted anything to do with my uncle. I had learned that there were just sick people in the world, and the hardest thing about life was that you had to survive them.

"What are we going to do?" Gabriel asked Lucian. I peeked over to where he was still sitting against the wall, his posture defeated.

Lucian lifted his head, his eyes haunted...but also angry. "We'll take him back to that warehouse and burn him. Then tell everyone that he got caught in the flames trying to help."

My eyes widened. "You really think that's gonna work? Isn't the fire already out?"

"The warehouse is huge, princess. It'll be easy to stash him in there, and just find him in the morning when we reconvene to keep looking through the damage."

Letting out a long sigh, he pushed to his feet. "I need to clean this blood off, and then I'll need your help, Gabriel. We can't bring anyone else into this."

Gabriel nodded resolutely. He didn't seem to be upset about his dead father either.

And I thought I'd had daddy issues.

"What are we going to do about Raphael?" Gabriel asked quietly.

Lucian shook his head. "I don't know. I had no idea that he felt that way. That he was planning to kill him. Right now, I don't feel like I know him at all." He sighed again. Then we locked eyes, and everything was different. A golden thread had begun to form between us when he comforted me the other night, but this, this had turned that golden thread into a rod of iron. Everything had changed. I wasn't quite sure yet what that meant, but I was never going to forget what he'd done for me today.

"Will you be okay for a while?" Lucian murmured, not seeming upset at all that I was plastered to Gabriel's chest.

I nodded, feeling exhausted…and numb.

"I'll get Emilia to come back over here and stay with you," Gabriel added.

That sounded good to me. I wasn't sure if I could stand to be alone in this place. And I definitely couldn't sleep in this room again.

"Sleep in my room tonight," Lucian suggested gently, as if he could read my mind. I nodded again.

Lucian left then, and after soaking up Gabriel's warmth, I reluctantly pushed away from him. My arm was still sore, but it felt a lot better, and I gingerly got up with Gabriel's help. He let me go for a minute to pull off his shirt, and it said how tired I was that lust didn't beat up my chest. He helped me remove my shredded shirt and then slid his shirt over my head. I breathed in deeply, coffee and amaretto flooding my senses. I headed for the door, and Gabriel put his arm around my waist like he thought I was going to fall. We walked out into the hallway and then out towards the living room.

There was no sign of Raphael, and my heart broke for him, remembering the torment in his gaze when he'd seen his father's body. Lucian wasn't the only Rossi son with secrets, it appeared. I wondered if I would ever discover them all.

Emilia was there ten minutes later, clucking over me in her mother hen way. Gabriel brushed a kiss across my forehead and gave me a sad smile as he joined Lucian in the entryway. Lucian had something black folded up in his hands, and I realized it had been some kind of body bag when they disappeared for a few minutes and then reappeared holding a long black bag that was now filled…with Carlo.

Emilia didn't comment as we watched them stagger into the elevator with the full body bag, and then disappear. As soon as the doors closed, she rushed to the kitchen and made me a steaming mug of hot chocolate, "with a little extra," she told me with a wink as I took a small sip and savored the splash of rum I could taste mixed in with the chocolate.

I tried to wait up for them to come home, anxiety ratcheting through my veins, but eventually, the stress of the afternoon became too much, and I fell asleep.

Where, of course, the monster lay in wait.

It was a beautiful perfect day when we buried Carlo. Like the whole world had decided to celebrate that he was gone. I was in a long, black stretch limo with Lucian and Gabriel, headed to the funeral. The ceremony was being held at St. Patrick's Cathedral. It seemed a little fitting that every major event in the Rossi life happened in the same place.

I hadn't seen Raphael at all this week, and neither had Lucian and Gabriel. Carlo's body was discovered the morning after the incident, everything about him burned except for half of his face, convenient for identifying him. His death had been written up in all the newspapers around town. The media just couldn't get enough of the story of the prominent businessman who had suffered an ugly death while trying to save some company property.

It was a much better story than he deserved, but as long as it protected Lucian and Gabriel, I was fine with it. The repercussions that would come if the wrong people found out that Lucian had been responsible for Carlo's death...dread shot through my spine just thinking about it. We pulled up in front of the familiar cathedral, and I couldn't help but look at Lucian, remembering that shit-show of a day. Lucian must have had the same idea, because he was already staring at me, a faint smile on his lips.

He'd seemed lighter in the last couple of days, like Carlo had been a heavy burden on his back that had finally been lifted.

"Valentina's going to be here today, right?" I asked, butterflies going crazy in my stomach at the thought of meeting their little sister. They were all very fond of her, even Raphael, which was saying something because he legitimately seemed to hate everyone.

"How's it going with her and The Outfit?" I asked. I certainly hoped it was going smoother than it had for me.

Gabriel frowned. "She's been quiet. She hasn't responded to a single text that I've sent. I had to call her asshole husband, Salvatore, to tell her about Carlo's death."

That didn't sound promising. Riccardo opened the door, and Lucian stepped out first, extending a hand as I struggled to get out of the car. I was wearing a tight black sheath dress that Emilia had bought for me, and it was a little too tight. Lucian offered me his arm, and I couldn't help but glance to where Gabriel was standing behind us, longing bleeding out of his gaze. I gave him a soft smile and then ripped my eyes away from his, concentrating on walking up the steps of the Cathedral without tripping.

Organ music was crooning a mournful tune as we walked in, and time hadn't changed how foreboding the chapel felt to me, with the stained-glass angels looking down on us like they could see all of our sins.

Most of the rows of pews were completely packed, the New York elite once again clamoring to make sure they were seen at another Rossi event. Everyone was salivating as we walked by, and I realized that people most likely weren't aware that Carlo was just a figurehead in the years preceding his death. Now that he was gone, they were all finally recognizing that Lucian was the man in charge. The piranhas had become sharks.

We'd made it to the front pew when a tiny sprite of a girl caught my attention. I knew it was Valentina right away. She had long, light brown hair and light blue eyes that were the same stunning shade as Raphael's. Her skin was smooth and tan, and she was practically hopping in place as we approached, her attention skipping between the three of us.

"La sorella," Lucian murmured, and she flung herself into his arms, much to the chagrin of the three imposing men she'd left, who were watching her closely like any minute she was going to be taken away. The three men were gorgeous, their looks rivaling the Rossi boys, which I hadn't thought was possible. They all looked close in age, and my eyes widened when I realized that two of them were twins. I didn't know much about the Chicago outfit, other than they didn't get along with the Cosa Nostra, but they all had the same big alpha energy that Lucian did. It was a little much having them all in the same room.

As soon as Lucian let Valentina go, she was in Gabriel's arms, and he brushed a kiss across her head. "Have you gotten taller?" he teased, and she lifted her head and rolled her eyes at him.

My heart clenched watching how sweet they were with her. It wasn't a shock seeing Gabriel like that, but even Lucian had a light in his eyes when he looked at his little sister.

"And you must be Dahlia," she said excitedly. I nodded, fidgeting with my hands, not knowing what to do. But she took over, throwing her arms around me. "I've always wanted a sister," she gushed, and I couldn't help but fall in love with her. I patted her back, a little awkwardly, but she didn't seem to care. Finally, one of the twins cleared his throat, and she sighed and released me, rolling her eyes again and mouthing "idiots" to me.

I couldn't help but giggle, and I had to slap my hand over my mouth, as I realized it probably wouldn't do to seem so light-hearted at a funeral, especially this funeral.

I saw Lucian surreptitiously glancing around, and I realized he must've been looking for Raphael. Valentina squeezed my hand and then started over to her three men, who all quickly surrounded her like they couldn't bear to be away from her. My eyes widened as I finally got it. She was with all three of them.

My throat burned thinking about having Lucian, Raphael, and Gabriel. But I quickly shook the thought away. It was my secret, one that I kept buried deep inside of me. One that I didn't even want to admit to myself.

I wished that I could've had all of them.

The organ switched songs then, moving to a darker, more depressing hymn, and the entire congregation turned towards the back of the church as the doors opened and Carlo's casket was carried inside by six men. I wondered if it was weird that the guys weren't carrying him in.

The mahogany casket was far nicer than Carlo deserved, if I'd had it my way, he would have been thrown in a tub of acid, until there was no trace that his dark presence had ever existed on this planet.

The priests started to file in from a side door, and the crowd began to hush. One of the priests glanced at Lucian, and I realized he was the same priest that had performed our wedding rites, at gunpoint. He was eyeing our pew like any of us could attack, and even from here, I could see the way his hands were shaking.

Poor guy.

Lucian gave him a slight nod and the organ stopped. Right as the priest opened his mouth, there was a banging sound, and I looked back to see that one of the giant bronze doors had been thrown open.

Raphael was standing in the doorway, and he was a mess. He was wearing a suit, but his shirt was unbuttoned halfway down his chest, and his suit coat was dirty and frayed like he'd been rolling in the sewer before he decided to attend. There was a rip in the knee of his suit pants.

His hair was all over the place, and his eyes were red-rimmed and glassy. He stumbled down the aisle towards us, stopping when he got to our pew. "Sorry I'm late," he said caustically, before pushing his way in, not stopping until he was by me.

I wrinkled my nose, because he smelled like the bottom of a tequila bottle, like he'd been doused in it.

"Raphael, what the fuck are you doing?" Lucian hissed. But Lucian's anger just made Raphael laugh, the sound of it seeming to ring through the cathedral.

I closed my eyes and winced. This wasn't good. I saw Valentina leaning over between her men, watching Raphael worriedly. He gave her a salute. "Oh hey, sis. Fancy seeing you here." His words were slurred, and Lucian was definitely one moment away from strangling him.

I pulled on Raphael's arm, and he turned to face me. "Well, hello there, little angel," he purred and leaned forward like he was going to fucking kiss me. Luckily, Gabriel grabbed his other arm and pulled him into the pew so he was sitting between the two of us. Lucian gritted his teeth then gestured at the priest who was watching us wide-eyed.

Unfortunately, under the circumstances, Lucian couldn't threaten the priest and force him to make the ceremony shorter. So we were in it for the whole thing, mass included.

This was going to be interesting.

It was hard to keep a straight face when the priest began to give a eulogy for Carlo. The man that he was gushing about had definitely not existed, and Raphael laughed outrageously when the priest went on and on about what a kindhearted man Carlo had been.

Lucky for all of us, Raphael fell asleep halfway through the funeral, his head falling to my shoulder. I glanced at Lucian, not sure what to do, but he just shook his head. I spent the next thirty minutes with him snoring softly in my ear with what felt like a million judging stares plastered on the back of my head.

By the time the funeral service ended, I was determined that I was never going to come back into this place unless it was my dead body being dragged in here.

Gabriel shook Raphael's shoulder, and he jerked up violently, pulling a knife from somewhere under his coat and looking around wildly.

"Cazzo," Lucian muttered. He didn't say anything to his brother though; he just slipped past to pay his respect to the nervous priest, who definitely could have done without Lucian speaking to him.

It took an hour to make it out of the cathedral. So many people were begging for Lucian's attention. I hadn't thought that it could get worse than our engagement dinner and the wedding, but that was just a taste of the pathetic these people all exuded. Valentina seemed nonplussed about it all, obviously used to her brothers getting this sort of attention. Gabriel spent the whole time trying to hold Raphael in place and prevent him from going off and doing something that would have people talking even more than they already were.

We finally got outside, where cars were waiting to take us to the gravesite. Valentina's men dragged her into a separate black limo that was waiting just behind our limo.

We piled into the limo, Gabriel and Lucian basically having to force Raphael into the car with us. Once we'd made it inside, Raphael immediately passed out on one of the benches.

None of us talked as we headed to the cemetery. Carlo was

going to be buried in the famous Green Wood Cemetery, where all of the Rossi family met their final resting place.

I looked out the window in interest as we pulled up in front of the gates that surrounded the cemetery. Beyond the gothic revival entrance gates, I could see rolling hills, green trees, and impressive monuments marking the famous residents who made the place their last home. Lucian gripped my hand tightly as we got out and made our way down the winding path.

"I hate this place," muttered Gabriel, as he struggled to keep Raphael on his feet. Raphael looked even more wrecked than he did at the cathedral, like the closer we got to Carlo's final good-bye, the closer he got to complete ruin.

What had Carlo done to him?

Valentina walked behind us, much more subdued than she'd been in St. Patrick's. Her three men surrounded her, their gazes vigilant as we walked.

I started to see the name Rossi pop up on the impressive-looking gravestones, and then we made it to where a large green tent was set up with chairs underneath. Carlo's elaborate casket was on a stand above a giant hole. A man I recognized but couldn't quite place went to the front and started speaking about how much Carlo had meant to him.

The mayor.

That's who that was. The furious peon that Gabriel and I had encountered at the restaurant that night.

It seemed like a lifetime had passed since then.

When the mayor finished speaking, people began to look at Lucian expectantly, and I realized that they probably thought he was going to give a speech.

Lucian had been holding my hand throughout the mayor's blusterous speech, and he squeezed it one more time before getting up from his seat and directing his attention to the crowd.

"Thank you all for coming to be with us on this very sad occasion. My father—" Lucian paused. "My father was a man that the world, and his family, will not soon forget. His influence will no doubt last for generations, and I know that he would be so honored to have you all here saying goodbye to him."

Lucian then turned and grabbed one of the roses from the enormous display set up by the casket. As he stood there and the casket began to be lowered into the hole, Lucian tossed the rose on top of it. He also spit on the grave, a move so smooth that you would've completely missed it if you hadn't been concentrating hard.

My eyes widened, but the crowd was still mostly silent, so they must've missed the move. The rest of us joined Lucian up front and grabbed roses to throw into the monster's grave.

"I hope you are burning in hell," I murmured as I threw the rose in. Valentina had taken two roses. One she threw in Carlo's grave, and the other she placed gently beside it, in front of her mother's grave. Her lip quivered as she stood there, having a silent conversation with the complicated woman I knew rested there until one of the twins put his hand on her lower back and gently guided her away. Raphael stood in front of Carlo's grave, his hands clenched, and his eyes sparking, momentarily clear. He'd crumbled up the rose into pieces in his hand, and he threw them in the grave violently, hate etched into his features.

We all waited by the side as people came by to pay their last respects, and then Gabriel sighed. "I can't believe we still have hours to go at the funeral reception."

I cringed just thinking about it. Lucian chuckled darkly, the mask he'd worn the entire day dissipating as people walked away.

He grabbed my hand. "I'm going to leave you to handle all of that, brother," he said to Gabriel, who looked at him in shock and dismay. "You and Valentina can take the reins, right?"

"Where are you going?" Valentina asked curiously as Lucian began to pull me away.

"Anywhere but here," he called to her over his shoulder. I stumbled behind him as we made our way out of the cemetery and back to the road where a gleaming black convertible was waiting in front of the limo we'd come in.

"You know how to drive, right?" Lucian asked with a boyish grin that should have been illegal because my heart definitely skipped a beat.

"On the wrong side of the road," I told him.

"Perfect." He threw me the car keys and I caught them, still staring at him wide-eyed.

"You're having me drive?"

"What's that saying, princess? Fuck the patriarchy? Let's go."

His smile was heart-stopping, life-changing...a miracle. I wanted to keep it so I jumped into the driver's side, trying not to freak out about all the buttons in this thing. It was like a spaceship.

I immediately stalled the car as I put it in the wrong gear, and Lucian laughed, the sound so light-hearted it made my heart sing.

I finally got the car moving, and we roared out of the parking lot.

Free of at least one of the monsters in our lives.

I could feel him watching me as I drove. I'd almost had a heart attack getting out of the city, stalling the car multiple times on the stop and go city roads. Lucian asked me if I knew how to drive, but he didn't ask how much experience I had.

Which was very little.

Luckily, he didn't seem to care, and I was practically creaming in my seat because I was getting the chance to drive this car. A Rolls-Royce Dawn. Swoon.

I made a mental note once again that I really needed to get one of them to show me the garage.

The air felt cleaner out of the city. The breeze blowing past my face smelled like summer and grass. I was tempted to ask if we could just keep driving, run away from all the problems that were waiting for us back in the city.

"You seem happier," I commented hesitantly, afraid that anything I said would make him withdraw.

Lucian was sprawled back in his seat, a pair of aviators on that was doing dangerous things to my insides. The waves in his hair were flying in the wind. And he was looking at me.

"It's a strange thing to live your whole life in the shadows and never realize it. I always knew my father was poison, but I didn't know how much of his poison was sliding into my veins until he was gone. It's liberating."

"Do you think anyone will find out?"

Lucian shook his head, not seeming worried at all. "No one's going to find out. No one in the city is sad that Carlo Rossi is gone."

I nodded.

"Turn left up at that sign," he commented, and I concentrated on not stalling the car as I downshifted. I turned onto the road, and we drove for about ten minutes before he pointed to a bed and breakfast to the left that advertised a restaurant on-site as well.

The bed and breakfast was in an enormous Victorian mansion. I could tell the outside colors had been updated, because they were a bright white and light blue, designed to be welcoming and nothing like the scary haunted houses I usually associated the style with.

I pulled the car into the small parking lot and let out a breath, thinking that maybe I'd have Lucian take over driving after this.

Lucian hopped over his door and jogged over to my side, opening my door for me and helping me out. His hand tangled with mine, sending sparks all over my skin. My heart felt like it was gasping for breath as it expanded under his watchful gaze. He was staring down at me with that damned smirk of his, the one that tested the endurance of my lace knickers. Damn man.

He led me around the house where I saw that an extension had been built onto the original structure. A sign above the welcoming doorway said *Nana's Kitchen.*

Lucian pushed through the door, and immediately, I was assaulted with the most delicious smells I thought I'd ever experienced.

My stomach groaned in hunger, and he looked back at me and winked. There were just a few people seated at the white shabby chic tables scattered across the gleaming white oak floor. The walls were whitewashed with gallery walls of mismatched frames and mirrors and trinkets that I could have spent hours looking through. There was a pair of white swinging doors on the back wall, and a tiny woman came barreling through them, a nest of white hair on her head. She locked eyes with Lucian and literally squealed. I'd never seen anyone have that kind of reaction to him. The woman was old, or maybe ancient was a better term for it. She had wrinkles upon wrinkles to match her snow-white hair, but her light blue eyes were full of life and energy, sparkling as she shuffled across the room.

"Oh, my boy, it's so good to see you," she said in a weathered voice. Lucian gave her a kiss on both of her cheeks, and she took his face in her age-spotted hands. "You haven't been eating enough. Much too skinny."

He smiled at her, and I didn't know how she didn't drop dead because the force of it was shocking to the system. Also, I noted that he didn't have any problem with her touching him. That was interesting.

She dropped her hands and turned her attention to me. "And who is this beautiful girl?" she crooned, clapping her hands in front of her in delight. I could feel the eyes of the other patrons on us, but unlike in the city, where it seemed like everyone was judging and speculating, they just seemed curious. It was a nice change.

Lucian slid his arm around me until he was gripping my hip. "Nana, this is my wife, Dahlia," he explained, sounding...proud.

Her mouth dropped open almost comically, and she squealed like a schoolgirl.

"We must celebrate! Go sit wherever you want. I'll tell Boris to start making some plates. This will be a feast like nothing you've seen before." She raced back towards the swinging doors and disappeared behind them, leaving me a little shell-shocked.

Lucian was staring after her fondly. After a second, he led me over towards an empty table in front of a large window that looked out to a beautiful, wild garden bursting with color.

Lucian pulled out my chair and I slid into it, and then he surprised me by moving his chair next to mine. When he sat down, the heat from his legs bled into my skin. The tingles I got every time he touched me were incredibly distracting.

"How did you find this place?" I asked.

"When I was sixteen, I was going to check on a new property about an hour away. I got caught in a storm, and my phone stopped working. Somehow, I found myself off the road in a ditch. I walked through the rain until I came across this place. They welcomed me in, put me in a room for the night, and stuffed me with some of the best food I'd ever had. I think it was the first bit of kindness I'd ever experienced in my life. I've tried to come back as often as I can ever since."

I frowned, thinking of Lucian as a child, never experiencing any type of real love.

Maybe we were similar in that way.

"You should've invited them to the wedding." He shook his head, his mood sobering. "I wouldn't bring these people around those sharks. They wouldn't last a minute."

I frowned at that, thinking how sad it was that we were forced to live in a world of people that we hated.

Before I could ask anything else, she was back at the table, loaded down with a tray filled with steaming bowls of chowder and a plate of sourdough bread that had obviously just been pulled out of the oven. She set the plate and bowls down on the table and kissed the top of my head before scurrying off again.

"You're going to fucking love this," Lucian exclaimed. I didn't think I'd ever seen him look this excited before. He grabbed a spoon and dug in, his eyes closing in apparent ecstasy as he scooped the chowder into his mouth.

"I think it gets better every time," he said after he'd swallowed. He scooped up another spoonful and then saw that I hadn't moved.

"Try it, principessa," he purred, and somehow Lucian got even more dangerous. Because when he used *that* voice with me, I wasn't sure that it was possible for me to say no.

I didn't like that. I didn't like that at all.

The soup smelled so good, and I had no problem spooning

some into my mouth. And then I had a mouth orgasm. It was clam chowder soup, but way better than anything I'd ever tasted. It was so creamy and rich that as soon as I swallowed, I was craving more. We ate in complete silence for the next couple of minutes, shoveling the soup into our mouths and scooping it up with the bread that was just as good.

"Please tell me that she has loaves back there that we can buy to bring back with us," I moaned, as I bit into a perfectly crisp bite.

"Oh, I'll make sure she loads us up with everything."

Nana was back soon after that, this time carrying salad plates bursting with various vegetables that she told us were straight from her garden. The dressing was homemade too, a light lemon vinaigrette that paired perfectly with the crisp vegetables that had been painstakingly cut up in tiny pieces. The croutons were made from the sourdough bread, and they were bursting with a delicious garlic butter flavor.

"It's official. I'm in heaven," I commented, and Lucian graced me with another one of those heart-stopping grins.

"Oops, there's a beet," he said suddenly, spearing one out of my salad.

I was silent as I watched him, wide-eyed. Because I knew I hadn't told him that I was allergic to them. I guess Gabriel could have, but I was developing another hypothesis. One that was sending butterflies floating through my insides.

The main entrée came out next, a lemon chicken piccata over homemade angel hair pasta.

"My favorite," Lucian practically gushed as he started shoveling it into his mouth, unaware of the epiphany I was experiencing.

Lucian was usually so proper when he ate, setting his fork

down in between every bite to clean off his face. It was hilarious to see him shoveling the food in his mouth as fast as he could like someone was going to grab it off the table at any moment.

I understood the feeling as soon as I took a bite and the flavors exploded in my mouth. I was already stuffed from everything we'd eaten, but I found myself clearing my plate. After there wasn't a scrap of food left, I leaned back in my chair and groaned.

"That's it. I'm done."

Lucian had finished way before me, and his arm was wrapped around the back of my chair. I shivered when he began to play with my hair while watching the people in the room. He'd been finding ways to touch me the whole day, and a slow heat was curling in my insides. Lucian was being so gentle...so sweet. It was making my head spin.

"You have to find a little bit more room. Nana's apple pie is worth the stomachache."

And somehow, when she brought out enormous slices of freshly baked pie with caramel and homemade vanilla ice cream on top, I found some room.

Like Lucian had said, it was definitely worth the stomachache.

Although Nana tried to tell him he didn't have to pay, when we got up, loaded down with containers of bread and soup, some more chicken piccata, and a whole apple pie, Lucian left five thousand dollars on the table. She looked near tears as she hugged me and then patted Lucian's face. "You stay out of trouble, my boy. And let this girl make you happy," she ordered as she walked with us to the door.

Lucian stared down at me, a look on his face that was hard to read but was definitely intense. "I'm thinking I should probably give that a try."

Fireworks joined the butterflies going off inside me at his words. I was trembling and trying not to read into it. I realized something then. Somehow, amidst all the pain, I was starting to fall in love...in love with all of them.

But falling in love with the Rossi men was like lighting a cigarette near an oxygen tank and hoping to God that you didn't explode.

Whatever path I was on, I didn't think I would survive.

Lucian held my hand tightly and led me towards the car. As he helped me into my seat, he gave me a surprisingly soft, lingering kiss that spelled my ruin.

After getting into the car, he lifted up the center console to grab some sunglasses and I spotted a receipt from Bergdorf Goodman. I wasn't trying to be nosy, but I couldn't help but see that it was for a Carolina Herrera dress and a pair of Christian Louboutin heels...the same brands as the surprise on my bed a few weeks ago.

Unable to stop myself, I grabbed the receipt, feeling like I was turning into a puddle of goo as my hypothesis became more of a concrete theory.

Lucian was frozen in his seat.

"Have you been sending me gifts, Lucian?" I asked quietly.

He was silent, and I thought for sure he was going to deny it, but he finally nodded slowly.

More ideas were flooding my head, because all of my gifts had been things that I'd saved on my Pinterest boards or in videos I'd seen on TikTok or Instagram. And if he'd been following me on those...what else was he responsible for?

"The wedding…and the engagement party, how much of that did you have a hand in planning?" I asked slowly.

His head fell forward, and then he turned to look at me, his gaze burning into mine.

"Would you believe me if I told you I'd had a hand in all of it?" he asked gruffly.

"Yes," I murmured, my hand reaching towards his cheek and watching, wide-eyed as he nuzzled into my palm.

"Would you believe me if I told you I've been obsessed with you since the moment I saw your picture, and I've done my best to learn everything about you that I could…so you could be happy here? Even if I've done a piss poor job of achieving that."

I searched his face for the lie, but it wasn't there.

"Yes," I finally answered, a roughness in my voice because I was having trouble forming words.

Just then his phone started going crazy. Ringing and beeping as texts and calls came in.

He frowned as he picked up his phone. "Fuck," he snarled after he read one of the messages. He pressed on the gas and then we were speeding down the road, going twice the speed limit as I held on tight to my seat.

"What's wrong?" I cried.

"Someone set the Rossi Inc. headquarters on fire. There are five crews out there trying to fight the flames." Lucian's voice was tight, the promise of retribution and death for everyone involved clear.

The ride back to the city seemed to take forever, even though I was sure it only took half as long with how fast he was driving. Surprisingly, we weren't pulled over by the police as we broke almost every driving law that existed.

Or maybe that wasn't surprising. Maybe the police could spot a Rossi vehicle immediately and know not to fuck with them.

As we got into the city limits, all the lightness he'd had today disappeared, and I was once again left with the cold shell he usually showed the world.

We sped towards the building, weaving in and out of traffic and almost getting in a wreck several times. And then we were there, and I gasped when I saw the fire eating away at half the building.

"What kind of devil is after you?" I murmured to Lucian as we both stared at the flames.

He was silent for a long moment. "The better question, Dahlia, is what devil isn't. There are only devils in this town. The only angel left is you."

Riccardo came running up to us then, and Lucian left him to guard me while he went to deal with everything.

We stood there for hours and watched as the flames destroyed the symbol of Lucian's hard work.

TWENTY-TWO

I was in the car with Gabriel, on the way to the animal shelter, when his phone rang.

"What's up?" he asked. I heard Lucian's voice speaking through the phone, but I couldn't make out what he was saying. "I'm with Dahlia still. You want me to bring her?" He looked surprised by whatever Lucian had answered. "Okay. See you in a few minutes."

He turned towards me after ending the call. "Lucian thinks he has a lead on who's behind everything. He wants us to meet him at the new offices to talk about it."

I nodded, feeling absurdly happy that Lucian was actually involving me in Rossi business for once. I bit my lip as I thought about everything that had happened over the last week. After the fire destroyed that building, all operations had moved to another building they owned, this one much less impressive looking, but with enough floors to hold all the departments.

Lucian had been gone around the clock, sleeping for an hour on the sofa in his office as he organized everything and tried to figure out who was behind the fire.

I'd missed him.

He'd sent me a few texts, but it wasn't enough. Not now that I'd seen that piece of him, the one that melted my insides.

An Emily Brontë quote got caught in my head. "If you ever looked at me once with what I know is in you, I would be your slave."

That quote may have been the most apt description that existed for what Lucian had managed to do.

I haven't seen Raphael either. Gabriel said he'd shown up after the fire, and he'd been helping with all the preparations, but he hadn't shown himself at the penthouse. I had a suspicion he was deliberately avoiding me.

"You need anything before we get there, bellissima?" Gabriel asked, squeezing my hand. There wasn't a minute now when I wasn't around Gabriel and he wasn't touching me in one way or another.

And I was okay with that.

"I'm fine," I assured him.

I kept waiting for it to fade, for him to lose interest. But as the weeks and months went by, he was still treating me like I was a priceless work of art that he was devoted to forever, and I was beginning to wonder if what he felt wasn't so temporary after all.

We pulled up to a building in an older part of Manhattan. This was where the previous Rossi headquarters were located when Carlo was fully in charge and Lucian was still a boy. We stepped into the lobby and saw workers everywhere, painting the walls and ripping up the outdated tile on the floors. There was very little left of the other building, and even though Lucian had vowed to rebuild, that process would take years. So this would have to do for now until something more suitable came along.

We rode up the elevator to the top floor where Lucian's office was…of course. This building wasn't nearly as tall as the other offices had been, but it was much wider, allowing for more departments per floor. I still had almost no idea what legal ventures the guys were involved in, but I guess I didn't know very much about their illegal ones either.

I needed to work on that.

My jaw dropped when the elevator doors slid open and revealed a pristine, modern office area that had been updated before anything else, judging by the thick paint smell that hung in the air and tickled my nose. Gabriel had obviously been here over the last few weeks because he didn't look surprised by anything as he began to lead me back towards where Lucian's office presumably was located.

As we walked, I realized I needed to use the loo, badly.

"Where's the loo?" I asked, and he gave me a stunning grin like he always did when I said something "British."

At this point, I was just using words in sentences so I could see his smile.

"It's back by the elevators," Gabriel answered. "I can come with you?"

"I think I can handle it," I winked. I moved away, but he was still holding my hand, biting his lip as he stared at my face.

"I really want to kiss you right now."

I blushed. "Me too," I whispered, thinking that the last few months with Gabriel were the most torturous forms of foreplay I could imagine.

I pulled my hand away and walked back towards the elevators. There was a delivery man in the lobby, his cart piled high with packages. The girls that had been at the desk when we'd first walked in were nowhere to be found.

That was weird.

As I made my way past the man, he stopped me. "Can you sign for these?" he asked in a gravelly voice.

"No, I'm sorry. I'm just visiting—"

Before I could finish my sentence, he reached up and I felt a pinprick in my neck. Immediately, the world began to spin...and then fade.

"Help," I gasped, my plea coming out in a whisper.

I was faintly aware of him grabbing me and carrying me to the elevator...and then everything went black.

GABRIEL

"What's taking so long?" I muttered, checking down the hallway again to see if Dahlia was on her way.

"Dahlia?" Lucian asked, trying to look like he was engrossed in the papers on his desk. He wasn't fooling anyone though. I'd seen the look of disappointment on his face when I walked in without her. He tried to be casual about that as well.

The man was gone.

Something wriggled around in my stomach and I wondered if now that Lucian seemed to be getting on board, what did that mean for me?

"Let's go meet up with her; we can show her around the building," said Lucian, still playing it cool.

Idiot.

We walked down the hall and got to the entrance. "Where're all the girls?" I asked, puzzled. Even if one of them took a break, there should still have been three more. I noticed the delivery cart with packages stacked up.

Lucian walked over to the desk and froze. "Fuck," he hissed. Without telling me anything, he rushed past me and barged into the women's bathroom, and I could hear him screaming her name.

Dread dripped down my spine as I went to look behind the desk, the dread morphing into fear when I saw the girls lying on the floor. I hurried over and checked their pulses. They were all alive but definitely knocked out.

Lucian burst out of the bathroom.

I already knew what he would say when he opened his mouth. She was gone.

Lucian pulled on his tie like it was choking him. "Call Raphael. Tell him to get his ass over here. I'm going to the surveillance room to see if we can see something." He disappeared into the elevators, and I pulled up Raphael's number.

"What?" he snapped in answer to my call.

"Dahlia's been taken," I told him roughly. Raphael was silent and then I heard the sound of things shattering. I needed to destroy something as well. Because right now I felt like I was going crazy.

I'd felt fear very few times in my life, but right now, what I was feeling could only be described as pure terror. "She went to the bathroom, now she's gone. All the secretaries were knocked out somehow. Get here now," I hissed before hanging up right as a text came in with a video message from Lucian. The clip showed Dahlia walking through the lobby and the delivery man asking her a question. I gritted my teeth when I saw him stick her with something and then carry her body into the elevator.

There were thousands of people in this building. How was it that no one was passing by? I shook my head in rage and raced towards the elevator to get to the surveillance room, texting Riccardo to meet us there as I flew down. I banged on the door, not feeling like taking the time to use the fingerprint scanner, and it was immediately opened by one of the tech guys. Lucian was standing in front of the thirty screens in the room, looking like he was losing it.

"See anything?" I asked.

"She was put in a van through the service entrance. I'm hacking into the street cameras to see if we can follow them."

"There. That's it!" Greg, the head of the security team snapped. "They're heading down 23rd St."

"Stream those cameras to my tablet," Lucian ordered, striding past me.

"Where are you going?"

"We're going to use the chopper to see if we can follow it better. We'd be too far behind in a car by now," he growled.

As we were walking down the hall towards the elevator that led up to the top of the building where three of our choppers were, the doors opened, and Raphael was standing there. I shivered a little bit looking at him. There was a nothingness in his gaze, a stillness about him that was like a predator right before he pounced. There were a lot of things that you could say about Raphael, but I'd never thought of him as cold. Right now, standing in front of us, he looked like a dark void.

"Did you find them?" he growled.

"We're going to take the chopper and follow the car."

We rode up the elevator in silence. Well, silence except for the sound of Raphael opening and closing his favorite knife. I could only imagine what he was going to do once we got these guys. There wasn't a place in my head for "if". I didn't know what would happen to us if we lost her.

I wouldn't want to live. It came to me clearly. I knew that I loved her, but it was more than that. She was necessary to my existence. I would be lost, a ship without an anchor. And I knew without a doubt that if I lost her, I'd follow her to the grave in hopes that she could be mine in the afterlife.

We got to the rooftop, and the wind whipped at our faces as we ducked our heads and rushed over to get in the chopper that Riccardo had started. The second we were all in, it lifted off the ground and headed up into the sky. Lucian threw on a headset and pulled a tablet from a shelf before climbing into the front where he slid into the copilot's seat.

"Let's go," Lucian barked, his screen turning on and displaying an aerial image of the white van. "40th Street," he directed Riccardo, who nodded and turned the chopper.

I was distracted by Raphael, who was calmly loading himself down with a variety of weapons from the weapons cache in this helicopter. "What are you going to do with the grenades?" I asked.

"Blow myself up if she dies."

Hmm. Good plan. I grabbed a grenade too…just in case, and Raphael and I locked eyes, twin expressions of resolution in our gazes. I'd never known anyone like I knew Dahlia. I knew that she only liked sweet potato fries. That she hadn't ever tasted ranch until coming to the city, and now she tried to put it on everything. I knew she hated the dark and always had to sleep with a light on… although I didn't know why. I knew her favorite color was pink, but she didn't like to wear pink because she thought it was too lighthearted for her. It was a million different things that I'd memorized about her until I felt like I knew her better than I did myself. I'd given her my soul a long time ago.

"There!" Lucian cried, standing up slightly in his seat as the chopper dipped.

"Fuck," growled Raphael, looking a little green. I forgot that helicopters always gave him motion sickness.

I looked out the window and spotted the van down below, weaving in and out of traffic. "What's our plan?" I yelled over the sound of the blades buzzing around us.

"Wait until they park and then kill every single one of the fuckers who participated in this," he growled. We all nodded resolutely.

Hang in there, bellissima. I'm coming.

DAHLIA

My head was pounding as I shifted; whatever I was lying on was hard as a rock. Had I fallen asleep on the marble floor? It took a second, but then everything came rushing back. We were at the office. I was going to the bathroom…and then the deliveryman.

My eyes flew open and I realized I was in some kind of van. My body was shaking as I looked around. There was a glass partition in between the back and the front where I could see two men sitting. We rolled over a bump and I flew to the side, knocking my knee. "Fuck," I whispered. That hurt.

Not to mention that I still really had to pee.

I tried to think. What was I going to do? Raphael's words came to me. *Make sure that when the next big and bad comes after us, you can fuck him up until we get there.*

Okay. I could do this. The drugs were making it hard to think. And the next bump had me banging my head against the floorboard, a soft moan slipping from my mouth.

I went immediately still, not knowing if they had heard me. I could hear the low murmur of their voices, but I couldn't make out what they were saying. I hoped that was the same for me.

They had tied my hands together in front of me, but not my legs. Maybe they thought that I'd be knocked out longer.

I looked for something to try and cut into the rope, but the back was completely empty.

All of a sudden, the van began to slow, and we turned left into a road that was paved with gravel judging by the rocks that were beating against the bottom of the van. The van turned once more, and then it stopped and turned off. The two men said something to each other, and then they got out. Okay, I was just going to have to wing it.

I still felt woozy as I moved right in front of the back door. When it opened, I'd just jump at him and try to get my arms around his neck. Except they didn't open the door right away.

I could hear the faint sound of voices outside the van as they continued to talk. I heard a yell, and then a shot was fired, and I swore when a bullet went right through the side of the van, barely missing my head.

I dropped to the floor of the van just in case anyone else started shooting, but the voices had stopped. And then I heard the sound of gravel crunching under shoes, and I crouched down in front of the door once again. The door opened, and I saw the delivery guy—or should I say the fake delivery guy?—but luckily for me, he wasn't looking at me. His attention was directed to the side. I flew at him, and my arms went around his neck. I pressed my forearms together as hard as I could so his head was caught in my grasp.

He'd been caught off guard, and he struggled to get me off. But as soon as I found footing on the ground, I wrenched my arms to the left just like Benny had ingrained in me, and I snapped the guy's neck. He fell to his knees and I went with him, my gaze scanning my surroundings for the second guy. It took me a moment to see the puddle of blood on the other side of the van, leaking from the body dressed in the same brown uniform as the guy I'd just killed.

I could do this. Just as long as someone didn't try and rape me, I'd be fine.

Or at least that's what I was telling myself. The sound of a helicopter overhead caught my attention, and I looked up as it got closer and started to descend. I covered my eyes as dirt, sand, and rocks started flying everywhere. Right as the helicopter landed, I heard the sound of a door bursting open behind me, and I barely fell to the ground in time as at least ten men dressed in black army fatigues came pouring out of a warehouse with machine guns and started to fire.

I glanced at the chopper, sure that everyone inside was dead, but to my surprise, I didn't see anyone inside.

I winced as a bullet pinged off the ground right in front of me, and I quickly scuttled under the van in an awkward army crawl thanks to my still bound wrists. I really needed to get this freaking rope off.

"Hi, angel," came Raphael's voice, and I jumped when I saw him on the ground a few feet away.

"You came," I whispered, although I wasn't sure how much good he could do with the amount of firepower currently going off around us.

His eyes devoured me, dancing over my skin worriedly.

"I'm not hurt," I assured him, and he nodded, relief clear in his gaze.

"Be right back," he snapped, and then he hopped off the ground, only to return one second later. "Cover your ears." He stood up again, and then I could only see his feet as they ran around the van. Were the others here? Were they alright?

Remembering what Raphael had told me to do, I covered my ears with my hands, and just in time, because the warehouse in front of me exploded, flipping the van all the way off me with the force of the blast. A piece of the siding smacked me in the head, and I whimpered as blood started to fall down my face.

"Principessa, I've got you," Lucian said from somewhere above me, and then he pulled me into his arms, his commanding energy brushing across my skin comfortingly.

I buried my head in his neck, soaking in his scent that was mixed with the smell of smoke.

Belatedly, I realized that it was completely quiet. I lifted my head and saw that arms and legs were sticking out of the debris that had exploded from the warehouse.

"She okay?" came Gabriel's frantic voice. "She's bleeding."

"Some of the siding hit her head. Thanks for that by the way, asshole."

"I saved our asses, didn't I?" Raphael replied from somewhere nearby. I was too tired to look up at him. I wanted a bath, a bed, and food...not necessarily in that order.

"We're going home," Lucian whispered soothingly. He was using that voice, the one that he'd used when he'd brought me out of my nightmare, the one that said he would kill all the bad guys, slay the dragons, and vanquish all the monsters.

And right now, I was thinking that maybe he was capable of all of that. Maybe they all were.

"Thanks for—" I started to say, and then everything went black.

I woke up in a bed made of clouds, or at least that's what it felt like against my aching body. I struggled to get my bearings for a second, until I realized I was in Gabriel's bed, and he was snoring softly beside me. The other two were nowhere to be found. I took stock of my body, noting that I was a little sore, but not as sore as I would've thought, and my head actually felt really clear. How long had I been out?

I slid off the bed as quietly as I could, not wanting to wake up Gabriel, and crept into his bathroom where I relieved myself and went and stood in front of the sink. For a kidnapping attempt, I'd emerged remarkably unscathed.

I was wearing an oversized shirt that I knew was Gabriel's based on the smell, and some knickers. Someone had cleaned up the cut on my forehead, and there was a butterfly bandage on top of it, all the blood gone from my face. I threw some water on my face to try and wake up a bit more, and then decided to go out to the kitchen to try and find some food.

But as I turned to leave the bathroom, Gabriel was there, his hair falling around him. He was shirtless, wearing a pair of low-slung gray sweatpants, the ultimate catnip for all women.

Especially when you had an elephant dick. Which I could see clearly outlined right now.

Not that I was looking.

Okay, I was definitely looking.

He stood there and stared at me. His intense gaze held mine for what felt like an eternity before he finally opened his mouth. "You're not allowed to leave me," he told me hoarsely.

"It wasn't exactly my choice," I tried to joke, but he wasn't seeing the humor.

"I can't breathe without you," he confessed. "I don't want to breathe without you."

I walked towards him, my heart feeling like it could burst with his words. I reached up to touch his cheek, and he nudged into my palm like he was just as in need of comfort as I was. His gaze slipped in intensity for a moment, and my heart stumbled. I saw it there, like I was standing in front of a mirror. All the love and need I'd been feeling since I met him reflected back at me.

I groaned and we lunged towards each other at the same time. Our lips crashed together, and suddenly, I was up against the wall, his mouth covering mine as his tongue licked over the curve of my lips and then thrust into my mouth with deep rhythmic sweeps. He groaned as he devoured me, his hands tangling in my hair, holding my head in place as he continued to kiss me like the sun couldn't rise without me. Like I was everything.

He pulled back, still staying close enough that our noses touched. "You taste so good," he breathed as he once again attacked my lips in a hard, hungry, controlling kiss that pulled a whimper from my lungs. His hand slipped between my thighs, and he pushed my knickers aside impatiently. I moaned when his fingers softly stroked over my skin before he plunged two fingers inside of me. His thumb caressed my clit, rubbing in gentle circles.

"Fuck, Bellissima. You're so tight." There was a groan in his voice, and a moan of relief slipped from my throat as his fingers worked in and out of me in a controlled rhythm, spreading me open.

I clenched my muscles involuntarily, and he chuckled darkly. "You have a greedy pussy, don't you?" he murmured, his fingers growing rougher inside of me. His muscles flexed and shifted with each thrust of his hand, a buffet of deliciousness that I was panting over. He forced a third finger inside of me, and I sobbed as he brutally stretched me.

I panted, arching, trying to allow his fingers in.

"I have to stretch you out so you're ready for me."

And I knew what he was talking about; the idea of fitting his dick inside of me was very exciting, but slightly terrifying at the same time.

He dropped to his knees, suddenly ripping my knickers and throwing the shredded cloth behind him. He grabbed one of my thighs and hooked it over one of his broad shoulders.

Before I could do anything, he was covering my sex with his mouth. Sucking and licking, he separated my folds with his hot tongue as he continued thrusting his three fingers into my clenching core. My hands were in his hair, pulling him closer and then pushing him away at the same time. He tilted his head back, and his hands reached around to squeeze my arse, directing me until I was literally straddling his face.

"Ride me, baby," he murmured as his stubble scratched my thighs. It was torture watching as his cheeks hollowed out, sucking rhythmically, and all my thoughts slipped from my mind.

There was only him. There was only this. My hips writhed against him as I moaned.

Admittedly, I had limited experience getting eaten out. But both Raphael and Lucian had seemed like experts. They hadn't given head like this, though. Gabriel ate me like he loved it. Like he couldn't get enough. Like he craved it. I didn't know if he was growling or moaning, but whatever he was doing was sending vibrations across my clit and into my core. Over and over.

I was whimpering a steady stream of pleas as everything inside me began to tighten, and he tongued my clit.

White-hot pleasure tore through me in a violent rush. I was a slave to sensations, my hips thrusting against his mouth desperately as I rode him. He licked and sucked eagerly, trying to get every last drop out of me as tremors continued to rock through my body. His fingers slipped out of my seam and then his tongue pushed in, over and over again, sucking me until I was seeing stars. He looked up, meeting my gaze, and that was enough to set me off on another tremor. It rocked through me, shocking me with its intensity.

"Never tasted anything so sweet, Dahlia. I want to spend the rest of my life eating your pussy." He stood up, and his lips sealed over mine, his tongue licking into my mouth so I could taste myself on his lips.

His movements slowed as he grabbed the back of my thighs and picked me up. I wrapped my legs around him, and my hands went around his shoulders. I watched as he slipped down his sweatpants, freeing his massive cock.

"You're huge," I gasped, a little worry leaking through my voice. He laughed, and I swore I was dripping so much that the floor had to be wet underneath me. He pressed his red, swollen head into my wet folds and began to rub it slightly, up and down, and across my clit.

"Please," my voice rasped.

"I'm going to take such good care of you, bellissima," he murmured, and I believed him.

The doubt that I'd been feeling since I discovered his disorder flew away, and in its place was a contentment and trust that I didn't think I'd ever experienced. Our eyes locked as he began to press in slowly. He paused after the first inch, and my breath stalled as I gasped. I really didn't know if he was going to fit. He began to pepper kisses all across my face, and his hand went down between us, slowly rolling across my clit and allowing me to relax enough for him to begin to push in more. My insides were screaming at the sheer size of him, and at only halfway in, I already felt full.

"Take deep breaths, baby. I'm going to make you feel so good." He rubbed on my clit again until he was able to slowly, steadily, push his way in. He was so deep inside of me, I swore he was tapping at my womb. All the while, his fingers kept massaging my clit.

"Breathe, baby. Breathe." His voice was hoarse from need. He stayed still inside of me for a moment, allowing my body to get used to him. His eyes were locked on mine, and it felt intimate, almost too intimate, like he could look into my soul. And I was afraid that he wouldn't like what he saw there. I liked how I looked in Gabriel's eyes; that was a lie, I loved how I looked in Gabriel's eyes. But he had me on a pedestal so high that it was just a matter of time before I disappointed him.

My dark thoughts flew away as he began to slowly withdraw, before slamming back into me so hard that it knocked the breath out of me.

"You're choking my dick," he moaned as he buried his face against my hair and took a deep breath. "Love how you take all of me." He moved his hips, and it hit my clit perfectly. His tongue traced from my pulse to my jawline.

"You're perfect. Better than I could've ever dreamed." He slowly withdrew until just his mushroomed head was inside me, and then he pushed in suddenly and I gasped at the feeling. Over and over again, he moved in and out of me as he brushed kisses across my lips. Locking eyes with me, he began to move slower as I clung to him desperately. His stare was so intense, it felt so intimate to be locked together like this, our faces just inches apart. He pushed my back straight against the wall and then began to thrust inside me harder. His hungry mouth devoured mine, his tongue plunging and demanding that I take it.

I was going to cum again.

"Dripping wet. Never been this good. I want you to come all over my big dick," he growled as he began to thrust harder and harder like he was pounding inside of me. I couldn't help but gasp every time he filled me all the way. I was moaning and fisting his hair. That seemed to do something for him, because he lost control. He began to pound into me, so hard that if I wasn't on birth control, he'd definitely be putting a baby in me.

"I want this every day. You gonna give it to me?" he asked as he continued to move in and out of me. He was so big that it hurt, which meant that my arousal level was spiking even higher. Every bite of pain brought me one step closer to orgasm. "Choke my cock, baby," he growled, and his dirty words sent me spiraling over the edge. The flames that were humming inside of me quickly turned into an outright forest fire, my whole body convulsing as pleasure surged through me.

"You're so fucking tight," he murmured. "Hottest girl on this whole fucking planet." His tongue kept taking deep licks into my mouth, and I whimpered as his rhythm changed. His forehead pressed against mine as he squeezed his eyes shut, continuing his pounding pace. His thumb went back down to my clit, and he began to press on it in time with his cock moving in and out of me. He moaned and then shuddered as he came with a loud gasp. I could feel him inside of me, hot liquid filling me up and once more sending me into an orgasm. His whole body trembled as he pushed in deeper. There was so much cum, it spilled out of me. He withdrew just a bit, a glimmer of satisfaction in his gaze when he saw his cum dripping out of me.

"You're so fucking perfect," he said again, brushing his lips across mine one last time.

When he withdrew, we both groaned, and he had to keep his hands on my hips because I'd forgotten how to walk. He carried me over to the sink and then grabbed a washcloth and got it wet with warm water before carefully cleaning me up. Gabriel put a kiss on both of my inner thighs, and then my stomach, and then the space between my breasts, and then on my lips.

"I want you to know that there's never going to be a day that I don't think about you. There's never going to be a minute when you're ever second choice or second place with me. I—" his voice trailed off.

I'd asked him to tell me when it would save me, but maybe he'd been saving me every day all along, making me stronger and less bound to the darkness of my past.

"I love you," I finished for him, and his breath hitched as he closed his eyes. When he opened them again, they were shiny, and I watched in awe as a tear trailed down his face.

"Dahlia, I love you. And I'll keep loving you until the end of this life, the next life, and any life after that." He put his arms around me, and his tears wet my shoulder. We stayed like that, just basking in what we'd found.

I slipped on a robe and Gabriel took my hand, leading me out to the hallway, promising to make me his spicy rigatoni again. We'd just stepped into the kitchen when light reflecting off of a glass in the living room caught my eye. Lucian was sitting there, a glass in his hand.

I knew he knew exactly what we'd done. But I didn't feel bad at all.

"Lucian?" Gabriel asked carefully, flicking on a lamp and lighting up the living room so I could see Lucian sprawled out on the sofa, his dress shirt unbuttoned halfway, looking like every girl's wet dream.

I couldn't believe myself right now.

"We received another package," he said before standing up and walking past us, disappearing down the hallway. I heard the sound of his door slamming shut, but I was preoccupied with the box sitting on the coffee table. This one was a shiny blue color, and I walked towards it hesitantly. Gabriel was there, with that trusty pair of tongs, and he lifted the lid up to reveal what looked like shattered glass. When I leaned in to look closer, I could see what looked like the heel of a shoe.

"Cinderella's glass slipper," I murmured. Of course there was a note. Gabriel carefully lifted the slip of paper out with his tongs.

When the clock struck twelve, Cinderella lost it all. Midnight's coming.

Well, I was certainly never going to look at fairytales the

same way. Dread shot through my bloodstream like a hit of cocaine.

A memory tried to force its way into my consciousness, but I couldn't quite grasp it.

Gabriel dropped the tongs and pulled me into his arms. I only realized then that I was shaking.

"Nothing's going to happen to you," he promised.

And that might've been the first lie that Gabriel ever told me.

TWENTY-THREE

Megan burst into the room, followed by Shelby Ray. "We've had our most successful week ever! Thirty animals were somehow adopted this week. I say we need to celebrate."

Shelby Ray was dancing around the room, and I watched her with a laugh.

"What did you have in mind?" I asked as I finished shoveling food into a new golden retriever's bowl.

"We're going out. We're going to go home, shower off the smell of dog shit, and dress up. And then we'll go to my favorite bar."

It sounded amazing… and kind of exhausting.

I hadn't slept well the last couple of nights, not even with Gabriel doing his best to wear me out. The sensation of knowing I'd forgotten something important was driving me crazy.

"What do you think?" Megan asked, and I looked up and saw

how hopeful she looked. Since I'd started working here, I learned that Megan was a single mom, and with the hours that she worked at the shelter, she probably didn't get out very much.

"What are you doing tonight, Shelby Ray?" I asked, giving one last pet to the adorable dog before I staggered to my feet, feeling about a hundred years old after everything I'd done today.

"I've got a date with Real Housewives and pizza," Shelby Ray said with a smile.

"That sounds like a plan," I said, and Megan jumped up and down like she was twenty years younger.

I bit my lip. "There's just one thing. I'm going to have to have someone tag along with me," I told her tentatively.

"I hardly think it'll be a shame to have some eye candy to look at all night."

I snorted, already plotting ways that I could get her laid tonight.

"What time do you want to meet?" I asked her.

"Let's go at seven," she said sheepishly. "Just in case I run out of steam."

I couldn't help but laugh. "It's like you read my mind."

I grabbed my stuff from the employee room, and I waved goodbye to Megan and Shelby Ray before heading to the front where Riccardo was on guard duty. He nodded at me solemnly when he saw me, quiet as usual.

As we drove back to the penthouse, I tried to psych myself into getting excited about tonight. I'd gone out to clubs in London, and Gabriel had taken me to some fun spots in the first couple of weeks, but I hadn't really done anything else since then.

Tonight, I was just going to forget everything and have some fun.

I hoped.

Gabriel held my hand as we bypassed the already long line and made our way past the bouncers and into a dimly lit bar. Megan assured me that it was the best bar in New York, and the dancing and drinks were fantastic.

Gabriel hadn't necessarily agreed with her assessment at all, but he told me he was just glad to be with me.

Of course, I swooned.

I was wearing the dress and shoes that Lucian had left on my bed a few weeks ago...and wishing he was coming tonight too. Evidently, I was greedy.

"You look so fucking hot," Gabriel purred in my ear as he grabbed my arse.

I smirked; he was the one who looked fucking hot. He was in a fitted dress shirt that was almost indecently tight. I could count every one of his abs through it.

The pair of dark jeans he was wearing looked amazing on his arse. Combined with the combat boots and the man bun, and I was already panting.

Megan gave a loud hoot when she saw us, and I saw there were already shots lined up in front of her.

Megan was wearing a tight black dress that showcased her impressively built legs perfectly, and her hair was down in waves. She looked gorgeous.

She waved us over. "Take a shot. Let's get this night started," she crowed.

"Go ahead," Gabriel said, pulling me in front of him and holding me by the waist as he guided me towards the bar.

"Are you going to have any?" I asked him.

He shook his head. "Designated driver tonight, Bellissima."

"But we have a driver?"

He didn't answer me, just smacked a kiss on my neck that had Megan's eyebrows raising.

To cut off any questions, I grabbed one of the light yellow shots, that kind of resembled piss, and threw it back.

Yum, a lemon drop. I'd always been a fan of those. Megan threw back the shot she'd gotten for Gabriel, and we headed to a table upstairs where we ordered more drinks and lots of greasy bar food, including cheese sticks, because those things were the shit.

As the night went on, I lost track of all the drinks I'd consumed. At one point, we discovered a shot that tasted exactly like a pink Starburst, and it was all downhill from there.

Megan had found some girl at the bar and brought her back to our table. They were currently wrapped around each other, and Megan was devouring her lips.

I wasn't any better. I was beyond horny, and Gabriel definitely wasn't minding it. I was straddling his lap, his hands on my arse as I rubbed against his hard dick as we made out.

Suddenly, I felt a vibration under my leg.

Gabriel moved his lips away from mine and sighed. "I'd better check who that is," he murmured reluctantly, pulling his phone out of his pocket.

"Yeah," Gabriel answered in an annoyed voice. "Right now? Can't it wait till morning? Yeah, I understand. I'll wait till he gets here."

Gabriel hung up the phone and groaned as his head fell back against the padded bench.

"We have to leave?" I asked with a frown. We hadn't even danced yet.

"I have to leave. Lucian's got some people he needs me to talk to. But you're going to stay here and enjoy your night. Raphael's going to switch with me."

I nodded, my nerves flaring up. I'd barely seen Raphael since the day I'd been kidnapped, and I was nervously excited to spend time with him.

He was still only speaking to Lucian when necessary, which meant that he spent most of his time away, doing who knows what.

"Maybe you can get rid of his bad mood," Gabriel said with a grin, and my cheeks flushed as I searched his face. Was he saying what I thought he was?

"I've always known I wasn't going to be the only one," he whispered in my ear. "Just as long as you always love me as much as you love them."

Love. I couldn't comprehend saying that to Lucian and Raphael...even if I may have felt it. Loving Gabriel was as easy as breathing though, a soft descent into warm water, laughter and sunshine, and a picnic under a perfect sky. Whatever I felt for Lucian and Raphael was wrapped in barbed wire, so complicated I felt like screaming every time I thought about it.

I slid off Gabriel's lap and grabbed one of the shots that had just been brought to the table.

This called for more alcohol. I tipped the shot back, but right as I did, a shadow fell over the table.

I looked up and saw that Raphael had just arrived.

Fuck. He was beautiful. He was wearing a fitted black Henley with dark jeans and boots, and his sleeves were rolled up to showcase his tattoos. The lights were reflecting off his gold hair, and everyone at the tables near us was staring at him. I could practically smell the lust hormones in the air.

Mine were definitely there.

"Angel, you look like pure sin," he murmured, his gaze solely locked on me.

Before I could answer, Gabriel tipped my chin towards him and claimed my lips in a possessive kiss, his tongue slipping in my mouth in aggressive licks that had me swooning.

When Gabriel pulled away, I couldn't help but look at Raphael. He didn't look jealous at all, just amused.

He clapped Gabriel on the back as he stood up and then quickly slid into his seat as Gabriel strode away.

I already missed him.

Raphael threw his arm around me and began to drive me crazy as he stroked my arm. He didn't seem as dangerous tonight; all the anger he'd been carrying around him like a cape was gone, or he was hiding it really well.

Raphael grinned at the show we were getting across the table. "I didn't know Megan was so freaky," he said. I couldn't help but giggle. Megan and her woman were getting so hot and heavy, I was afraid she was about to be laid out on the table and I was going to see something I couldn't forget.

"Want to dance?" Raphael asked, his hand sliding down my arm.

"Yep," I squeaked. I grabbed another shot and threw it back, the fruity flavor sending heat soaring through my bloodstream. My head felt light and my nerves relaxed. Yep, that hit the spot.

I didn't know what it was about Raphael that always had me on my guard, but even after months, I never knew what he was going to do next. Probably should've known that after he took my virginity on the plane.

"What about your virginity?" Raphael purred, his breath warm on my ear.

Whoops, I'd said that out loud.

Raphael slid out and then helped me out of the booth. He led me by the hand down the stairs and then onto the dance floor that was writhing with people. Raphael took us to the farthest corner of the club, which also happened to be the darkest. He tugged me until my arse was nestled against him. "Show me your moves, angel," he murmured.

One of his hands moved from my hip up to the base of my neck, and my breath caught as I thought about the other times that his hand had been there. His fingertips were dragging along my collarbone, and when I looked up, I lost my breath when his eyes met mine and I saw the dark possession that was there. His hand that wasn't sliding across my skin and driving me crazy yanked my hip back roughly against him. The alcohol was hitting me hard by this time, and combined with his breath on my neck and his lips that had begun to ghost over my skin, I was on fire. My knickers were soaking wet. Not that they hadn't already been wet before he'd gotten here because of Gabriel…but at this point, it was embarrassing.

He began to guide our movements, and I relaxed against his body as I let him take the lead.

His body was curved around mine, like a shield, and I couldn't help but melt against him. My eyes closed as I breathed him in. I'd missed his scent. The Weekend's "Blinding Lights" began a pulsing beat, and I was consumed. Our bodies were in perfect sync as we moved, and I could feel his hard cock against my arse. One of his hands glided across my skin, slowly exploring my entire body.

"I've missed you," I blurted out, immediately embarrassed.

Raphael froze at my admission. He moved his hand to my stomach and pushed into me until his dick was sliding into the crease of my arse. I was already plastered against him, but I put my arm around his neck, needing him to ground me because I felt like I was going to float into the sky with how loose and free I felt.

"I'm always watching you, angel. Can't fucking stand being away from you for too long. Makes me go crazy."

I continued moving against him, but I was really confused. When was he watching me?

"I'm obsessed with you. Can't get enough. I think about you every second of every day." His voice was pure sex as he rasped into my ear.

Everything was getting fuzzy, and my body felt like liquid heat.

I didn't know if I could say no if he decided to fuck me right here on the dance floor in front of everyone. He was making me that crazy.

"Let's get out of here," he whispered, and I quickly agreed, forgetting any reasons why I shouldn't.

He began to lead me off the dance floor. "Wait, Megan," I cried.

"Riccardo's going to stay and watch over her, make sure the girl isn't a creeper."

I relaxed against him.

"Okay."

His arm was around my waist, keeping me from falling as we headed out the front into the night air.

Raphael kept me captive, a possessive hand on my hip as we made our way to where a midnight blue Lamborghini was parked right in front of the club.

"How do you guys always get the best parking spots?" I asked, a little slowness in my voice.

Raphael's arms wrapped around me from behind, and his body was flush against my back as he moved me towards the car. It was about to melt into a puddle. He was going to have to scrape me off the sidewalk from just the feel of his breath on my neck.

"Tonight, it's called a valet," he said, amused.

That made sense.

He opened the door and squeezed my arse as he helped me inside before closing it and hustling around the car. It smelled like him. That smoky orange scent that I'd been obsessed with since the moment I breathed him in. I was afraid that I was going to leave a wet spot on the leather just from how turned on the smell made me.

I was really drunk. Raphael took hold of my hand and held it under his while he shifted gears. I wasn't sure what they called the gear lever here in the states, but it was sexy how he kept our hands like that the entire way home.

But then again, I'd probably think that anything he did was sexy right now.

My, how things had changed.

He was being so touchy-feely tonight; it was making my head spin even more than the alcohol was.

I wasn't sure how I'd gotten here, hating his guts as he walked away from me at the airport, to wanting to jump on his lap and ride him like a pogo stick now.

The thought made an image pop into my mind, of me on a pogo stick with Raphael's eyes attached. It made me giggle, and Raphael glanced at me, amused, before turning his attention back to the road. It's not like Raphael had been sweet. Every single circumstance I'd had with him had been wild, insane. Not healthy in the least bit. But maybe whereas Gabriel made me feel safe and gooey, Raphael called to the craziness inside me. He saw all the twisted things about my soul, and it made him want me even more.

That was probably it.

We pulled up in front of our building, and the doorman was there to let me out. One of the same ones who had watched me struggle on the sidewalk, most likely at Lucian's direction.

He wasn't ignoring me now. Raphael growled when he got to my side and saw the doorman's eyes were lingering on my legs a little too long. I giggled when the guy stumbled backward, almost falling to the ground, and then I let Raphael lead me into the building. When we got inside the elevator, and the doors had closed, Raphael wasted no time pinning me against the mirrored wall until his body was completely flush against mine. He moved against me, teasing me with his hard cock, and then his lips sealed over mine, a slow and penetrating rhythm that reminded me of how he liked to fuck.

I was so aroused, I thought I might die.

But what a way to go. We were still wrapped around each other as the elevator doors opened and we spilled out into the entryway. I was barely able to stand, and Raphael hoisted me into his arms. I wrapped my legs and arms around him as he walked us forward, not stopping until we were in the living room.

A little voice tried to tell me the living room wasn't where we should be doing this, but I was too far gone. Between that last Starburst shot, or maybe it was all the shots before that, combined with the way both Gabriel and Raphael had played my body; I didn't care where we ended up. He laid me on the sofa and looked down at me.

"Hurry," I whispered, grabbing onto his shirt and trying to pull him towards me. I released his shirt, and my hands slipped underneath gasping at his obscenely defined abs. I found his nipples and pinched them. His eyes closed as a hot moan fell from his lips. He sat back on his haunches and began to trail his hands up my thighs until he reached the hem of my dress. Then slowly, so slowly it had to be intentional, he pushed my dress up, higher and higher until my barely-there knickers were revealed, and then my stomach, and then over the swells of my heaving breasts.

"Sit up, angel," he ordered gruffly, and I moved so that he could slip the dress over the top of me until I was laying there in nothing but some black lingerie.

"I like this," he commented as he fingered the front clasp on the bra. I'd never had one of those before, but it was sexy as fuck when he flipped it open, and it slid off, my nipples pebbling even more under the cool air. I slid the straps off and then laid back down, my skin burning as his gaze ate me up.

His hands kneaded my breasts hungrily. And then he squeezed my nipple roughly and I almost spiraled into an orgasm.

After he tortured me for a moment, going back and forth as he suckled on my breasts, he pulled back, and I whined, desperate for more. Finally, he took pity on me and began to slide my knickers down my legs.

The sound of glass shattering on the floor made both of us freeze. I peered around Raphael and gasped when I saw Lucian standing there in the living room, a broken tumbler scattered all over the floor. He didn't seem to notice the broken glass though. His chest was heaving, his gaze on fire as he took me in. Raphael was frozen in place, a growl on his lips. He was ready to put up a fight if Lucian tried to end this.

But to both of our surprise, Lucian came and sat on the sofa a few feet away from where I was laying. The moon was shining through the window, almost a spotlight on my chest, and I found myself gushing just being under the intense stares of both men.

"Spread her legs so I can see her pretty pussy," Lucian ordered in a low, dark voice.

Raphael was still frozen in place, and I watched in breathless, drunk anticipation to see what he would do.

Slowly, Raphael began to spread my legs, his fingers trailing up my thighs.

"I want to see you suck on those pretty tits first. Prettiest fucking tits I've ever seen," Lucian ordered.

Raphael growled, but he did what Lucian had commanded and moved in between my legs, back up to my chest that he'd been working so good before.

His head lowered, and his breath tickled my still wet nipples. He leaned down, and I moaned when I felt the heat of his mouth moving over my sensitive peak.

"Suck it harder. I want her screaming under your tongue."

I arched as Raphael's suction increased. He added a scrape of teeth, and my core tightened with every streaking jolt to my throbbing pussy.

"Good girl. You like him sucking your pretty fucking nipples, don't you?"

I'd closed my eyes, but they flew open, and I looked up to see Lucian sitting closer now, his eyes twin sparks in the darkness of the room.

"Answer me," he said silkily.

"Yes," I moaned as Raphael released my tip, licking a path

across my chest to my other nipple, his fingers kneading and pinching my abandoned wet one.

"Harder," Lucian ordered, and Raphael's cheeks hollowed as he sucked my nipple deeply into his mouth, plunging me into an orgasm so good that I screamed.

I felt a hand stroking my cheek softly. "Such a good girl. It's not over yet, principessa. Look at you. We're so fucking lucky."

I stared up at the ceiling, the room dancing around me. This felt like a dream. The most delicious dream ever that I never wanted to wake up from.

Now if only Gabriel was here.

"He's going to eat your pussy now. Would you like that, Dahlia? Are you going to let him make you feel so good?"

I moaned in answer, unable to form words.

"You heard our girl, brother. She's ready for you to fuck her with your tongue."

Raphael's pupils were blown out. I would have never expected him to be into something like this, especially when it was Lucian giving the orders, but it was obvious how turned on he was.

Raphael obediently put his face between my still spread legs, and then he let out a deep groan as his hot, wet tongue slid between my folds.

"She tastes so good, doesn't she?"

Raphael just moaned in response as his tongue began to circle my clit, sliding back to plunge in my opening.

"Get every last drop. Nothing on this planet tastes as good," Lucian murmured as Raphael went to work consuming every drop of my cum that was practically gushing from my core.

My breath was nothing but gasps until Raphael began to

press and rub on my clit; all I could do was moan after that, my core tightening in response.

The sound of Raphael eating me filled the whole room in an obscene soundtrack I wanted to hear over and over again. I heard the sound of a zipper sliding down, and my eyes popped open to see that Lucian had pulled out his long, perfect dick and was moving his hand slowly up and down as he watched me get worked over.

Lucian's expression was starving, and I would have loved for him to join in.

But this was good too.

As Raphael sucked hard on my clit, I kept my gaze locked on Lucian's tattooed hand as he slid it up and down his length, the mushroomed head purple and angry looking with a drop of pre cum I was suddenly desperate to taste.

I had to close my eyes as an orgasm crashed over me. This seemed to spur Raphael on because he was suddenly ravenous.

"Push her harder, Raphael. Let's see if she likes having her sweet little asshole played with."

I froze at that direction, because I wasn't sure I could do arse play. Not after what my uncle had done, over and over again until I was almost always bleeding.

But Raphael didn't give me any time to think about it.

He brushed his thumb softly over my arsehole, and I shivered at the sensation.

While his thumb massaged my opening, Raphael began pushing his fingers into my swollen pussy. I'd gotten tighter with each orgasm, and even one finger was enough to have me gasping for breath.

"Add another one," Lucian murmured, a rough edge to his voice that had me immediately watching him once again.

Raphael slid another finger in, and I gritted my teeth, a soft whimper slipping out.

He jerked them in and out of me a few more times before he abruptly pulled out.

I moaned as I felt a slick finger replace his thumb and start rubbing over my puckered flesh.

Evidently, I was a fan of arse play...if the Rossi men were involved, because I lost my mind, beginning to thrust against his finger as his other hand worked on my clit and began to scissor in and out of me.

Lucian looked feral behind me. "Cazzo," he murmured, pinching the tip of his dick.

Raphael suddenly pushed through my tight ring of flesh, and I screamed. The pinch of pain was immediately gone though, and then all I could feel was his thick finger as he began to work it in and out, rubbing over my nerve endings and making me hornier than I'd ever been before. It had never been like this. This was incredible.

I was faintly aware of the pleas spilling from my mouth as my body began to shake. Lucian was suddenly right above me, his eyes bright as his strokes got faster.

I screamed as the most intense orgasm of my life washed over me, almost making me black out, and then I felt a spurt of hot liquid splash my face as Lucian came.

Raphael moaned from in between my legs, and my pussy twinged in response.

I was a limp, mindless mess, incapable of even opening my eyes as Raphael pulled his fingers out of my core and arsehole. A minute later, I felt a warm, wet cloth on my face, wiping off Lucian's cum, while another warm cloth cleaned up my aching core. I winced, my eyes fluttering as it moved over my sensitive clit.

"We've got you, principessa," Lucian murmured, and I was gathered into someone's warm chest. I wasn't even sure whose it was. I didn't have the strength to try and find out. I tried to hang on to consciousness, but I was too far gone.

And soon, I slipped into a blissful, dreamless sleep.

TWENTY-FOUR

I woke up in Gabriel's bed, oddly enough, my brain ratcheting against my skull. Gabriel was nowhere to be found, but the bed was still warm beside me.

Way too much alcohol—holy fuck...last night wasn't a dream.

Fuck. Fuck. Fuck.

My core began to throb just thinking about it.

I wanted a repeat. A million repeats. Nonstop forever, please.

Before I couldn't stop myself from touching my throbbing clit, I got out of the bed, my body aching all over. I was dressed in nothing but an oversized t-shirt that, judging by the smoky orange scent, belonged to Raphael...no knickers underneath.

I grabbed some of Gabriel's boxers from his drawer and slipped them on before stumbling out into the hallway, desperate for some food...and some aspirin.

Why was it so fucking bright?

I stopped short when I got to the kitchen and saw that all

three of the Rossi men were standing there with Emilia who was fussing over them. Of all days for them to actually be around…

My eyes suddenly were glued to the floor, and I could feel the blush staining my cheeks.

One of them chuckled, and I decided today might be the day that I died…from embarrassment.

"Oh, dearie. You're looking rough this morning. Let's get you some food," Emilia said while scooting me towards a barstool at the island.

She moved around the kitchen, opening and closing cabinets before bringing me over a drink that smelled like wet dog and cabbage.

"A little hair of the dog to get you right this morning," she explained as I eyed it dubiously.

"Drink it down, angel. It's an old family secret and works like a charm," added Raphael.

I didn't answer him…or look at him. I just picked up the drink and began gulping.

It didn't taste better than it smelled, and I had to work to keep it from coming back up. I quickly figured out that the only way for me to drink it was by plugging my nose.

I don't think I'd ever drunk something so fast.

I winced when I set the empty glass down a little too hard, and I heard the guys chuckling.

"You're too cute, bellissima," Gabriel murmured as he slid a kiss across my cheek. My eyes widened and darted over to where Raphael and Lucian were leaning against the counter.

But they didn't look upset about it. Apparently, this was a thing we were doing now.

The drink was already starting to work and, combined with

some aspirin, I was able to eat the eggs and toast that Emilia set in front of me.

"Does your dress need to be steamed?" Emilia asked a few minutes later.

I looked at her in confusion. "My dress?"

"Cazzo," Lucian muttered. "We have that benefit tonight."

"Let's just send a check. It can be a really big check, but I'm definitely not in the mood to fucking have to schmooze all night," griped Raphael.

"What's the charity?" I asked.

"An organization that fights against child abuse, I think," mused Gabriel absentmindedly. He'd somehow ended up next to me with my hand stretched out in front of him, and he was doodling patterns on my skin with his finger. Of course, it was giving me goosebumps.

I froze. "We need to go," I blurted without thinking. Eight eyes were suddenly locked on my face, and I got even redder because I could only guess what they were all thinking. I couldn't help but sneak a glance at Lucian who was staring at me intensely, a tic in his cheek. He knew why something like this would be so important for me to attend.

"Well, I think the lady has spoken," said Lucian lightly. "I'll make sure that a dress is sent up, but we're all going." He strode out of the kitchen without another word, and I wondered what kind of demons he was running from right then. Gabriel shrugged over Lucian's seemingly weird behavior and then went back to tracing patterns on my skin.

I continued munching on my toast, very well aware of the watchful gazes of Raphael, Gabriel, and Emilia.

Fuck.

LUCIAN

Dahlia was a mess tonight, a beautifully, perfect mess.

You could tell that everything about this night was a trigger for her. She was jumpy and distracted, only picking at her food even though it had been catered from one of the best restaurants in the city. Gabriel had asked her if she wanted to dance but she'd just shaken her head no. She was now listening with rapt attention to the MC of the event, Justine Goodman, one of the bigger local news anchors. Justine was in her element, dressed up in a big poofy gown with her hair in a complicated updo, and a fucking crown on her head. She and Gabriel had a brief affair if I was remembering right, and I didn't miss the longing looks she kept throwing at our table.

Of course, Gabriel was completely unaware; his attention was locked on Dahlia, and I could see the tension in his muscles from being unable to touch her.

My attention was locked on her too, though. She was dressed in a skintight black dress with a halter neck, and a slit that went past her knee and showcased her gorgeous legs when she walked. Her hair was down in loose curls, and a splash of red stained her full lips.

And she looked so fucking sad.

I actually hadn't forgotten tonight, I just tended to stay away from things with this subject. I had to keep my eyes on her at all times to stay grounded right now, and so I didn't miss the way she was pressing down on her hip like she always did when she was upset.

Unwillingly, flashes of last night shot through my brain. I'd never been so turned on as I had been watching my brother work her over. I was definitely a sexual deviant, but that was a first for me; I'd never known voyeurism was my thing. Or maybe it was just my thing when it came to Dahlia.

My cock stiffened in my pants just thinking about it, and I had to move my legs to make sure that I was firmly hidden under the table.

Justine stopped speaking and the music struck back up, and I just wanted to do anything I could to get rid of the frown on Dahlia's face.

"Dance with me?" I asked. She'd already said no to Gabriel, but it almost felt like dancing was our thing. Our dance at the mess of an engagement party was the first time that I'd seen the spark of interest in her gaze.

"Okay," she said glumly, and Gabriel rolled his eyes at me from behind her, miffed she'd agreed to dance with me when she'd refused him. I winked at him, and then grabbed her hand and led her over to the dance floor, pulling her as close as I could without making a scene.

"You look fucking gorgeous tonight, principessa," I murmured into her ear. She softly sighed and relaxed in my arms, and I couldn't help but think of her trusting me in a different way.

"Last night...was interesting," she suddenly whispered, and my eyes widened, surprised she was bringing it up with how embarrassed she'd been to see us this morning.

"Last night was fucking hot," I responded.

She giggled, and I savored the sound.

"You know I want more from you."

I stiffened and missed a step. "Dahlia—"

"How do you know I can't be what you want?" she asked, pulling away from me a little bit so she could look me in the face. I'm sure she could see all the want and need in my gaze because there was nothing more I wanted than to have her tied up on my bed, feeling my dick sliding in and out of her perfect, wet heat.

Sometimes I wondered if she'd be up for the stuff that I needed. She'd certainly seemed up for anything last night.

Before I could say anything else, the sound of shots firing from out in the hallway outside of the ballroom filled the air. I immediately pulled Dahlia to a crouch as people began screaming and running around. Trying to stay calm, I pulled out my gun from under my tuxedo jacket.

Dahlia looked terrified, and I took her hand and started moving her towards the exit on the other side from where we'd heard the shots. Suddenly, men began pouring into the room from the hallway opposite of where we were headed, black masks covering their heads.

"Fuck," I hissed. I could see Gabriel crouched down behind our table; he was trying to search for us while keeping one eye on the men scattering through the room.

I couldn't think of many reasons why someone would put out a hit on an event like this, other than something having to do with me.

Which meant that we needed to get out of here, now.

We'd almost made it to the doorway when one of the men spotted us. He lifted up his gun, but before I could even fire, he was shot in the chest, and crumpled to the ground. I looked over to see Gabriel, crouched down closer than before, a gun in his hand.

We nodded at each other, completely unified in our goal to keep Dahlia safe at all costs.

The exit was right up ahead. As we moved towards it, more

shots rang out from behind us, and I felt the hot sting as a bullet grazed my arm.

We made it through the doorway, and I pulled Dahlia behind me as I peeked back into the ballroom and started to fire shots. I'd gotten three of them before they realized where the bullets were coming from, and then they were running at us en masse, at least five of them, firing the whole way.

I pulled Dahlia to the ground, telling her to start making her way towards the glass doors just ahead that led into the street. Bullets were whizzing through the wall a few feet above us, and Dahlia took a deep breath before listening to my instructions.

She cried out when a bullet came through the wall right in front of her.

I leaned back into the ballroom and shot at the asshole who was closest to us, striking him right in the forehead so he immediately collapsed to the ground.

"Go," I yelled at her when she stopped in front of the doors and looked back at me. "I'll be right there," I promised her.

And I hoped that I hadn't just told her a lie.

DAHLIA

I was shaking as I stumbled through the glass doors, everything in me screaming for me to go back to Lucian. But I knew I'd just be a distraction. And what I needed was for him to make sure that Gabriel got out of that room.

I was suddenly caught in a pair of arms, and I flinched before smoke and oranges filled my senses. I looked up to see a pale-faced Raphael.

"Are you hurt?" he snapped worriedly, his hands feeling all over me for a wound.

I shook my head, my breath coming out in gasps.

He pulled me towards him and wrapped his arms around me so tight that it was hard to breathe, burying his face into my hair.

"I'm so fucking sorry," he whispered.

I sniffed, my eyes burning, but of course, no tears came out.

"For what?"

"That I wasn't there," he said. "I was out talking to one of the city councilmen who was taking a smoke break when I heard the bullets. They barred the exit on that side though, so I was on my way over here to come find you. Let's get out of here." He abruptly released his octopus hold on me and tried to get me to walk with him.

I dug in my heels. "They're still in there. We can't leave without them," I told him insistently. Police sirens rang in the air, and at least ten cop cars came screeching to a halt in front of the hotel where the event was being held. Police officers poured out of their cars, ignoring the dazed guests wandering around the grounds.

Suddenly, I started to panic. How long had it been? They still weren't out yet. I began to pull Raphael towards the door. "We have to go in and help them," I cried. But he just grabbed me and dragged me back into his arms. I tried to beat on his chest, but he held me still. "I can't let you go back in there. You know they would never be okay with that."

I was thinking about stabbing him when I heard Lucian's voice. He was helping hold Gabriel up while a police officer asked them questions.

"They're out," I cried, pushing loose from Raphael's grasp and running towards them. Fear shot through me when I saw that there was a hole in Gabriel's pant leg and the fabric was darkened with blood.

"You're hurt!"

Immediately, both Gabriel's and Lucian's eyes were locked on me.

Lucian pushed past the police officer and began to stride towards me as fast as he could with Gabriel. I was barefoot by now, and I met up with them, stopping myself from jumping at them in case they had other injuries I couldn't see.

"Are you okay?" I asked Gabriel. He tried to smile, but it looked more like a grimace. "Nothing that Riccardo can't fix up, baby," he told me in a tired voice.

"No, we need to take you to the hospital," I argued.

"Riccardo was a trained medic in the Army. Gunshots happen to be his specialty," said Lucian soothingly.

"Are they all dead in there?" I asked.

Lucian nodded his head, his eyes glimmering darkly.

"All of them. I just wished I'd been able to grab the last one to question him. He shot his brains out right when I got up to him."

I felt Raphael come up behind me, and he slid his arms around my waist, putting his chin on top of my head.

"I did suggest we not come tonight," Raphael drawled, and I began to giggle, for no reason at all, because really, what we'd been through was not funny. At all.

But my giggles soon turned hysterical, and all of them stared at me worriedly.

"Let's get you home, angel," Raphael murmured, scooping me up in his arms. Lucian dragged Gabriel behind us, and we piled into the car where Riccardo was waiting.

"We'll get that patched right up, sir," Riccardo assured us

after we'd all piled in. Gabriel nodded at him gratefully, and we sped off into the night. Safe and sound.

At least for the moment.

We made it to our building, and we were walking through the lobby when Lorenzo strode towards us worriedly, holding a familiar-sized box that filled my gut with dread.

"This was left outside the doors, sir," he told Lucian, looking pale.

"Cazzo," Lucian barked, grabbing it from Lorenzo's shaking hands. He dropped it to the ground and the lid of the box slid off.

"Fuck, Fuck, Fuck," he muttered, running a furious hand through his hair. We crowded around the box, and I immediately wished that I hadn't. The head of the MC from tonight's event, the one that had dressed up like an over-the-top Cinderella was staring at us unseeingly from inside the box. That meant sometime in the last hour, when all the craziness was happening, she'd been captured and killed, and this box delivered.

I felt a little faint and stumbled backward, right into Raphael's comforting embrace. I was expecting there to be a note under the head, but when Lucian used Lorenzo's pocket square to lift the head out by its hair, he immediately growled and dropped it back in with a loud *thunk* that made me jump.

"What did it say?" I asked, but Lucian shook his head, his eyes burning as he bit his lip.

He and Gabriel exchanged dark looks.

"Okay, you're scaring me."

"It was a pair of your panties," Lucian growled. "Covered in..." His voice trailed off, but he didn't need to finish the sentence. I turned to the side and immediately vomited all over the floor.

Raphael pulled my hair back as I continued to puke up the

little I'd been able to eat that day. When my stomach was done spiraling, I stood back up and wiped my mouth with the back of my hand.

"So they've been in our place again. I thought there was no way they could bypass the new security?"

"I'm sure it was taken before. It was a pair you'd brought with you from London," soothed Lucian, evidently very familiar with my knickers.

"There's not a person in the world who could bypass our security," added Raphael.

I hoped he was right, but it all still made me sick. Gabriel hissed as his leg buckled, and Lucian and Riccardo just caught him before he fell to the floor.

"Let's get upstairs," Raphael growled, darkness wrapped around his voice like barbed wire.

We all trudged upstairs where Riccardo did indeed patch Gabriel up.

But I couldn't help but think…what was going to happen next?

I'd been asleep in Gabriel's bed when I woke up in desperate need of a glass of water. It was still dark outside, only 4 AM. I slipped out of the bed quietly amongst Gabriel's soft snores. He rolled over to where I'd been sleeping, and a whisper of my name slipped from his lips. When I was confident that he was still asleep, I tiptoed out of the room and went to the kitchen to get a drink.

I'd just taken my first sip when I heard what sounded like a shout coming from down the hall. Tentatively, I set my glass down and wandered towards the noise. I heard it again, louder, and I realized that it was coming from Lucian's room.

Taking a shaky breath, I slowly opened up his door and peered inside.

Lucian was thrashing around on his bed, whimpers and shouts flooding the room. I hesitated for a moment before stepping all the way inside and closing the door behind me.

Staying far enough that he couldn't reach me if his dream turned violent, I called to him.

"Lucian! Lucian!"

He moaned and whimpered my name.

"Lucian," I said one more time, louder, and he shot straight up, his chest heaving and his skin dotted with sweat.

He gasped for air like he hadn't been breathing, and then his eyes fell on me.

"Fuck," he growled. "What are you doing in here?"

I took a deep breath and then made a decision, taking one step towards him, and then another. He tracked me as I walked, like a panther about to pounce on its prey...but he didn't tell me to go away.

When I got to the edge of the bed, I slowly lowered myself to my knees. Then I placed my hands on my knees, palms facing up...my body shaking.

"Take back your power," I told him, keeping my gaze on the floor submissively. "Use me to do it."

I could feel his stare on my skin and it seemed to stretch on forever. "Dahlia," he said roughly.

"I'm here. And I'm not going anywhere. No matter what."

He stayed still for so long that I thought for sure he was going to refuse me. Then finally, he stood up and stepped from the bed to the floor.

"Get on the bed," he ordered, his alpha energy rolling over my skin.

My tremors increased as I rose off the floor and carefully crawled onto the bed. After situating myself, I looked up at him expectantly.

One side of his face was thrown into sharp relief by the light streaming in from the window. He's split down the middle, light and dark, good and evil, as if the devil was whispering half-truths in one ear and he was falling victim to temptation.

"I can't decide if you're an angel here to save me, or a demon sent to ruin me," he murmured. He reached out with a trembling hand and softly touched my cheek. I couldn't help but sigh as I nuzzled into him.

"Why can't it be both?" I whispered.

He had my heart. He and his brothers owned every piece of me.

But he obviously didn't know that, because right then, he looked nervous. An emotion that didn't belong on Lucian Rossi's perfect face.

"I want to own you," he whispered, staring at me intensely.

His possessiveness lit a match within me until a slow and steady heat started to flicker inside. "You already do," I admitted.

"You're the most important thing in my life," he breathed, and his brow crumbled as he stared at me, almost confused, like he didn't know how that had happened.

"Tell me what you need," I whispered. My gaze flicked to his chest, really taking in his tattoos for the first time. In the center of his chest, there was a figure bound in chains, his heart showing from a hole in his chest.

My poor Lucian. I wanted him. With every fiber of my being. I wanted the good and the bad. The man who would kill for me. I wanted him open and raw and aching with a primal drive to imprint himself into my soul. I want to fall apart in his hands.

I'd always thought that I wanted to be free.

But it turned out, all I really wanted...was to be owned.

"Take off your shirt," he murmured.

I was quick to obey, sliding off my shirt until I was in front of him in nothing but a pair of knickers. My skin burned under his hot appraisal, and I had to resist the urge to rub my thighs together as he walked over to his nightstand and opened a drawer.

"Trust me," he said, no question in his voice. He lifted up a black rope from the drawer and held it up for me to see.

I didn't even have to think. I immediately offered up my hands. He appeared stunned by my easy acquiescence. His lips parted to speak, but then he changed his mind and he immediately slipped the rope around my wrists, wrapping around twice, and with a gentle tug, I was laid back on the bed, with my hands above my head and tied to the headboard.

"Just as long as you don't leave me like this again," I quipped, and a party broke out inside of me when a small smile graced his lips.

"No promises," he whispered as he brushed his lips against mine, and then he pulled the rope taut, so the tight hold dug into my skin. Just a speck of pain though, enough to fuel my need.

I squirmed as I felt some wetness slide down my leg.

"So fucking perfect," he growled as he traced a finger along the curve of my elbow and down to curl around my nipple. I swallowed a cry when he flicked it, and I lifted into his touch.

"In a moment, principessa," he whispered, laying his forehead on mine. "First, I want to ruin you."

He stood back up and reached into the drawer, this time

pulling out a red cloth and something that looked suspiciously like a plug...for my arse.

I immediately squirmed, remembering how good it had felt to have Raphael's finger inside of me.

He set the items down, and then slowly slid off the black briefs he'd been wearing.

My pulse skyrocketed as I took him in. He was hard everywhere, so fucking perfect it was hard to believe he existed.

He got up on the bed and moved so that he was straddling me. He grabbed his cock, stroking it up and down much harder than I would know to do, and then he leaned forward so it was just inches from my face.

"Finally," I whimpered, remembering how much I'd wanted it the other night. His face was hard to read. It was like he was at war with himself, the need to use me and love me seemingly at odds.

Little did he know, they were the same.

I flicked out the tip of my tongue and caressed his swollen head. He moaned and then abruptly grabbed my hair with one hand while he fed me with the other in a slow drive forward. He pushed in and out in short strokes until finally, his control slipped, and he went all the way to the back of my throat. I gagged, and he smoothed the side of my face.

"Relax, sweetheart. Let me in," he soothed.

His tone was what broke me. I couldn't help but begin to lick and suck desperately, urging him deeper with the curve of my tongue, breathing in his delicious musk.

I loved this. I...loved him. Watching him lose his mind as he fucked my mouth absolutely demolished me.

"You look so pretty swallowing my cock," he whispered as he gazed down at me with his glimmering green eyes.

He flexed his hips, and his muscles coiled beneath him as he started to jerk faster and faster. His eyes glassed over. And even though I was desperate for him to fuck my aching core, I was also desperate to taste his cum.

I whimpered as he fell forward, his hand braced against the headboard as he punished my mouth, almost angrily. Like he hated me for making him lose control like this.

I was so full and yet so empty at the same time. Each thrust, every swirl of his hips was a direct line to the throbbing beat that taunted my insides. My body was a live wire, and I just wished he would touch me. Make me cum. Make me scream. The only part of him that was touching me right now was his cock.

He moaned and stiffened as he came, pulse after pulse, so much cum that it spilled out of my mouth as I was desperately trying to get every drop.

He panted, trying to recover, until I swirled my tongue over his crown. Growling, he pulled out.

"Fuck. I hadn't meant to do that. You're a naughty girl, principessa."

I squirmed under his hot stare. He was still hovering over me, holding his giant erection at the base.

He reached behind him to slide his fingers into my slickness. A pleased sound slipped from his lips, and he murmured, "So wet" as he dipped teasingly through my folds.

And then, as his lids sank into a look that should have frightened me, he slapped my aching core.

I squeaked, not understanding how I was suddenly so close to cumming.

I fidgeted underneath him, tugging at my arms in desperation.

His answering smile was dark and dangerous, and it made me just want to spread my legs and hold on for the ride.

"Do you want to come?" he purred, his smile still in place as he stretched out until we were pressed together, his somehow still hard length next to my wet heat.

"I'm going to take such good care of you," he murmured, an echo of the other night. Except Raphael was the one who took care of me then.

I didn't mind this level of attention.

Lucian licked at my lips, and then sucked on my tongue until I was writhing underneath him, my hips bucking up as my insides lit up like fireworks in the sky.

He moved his lips from mine and my head went up, trying to follow him. He just laughed...evilly and slid off me all the way.

Lucian picked up the cloth from the nightstand and moved over me. "Lift up your head, principessa," he murmured, and when I did what he asked, he put the cloth over my eyes and then tied it behind me.

I couldn't see anything, and I bit my lip nervously.

"Trust me," he breathed. I couldn't see him...but I could feel him, like his stare was a physical caress.

He lifted off the bed once more, and I heard him reach into the drawer again.

"What are you going to do now?" I choked out, hating that I couldn't see.

He squeezed something, and I tensed a moment later when I felt the air move, and then he was touching my ankle lightly. The bed shifted, and my legs automatically spread for him.

I jerked when his tongue licked my clit, hot and wet, sliding down to my arse, teasing around my tight rosebud.

His hands gripped my arse, thumbs slipping into my crack, spreading my cheeks wide, exposing me.

A bleating whimper burst out of me.

His tongue began to massage my puckered flesh, and I shivered, my breath coming out in stuttered gasps. His fingers moved to my clit, coating it with my slickness. He palmed my breast with his other hand, softly kneading and thumbing my nipple into a hard peak.

"Going to eat you every day," he murmured, and my thoughts flashed to when Gabriel had said something similar. My vagina was going to be busy.

And I was pretty okay with that.

He moved away from me, and I whimpered again, needing his touch.

Something wet dripped down my crack, and I jerked in alarm.

"It's just some oil, principessa," he rasped. His fingers spread the oil around my arsehole, and I clenched up at the sensation.

Was this happening? Was he about to fuck my arse? I froze as memories assaulted me, memories with *him*, and what he'd done to me.

"Stay still, pet. This will feel so good." Blinding, sharp pain ratcheting through my body.

I was gasping as I struggled to calm myself down.

He wasn't here. I could erase that memory, right now.

"Relax, Dahlia," he purred, a sound that went straight to my core. He slipped a thick finger inside, and I jumped, my skin tingling and hot. Everything was amplified without my sight. All I could do was just lay there and feel.

He slipped a second finger in and began to scissor them in and out, stretching me. His breathing was ragged; he was definitely turned on…which turned me on even more.

This was so different than what *he'd* done.

He moved away from me for a second, and then I felt something hard pressing against my opening, definitely not his dick.

Yep, that had definitely been a butt plug.

"Shhh. Just take it, baby." He began to massage my clit, and then it popped into my opening. I lost my breath and cursed at how full I felt.

I whimpered and thrashed until he pressed on my lower stomach and began to move the plug in and out of me. I cursed and moved against it, trying to arch my hips.

His fingers suddenly ran over my patch of scars, and I froze.

"Never again, baby. Going to make you feel so good...so happy, you won't ever have to again."

His words worked on my insides, and my breath hitched as he pushed the plug all the way in and then left it there as he began to move up my body.

"Most beautiful thing I've ever seen," he murmured as he dragged his tip through my swollen flesh. He pushed against my entrance, and I gasped. I already felt so full with the plug. How was I...? He slowly pushed in, and I cried out. It was too much, way too much.

"Breathe," he ordered, nipping at my jaw and neck, bringing me back down to earth. He sucked on my pulse, and I bit my lip so hard that it bled.

Lucian lapped at the blood, and I shivered.

"You're going to feel me tomorrow. You're going to be reminded who you belong to every time you move," he promised.

My lips curved into an unbidden smile. "I can't wait," I murmured.

He sunk all the way into me, and I couldn't help it—the words slipped out. "Please. Let me touch you," I begged.

He withdrew, and there was nothing but cold air until suddenly I was twisted onto my stomach.

"I'm sorry," was his response as he surged into me again. Faster and faster. Every thrust seemed deeper than the last, pushing and pulling at the plug in my arse.

My insides were burning with need as he pushed me closer and closer to the edge.

I went out of my mind, begging him to go harder, faster...to never leave.

He smacked my arse and I moaned, but somehow, he never missed a beat. He bent over me and savagely bit my neck, like he was a wolf from one of my sexy shifter books.

I keened, and he laughed. "Want to mark you all over. Cover every inch of your body with my touch."

"That's it, you're right there, principessa." Lucian was grunting with every stroke, grinding me into the mattress perfectly, the sheets rubbing against my clit.

The room was filled with the sound of us, the slick sounds my body made as my pussy tried to suck him back in, my cries, my pleas, his ragged breaths. He pushed on the plug, and that did it...I was done. I came so hard that I screamed as he continued to ride me.

On and on he went, extending my orgasm until it felt never-ending. His hand grabbed my breast and started to pull and pinch at my nipple, and the pleasure surging through my body was too much. I couldn't do it.

"Say you'll never leave me," he growled. "Promise me." He stroked in and out, long and short, fast and slow.

"Never going to get enough," he whispered. We were both sweat-drenched, and it only added to the sensations. "Come for me one more time."

I just whimpered in response...I really didn't think I could. But then he started to move harder, driving himself inside of me, and all I could do was hang on and get swept up by the ride.

"Fuck," he growled as he brutally thrust a few more times before I felt his release filling me.

But he wasn't done yet. Still inside of me, he licked up my spine and turned my head to kiss me. Long, desperate drags of his tongue as he began to massage my clit.

I was so full, so overwhelmed, so...everything.

"Feels like a dream. You're so hot. So perfect. My plug in your ass, your body splayed out just for me. Better than anything," he growled.

I whimpered as he moved faster, somehow still hard in me as he worked my clit. Abruptly, he pulled out and flipped me back around so that my back was on the bed. I was screaming when his lips replaced his finger on my clit.

"I can't," I gasped.

And then that was it, the world exploded, a white-hot flash of light as my body came undone like it never had before.

I was faintly aware I was screaming, but the world was fading to black and then I—

Faded into nothingness.

Completely ruined.

When I came back to life, my hands were free and I was wrapped snugly in the blankets, my body completely destroyed and aching in the best possible way.

Lucian was lying beside me.

But he wasn't asleep. Instead, he was staring up at the ceiling, a haunted look in his gaze.

My heart crashed and burned because he looked devastated.

"Baby," I murmured, the endearment slipping out. I want to assure him I loved him. Smother him in my love so he never hurt again.

Because what we just did was everything. He split my insides apart and remade me.

He doesn't say anything, and I frown.

"You know...you can tell me anything," I whispered, as I held perfectly still, hoping this was when he would open up.

But he didn't. Instead, he stiffened and then rolled off the bed.

"Lucian." He flinched at the ache in my voice.

"There are some secrets that have to stay buried. Everyone has something they keep hidden, even from the ones they love the most. Because once those secrets are out, nothing can ever be the same."

It was the closest he'd ever come to admitting he loved me.

And then I watched him walk away once again.

But I guess at least this time he hadn't left me tied up.

TWENTY-FIVE

A few days passed, and I didn't know what it was, but I was even more on edge than normal, like I was preparing for the world to fall apart. Gabriel was up and walking around, and we hadn't had any more terrible packages delivered…but it felt like the calm before the storm. Or maybe the calm before the hurricane.

Lucian had been avoiding me. Of course.

And today, I'd decided I'd had enough.

No more hiding. No more running. We were having it out until he came back to me…and stayed there.

"Can you drive me to the office?" I asked as I got into the car after a few hours of work at the shelter. Megan was in love, head over heels for the girl she'd met at the club. She flitted around the shelter with her head in the clouds, and I loved that for her, but it was a lot with how twitchy I was feeling.

One thing I loved about Riccardo, he'd developed a soft spot for me. I'd learned it was almost impossible for him to say no to me. So of course, he immediately headed in the direction of the office.

I sniffed at my hair, wrinkling at the smell of wet dog from the baths I'd given over the past hour.

Oh well, I was coming here to argue, not to get fucked.

Okay…maybe I was hoping I could get fucked.

We pulled up to the front of the building, and Riccardo acted as my silent sentry as we made our way through the now fully remodeled lobby and into the elevator. We'd just reached the top floor when Riccardo's phone chimed. He sighed. "Raphael needs me to pick up a package across town."

"Go ahead and go. I can make it to his office," I said. It was after hours, so the girls, and probably most of the employees were gone for the day. The new security measures they'd put in place after my kidnapping had made this place harder to get into than Kensington Palace.

"I'll just make sure you make it to his office door," he said with a frown, and I nodded as he followed me down the hall, stopping and watching me walk all the way to Lucian's office.

I waved at him, and he nodded at me and then left. Someday I was going to get him to talk to me.

I was quiet as I twisted the doorknob, wanting to surprise him, but as soon as the door opened, I realized he wasn't alone.

Raphael was in there with him.

"When did you realize?" he asked, a dangerous edge to his voice that had me shivering.

I don't know what made me continue to stand there and not go in, but something had me frozen in place.

"When you disappeared the night of the gala. I know you, Raphael. You don't just disappear to talk to councilmen, especially when *she's* around."

Raphael chuckled, and I tried to peek through the crack, but all I could see was Raphael's back.

"She almost got shot, you fucking bastard," Lucian hissed.

"I would never hurt her," Raphael growled.

Lucian hummed and Raphael tensed even more.

"I had the team get me the security tapes from all around the building, and you were nowhere to be seen. That wasn't enough to confirm anything, of course, and you're my brother, so I wanted to believe otherwise. But when you happened to be gone every time I needed you, I decided to set a little trap, just to make sure it wasn't you."

"And what was that?" Raphael said lightly.

My heart was thumping against my rib cage as I struggled to comprehend what they were talking about. Surely it wasn't what I thought it was. I was just misunderstanding.

"The latest shipment of guns from the factory in South America...You were the only one who knew when and where it was coming in, besides me. I made sure of that." Lucian sighed, and I could just picture him shaking his head in dismay. "Imagine my disappointment when a crew turned up to intercept the shipment."

Raphael threw his head back and laughed. "Well, I guess you caught me, brother. I must say, it's taken you way longer than I thought. Watching you run around, falling apart more and more every day has been a treat."

I was shaking as I stood there. Goosebumps peppered my skin. I thought about all the times Raphael had disappeared, how most of the time lately he'd seemed to show up after the chaos had already happened. It all seemed clear now, but my heart just couldn't believe it.

"Why?" Lucian asked quietly. "Why would you do this?"

Raphael's body stiffened. "Why? The fact that you would have to ask that question shows what a worthless asshole you really are."

"Rafe—"

"Don't fucking call me that," he spat, and the venom in his voice made my insides hurt.

Raphael's body trembled as he stood there. "Carlo killed my mother," he said hoarsely. "She'd kept me a secret for years, and when we were finally about to be on the streets, she went to him and told him about me, hoping he would help us. And his answer was to shoot her while I sat in a chair across from them. I wish he would have just killed me too."

"Raphael—" Lucian's voice dripped with pity.

"Until I was big enough to fight back, he tortured me, made every day of my life a living hell. And you, the heir to the throne, drifted along, blissfully unaware of anything. That was my kill. I had a plan. And you took it from me! Just like you've taken everything from me my entire life." He took a deep breath, and I watched in horror as he pulled a gun from underneath his suit coat and pointed it at Lucian.

I threw open the door, and Raphael whirled on me, a manic gleam in his eyes. "What are you doing here?" he roared, panicked. "Get out of here! Get the fuck out of here!"

Lucian moved, and Raphael whirled, taking a few steps back so that he could keep both of us in his sights.

"Get out of here, Dahlia," Lucian barked, but I shook my head, my mind racing as I tried to think what to do. Since Raphael was the one with the gun, I slowly edged my way towards Lucian.

"Raphael, you don't need to do this. This isn't you," I pleaded.

He laughed, the sound ugly and hard.

"You should know that isn't true. Have you told your husband our little secret?" he said cruelly.

"I don't think it matters now, Raphael. Lucian seems to be good with sharing."

"Oh, I think he'll care. Stop!" he barked, and I saw that Lucian had been reaching for his gun. "Hands on the desk."

"Or what? This is ridiculous. You're not going to shoot me," growled Lucian, but he put his hands on his desk anyway.

"I fucked her on the flight here. She gave away her virginity to a stranger because she couldn't bear to give it to you," Raphael growled.

Lucian looked stunned, but again, this was all water under the bridge.

A litany of emotions crossed his face like a dark parade...and all that was left at the end was acceptance.

"Raphael, I forgive you," Lucian finally said quietly, and Raphael looked shaken for a moment, his hand that was holding the gun, trembling.

"I don't need your forgiveness," Raphael whispered, his hand steadying. "I've been working to dismantle Carlo's empire...his legacy. And it's time to get rid of the biggest piece. You."

It happened in a blink of an eye. Raphael gave Lucian a blood-soaked smile, and I darted forward...right as Raphael fired.

The bullet struck me in the chest, and it felt like I was suspended in the air for a second before I felt myself falling back. I hit the ground like a crumpled piece of paper, and I stared up at the ceiling, a chill beginning to spread through my veins, paralyzing me in place.

An inhuman sound like an animal dying filled the air. It took me a moment to realize that it was Raphael.

He was there then, hovering above me, his face pale and wide-eyed, like a soldier returning from war.

"No. Please. I'm so sorry," he whimpered, his hands pressing on my wound, desperately. I hated seeing him like that. I tried to move my hand to comfort him, but it felt disconnected. I was dimly aware of Lucian nearby, talking to someone urgently, but it felt like I was floating underwater, the sounds discombobulated and stilted.

"Was any of it real?" I whispered to him with a soft, sad smile as he tried to stop the blood pouring from my wound. Now that it was all over, I wanted to know if there was anything but sad smiles, or if we were all so tainted by our pasts they couldn't be anything else. I wanted to know if the love affair had maimed him too, or if it was just me who was lying here, draped in desolation.

"Every bit of it," Raphael sobbed, tears dripping down his face before he was ripped away by Lucian who threw him to the ground and stumbled to my side.

"Principessa," Lucian choked. My Lucian looked lost, and I couldn't take that.

"I love you," I whispered to him, giving him my last breath as the colors of the world began to fade into a heartbreaking black and white tapestry.

And then everything faded away.

TWENTY-SIX

Beeeeeep. Beeeeeep. "Code Blue. Code Blue."
Strangers' faces hovered over me. A shock tore through my chest.
A long tone.
Darkness everywhere.

Tap. Tap. Tap.
Someone needed to stop that.
Tap. Tap. Tap.
I moaned, and something crashed nearby.
"Dahlia," a familiar voice cried.
I tried to hold on, tried to grasp how I knew that voice.
But it was too hard.
Sleep. I would just sleep a little longer.

GABRIEL

All the light was gone. I was a dried-out husk, moving around in the darkness, waiting for the end to come.

Thirteen days she'd been asleep. Thirteen days my life was tied to the pale, beautiful girl lying in the medical bed next to me.

Sometimes I could feel her, like a ghost, settling on my skin and telling me everything would be alright.

But that was only in my dreams.

I'd follow her if she left. I'd end my life in an instant because there was no other path I could take; there was only the path that led to her.

Even if it was broken right now.

They'd told us that it was a bad sign that she hadn't woken up yet, that we should start saying our goodbyes.

But I was still waiting for the miracle.

Or at least that's what I was telling myself while I stared out the hospital window, feeling like it was me that was dying. It was me that was trapped in a faith-forgotten land.

I hadn't known you could grieve for the living.

But now I did.

It was early morning, the sky still dark and endless, when I heard it. A rustle, and then a soft moan.

I flew to her bedside, my gaze attached to her face like it held the secrets of the universe.

And then she opened her eyes, glimmering waves of blue that restarted my heart.

It had felt like a never-ending night since she'd been gone.

But now...I could see daylight.

And it was the most beautiful thing I'd ever seen.

DAHLIA

I opened my eyes slowly, bright lights glaring at me as I tried to figure out where I was. There was a steady beeping sound that sparked something, but I couldn't quite grasp it.

"Dahlia," a voice whispered reverently. My eyes flicked to my left, and Gabriel was there. Except it was a gaunt-looking Gabriel with red-rimmed eyes, who looked like he'd just journeyed through hell.

"Water," I tried to whisper until I realized that something was down my throat and the words couldn't come out. I began to panic, trying to get it out.

"Calm down, baby. Please," Gabriel begged, tears slipping down his face. Something burned in my arm as I pulled at a tube.

Nurses and doctors rushed in, and I stared at them wide-eyed as they buzzed around me, pulling and prodding until I was shaking. They pulled a tube out of my mouth, and I immediately began coughing. Gabriel was hovering on the edges of the room, his gaze a lifeline that I held onto as tightly as I could.

Because it was all coming back to me, in sepia tones, every word, every look. Lucian. Raphael.

My heart began to seize, and my eyes rolled back in my head.

"She's having a seizure. Turn her over, turn her over."

My body was shaking, all thoughts gone.

It went on and on, an endless pain.

And then I went still.

Everyone was buzzing around me even more urgently, and

fear was licking at my soul. But then I felt a touch on my feet, and Lucian was there, holding onto me so that I didn't fly away.

Everything inside me settled at his touch.

"I'm here," he whispered.

And then I drifted off to sleep.

The days had drifted in and out. I was only able to stay awake for short periods at a time. The bullet had nicked my lung and hit my heart. My lung had collapsed, my heart had stopped beating, and my organs had started shutting down. I'd been in surgery for hours, and as the doctors and nurses kept telling me...it took time to recover from something like that.

But at least I was recovering. That was a miracle in itself.

I'd literally almost died of a broken heart.

How fitting.

Today though, I felt clear-headed for the first time, and that was the only thing I could think of to explain the gaping hole I felt in my chest that had nothing to do with my injury.

No pain medicine could numb the fact that I felt the loss of Raphael all the way down to my bones.

"Has anyone seen him?" I blurted out while Gabriel bustled around my bed like a mother hen and Lucian directed his empire from the table workstation he'd set up in the hospital suite they'd set me up in.

From what I'd gathered from listening to Lucian's phone calls, all the attacks on the supply chain had stopped, and everything that had gone missing had been returned to various Cosa Nostra warehouses around town.

Including all the men who'd left Lucian to go with Raphael.

They'd been bound in ropes and dumped in one of the warehouses, a giant "T" carved into their skin. For traitor, I presumed.

Lucian had killed them all.

I wasn't sure how I felt about that. I knew firsthand how very persuasive Raphael could be when it came down to it. But I did understand that Lucian would never have been able to trust them again. Once a traitor, always a traitor.

Except it was still hard to think of Raphael like that. A traitor.

There must have been something wrong with me, that I still cared…that he still owned a part of me.

But I felt marked like the traitors had been, like Raphael had carved his name into my soul, right beside Lucian's and Gabriel's.

I wasn't sure what it would take to get rid of that.

Gabriel and Lucian were feeling it too, though. Besides how they felt about me almost dying, the melancholy we were all experiencing was so thick in the air, it felt hard to breathe.

Which was not good since I was still having trouble breathing with my lung injury as it was.

"He's lost in the wind. There aren't even rumors of people seeing him," said Lucian, leaning backward in his chair. "Not that we've been trying to advertise that he was behind everything." Lucian rubbed his temples, looking more stressed than I'd ever seen. He also looked like he hadn't slept in a month. He would fall asleep for a moment in his chair, and then jerk awake a second later, like he was afraid of what was waiting for him on the other side.

"Behind everything" filled me with a chilling thought. "Do you think he was responsible for the boxes?" I asked quietly, feeling like I was going to throw up even though they'd been pumping me with anti-nausea medication.

Both Gabriel and Lucian said "no" practically at the same time.

"I'll be the first one to admit that I didn't know Raphael like I'd thought…but his panic when he shot you, his self-hatred…he wasn't faking that. I can't imagine him ever wanting to scare you or hurt you like that," said Lucian.

I nodded, except Raphael had been about to take away something that would have hurt me more than anything—Lucian.

"Church has been blowing up your phone, Dahlia. Is it alright if I text him?" asked Gabriel, holding up my phone that I hadn't bothered to look at once in the hospital.

"Shoot. I'd better call and explain," I said, holding out my hand.

Gabriel handed me my phone, and I immediately dialed Church's number. Benny, of course, picked up.

"Why are you ignoring me?" he snapped as soon as I'd said hello. "Has it been that bad? Should I come get you?"

"It's kind of a long story. I'm actually in the hospital right now thanks to being shot."

I heard Church's voice in the background, obviously listening to the conversation since he was panicking at the news.

"Shit. Are you going to be alright? Who do I need to fuck up?"

I smiled and realized that all the anger I'd been holding on to for my brother abandoning me…I wasn't feeling that for once. I was beginning to understand that most of the people on this planet were just trying to do the best they could. And maybe most of the time it was impossible for that to be the best thing for you too. But it didn't mean that they didn't care.

"I'll be fine," I told him, not knowing if that was a lie. "I'm getting better every day."

"Who shot you?" asked Benny, and I heard a woman's voice in the background asking a question.

"Just someone I used to know," I told him sadly, and he didn't ask any more questions after that.

After telling my brother I'd call soon, I hung up and sank back against my bed, exhausted just from that much effort.

"Emilia is in the lobby with some coffee," said Lucian, getting up from his chair and stretching. "I'm going to go grab it."

I nodded and had just begun to relax when a nurse in bright blue scrubs came hustling in to check my vitals.

"Getting better every day," she said after listening to my heartbeat.

I nodded, wondering if that would eventually happen with the ache that was a living, breathing thing in my chest.

She left the room, and I shifted in the sheets, frowning when a folded piece of paper rustled at the end of the bed.

Had the nurse dropped it?

I leaned over to grab it, and Gabriel looked up from the tablet he'd been working on.

The paper was folded in half, and as I opened it, my heart felt like it was breaking all over again. In a swooping familiar scrawl, it read:

I'm sorry, angel. No matter where I end up after this life, I'll always be looking for you.

My hands shook as I read the words over and over again.

"What is it?" Gabriel asked gently, and I looked at him, blind panic firing through my veins.

"It's from Raphael. I think he's going to kill himself. We've —we've got to find him!"

I struggled to get off my bed as Gabriel sprang from his chair.

"Dahlia, you need to get back in the bed. You're not supposed to be up," he cried.

"We've got to find him. We have to!"

Lucian walked in with a tray of coffees, throwing them on a table when he saw that I was up.

"Dahlia, what are you doing?"

I shoved the note at him with shaking hands, and he cursed after he read it.

"Stupid fool," he muttered.

"We have to find him," I insisted.

"Why? So he can shoot you again? Or shoot Lucian this time?" Gabriel hissed.

"I can't give up on him," I said softly. "I don't know how."

"Fuck," Lucian said. "Are we just going to drag your IV along with us?"

"Yes," I said stubbornly.

"Sweetheart, you might want to put some pants on first," said Gabriel dryly.

I flushed, realizing that I was just wearing a long t-shirt... with just a pair of knickers...I probably shouldn't go out like that.

My heart was pounding in my ears as Gabriel helped me get dressed. What if that paper had been there for days and I hadn't noticed? What if he was already dead?

Gabriel was taking his time, and it was hard for me not to snap.

"Why aren't you feeling the same urgency that I am right now? He's your brother."

Gabriel looked at me like I was crazy.

"Because he hurt the one thing I love more than anything else in the world. I don't know how you come back from that,"

Gabriel responded fiercely as he slipped the IV fluid drip off the metal pole.

I didn't know what to say to that, but luckily Lucian was there to usher us out of the room, IV fluid sac and all.

"Where are you taking my patient?" one of the nurses said as she dashed towards us, looking shocked.

"We'll be back," said Lucian firmly, and his voice was so commanding that she actually seemed to lose hers. We were able to get to the elevator without incident.

Except…I was exhausted. Already.

Gabriel must have read it in my face because he swooped me into his arms. I snuggled into his neck, breathing in his comforting scent while Lucian's gaze softly caressed my skin.

As was the Rossi way, Riccardo was out front already with a car, this one a large Escalade "so I could lay down," according to Gabriel.

We got in the car. "I'm glad to see you looking a bit better," said Riccardo, real concern in his gaze.

"Thank you," I said softly before turning my attention to the problem at hand. "Where would he even be? You said that no one had seen him!"

Gabriel stroked my hair reassuringly, but I was already spiraling.

I'd heard the pain in Raphael's voice as he was talking to Lucian. But what Raphael hadn't realized is that he had far more in common with Lucian than he thought he did.

"I think I know where he would be," said Lucian, looking haunted. "My father's residence." My stomach felt like it was filled with lead, because I was pretty sure that most of the demons in this family stemmed from things that happened in that place.

Riccardo pulled out and began to drive.

None of us talked, but we were all thinking so loudly that we might as well have been screaming.

"I'm sorry, Dahlia. This is all my fault. I ignored things as a kid, and then as a teenager. I didn't feel like I could help him when I was just trying to survive." Lucian's voice was laced with regret.

I reached over for his hand.

"Sorry isn't something you ever have to say to me, Lucian," I murmured. "But maybe you can say it to him."

The mood tangibly darkened the longer we drove. When we finally pulled up to the front of the imposing brownstone, I was convinced that the devil lived there. That's how much I'd built it up in my head.

Thinking of Carlo hovering over me, I was thinking I wasn't that far off.

Lucian had his door open before we'd even stopped, and he jumped out of the car and ran up the brick steps to the large double-doored entrance.

"Is there any way that I can convince you to stay in the car?" asked Gabriel.

I flashed my teeth at him, and he shook his head before scooping me up in his arms again and heading towards the entrance that Lucian had just disappeared through.

It hadn't been that long since Carlo's death, but the place felt like it had been empty for years. There was dust covering everything, and there were foot imprints where Lucian had walked.

The air felt oppressive as we went through the elegantly decorated rooms, looking for some sign of Raphael. "Are there other entrances he could have used?" I asked worriedly when I saw that everything looked undisturbed, no sign that he'd been there or anyone else for that matter.

"There's a fire escape," Gabriel said suddenly. "Lucian! He could be on the roof."

Lucian pushed past us and started to dash up the stairs while Gabriel carried me down a hallway.

"Where are we going?"

"There's an elevator right here," he answered, and sure enough, we turned a corner, and there it was.

"Set me down," I ordered once we'd gotten inside. The anxiety rushing through me was getting to be too much, and I needed to be able to move or I'd go mad.

The elevator doors opened, revealing a rooftop garden and entertaining area. And just beyond the flowers, and the sofas, and a bar area…was Raphael.

He was sitting on the edge of the roof, his back to us and his feet dangling over the edge. A brown bottle of liquor next to him.

Lucian burst through a door next to the elevator a second later, but Raphael didn't even act like he'd heard us.

We walked closer, but he still didn't turn around.

"Raphael," I called in a pleading voice, and his whole body shook at the sound of my voice.

"Go away, Dahlia," he responded in a hoarsely.

"I'm sorry," Lucian suddenly said when he was just a few feet away from him. Raphael froze. "I'm sorry for everything. I'm sorry I ignored what he was doing. I'm sorry I turned the other way." Lucian's voice cracked.

He looked at me, and I nodded at him to go on, but he was frozen in place, his gaze distant, like he was locked in a memory.

"I just want it to be over. I don't want to feel this anymore," said Raphael roughly.

That seemed to spark Lucian back to life, probably because me and him, we'd lived that feeling over and over again.

"The year after you arrived, I was drugged and taken by some of Carlo's associates from a party that Carlo was throwing here." Lucian's hands were trembling as he paused and took a deep breath. "For the next two weeks, those men raped me over and over again, nonstop. They kept me drugged the whole time, but I was awake, I could feel everything they were doing to me." Lucian fell to his knees, his whole body wracked with sobs. "They finally left me on the doorstep, a bloody, broken mess…And I've just been trying to survive since then."

Gabriel was frozen next to me.

And me…I was crying. For the first time since I was a little girl, I was crying. For Lucian, for Raphael, for Gabriel…for me. Hot, wet tears were streaming down my face. My heart felt torn open, like the bullet hole they'd patched was actually a deep fissure of pain.

If Carlo were still alive right now, I would have shot him in the face myself.

It took a long time for Lucian to recover, but after he got off his knees, it was like he'd been brought back to life, like the clouds had disappeared.

We never realize how heavy the secrets are that we keep, until we let them go.

I was seeing that truth in Lucian right before my eyes. He was free.

"Instead of trying to destroy what Carlo left, join me in making it our own, so no one ever utters Carlo's name again because we've eclipsed anything he could have dreamed of accomplishing."

Raphael was standing now, a beautiful wreck who looked like he'd walked through hell and barely survived.

"I've spent so much of my life hating you..." his voice trailed off, and I could see the shame embedded in his skin. "How do I come back from what I've done? How do I fix this?"

His eyes flicked to me desperately, begging for me to grant him absolution for his sins.

But he didn't need to worry; I'd forgiven him as soon as that shot was fired.

"Maybe you can't. Maybe you have to take the ruined wreckage of this family and make something completely new. Maybe that's the only way forward," I murmured.

Raphael watched Lucian warily as he slowly approached him.

And then...Lucian put his arms around him and hugged him, and those two big bad mafia men wept together.

It was beautiful.

After a long embrace, Lucian clapped him on the back and stepped away, and then Gabriel was there.

And to my surprise, he reared back and punched Raphael right in the mouth.

"Gabriel!" I cried as Raphael fell to the ground and gave us a bloody grin, his lip destroyed by the force of the hit.

"That was for almost taking away what's most important in my life," Gabriel growled. "But I forgive you...only because she lived."

Raphael nodded solemnly. "You owe me a lifetime of those, little brother."

I shivered, and then my legs completely failed me, and I began to fall. Somehow, Lucian managed to catch me before I crashed to the ground.

"We need to get you back to the hospital, principessa," Lucian murmured, concerned as Gabriel and Raphael hurried towards me.

"Haven't you figured it out by now, Lucian? Our girl's not a principessa. She's a mother-fucking queen," Gabriel announced.

"That she is," Lucian agreed, rubbing my chin softly with his thumb and turning my limbs into butter.

I could feel Raphael's heavy stare on me as we used the elevator to go back down, and I knew there was so much we needed to say. But right now, I needed a nap. And some pain meds. And then I wanted a bacon burger delivered to the hospital from that place down the corner from the penthouse. All of the things.

I felt noticeably lighter as we stepped out into the sun and left that house of misery. And if it happened to burn to the ground soon...I wouldn't be mad about that either. I would probably throw a party.

Riccardo was standing in front of the Escalade when we came out. When he saw Raphael, he burst into tears, took Raphael's hands in his, and nodded at him through tear-stained eyes, a huge smile on his face.

Who knew Riccardo was such a big softie?

Lucian and Gabriel got in the backseat with me, and Raphael got in the front...and we were off.

I put my head in Gabriel's lap, and he stroked my hair as I listened to the buzz of voices of the men I loved the most.

We pulled up in front of the hospital and got up to my room, and I sank into the bed with a sigh.

Gabriel and Lucian came into the room, but Raphael hovered in the doorway, looking anxious.

"Raphael," I murmured, holding out my hand to him from the bed.

He walked toward me tentatively. "Take a nap with me?" I asked.

Raphael shook his head. "How can you still want me after— after I almost killed you?"

His eyes were watering, and because I'd suddenly regained the ability to cry today, my eyes watered too.

"Because I know all about destroying everything good in your life because of the pain. I just aim a little smaller with my destruction." I tried to smile through the tears blurring my vision of him standing above me. "Plus, dying on the operating table makes you realize that tomorrow's not promised. And since that's the case, I need to make sure that I spend all of my todays how I want. And what I want…is all of you."

"Fuck, angel." His eyes closed, and when he opened them, there was a look of sweet surrender that I wanted to remember for the rest of my life.

He carefully slid into the bed and put his arms around me.

And there, under the watchful eyes of Lucian and Gabriel, we fell asleep.

TWENTY-SEVEN

I was released from the hospital a few days later with the condition that I avoid basically anything for at least a month. And over the next month, we did our best to start a new chapter. One filled with movie nights, laughter, and giving each other the secrets of our souls so that the mistakes of the past would never be made again.

I'd told them about what my uncle had done to me, and we'd needed to replace half the living room after Gabriel and Raphael destroyed it. And I'd basked in the destruction, because I'd never had anyone in my life besides them, who wanted to destroy the world when I cried.

After a month, Raphael was finally smiling again, the shadows in his eyes still there, but lighter. We were all a work in progress, and that was alright.

And finally…I was released by the doctor to engage in… extracurricular activities.

So there I was, standing in Raphael's room, waiting for him

to come in…in his favorite pair of black lingerie. I thought my new gnarly scar only added to the sex appeal.

He walked into his room, talking to someone on the phone. And then he saw me.

He abruptly ended the call without a goodbye and dropped his phone on the floor while he stalked my way.

A second later, I was in his arms, my hands tangling in his hair as I clung to him. My lingerie disappeared in a second, ripped to threads, and his clothes followed a moment later.

Nothing separated us, and we came together, skin against skin. His arms completely enveloped me as he worshiped my mouth with his. My body heated under his hands, and our groans mixed together in the air. I whimpered as he kissed across my cheek and down my neck, nibbling at the hollow above my collarbone. I touched him everywhere I could, well aware of the miracle it was that we were both there right now.

Without warning, he pushed me to the bed, but he didn't come with me. Instead, he stood in front of me, his gaze brushing against my skin slowly and deliberately. "This feels like a dream and any minute I'm going to wake up," he said roughly as he began to stroke his rock-hard cock up and down. "I don't deserve this, don't deserve you, angel," he whispered, and his eyes changed from veneration to a passionate need as he drank me in.

"Dahlia," he breathed, like my name was a prayer and I was the altar he was praying to. He climbed onto the bed until he was lying beside me, and then he leaned in, his mouth hovering over mine and barely brushing against me.

"Raphael," I whimpered as he began to knead and caress my breasts, pinching and pulling until I was a moaning mess as my core began to flutter.

"Need to feel you, angel. I'll do it slow next time," he promised.

"Just as long as there are knives involved," I murmured, and the passion in his eyes turned into a wild need. That mirror action had been fucking hot.

He moved on top of me, and in one swift move, he slid inside me, and a garbled moan slipped out as I tried to get used to the fullness. Before I could catch my breath, Raphael flipped us over so that I was on top and straddling his hips.

I liked this position. I liked it a lot. He was stretched out before me, a decadent canvas of ink and perfect muscles that made me want to lick him all over. Especially the new pair of angel wings in the center of his chest that he'd gotten just for me. Straddling him like this, he was reaching inside me in a new way, a full, tormenting stretch that had me panting like a bitch in heat.

We groaned together when I rotated my hips, and we groaned together as I sunk even deeper on his dick. I leaned over him, and our eyes locked, and I could feel it then, that broken heart I'd been trying to put together over the past couple of months…it finally mended.

"I love you, angel. Never loved anything or anyone else in my life. But I love you. The only thing I ask is that you make sure to outlive me, so I never have to go a day without you."

My tears dripped down my face as I let myself feel his love.

"I love you too," I whispered in a choked voice, and then I began to make love with Raphael Rossi. My hips moved, rounding gently at first, and I pulled him in and out at a tortured, perfect pace that had our breaths gasping together as our bodies joined, again and again…and again.

I sat up, and I sunk down on him further, a new depth that had me biting my lip in delirium. Our rhythm changed, and his hands went to my hips, moving me up and down until we were at the perfect cadence.

It all felt so achingly sweet.

"Raphael," I whispered as our eyes met, and I got lost in the gaze that had held my attention since the first moment that I'd met him.

All thought disappeared as the tension built. I cried out as he began to pump into me, thrusting his hips until I felt like I was rocketing into the sky with how high he was taking me.

And then I came.

I erupted around him, and he followed me over the cliff.

And I swore I felt our souls brush against each other.

I fell onto his chest, feeling completely destroyed in the best possible way.

His hands moved all over me, holding me tight as our breaths slowed.

"I love you," he murmured as he brushed a kiss against my lips.

I smiled, because I knew he meant it.

All of it.

TWENTY-EIGHT

1 month later

I hummed as I fed our latest guest, a gorgeous cocker spaniel that you couldn't help but love. She would get adopted fast, I just knew it, so I was soaking up all the time I could with her.

"You're a good girl. Aren't you, sweetheart?" I murmured since Gabriel wasn't here to make fun of me.

It was Friday afternoon and I was looking forward to a weekend with my men. They'd told me they had a surprise for me, and I couldn't wait to get home and find out what it was.

I hoped it was sex. Lots and lots of sex.

Only one more row of animals to feed.

Bang.

I dropped the dog bowl on the ground, the small pieces scattering all over the floor.

What was that? It had almost sounded like…

Bang. Bang.

Gunshots. At the front of the shelter.

Riccardo was up at the front. He'd been helping Shelby Ray with her English homework.

I was in the very back room, so everything sounded muffled in here. But I knew I wasn't hearing things.

My gun and my phone were in my purse in my employee lockers…two rooms away. So I started to scan the room for a weapon.

Besides dog food bags, I didn't see anything—until yes, a screwdriver, over on the counter.

I quickly grabbed it and slowly opened the door, peeking out to see if I could see anything. The animals in the next room were going crazy, but the room was clear of anyone.

I walked inside and tiptoed to the next door, I just needed to get through this and then I could get my phone. I slowly twisted the doorknob and peered through the crack.

It was perfectly silent in there.

I took a deep breath, trying to control my out-of-control heart, and I pulled the door open farther to slip inside. On the other side of the room was the doorway to my locker. And then past that, another exit.

I was almost there.

I crept over to the room and paused in front of the doorway before cautiously poking my head inside.

No one was there. I let out the breath I hadn't known I was holding and took a step inside.

I was reaching in the locker for my phone when I heard it— heavy breathing right behind me.

And I knew who it was.

Because even though life had felt like some kind of fairy tale the last little while, my fairy tales never ended with a happily ever after.

"I've missed you," he murmured, and a tear slid down my cheek because I would have rather died than ever seen him again.

His hands curled in my hair and pulled, and I squeaked as my head was wrenched back.

He licked my cheek with his slimy wet tongue, and I had to bite my cheek to keep from crying out.

I was twisted around and thrown against the locker, my head slamming so hard against the metal that I saw stars.

And when the blasted things disappeared, there he was. The monster behind every scar that lined my body and my soul.

He was much older than I remembered. My mind had kept him frozen at the same age that I'd last seen him. But now there were more lines to his forehead, age spots, and a yellowish tint to his skin that spoke of a bit too much whiskey.

My uncle was still big, though; still muscled, ugly, and awful. Salt and pepper hair and freckled skin. Watery, pale blue eyes that I swore were the devil's.

"How are you here?" I gasped, flinching as the words left my mouth.

"Couldn't let my favorite girl go across the pond without me, now could I?"

I was trembling, an automatic ingrained reaction from years of suffering.

I'd set the screwdriver down when I was opening my locker, and it was off to my right. I didn't look at it, hoping that he wouldn't notice the tool and maybe…I'd have a chance.

"I've missed you. No one else screams as pretty. No one else cums so good at my touch."

A hitched sob tore out of my chest as a million flashbacks came at me with the many times that my body had betrayed me at his hands, and bile filled my throat. I choked on the sour, sharp taste.

He smiled. His teeth glinting like a demon come to life out of the pages of a horror novel.

"Did you like the presents I've been sending you?"

Hadn't my gut known it was him? And I pushed it aside like a wishful child hearing that Father Christmas wasn't real.

My mind flashed to Shelby Ray…to Riccardo. What had he done to them?

"I didn't know you were such a fan of fairy tales," I told him, trying to hold my head up high.

"Don't you remember, pet? All the stories I would read to you while we 'played.'"

Hot bile flooded my mouth. Because I did remember now. My mind must have blocked it out. The trauma too much. But now it felt like I was being raped all over again as the images flooded my mind.

Me forced to suck on his cock while he read *Cinderella*.

Him sliding giant dildos in my arse while he read *Rapunzel*.

On and on, each one more horrific than the last.

The stories were all there.

Maybe that's why my nightmares were always worse after Disney movies…

"I think I've waited too long, little Dahlia. It's time to play," crooned my uncle, bringing me back from my walk down a memory lane filled with horrors.

He threw me down on the bench in front of the locker and began to tear at my clothes.

My body went limp as panic sliced through me, the world spinning and fading, and I was just wishing I was dead.

Worthless. I was worthless. I let this happen. I couldn't stop it.

The words beat in my head, destroying me.

But then my limp fingers brushed against something hard, and the darkness receded, just for a second.

My hand curled around the screwdriver as he split my shirt open and groped at my bra.

"Our girl's not a principessa. She's a mother-fucking queen."

The words cut through the haze and the self-loathing, giving me the strength I'd never had before, because I was a fucking queen. And I was done giving anyone power over me.

Especially *him*.

I swung the screwdriver right into the fucker's neck as hard as I could. It ripped through his skin and his muscle.

Shock sliced through his features…and then fear. The only time that I'd ever seen him look scared.

He struggled to sit up, but he couldn't. I'd hit something good. Blood began to gurgle out of his mouth, staining his teeth, and staining me as I held his gaze until all the life was bleached out of him.

I was shaking as I pushed him off me, and he crashed to the floor. I sat up, and I was faintly aware of voices and the sound of stomping feet as I rocked back and forth on the bench.

Killing monsters was hard work.

My gaze kept flicking to where he had fallen, expecting him to get up at any minute and continue the nightmare. But he never did.

I heard the voices of Shelby Ray and Riccardo drawing nearer, and I sagged in relief. They were okay.

I was okay.

The guys rushed in, and I was pulled against a hard chest as they all tried to touch me…

In that moment, I realized I was finally free.

And the best part was…I'd freed myself.

EPILOGUE

LUCIAN

She approached me slowly, one foot in front of the other until she was standing at the edge of the bed. There was a tie in her hand, and I watched with a little trepidation… and a whole lot of arousal, as she slid it between her fingers.

"Do you want to play with me?" she murmured. I swallowed, unable to form words as she climbed up onto the bed and began to crawl up my body.

We'd been leading up to this for months. First, her being able to touch me, and then more and more until here we were.

I watched in awe as she pulled on my zipper and slowly began to slide it down. I didn't have anything on underneath, so my cock strained towards her immediately. Like the goddess she was, she began to lap at my tip, teasing me until I was gasping.

"Suck me," I growled, and I watched as she licked away a

bead of pre cum, the sexiest thing I'd ever seen. She looked up at me through her lashes as she began to suck on my throbbing head like it was a lollipop.

"Cazzo," I hissed as her lips slipped off my dick and began to move over my body.

I never knew that it could be like this, that I'd ever be able to be touched and want more.

The nightmares still came, but she was always there to chase them away.

She pressed words into my skin as she kissed me all over— words of love, devotion, and light that only she could give me.

She finally got to my lips, and she hovered above them, our lips just an inch apart.

"Hands above your head," she murmured, and for a moment, something tried to push through, to ruin this moment. But then she was there, running her fingers over my skin, and I remembered that no matter what, I'd always be safe with her.

She tied my wrists together, much looser than any I'd done on her, and I groaned as her breasts slid against my face as she worked on the knot.

"There."

She sat back with a smug expression, and I made no move to try and get out; the last thing I ever wanted was to escape from her.

Dahlia finally gifted me with a kiss and then moved until she was sitting on my aching cock. I groaned when she ground against me, a mimicry of what I was so desperate for her to do.

Instead of sliding me into her wet cunt, she moved back down my body and pulled my cock back into her mouth, this time all the way.

My heart was pounding against my rib cage as her fingers

slid under my balls, and she flicked the smooth skin underneath my testicles before moving to lightly press on my asshole—something that took me forever to admit I loved.

I was a trembling mess as pressure began to build as she bobbed up and down on my dick.

She was perfect. So fucking perfect. Fuck.

Abruptly, she released my cock just as I was about to cum, and she wrapped her hand around my slick shaft, moving up and down.

I was so fucking close.

She moved again, until she was positioned right above me, and then she began to fucking touch herself, caressing her breasts that I was desperate to lick.

"Can you feel how wet I am for you?" she smiled, rolling her hips against my bare cock so I could feel her dripping heat.

Her hands moved from her breasts, down her stomach, and then to her clit. I was a captive audience as she slid a finger through her folds and into her opening, gasping as she fingered herself.

She tortured me for another minute before she pulled her finger out and offered it to my lips. I eagerly lapped and sucked on her finger, her taste something I could eat for breakfast, lunch, and dinner.

And then she slowly sank down, all the way, and she began to ride me, her head thrown back in ecstasy as we both lost ourselves to the sensations. Our fumbled words and grunted cries were like music, and they drove me to buck into her faster and harder.

Her pale skin was flushed, a light sheen of sweat on her body, and I'd never seen anything so fucking sexy in my life.

And then I'd had enough. I pulled my wrists from the tie,

grabbing her and flipping us so that her back was pushed against the mattress.

"My turn," I murmured, and her eyes shone with delight, her love so vibrant, I could barely breathe.

As I slid into her again, I knew that I wasn't worthy of this gift.

But I was never letting her go.

Long before I'd known her, I'd wanted to ruin her, and instead, she'd ruined me.

And I never wanted anything else.

Later, as we were lying there, intertwined and happy, I took her left hand in mine and slowly began to slide off her ring.

She looked at me in alarm, but then relaxed when she saw the look on my face.

"Marry me," I murmured.

"I think I already have," she said with a laugh.

"Marry me again. Not because you have to. Not because of your family. Not because of the treaty. Marry me because you've become my entire world, and I can't breathe without you."

Her gorgeous blue eyes filled with tears as she nodded, and I slid a new ring on her finger, this time sealing a promise I'd never break.

I knew Gabriel and Raphael had rings they would be giving her soon too.

We'd also enrolled her in college classes, which was hell for security, but just right for our girl. She'd be finding that out soon as well.

"I love you," she told me as her lips moved to mine.

I rolled back on top and slid inside of her again. I didn't stop worshipping her for a very, very long time.

.

The End

Gabriel's Spicy Vodka Rigatoni Recipe

Ingredients

- 3 tbsp salted butter
- 2 shallots minced (or substitute ½ sweet onion, minced)
- 3 cloves garlic minced
- ½ cup tomato paste
- 1 tsp Calabrian chili or substitute for ½ tsp red pepper flakes
- ½ shot vodka
- ¾ cup heavy cream
- 1 cup grated parmesan divided
- Kosher salt
- 1 lb. tubed pasta such as penne or rigatoni

Instructions

1. Add 1 lb of Rigatoni to salted water and cook pasta until it's al dente. Strain and reserve two cups pasta water and set aside.

2. Meanwhile, melt butter in a large sauce pan over medium heat then add shallots and garlic. Cook down for a few minutes, stirring often, until the garlic and shallot are soft and fragrant but not browned.

3. Next, add tomato paste and Calabrian chili paste to the pan and continue stirring until everything is incorporated and the tomato paste has darkened slightly; about 5 minutes.

4. Now add the vodka and stir vigorously for another 3 minutes until the pan has been completely deglazed and the sauce has come together.

5. Turn the heat to medium-low and add heavy cream and stir until incorporated. Let it simmer on low for 3 minutes then add in ½ cup of parmesan cheese and continue stirring until it's melted.

6. Now add in the al dente pasta and toss it with the sauce. Then add ½ a cup of pasta water until the sauce becomes smooth and creamy! If it still looks dry, add more of the reserved pasta water, little by little, over medium-low heat until the sauce looks silky and smooth.

7. Add a few scoops of the pasta to each bowl and top with remaining parmesan cheese!

Author's Note

To say that this book took me beyond my comfort zone is the understatement of the century. I tackled a lot of topics in Ruining Dahlia that I've never touched before, and it was definitely a challenge. This book was so dark that I had to take frequent breaks to calm myself down and I definitely cried through many parts.

Dahlia has been all I can think about for the last few months. I love her and her guys so much.

And I hope you did too.

A note of thanks…

First, I want to thank my fellow Mafia Wars authors. I'm so in awe of your talent, and I feel so privileged that you included me in this project. I've enjoyed every second of it and truly value our friendships.

Another huge thank you to Jasmine Jordan for coming in clutch with edits. This was a huge book and she worked so hard!

A special thank you to Summer, Caitlin, and Mila who are

true ride or die friends, always there when I need them. Love you girls so much! This book is for you! You guys have gotten me through the last few months. So thankful for our friendship.

Thank you to my readers. I love you so much. You allow me to live my dreams. Thank you from the bottom of my heart.

Until next time…

PREVIEW OF THE SOUND OF US

Keep reading for a look at the first chapter of The Sound of Us Complete Collection, my reverse harem rockstar romance.

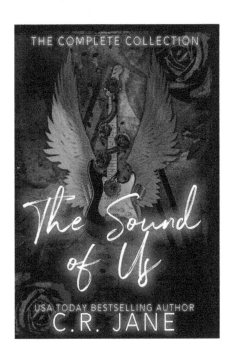

C.R. JANE

Grab the complete collection today!

The Sound of Us
Complete Collection

Blurb

They are idols to millions worldwide. I hear their names whispered in the hallways and blasted through the radio. Their faces are never far from the television screen, tormenting me with images of what I gave up.

To everyone else, they're unattainable rockstars, the music gods who make up The Sound of Us. But to me? They'll always be the boys I lost.

I broke all our hearts when I refused to follow them to L.A., convinced I would only bring them down. Years later, after I've succumbed to a monster, and my life has become something out of a nightmare, they are back.

I'm no longer the girl they left behind. But what if I've become the woman they can't forget?

PROLOGUE
BEFORE

According to the Sounds of Us Wikipedia page, the band hit almost instant stardom as soon as they finished recording their first album. A small indie band that had gained only regional notoriety, Red Label had taken a huge risk by signing them. The good looks and the killer voices of the three band members combined with the chance at a larger platform ended up making Sounds of Us the Label's most successful band in history. They released their first album, Death by Heartbreak, in 2013, and the first single, Follow You Into the Dark, made it to the Billboard Top 100 immediately.

It was their second single that propelled Sounds of Us to legend status though. Cold Heart was number one on the charts almost the second it was released. That led to four other songs ending up in the top ten. Three of them reached number one, with a fourth hitting number two on the charts. That album was torture in its finest form for me. Partly because I had lost them, but also partly because every one of those songs was about me.

And that was just the hits. There were a lot more references in the songs that never got released as singles. It was a sharp stab in the chest to hear songs blaring from radios – songs whose lyrics contained exact words each of them had said to me, and that I had said to them.

And while some of the songs were wistful and pained, others were angry. Pissed-off. Occasionally enraged. It was uncomfortable. Actually, it was excruciating. At least for the first couple of months. I stopped listening to music eventually, something that had meant the world to me my entire life. I just couldn't handle the reminder of them anymore. My heart couldn't take it.

But every so often, a car would go by with its window down, or I'd walk past a motel room playing the radio, and I'd hear one of their voices and it would be an unexpected jolt of pain all over again.

After the release of their album, the band embarked on a short European tour, then followed it up with a much larger American tour. They started selling out stadiums. They appeared on every late-night show there was. Everyone wanted a piece of them. They were like this generation's Beatles, probably even bigger. The next two albums certainly were bigger, although those were easier for me to listen to since the songs about me faded as time went on. They were the most celebrated band in the world and there was no sign of their success slowing down anytime soon. It was everything they had ever dreamed about and that I had dreamed about with them.

They lived up to the bad boy image their label wanted to sell. Rumors of drug use and rampant women kept the gossip sites busy. I tried to ignore the magazines in the store racks by the checkout stand, but some of the pictures of the guys stumbling out of clubs with five girls each were a little too damning to be completely unfounded. And of course, there were the rumors that Tanner had secretly been in and out of rehab for the last two years in between tours. Tanner had always struggled with addiction but had only dabbled in hard drugs when I knew him. It wasn't hard for me to picture him struggling with them now that he probably had easy access to whatever he wanted from people desperate to please them all.

I often wondered if any part of the boys I knew were still around after I let myself give into my own addiction of catching up on any Sounds of Us news I could find. And then I would hear about them buying a house for someone who had lost everything in a natural disaster or hear of them participating in a charity drive to keep a no-kill shelter up and running, and I would know that a part of them was still there.

I've never made peace with letting them go. I never will.

CHAPTER 1
NOW

I hear the song come on from the living room. I had forgotten I had read that they were performing for New Year's Eve tonight in New York City before they embarked on their North American tour for the rest of the year. I wanted to avoid the room the music was coming from, but not even my hate for its current occupant could keep my feet from wandering to where the song was playing.

As I took that first step into the living room, and I saw Tanner's face up close, my heart clenched. As usual, he was singing to the audience like he was making love to them. When the camera panned to the audience, girls were literally fainting in the first few rows if he so much as ran his eyes in their direction. He swept a lock of his black hair out of his face, and the girls screamed even louder. Tanner had always had the bad boy look down perfectly. Piercing silver eyes that demanded sex, and full pouty lips you couldn't help but fantasize over, he was every mother's worst nightmare and every girl's naughty dream. I devoured his image like I was a crack addict desperate for one more hit. Usually I avoided them like the plague, but junkies always gave in eventually. I was not the exception.

"See something you like?" comes a cold, amused voice that never ceases to fill me with dread. I curse my weakness at allowing myself to even come in the room. I know better than this.

"Just coming to see if you need a refill of your beer," I tell him nonchalantly, praying that he'll believe me, but knowing he won't.

My husband is sitting in his favorite armchair. He's a good-looking man according to the world's standards. Even I have to admit that despite the fact that the ugliness that lies inside his heart has long prevented me from finding him appealing in any way. His blonde hair is parted to the side perfectly, not a hair out of place. Sometimes I get the urge to mess it up, just so there can be an outward expression of the chaos that hides beneath his skin.

After I let the guys go, there was nothing left for me in the world. Instead of rising above my circumstances and becoming someone they would have been proud of, I became nothing. Gentry made perfectly clear that anything I was now was because of him.

Echoes of my lost heart beat inside my mind as another song starts to play on the television. It's the song that I know they wrote for me. It's angry and filled with betrayal, the kind of pain you don't come back from. The kind of pain you don't forgive.

Too late I realize that Gentry just asked me something and that my silence will tell him that I'm not paying attention to him. The sharp strike of his palm against my face sends me flying to the ground. I press my hand to my cheek as if I can stop the pain that is coursing through me. I already know this one will bruise. I'll have to wear an extra layer of makeup to cover it up when Gentry forces me to meet him at the country club tomorrow. After all, we wouldn't want anyone at the club to know that our lives are anything less than perfect.

The song is still going and somehow the pain I hear in Tanner's voice hurts me more than the pain blossoming across my cheek. Would it not hurt them as much if they knew everything I had told them to sever our connection permanently was a lie? Would they even care at this point that I had done it to set them free, to stop them from being dragged down into the hell I never seemed to be able to escape from? At night, when I lay in bed, listening to the sound of Gentry sleeping peacefully as if the world was perfect and monsters didn't exist, I told myself that it would matter.

"Get up," snaps Gentry, yanking me up from the floor. I'm really off my game tonight by lingering. Nothing makes Gentry madder than when I "wallow" as he calls it. As I stumble out of the room, my head spinning a bit from the force of the hit, a sick part of me thinks it was worth it, just so I could hear the end of their song.

Later that night, long after I should have fallen asleep, my mind plays back what little of the performance I saw earlier. I wonder if Jensen still gets severe stage fright before he performs. I wonder if Jesse still keeps his lucky guitar pick in his pocket during performances. I wonder who Tanner gets his good luck kiss from now.

It all hurts too much to contemplate for too long so I grab the

Ambien I keep on my bedside table for when I can't sleep, which is often, and I drift off into a dreamland filled with a silver eyed boy who speaks straight to my soul.

The next morning comes too early and I struggle to wake up when Gentry's alarm goes off. Ambien always leaves me groggy and I haven't decided what's better, being exhausted from not sleeping, or taking half the day to wake up all the way.

Throwing a robe on, I blurrily walk to the kitchen to get Gentry's protein shake ready for him to take with him to the gym.

I'm standing in front of the blender when Gentry comes up behind me and puts his arms around me, as if the night before never happened. I'm very still, not wanting to make any sudden movement just in case he takes it the wrong way.

"Meet me at the club for lunch," he asks, running his nose up the side of my neck and eliciting shivers...the wrong kind of shivers. He's using his charming voice, the one that always gets everyone to do what he wants. It stopped working on me a long time ago.

"Of course," I tell him, turning in his arms and giving him a wide, fake smile. What else would my answer be when I know the consequences of going against Gentry's wishes?

"Good," he says with satisfaction, placing a quick, sharp kiss on my lips before stepping away.

I pour the blended protein shake into a cup and hand it to him. "11:45?" I ask. He nods and waves goodbye as he walks out of the house to head to the country club gym where he'll spend the next several hours working out with his friends, flirting with the girls that work out there, and overall acting like the over-whelming douche that he is.

I don't relax until the sound of the car fades into the distance.

After eating a protein shake myself (Gentry doesn't approve of me eating carbs), I start my chores for the day before I have to get ready to meet him at the country club.

My hands are red and raw from washing the dishes twice. Everything was always twice. Twice bought me time and ensured there wouldn't be anything left behind. An errant fleck of food, a spot that hadn't been rinsed – these were things he'd notice.

Hours later, I've vacuumed, swept, done the laundry, and cleaned all the bathrooms. Gentry could easily afford a maid, but he likes me to "keep busy" as he puts it, so I do everything in this house of horrors. I repeat the same things every day even though the house is in perfect condition. I would clean every second if it meant that he was out of the house permanently though.

I straighten the pearls around my neck and think for the thousandth time that if I ever escape this hell hole, I'm going to burn every pearl I come across. I'm dressed in a fitted pastel pink dress that comes complete with a belt ordained with daisies. Five years ago, I wouldn't have been caught dead in such an outfit but far be it for me to wear jeans to a country club. I slip into a pair of matching pastel wedges and then run out to the car. I'm running late and I can only hope that he's distracted and doesn't realize the time.

As I drive, I can't help but daydream. Dream about what it would have been like if I had joined the guys in L.A. Bellmont is a sleepy town that's been the same for generations. I haven't been anywhere outside of the town since I got married except to Myrtle Beach for my honeymoon.

The town is steeped in history, a history that it's very proud of. The main street is still perfectly maintained from the early 1900s, and I've always loved the whitewashed look of the buildings and the wooden shingles on every roof. The town attracts a vast array of tourists who come here to be close to the beach. They can get a taste of the coastal southern flavor of places like Charleston and Charlotte, but they don't have to pay as high of a price tag.

It's a beautiful prison to me, and if I ever manage to escape from it, I never want to see it again.

I turn down a street and start down the long drive that leads to Bellmont's most exclusive country club. The entire length of the road is sheltered by large oak trees and it never ceases to make me feel like an extra in Gone With the Wind whenever I come here. The feeling is only reinforced when I pull up to the large, freshly painted white plantation house that's been converted into the club.

My blood pressure spikes as I near the valet stand. Just knowing that I'm about to see Gentry and all of his friends is enough to send my pulse racing. I smile nervously at the teenage boy who is manning the stand and hand him my keys. He gives me a big smile and a wink. It reminds me of something that Jesse used to do to older women to make them swoon, and my heart clenches. Is there ever going to be a day when something doesn't remind me of one of them?

I ignore the valet boy's smile and walk inside, heading to the bar where I can usually find Gentry around lunch time. I pause as I walk inside the lounge. Wendy Perkinson is leaning against Gentry, pressing her breasts against him, much too close for propriety's sake. I know I should probably care at least a little bit, but the idea of Gentry turning his attentions away from me and on to Wendy permanently is more than I can even wish for. I'm sure he's fucked her, the way she's practically salivating over him as he talks to his friend blares it loudly, but unfortunately that's all she will ever get from him. Gentry's obsession with me has thus far proved to be a lasting thing. But since I finally started refusing to sleep with him after the beatings became a regular thing, he goes elsewhere for his so-called needs when he doesn't feel like trying to force me. At least a few times a week I'm assaulted by the stench of another woman's perfume on my husband's clothes. It's become just another unspoken thing in my marriage.

Martin, Gentry's best friend, is the first to see me and his eyes widen when he does. He coughs nervously, the poor thing thinking I actually care about the situation I've walked into. Gentry looks at him and then looks at the entrance where he sees me standing there. His eyes don't widen in anything remotely resembling remorse or shame...we're too far past that at this point. He does extricate himself from Wendy's grip however to start walking towards me, his gaze devouring me as he does so. One thing I've never doubted in my relationship with Gentry is how beautiful he thinks I am.

"You're gorgeous," he tells me, kissing me on the cheek and putting a little too much pressure on my arm as he guides me to the bar. Wendy has moved farther down the bar, setting her sights on another married member of the club. It's funny to me that in high school I had wanted to stab her viciously when she set her sights on Jesse, but when she actually sleeps with my husband I could care less.

"My parents are waiting in the dining hall. You're ten minutes late," says Gentry, again squeezing my arm to emphasize his displeasure with me. I sigh, pasting the fake smile on my face that I know he expects. "There was traffic," I say simply, and I let him lead me to the dining hall where the second worst thing about Gentry is waiting for us.

Gentry's mother, Lucinda, considers herself southern royalty.

Her parents owned the largest plantation in South Carolina and spoiled their only daughter with everything that her heart desired. This of course made her perhaps the most self-obsessed woman I had ever met, and that was putting it lightly. Gentry's father, Conrad, stands as we approach, dressed up in the suit and tie that he wears everywhere regardless of the occasion. Like his son, Gentry's father was a handsome man. Although his hair was slightly greying at the temples, his face remained impressively unlined, perhaps due to the same miracle worker that made his wife look forever thirty-five.

"Darling, you look wonderful as always," he tells me, brushing a kiss against my cheek and making we want to douse myself in boiling water. Conrad had no qualms about propositioning his son's wife. I couldn't remember an interaction I'd had with him that hadn't ended with him asking me to sneak away to the nearest dark corner with him. I purposely choose to sit on the other side of Gentry, next to his mother, although that option isn't much better. She looks me over, pursing her lips when she gets to my hair. According to her, a proper southern lady keeps her hair pulled back. But I've never been a proper lady, and the guys always loved my hair. Keeping it down is my silent tribute to them and the person I used to be since everything else about me is almost unrecognizable.

Lucinda is a beautiful woman. She's always impeccably dressed, and her mahogany hair is always impeccably coiffed. She's also as shallow as a teacup. She begins to chatter, telling me all about the town gossip; who's sleeping with who, who just got fake boobs, whose husband just filed for bankruptcy. It all passes in one ear and out the other until I hear her say something that sounds unmistakably like "Sounds of Us."

I look up at her, catching her off guard with my sudden interest. "Sorry, could you repeat that?" I ask. Her eyes are gleaming with excitement as she clasps her hands delicately in front of herself. She waits to speak until the waiter has refilled her glass with water. She slowly takes a sip, drawing out the wait now that she actually has my attention.

"I was talking about the Sounds of Us concert next week. They are performing two shows. Everyone's going crazy over the fact that the boys will be coming home for the first time since they made it big. It's been what...four years?" she says.

"Five," I correct her automatically, before cursing myself when she smirks at me.

"So, you aren't immune to the boys' charms either..." she says with a grin.

"What was that, Mother?" asks Gentry, his interest of course rising at the mention of anything to do with me and other men.

"I was just telling Ariana about the concert coming to town," she says. I hold my breath waiting to hear if she will mention the name. Gentry's so clueless about anything that doesn't involve him that he probably hasn't heard yet that they're coming to town.

"Ariana doesn't like concerts," he says automatically. It's his go-to excuse for making sure I never attend any social functions that don't involve him. Ariana doesn't like sushi. Ariana doesn't like movies. The list of times he's said such a thing go on and on. I feel a slight pang in my chest. Ariana. Gentry and his family insist on calling me by my full name, and I miss the days where I had relationships that were free and easy enough to use my nick-name of Ari.

"Of course she doesn't, dear," says Lucinda, patting my hand. The state of my marriage provides much amusement to Lucinda and Conrad. Both approve of the Gentry's "heavy hand" towards me and although they haven't witnessed the abuse first hand, they're well aware of Gentry's penchant for using me as a punching bag. Gentry's parents are simply charming.

I pick at my salad and listen to Lucinda prattle on, my interest gone now that she's off the subject of the concert. Gentry and his dad are whispering back and forth, and I can feel Gentry shooting furtive glances at me. I know I should be concerned or at least interested about what their talking about, but my mind has taken off, thinking about the fact that in just a few days' time, the guys will be in the same vicinity as me for the first time in five years. If only….

"Ariana," says Gentry, pulling me from my day dream. I immediately pull on the smile I have programmed to flash whenever I'm in public with Gentry.

"Yes?"

"I think you've had enough to eat," he tells me as if he's talking about the weather and not the fact that he's just embarrassed me in front of everyone at the table.

I shakily set my fork down, my cheeks flushing from his comment. I was eating a salad and I'm already slimmer than I should be. But Gentry loves to control everything about me, food being just one of many things. I see Lucinda patting her lips delicately as she finishes eating her salmon. My stomach growls at the fact that I've had just a few bites to eat. I have a few dollars stashed away in my car, I'll have to stop somewhere and grab something to eat on the way home. That is if Gentry doesn't leave at the same time as me and follow me.

When I've gotten my emotions under control, I finally lift my eyes and glance at my husband. He's back in deep conversation with Conrad, their voices still too soft for me to pick anything up. Looking at him, I can't help but get the urge to stab him with my silverware and then run screaming from the room. The bastard would probably find a way to haunt me from the grave even if he didn't survive. Still, I find my hand clenching involuntarily as if grasping for a phantom knife.

After that one terrible night when it became clear that I couldn't go to L.A. to meet up with the guys, I was lost. I got a job as a waitress and was living in one of those pay by week extended stay motels since there was no way I could stay in my trailer with *them* anymore. I met Gentry Mayfield while waitressing one night. He was handsome and charming, and persevered in asking me out even when I refused the first half a dozen times. My heart was broken, how could I even think of trying to give my broken self to someone else? I finally got tired of saying no and went on a date with him. He made me smile, something that I didn't think was possible, and every date after that seemed to be more perfect than I deserved. I didn't fall in love with Gentry, my heart belonged to three other men, but I did develop admiration and fondness for Gentry in a way that I hadn't thought possible. After pictures started to surface on the first page of the gossip sites of the guys with hordes of beautiful women, and the fact that my life seemed to be going nowhere, marrying Gentry seemed to be the second chance that I didn't deserve. Except the funny thing about how it all turned out is that my life with Gentry turned out worse than I probably deserved, even after everything that had happened.

Three months after we were married, I burnt dinner. Gentry had come home in a bad mood because of something that had happened at work. Apparently, me burning dinner was the last straw for him that day and he struck me across the face, sending me flying to the ground. Afterwards, he begged and pleaded with me for forgiveness, saying it would never happen again. But I wasn't stupid, I knew how this story played out. I stayed for a week so that I could get ahold of as much money as I could and then I drove off while he was at work. I was stopped at the state lines by a trooper who evidently was friends with Gentry's family. I was dragged kicking and screaming back home where Gentry was waiting, furious and ready to make me pay. Every semblance of the man that I had thought I was marrying was gone.

I had $5,000 to my name when I met him. I'd gotten it from selling the trailer that I inherited when my parents died in a car crash after one of their drunken nights out on the town. Gentry had convinced me that I should put it in our "joint account" right after we got married and stupidly, I had agreed to do it. I never got access to that account. Gentry stole my money, he stole my self-esteem. No, he didn't steal it, he chipped away at it and just when I thought I'd crumble, he kissed me and cried over me and told me he'd die without me.

I tried to get away several more times, by bus, on foot, I even went to the police to try and report him. But the Mayfield's had everyone in this state in their pocket, and nothing I said or did worked. I eventually stopped trying. It had taken me a year of not running away to get my car back and to be able to do things other than stay home, locked in our bedroom, while Gentry was at work.

Gentry stood up from the table, bringing me back to the present. A random song lyric floated through my mind about how the devil wears a pretty face, it certainly fit Gentry Mayfield.

"I'm heading to the office for the rest of the day. What are your plans?" he asks, as if I had a choice in what my plans were.

"Just finishing things around the house and going to the store to get a few ingredients for dinner," I tell him, waving a falsely cheerful goodbye to Gentry's parents as he walks me out of the dining area towards the valet stand. We stop by the exit and he pulls me towards him, stroking the side of my face that I've painted with makeup to hide the bruise he gave me the night before. My eyes flutter from the rush of pain but Gentry somehow mistakes it as the good kind of reaction to his touch. He leans in for a kiss.

"You're still the most beautiful woman I've ever seen," he tells me, sealing his lips over mine in a way that both cuts off my air supply and makes me want to wretch all at once. I hold still, knowing that it will enrage him that I don't do anything in response to his kiss, but not having it in me to fake more than I already have for the day. He pulls back and searches my eyes for something, I'm not sure what. He must not find it because his own eyes darken, and his grip on my arms suddenly tightens to a point that wouldn't look like anything to a club passerby, but that will inevitably leave bruises on my too pale skin.

He leans in and brushes his lips against my ear. "You're never going to get away from me, so when are you going to just give in?" he spits out harshly. I say nothing, just stare at him stonily. I can see the storm building in his eyes.

"Don't bother with dinner, I'll be home late," he says, striding away without a second glance, probably to go find Wendy and make plans to fuck her after he leaves the office, or maybe it will be at the office knowing him.

I wearily make my way through the doors to the valet stand and patiently wait for my keys. It's a different kid this time and I'm grateful he doesn't try to flirt with me.

On my way back from the country club I find myself taking the long way back to the house, the way that takes me by the trailer park where I grew up. I park by the office trailer and find myself walking to the field behind the rows of homes. Looking at the trash riddled ground, I gingerly walk through the mud, flecks of it hitting the formerly pristine white fabric of my shoes. I walk until I get to an abandoned fire pit that doesn't look like it's been used for quite a while. For probably five years to be exact.

I sit on a turned over trash barrel until the sun sits precariously low in the sky and I know that I'm playing with fire if I dare to stay any longer. I then get up and walk back to my car, passing by the trailer I once lived in. It's funny that after everything that has happened, at the moment I would give anything to be back in that trailer again.

Discover the rest of this **COMPLETED** series HERE!

About C.R. Jane

A Texas girl living in Utah now, I'm a wife, mother, lawyer, and now author. My stories have been floating around in my head for years, and it has been a relief to finally get them down on paper. I'm a huge Dallas Cowboys fan and I primarily listen to Beyonce and Taylor Swift…don't lie and say you don't too.

My love of reading started probably when I was three and with a faster than normal ability to read, I've devoured hundreds of thousands of books in my life. It only made sense that I would start to create my own worlds since I was always getting lost in others'.

I like heroines who have to grow in order to become badasses, happy endings, and swoon-worthy, devoted, (and hot) male characters. If this sounds like you, I'm pretty sure we'll be friends.

I'm so glad to have you on my team…check out the links below for ways to hang out with me and more of my books you can read!

FOLLOW ME

Stay up to date with C.R. Jane by joining her Facebook readers' group, **C.R.'s Fated Realm**. Ask questions, get first looks at new books/series, and have fun with other book lovers!

Visit my **Facebook** page to get updates.

Visit my **Amazon Author** page.

Visit my **Website**.

Sign up for my **newsletter** to stay updated on new releases, find out random facts about me, and get access to different points of view from my characters.

Books by C.R. Jane

The Fated Wings Series

First Impressions

Forgotten Specters

The Fallen One (a Fated Wings Novella)

Forbidden Queens

Frightful Beginnings (a Fated Wings Short Story)

Faded Realms

Faithless Dreams

Fabled Kingdoms

Fated Wings

The Rock God (a Fated Wings Novella)

The Darkest Curse Series

Forget Me

Lost Passions

The Sounds of Us Contemporary Series (complete series)

Remember Us This Way

Remember You This Way

Remember Me This Way

The Sound of Us Boxed Set

Broken Hearts Academy Series: A Bully Romance (complete duet)

Heartbreak Prince

Heartbreak Lover

The Heartbreak Prince Boxed Set

Ruining Dahlia (Contemporary Mafia Standalone)

Ruining Dahlia

Hades Redemption Series

The Darkest Lover

The Darkest Kingdom

Monster & Me Duet Co-write with Mila Young

Monster's Plaything

Academy of Souls Co-write with Mila Young (complete series)

School of Broken Souls

School of Broken Hearts

School of Broken Dreams

School of Broken Wings

Fallen World Series Co-write with Mila Young (complete series)

Bound
Broken
Betrayed
Belong

Thief of Hearts Co-write with Mila Young (complete series)

Siren Condemned

Siren Sacrificed

Siren Awakened

Siren Redeemed

Kingdom of Wolves Co-write with Mila Young

Wild Moon

Wild Heart

Wild Girl

Wild Love

Wild Soul

Stupid Boys Series Co-write with Rebecca Royce

Stupid Boys

Dumb Girl

Crazy Love

Breathe Me Duet Co-write with Ivy Fox (complete duet)

Breathe Me

Breathe You

Rich Demons of Darkwood Series Co-write with May Dawson

Make Me Lie

Make Me Beg